The
LUMINOUS
HEART of
JONAH S.

BY GINA B. NAHAI

©2014 Gina B. Nahai
Hardcover ISBN: 978-1-61775-321-3
Trade Paperback ISBN: 978-1-61775-320-6
Library of Congress Control Number: 2014938697

Akashic Books
info@akashicbooks.com
www.akashicbooks.com

Giti and Francois Barkhordar, for your faith and courage
David Nahai, for our life, and everything in it
Alex, Ashley, and Kevin Nahai, for giving me the world—every day

SOLEYMAN FAMILY TREE

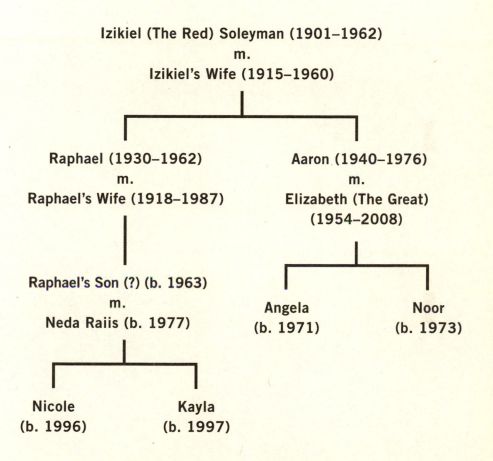

LOS ANGELES

Monday, June 24, 2013

Raphael's Son died alone in his car, sitting upright behind the wheel with his safety belt on and his throat slashed from right to left—a clean, some would say artful, cut of almost surgical precision. His body was discovered at 4:45 a.m. on Monday, June 24, 2013, by Neda Raiis, his wife of seventeen years who, according to her statement to the police, had found him cold and unresponsive in his gray, two-door Aston Martin with the personalized license plate—I WYNN—as it sat idling against the wrought-iron gates of their house on Mapleton Drive in Holmby Hills. Nearly one hour before that, Neda had been awakened by the sound of what she imagined was a car accident—metal crashing against metal—on the street. She had spent the next fifty minutes drifting into and out of sleep. Then, finally, she had decided to investigate the source of the earlier disturbance, risen from bed, and walked the length of the yard to the front of the estate. The sound she had heard was that of the Aston Martin crashing head-on into the gate.

The driver's window was lowered all the way. Through it, Neda could see a trail of blood that had spilled out of the wound in Raphael's Son's neck down along his chest and stomach, onto his short, portly thighs, and gathered in a pool on the Italian leather of the car seat. Raphael's Son's eyes were open and his mouth was slack, and he looked as gray and hollow as an inflatable toy animal with the air let out—like he had finally lost those extra thirty pounds he had carried so imperfectly for so long around the middle and that made everything he wore—those $2,800 Zegna suits from Saks Fifth Avenue and $700 jeans from Barney's and, on Sundays at the Sports Club in West LA, those black Nike shirts that he had to buy in extralarge, so they fit around the waist but hung too low over his knees—appear as if it belonged to an older, much taller brother.

To find out if her husband was alive, Neda had reached through the window and shaken him gently by the left shoulder. When he didn't move, she left him in the car and went back into the house to call the police.

* * *

This, at any rate, was the story that circulated within the Iranian Jewish community of the United States in the first two or three hours following the alleged discovery of the body. By nine o'clock Monday morning, word had spread to Canada and Israel. By noon, the closed-circuit, Persian-language satellite radio stations broadcasting from LA to Iran and elsewhere in the Middle East were receiving calls from Tehran asking to confirm the rumor.

Raphael's Son was not the first Iranian Jew to be murdered in America, but he was by far the most high profile, hated, and, according to his enemies, deserving of a painful and untimely death. So the story, which would have been sensational in any case, circulated with even greater speed and urgency, the details becoming more bloody and brutal with each telling until the single wound at the throat had morphed into multiple stabbings, then a beheading, then a complete dismemberment. Accounts varied as to the immediate motive for the killing and whether he had been robbed of his wallet, the five-karat diamond pinkie ring he wore instead of a wedding band, and the $30,000 gold Rolex Daytona he had bought a few years earlier at the Aramaic brothers' jewelry store on Pico and Sepulveda. The watch, Raphael's Son had announced to the Aramaic brothers, would serve as a memento of his incontrovertible triumph in the fifty-two-year, scorched-earth, take-no-prisoners, only-one-of-us-is-walking-out-of-here-alive, legal and psychological battle he had waged against his wife's family, the Soleymans of Tehran who, he was proud to claim, had suffered endlessly at his hand.

Meanwhile, a continual string of celebrity murder trials and incessant reruns of CSI on cable having turned the entire population of LA's West Side into prosecuting attorneys and forensic crime–solvers at once, every bit of information that seeped into the ether was analyzed and employed to draw conclusions about the killer's identity, motive, and modus operandi.

It wouldn't take a detective, of course, to figure out that Raphael's Son could have been murdered by any number of bitter enemies he had toiled so restlessly during his entire adult life to create—from former "enemies of the revolution" in Iran that he had handed over to the ayatollahs only so he could secure their release in exchange for a "service fee," to every business partner he had defrauded then sued for fraud, to the thousands of Iranian Jews and a few American ones he had most recently swindled out of half a billion dollars. And those were just his adversaries; his allies were even more likely to want him dead.

For years, Raphael's Son had run what proved, during the great financial meltdown of 2008, to have been an especially smart variation on a Ponzi scheme that targeted mostly Iranian Jews. Because of him, entire families had slipped into poverty or suffered irreversible financial setbacks. When pressed about how he had managed to "lose" all the investors' money, he blamed the worldwide economic meltdown and reminded people that, with Greece and Iceland also bankrupt, he was, indeed, in good company. When asked if he felt he should be held accountable for any of the pain that had been caused, he sighed and said he wished he were held accountable—just as accountable as Hank Paulson, Ben Bernanke, Timothy Geithner, and all those Wall Street CEOs who either got reappointed to their cabinet posts or received huge bonuses for presiding over a global financial fiasco.

Like those CEOs, Raphael's Son had emerged from the collapse of the Ponzi game richer and more self-righteous then ever. Five years after he was officially broke, he still lived in a $52 million house—2.6 acres in one of the city's most vaunted neighborhoods, just across Sunset Boulevard from the Playboy Mansion with its peacocks and swans and naked twins running loose, a stone's throw from Aaron and Candy Spelling's fifty-six-thousand-square-foot, $150 million pad with the leaky roof (recently sold to a twenty-two-year-old Russian "heiress" for half that amount), down the street from the forty-five-thousand-square-foot, $125 million "Little Versailles" of that nice Jewish couple who spent five years building the house and divorced the minute it was completed.

Raphael's Son's house had eight bedrooms, a six-thousand-square-foot guesthouse, an outdoor basketball court, indoor bowling alley, outdoor tennis court, indoor lap pool, outdoor pool and cabana, three kitchens (one, the size of the Taj Mahal, where no cooking was done; a smaller, restaurant-caliber, for household use; and a third, catering-style kitchen for large parties), three regular bars, a dry bar, two dining rooms, a thousand-square-foot breakfast "nook," plus the obligatory library, dome-roofed greenhouse, and thirty-two-seat projection room.

Substantial as that may seem to any reasonable person, Raphael's Son had the gall to deem the house a "disappointment." It was big, yes, by most people's standards, but in Los Angeles, it was not what one would call jaw-dropping—not when Little Versailles boasted a three-and-a-half-mile jogging track, the Spelling house came with a stable of thoroughbred horses, and the Playboy Mansion had Hugh Hefner and a few sets of twin bunnies.

Raphael's Son had said this to the Aramaic brothers the day he went to buy the Rolex. Hoping to remind him that he was too rich to ask for a discount, they had inquired, ever so discreetly, if he enjoyed living in Holmby Hills.

"Oh yeah!" Raphael's Son had responded ironically. "We have no cell phone reception because AT&T is a rip-off, and the lights go out every time there's wind or rain because the power lines are old and decrepit, and our neighbors are all useless derelicts."

The people at the Playboy Mansion threw parties seven nights a week. They blasted the music loud enough to create an earthquake, let their guests park their cars in the middle of the street, and didn't bother to answer the phone or open the door whenever Raphael's Son went over to complain. And you're naive if you think the police were any help; they actually looked forward to being called to Hefner's door. They got to stand around in the foyer and watch the naked bunnies, throw back a couple of apple martinis, and leave with a nice tip from one of the mansion's many good-looking gay gatekeepers.

The old woman next door, heir to some cigarette fortune, had built a lake in the middle of her lawn, and she insisted on filling it right up to its sandy banks, never mind the rest of the city was facing a water shortage. Her daughter, married twenty years and a mother of three, lived with her and made a point of sleeping with every plumber, handyman, and eighteen-year-old delivery boy who showed up with a pizza. Across the street an Indian pharmaceutical mogul kept building the same ugly mustard-yellow house with 1,700 little windows, tearing it down just as it was nearly complete, and starting over; and a Russian mobster who, after attending one too many Landmark Forum seminars, confessed to his wife that he had cheated on her exactly 1,112 times. A few weeks later, his body was found, sliced in half, on a beach in Cancún.

Raphael's Son had sued the cigarette lady for using too much water, Hugh Hefner for creating a noise disturbance, and AT&T for providing generally awful service, and he planned to sue the Department of Water and Power as well, for its crumbling infrastructure and high rates.

"I feel like I'm living in a third-world country," he told the Aramaic brothers. "One person hordes all the water, the cops are on the take, and I have to buy my own generator or sit in the dark at night."

None of this helped explain why Raphael's Son had been able to maintain ownership of the house and God only knows what else, while some of his former "investors," having lost their life savings, were reduced to living in their cars or neighbors' garages. What seemed evident was that, in the ten years leading up to the bankruptcy, he had slowly ferreted half a billion dollars into the savings accounts of a ragtag army of his maternal cousins, their spouses, and their children. Forever impecunious until they fell into Raphael's Son's orbit, the gang known as the Riffraff Brigade had lived in near poverty in various provinces in Iran, then in cinder-block homes in Israel's "occupied territories," and finally in three-hundred-square-foot apartments in North Hills and Agoura in Los Angeles. Then all at once, starting in 2003, they began to buy ten-thousand-square-foot houses in Brentwood and Beverly Hills. Their wives' miniscule diamonds suddenly grew to ten carats, their children enrolled in expensive Jewish day schools, and if you asked them where all this came from, they said with a straight face that it was "old money" from Iran because, didn't you know, their fathers were all millionaires? That they owned land and horses and enough jewels and antiques to fill a museum?

The creditors believed the Riffraff were helping Raphael's Son hide the stolen money—that they would hold on to it for a few years, then quietly return it piecemeal, minus their own commission, in creative configurations. It was easy, transparent, and, much to everyone's amazement, extremely effective. The "investors" who had lost everything could hardly afford a lawsuit against Raphael's Son or his cousins; the ones who had been robbed of a few million but had more to spare had all been promised, in secret, that they would get their money back if they didn't go to the authorities or sue. The district attorney, who believed that all "Eye-ray-nians" were rich and entitled, had no interest in pursuing a criminal case in which some of them had stolen from the rest. The bankruptcy trustee was having a blast billing for time—four years, so far—he spent "looking into" the case, and the news media had their hands full covering celebrities who got drunk and crashed their cars, or killed their wives or themselves.

Raphael's Son's only punishment for the damage he had wrought was to become a pariah everywhere on the West Side, but that wasn't as big a deal as it might seem because he had never been held in very high regard anyway. He was called "The Bandit of Holmby Hills" and "The Thief Who Came for Dinner" in a blog post or two, which he doubted that anyone of consequence actually read. His wife and daughters hated him, but that was neither new nor relevant. His Riff-raff cousins prayed daily for his demise so they could keep all the money they held in trust for him, but they were too terrified of him to withhold so much as a dollar when the time came.

In the end, it was safe to say the only person who might have harbored any affection for Raphael's Son was his mother, but she was dead and buried in Israel—and besides, she had been no Queen of Congeniality herself. He did not relish being universally despised, but he did enjoy having all that money—tax-free—in his offshore accounts. More than that, he reveled in the harm he had inflicted upon everyone else, the fact that he had gotten away with it so easily, and the certainty that, once the dust had settled and his creditors had tired of crying over their lost money, memories would fade and his commercial credibility would be restored merely by virtue of his hundreds of millions. He was already making backroom deals and buying up foreclosed properties using the Riffraff as a front, paying all cash and hiding the assets in unregistered corporations and having a grand time of it all—let the creditors eat stale bread, there's money to be made in a recession—when he encountered, in 2011, a glitch in his plan.

Two of Raphael's Son's "investors" managed to convince the DA that he could make a strong case for wire fraud and money laundering. The amount involved was small—$30 million—but the investors were American, which meant they had asked Raphael's Son for more than a handshake to verify and track their deposits. Thus nudged out of complacency, the DA pressed charges, and almost simultaneously offered a plea: if convicted, Raphael's Son could get up to twenty years in a federal prison, and have to return the money; if he agreed to settle, he would do six years and return the money.

Raphael's Son's attorneys urged him to accept the deal; he fired them summarily for being cowardly and incompetent, then hired a cheaper set. He told them that if the heads of Goldman Sachs and Bank of America were sleeping in their own beds, his case should be a cakewalk. He told his second team of attorneys that he would never be convicted by a court because he was an observant Jew who served on many boards. Then he fired them too and hired a third team.

A trial date was set for Monday, July 8, 2013. As the pressure intensified and the lawyers swore to him that he was no Lloyd Blankfein and that even he—Blankfein—wouldn't escape conviction and imprisonment if the government wanted it, Raphael's Son began to contemplate parting with some of other people's hard-earned money. He instructed his lawyers to go back to the DA with a plea deal that involved his returning the money but not serving time. He said he would have to "borrow" the money from his cousins, the Riffraff. A meeting was set at the DA's office for Monday, June 24, at ten a.m. He died approximately five hours before that.

His enemies barely had time to process this information when, at 12:15 p.m. the day of the murder, they were struck by a second, much more disturbing, news bulletin.

In response to Neda's call to 911, the ambulance had arrived quickly. It was greeted at the top of Mapleton by a hysterical Latina in a floor-length silk robe with lace trimmings, a pair of gold slippers with three-inch heels, and half a dozen rings in each ear. In between hacking sobs and mutterings of "Oh Mister, poor Mister," she introduced herself as Esperanza Guadalupe di Chiara Valencia, "the children's governess," and led the paramedics to the scene.

Neda Raiis, 5'1", small-boned, and meek as a canned sardine, was shivering quietly in a bloody bathrobe as she stood next to the car. A pair of teenage girls—Neda and Raphael's Son's daughters—stood barefoot and barely dressed next to the pedestrian gate. The Aston Martin was in park, the engine still running.

The paramedics saw a great deal of blood on the driver's seat and on the floor mat beneath the steering wheel. They saw Raphael's Son's jacket draped carefully on the passenger seat. They did not see a Rolex or a pinkie ring but that was hardly an issue because what they also did not see—dead or alive, injured or whole—was Raphael's Son.

He had been there, Neda explained to them plainly from between chattering teeth. He had been in the car and his throat was cut, it was definitely him and he was definitely dead when she left him and went into the house to call the cops. When she came back, he was gone.

Gone. As in: faked his own death and, with the help of his wife who has always been under his thumb, avoided the trial and absconded with everyone's money.

Gone. As in: probably skipped the country by now, off to Israel or Iran where he'll lie on the beach in Eilat or at the Caspian, wait out the storm, and turn up somewhere else in the world in a few years, still rich and fat and pretending to be a good Jew.

As in: the son of a bitch wins again.

News of the missing body was announced on the Tumblr page of Angela Soleyman, an Iranian Jewish attorney who despised Raphael's Son and was happy to say it. She attributed the bulletin to the website of the *Los Angeles Jewish Herald*.

No sooner had Angela's Tumblr post gone live than the *Herald* began to receive calls from livid readers denouncing the publication, Tumblr and all social media, and, especially, Angela Soleyman. She, the callers informed the nineteen-year-old intern who had the misfortune of working the switchboard that day, was a loose cannon with too many college degrees and not an ounce of common sense to help her get along in the world. She was also a monstrous liar who had left out of her so-called reporting (since when does anyone with Internet access become Peter Jennings?) the rather relevant fact that she was an unhappy soul with a very sharp ax to grind against the Iranian community because she was in her early forties and had not managed to find a man stupid enough to marry her. That she had spent years trying to embarrass Iranian Jews and give them a bad name. She should be fired by the *Herald*, banned by the State of California from ever touching a keyboard again. That's what the Iranian callers said.

The Americans who called wished to express: a) the depth of their disinterest in whatever fate had befallen yet another rich Iranian; and b) their abiding resentment of the entire community for being bold enough to live in the most desirable neighborhoods of Los Angeles, send their children to the most competitive schools, and excel in the most difficult and lucrative professions while, at the same time, keeping mostly to themselves and each other, speaking Persian everywhere they went, and insisting that their children marry other Iranians. It was simply too cheeky, too unimmigrant-like, for these Eye-ray-nians to be living next door to and eating in the same establishments as the icons and avatars of American culture. The women get their nails done at the same Vietnamese-owned-and-operated, sixteen-dollars-for-a-manicure and you get to pass right through the paparazzi lines even though you're not a celebrity—yet—shop on Bedford Drive in Beverly Hills that Kim Kardashian, that goddess of LA culture, frequents. First-generation immigrants must live in undesirable areas and work their fingers raw doing laundry or selling noodles, or slave in factories and eat cabbage, so that their children can go to school and become middle class. That's what all the Russian and Polish and Western European Jews did when they first arrived on these shores. Only these Eye-ray-nians don't know how to take a number and stand in line.

The collective response to the news of Raphael's Son's missing corpse alarmed the *Herald*'s editor, an American who had never understood his fellow white people's visceral resentment of the Iranian population in LA.

"I would note," he said politely to the first few callers before he realized it was a losing battle and told the intern to take messages, "that Ms. Soleyman is not affiliated with this publication and does not represent its views."

The Americans concluded, once again, that the *Herald* was too liberal and hung up. The Iranians insisted that, regardless of who paid her bills, the *Herald* had provided Ms. Soleyman with "fake news"—an act that was especially egregious given that Angela had always had a way of turning any message—good, bad, or indifferent—into a source of anguish and embarrassment for her own people.

Angela S. was a 5'9", 138-pound, Princeton undergrad, Yale law (but she wasted all that education and gave up her $180,000-a-year job at a private law firm to become a writer because she believes in truth, justice, and being poor), Iranian Jewish woman of a certain age— forty-one—who had offended just about every person in the upper-income bracket of the community in LA (and most of Long Island) because she was, in the most aggravating sense of the word, frank. That's the American and European way to describe her; in Persian, she was tactless, offensive, angry, bitter, and merely out to embarrass her own kin. She was born in Iran but left when she was barely eight years old, and it's true that she didn't have an easy time of it (Who did? There's a reason they call it "exile" instead of "resort vacation.") but personal hardship is no excuse for unhinging one's jaw and letting just anything spill. And besides, she had fared better in the US than she ever would have in Iran.

She finished high school in LA and took off, full scholarship and all, for the East Coast, came back seven years later, and went to work in a private criminal defense law firm, and that should have been the last anyone heard from her except she decided that all defense attorneys were sleazy bastards and joined the DA's office, decided that all district attorneys were crooked assholes, and, in 2008, quit that job too. This time, she decided that the American people were not well-served by the three hundred thousand–plus new books published in the US every year, and that what the country needed in the midst of two wars, a near depression, and young people killing each other with machine guns on the street every night, was one more book. Entitled *Two Continents, One Thief*, the magnum opus was intended as a tell-all, unmask-the-scoundrel, shoot-the-guy-in-both-knees-and-watch-him-crawl-to-libel-court exposé of Raphael's Son and his cast of Shakespearean co-miscreants. Never mind there were more writers in LA than people who read books, or that, outside of the Iranian Jewish community, hardly anyone knew or cared to know Raphael's Son.

Even *this*—writing a book that, if read by a single LA native, was "bound to embarrass and belittle all Iranians everywhere in the world because, as you know, *they* are going to think we're all like Raphael's Son and the Riffraff"—might have been bearable (at least it would take her and her mouth out of circulation for a couple of years). But then she went and signed up for a private workshop taught by a fat-and-unhappy, never-published-a-book-in-her-life-but-claims-she-can-teach-others-to-write Russian woman named Babette, who lived with her thin but equally clueless fiancé and their grew-old-and-died-years-ago-only-his-owner-is-too-stupid-to-notice dog in a downtown studio. Angela could stand the smell of urine everywhere in Babette's apartment/classroom, and she could (just barely) stand the obsequious praise the two women heaped on each other, but she quickly caught on that, rather than a real writing course, this was yet another LA-style self-improvement scam (green juice, Pilates, a memoir) by a person who clearly was in dire need of taking one of those classes herself. "In short, she's no Nabokov." The only thing Angela took away from the course was that to get a book deal, writers must engage in a form of self-prostitution No Nabokov called "platform building" (slang for "get someone interested in buying the damn book or use your own money to publish it"). Hence the creation of Angela's blog on Tumblr.

For some reason she thought she was an expert on the social and cultural anthropology of Iranian Jews anywhere, and that the cure for any of their ills was to expose, "without fear or favor," their every seminal secret or insignificant minutiae before the world. It's true she went to great pains to insult Americans as well, but no one cared about that because white people don't have to worry about their reputation. Minorities, on the other hand, are always judged by their lowest common denominator. No one cared, either, that Angela had as many good things to say about the community as bad. Utter a dozen words of praise and one of criticism, a wise rabbi once said, and they'll remember the one and hang you for it.

She had a conviction, fashioned, no doubt, out of resentment of the fact that she was childless and unmarried and without prospects, that Iranian Jews had been silent and insular and fearful of the judgment of others for too long—first, because they were persecuted minorities who survived by remaining invisible, and later, when they were allowed out of the ghettos and into the top echelons of Iranian society, because they had an image to cultivate and maintain—and that they needed *her* to bring them all out of the shadows so they could shout from every laptop their own and their neighbors' personal histories, their secrets and flaws and differences, their confessions and complaints and all those other so-called facts they had tried for three thousand years to conceal.

The question of who died and made Angela truth-teller extraordinaire remained, as yet, unresolved, but it was one thing for her to "speak frankly" to one or two or a dozen other people, and something entirely different—indeed, reckless—to begin to operate an instrument of mass destruction.

In the blog, she was always digging, always trying to expose one cultural flaw or another in every major segment of LA's population. She picked on Iranians and Koreans, Jews and Muslims and Presbyterians. Not that she was especially wrong about things, but she didn't understand the art of the unstated—of knowing what to express in words and what to leave implied, what to hint at and to deny in spite of the evidence—all in the interest of keeping unity and harmony within a population.

She would have been ignored or shunned by most people a long time ago were it not for the fact that her late mother, Elizabeth "The Great" Soleyman, was one of the most adored and respected members of the Jewish community in Los Angeles. "The Great" was a title conferred upon her by popular disposition some ten or so years earlier, when a profile of her appeared, without her cooperation or consent, in *Fortune* magazine. Until then, people had known that she was a self-made woman who had achieved remarkable success without having so much as a high school diploma. Just how remarkable that success had been became clear when the article divulged her after-tax worth as $2.7 billion, all of which, amazingly, she had come by honestly.

But while Elizabeth's wealth and popularity provided some level of tolerance for Angela in the community, they did not serve as a significant restraint on her actions. For one thing, Elizabeth had acted in a manner entirely contrary to any Iranian or Jewish parent when she bequeathed, in a will devised by her in-house attorneys, her entire estate to her charitable foundation. To her daughter and only heir, she left half a million dollars, Warren Buffet–style, and the obligation to serve as second fiddle to the foundation's executive director.

Not that Iranians were loathe to give to charity; far from it. They just left more to their children than to perfect strangers. Then again, neither Elizabeth nor Angela had ever understood how much fun being rich can be.

Angela's blog on Tumblr, *The Pearl Cannon*, was named after a real piece of artillery built by a Jewish blacksmith in nineteenth-century Iran. Like her, the cannon spewed a great deal of ammunition every time it was fired up. Like her too, it had its own mind and went against the grain: instead of shooting its explosive charge forward through the muzzle, the real Pearl Cannon exploded through the back and lay waste to its own team.

The only difference was that the Pearl Cannon, having revealed its fatal flaw at the first try, was permanently retired from battle. Angela, on the other hand, kept writing. She picked on every cornerstone of Iranian Jewish culture, and made it look draconian and insidious. Close family ties meant codependence, conservative values were designed to keep women in chains, respect for one's elders robbed the young of the opportunity to pursue their own dreams. The young, meanwhile, were a bunch of spoiled, entitled mama's-boys-and-girls who would never grow out of their high school mentality or conceive of an original idea that didn't have to do with making money. Women were complicit in their own enslavement because they traded their freedom for financial security. And family ties . . . well, about that, Angela could have written a few volumes and still have more left to say.

A good number of those volumes would doubtless reflect her special enthusiasm for exposing the truth about the Soleymans' sworn enemy, that reptile-in-Ferragamo-loafers, Raphael's Son. Angela wasn't the only person who had loathed the bastard long before his so-called bankruptcy, but she was certainly the loudest and most prolific and, once the Ponzi scheme was unearthed, the greatest proponent of sending him to jail for fifty years before hanging him from a crane. Long before the rest of the community came to see the light, she had concluded that anything he did—financial, social, or personal—was morally corrupt and legally dubious at best. Later, she applied the full force of her bulldog spirit to identifying the Riffraff as the sort of vermin who gave all Homo sapiens a bad name.

"Let me say it like it is," she wrote in the closing lines of her column that Monday. "The wolf in a seal's body is about to pull his biggest rip-off yet, his wife and the Riffraff are going to help him disappear with everyone's money, and the cops in this town are too incompetent and unmotivated to care."

That last comment, about the cops, dug deep into the detective who was called to the scene that Monday. Leon Pulitzer was another LA writer who thought he was doing time in an ordinary job until fame and fortune caught up with him. He had been in law enforcement for twenty years, never finished a book, and still fancied himself a "crime writer in training." At six o'clock on the day of the murder, he was summoned to the site when his boss, Detective III Jay O'Donnell, found out that the victim and his family were Iranians.

"Get over here and tell me what the wife's saying," O'Donnell had ordered Leon, who was still in bed. "These people all speak English but make no sense."

Leon was about to protest that he was neither a translator nor a mind reader when O'Donnell mentioned Raphael's Son's name.

He arrived on Mapleton to find it swarmed with police cars and spectators, television news vans and camera crews and paparazzi, and all the usual hangers-on who popped out of the ground every time there was a hint of celebrity-related news anywhere in Los Angeles. In the case of Raphael's Son, the Holmby Hills address was enough to attract a good amount of media attention, given the neighborhood's famous living residents and especially its most renowned dead person— Michael Jackson—who had been "put to sleep" in 2009 with the help of his in-house physician, in a rented mansion around the corner from Raphael's Son's. More recently, the drama surrounding the divorce of the couple who owned the LA Dodgers had made the area a paparazzi favorite. The Dodgers couple, court papers revealed, owned two houses in Holmby Hills, two in Malibu, and three elsewhere in the country. According to the wife—a smart but starved-looking little critter with a chihuahua's nervous demeanor who, before the divorce, had paid a hair dresser $10,000 a month to dry and comb her and her husband's hair—the first house, purchased for $21 million, was intended as their residence; the second house, immediately next door to the first and purchased for $6.5 million, was used for doing "extra laundry."

Outside the house, Neda stood in her bloodied white terry cloth bathrobe purchased for $275 at the spa of the ugly and expensive Montage hotel on Cañon Drive in Beverly Hills, and her bloodied white terry cloth slippers with the single pink rose, purchased for $5.99 at the Rite Aid (where all the pharmacists are Iranian, the cashiers are Filipino, and the store clerks are Latino; white people, it seems, do not work at Rite Aid) across the street from the hotel.

Glassy-eyed and terrified, she had already given her statement to the uniform, Jose Montoya, who had arrived on the scene in his black-and-white, and was now repeating it for O'Donnell.

Leon stood next to him and listened: the last time she saw her husband alive, Neda explained, was Friday evening. At the time, they hadn't been on speaking terms for about ten days, which wasn't unusual for them, though she couldn't recall the reason for the latest estrangement. Her husband had been unusually busy at work, and his bedroom, separate from hers, was situated at the opposite end of the house, so that he could have come and gone half a dozen times in one night without her taking notice.

On Sunday night she had eaten dinner alone, in the "functional" ground-floor kitchen (not to be confused with the other, more expensive "just for show" kitchen also on the ground floor). After dinner she had watched an old episode of *The Borgias* on Showtime in the family room, then retired upstairs to her bedroom by ten p.m.

She had not seen the girls before she went to bed Sunday night either. She thought the older one had been studying at the library, and that the younger one—well, to be honest, she had no idea what the younger one had been up to. As had become her routine in the last three and a half years—since Raphael's Son had made himself and his family social pariahs—Neda had downed two Xanax, plus half an Ambien, plus two melatonin gelcaps, to fall asleep. Hours later, a loud noise had awakened her. She believed the time was "three thirty-something," but she could be wrong. The Xanax had worn off and the melatonin was useless, but she was still groggy from the Ambien, so she had drifted in and out of sleep for the next hour before she finally got up, driven, she said, by the "feeling that something had happened," and ventured out of her room to investigate the source of the disturbance.

Without first checking the house, she went straight into the yard, hiked down to the gate, heard the sound of the Aston Martin's engine still running, and saw the front of the car pressed against the metal bars.

Here, Neda stopped, drew a hollow, stunted breath, turned more ashen, and told O'Donnell, "I'm sure he was dead."

At this, O'Donnell smiled broadly and turned away from Neda toward the ever-growing circle of onlookers at the edge of the police tape. Like any normal Angeleno, O'Donnell hated the paparazzi, thought they were less than pond scum, that they should have their cameras confiscated and their asses kicked to the curb as long as they were chasing other people. But if it was he they chased . . . well, in that case . . . O'Donnell's heart quivered at the thought that he might be quoted, even featured, on TMZ or E! or—who knows, stranger things have happened—invited to appear on his own reality show, *The*

Real Cops of Holmby Hills. So he sucked his stomach in and stood with his feet wide apart, wiped his face every few minutes, and did his best to look professional and photogenic.

"Ma'am," he said, one eye on Leon and the other on the television cameras, "this is Detective Pulitzer. I believe he speaks Farsi. In case you're more comfortable."

The security cameras outside the house were dummies intended to scare off inexperienced thieves. Raphael's Son had disabled them when he bought the house because he didn't want any record kept of his own comings and goings. The lights that should have illuminated the driveway and the gate had been dark since the Department of Water and Power launched its Compact Fluorescent Energy-Efficient Lightbulbs campaign in 2009; the lightbulbs conserved energy by going dark after a week or two, or breaking as they were being installed. They were significantly more expensive than regular lightbulbs, and they had to be changed so much more often that, in the end, the consumer spent more than he saved on the power bill. In Neda's house, Gerardo, the gardener who usually changed the bulbs as a favor, finally drew the line and insisted that he should be paid for his time and the use of his ladder. Raphael's Son responded that Gerardo was getting way too much money for walking around with a leaf blower. They had a hearty argument, Gerardo quit for the twelfth time that year, and the lightbulbs remained dark thereafter.

O'Donnell sent Neda into the house with a female cop to change out of the bathrobe and slippers that were now evidence, told Leon to follow her in and "see what you can squeeze from her between pals," then sauntered with as much reluctance as he could feign toward the Channel 9 news van.

The path from the gate toward the main building led up a slowly rising, pleasantly winding walkway paved with smooth white stones and lined on both sides by an emerald-green lawn dotted with giant palm trees and white marble benches. On the left, a dark blue infinity pool lay above a sharp slope toward a terraced area with a tennis court and, below it, an orchard. On the right, a massive river gushed out of a set of polished black rocks and into a tropical pond complete with a bamboo bridge, waterfall, wet bar, fire pit, and a cabana.

The front door was twelve feet high, made of black oak with shiny brass hardware; the foyer was as large as a decent-size hotel lobby. The family room, where Leon met Neda once she had changed out of her bloody clothes, was as large as his house. Divided into three sets of sitting areas, it was furnished with oversize armchairs, wrought-iron-and-glass coffee tables, heavy drapes and fine Persian rugs, and, here and there, mammoth books with titles like *Tuscan Villas* and *The Jewels of Elizabeth Taylor*.

The house had been decorated by an Israeli man who pretended he was French, and who had become the flavor of the year among Iranian homeowners on the West Side. He was tall and glib and painfully transparent. He wore his shirts with the top four buttons undone, hoping to assume that Tom-Ford-on-the-big-billboards-above-Sunset-Strip look, but it was a close call with John-Travolta-in-the-disco-age. Since most of his clients were bored, middle-aged women with grown children, no jobs, and rich husbands who ignored them, Disco Tom regaled them first with stories of his own perfect marriage that involved, among many other romantic marvels, the daily presentation, by him to his wife of twenty-four years, of "a single black rose, raised in my own farm in Ecuador, and adorned only with a string of raffia tied in a bow around the stem." Since none of his clients' husbands were thoughtful enough to do the same, it was only fair that he—the husband—should pay through the nose for rugs and drapery instead. From there, Disco Tom was only too happy to provide the wives with exactly what he knew they wanted: they wanted exactly what their friends had, only better.

Perched on a giant sofa with light-blue and lime-green upholstery, Neda looked like a small stuffed animal afraid it would be picked up by a maid and thrown in the trash before its owner could save it. She had traded her bathrobe for a black Juicy Couture sweat suit that she had bought at Cabazon Outlets outside Palm Springs the previous Christmas. She had cleaned the blood off her face and hands, but she hadn't managed to rub the smell out entirely, and thus she remained: head slightly cocked to the right, hands abandoned on her lap, staring at the coffee table in front of her with that dull, steady gaze of the overly medicated or the lobotomized which she had perfected over the years.

When he approached her, Neda looked right past Leon and offered a faint, friendly smile. "Welcome, sir."

* * *

Neda told Leon she had no idea who would have wanted Raphael's Son dead. It's true he had "differences" with some people, but he was an observant Jew, she said, as if this alone might make him immune to harm. There had been a fight with the gardener, Gerardo, the previous week, over a $1,600 "landscaping" bill that Raphael's Son had laughed at and thrown out—"Give me a break, all the guy ever does is cut the rosebushes down to the roots as soon as a flower is about to bloom, and he planted some impatiens where I told him not to—how does that make a leaf blower into a 'landscape artist'?"

There had been some yelling, Neda recalled, then Gerardo had quit, once again, and issued a warning: "You send me a check," he had yelled in front of Neda and the maid, "or I'll come back and make you pay!"

Neda hadn't seen Gerardo since last Wednesday; she didn't know his last name and didn't have a cell phone or a landline number for him. She thought, but wasn't certain, that he drove a red, beat-up old pickup truck—every gardener in LA drives one—with a lawn mower hanging precariously off the flatbed, no insurance, no driver's license, and why would you ask for a Social Security number when you already know it's fake?

She had no idea what country Gerardo was from, maybe Guatemala, or El Salvador, or Mexico. Yes, of course he was illegal, good luck trying to find a gardener who isn't. Home address? What for? These illegals change domicile every five minutes, move out of one aunt or cousin or boyfriend's house and into another, and they never give the employer the correct information anyway, just in case something comes up that would make them not want to be found.

Neda didn't remember how she had come to hire Gerardo. She thought the maid, Esperanza, might have recommended him. Esperanza herself was a cousin of someone who worked for one of Neda's relatives. That woman, in turn, was hired from the bus stop on Sunset and Benedict Canyon, right in front of the famed Beverly Hills Hotel, where every Monday and Tuesday morning anyone looking for work waited on the sidewalk for potential employers to drive by and select from among them. Then again, Esperanza might have come from an agency, Neda said, though she had no idea what the name of the place would be, and besides, what's the difference? Those agencies are here today, gone tomorrow. They're one-room operations in some strip mall in the Valley; some Latina or Israeli housewife's idea of taking advantage of other housewives' naïveté. They open their doors at around eleven in the morning because the muchachas—the would-be employees—are often not early risers. Muchacha might mean "young girl," but that's how domestics refer to one another, even if they're sixty years old. You never know their real age anyway, they lie about it like they lie about everything else, including having "papers." The only people who even bother to ask for papers, or believe that the agency actually does the background checks it charges for, or—this is the most ridiculous thing—don't realize that the "previous employer reference letters" the agency provides are all written by the muchacha's first cousin or next-door neighbor, are young American mothers who refer to the maid as "the nanny."

Better realize you're letting potential ax murderers and jewel thieves into your garden and bedroom than live with a false sense of security.

By midmorning, Neda's shivers had stopped and some color had seeped back into her face. Drops of perspiration moistened her hairline and slid down her temples, and the scent of humidity mixed with dried blood rose from her like rot in an old, enclosed place. When she had answered all of Leon's questions, she gave him permission to talk to her daughters.

The older girl, Nicole, had bright red hair and hazel eyes, and the smooth, round face, impeccable white skin, and softly aquiline nose of the girls in dreamy fashion magazine photos. She was the type of child—quiet, kind, smart, and studious—most parents dream of having, then spend years worrying about: her quietness made her insipid, her kindness allowed others to take advantage of her, her intelligence frightened boys, and her studiousness meant she had no friends.

Nicole was a senior at the Brentwood School. She got a near-perfect SAT score the first time she took the test, ran cross-country, and was a concert pianist. But she was always alone, at home or in the library, chewing at her nails and avoiding the gaze of others—crushed, it seemed, under a weight so exacting, she needed every last breath with which to fight it.

She told Leon she had been at the library till nine o'clock the night before. She had come home through the garage and gone straight to her room, where she had stayed till she was awakened by Esperanza's barking through the foyer as she spoke to the emergency operator on a cordless phone. Nicole hadn't seen anyone when she came home, didn't remember if her parents' cars were in the garage. She had no idea who else was at home, but that again wasn't unusual for their family.

"We're not the communicative type," she explained. "Most of the time, everyone's in their own room with the door locked."

She spoke with her eyes cast down and her skin blushing a faint pink. She hadn't heard the crash that awakened Neda, didn't know what time Esperanza started to scream. Asked if she had any idea who might have wanted to harm her father, Nicole studied Leon's face, then shrugged ever so slightly and said, in a voice that was at once removed and ridden with heartache, "Everyone."

The younger sister, Kayla, was tall and busty, with long, shapely legs and wavy, light-brown hair. She sat on her bed wearing a pair of old Uggs, very short frayed shorts, and a thin, loose top that, depending on how she moved, revealed or covered the chai tattoo on the curve of her lower back. She had large brown eyes, still painted heavily from the night before, full lips, perfect teeth, a second tattoo on the tip of her left shoulder.

She had been "out" till about three the previous night, first at one friend's and then another's, "and then we went to Hyde because my friends wanted to go but I don't like that place. We got a table and ordered a magnum, but we got bored and left after a half hour."

A table at Hyde cost anywhere from $3,000 and up. The tab was picked up by Kayla's friend Ati, the daughter of an Indonesian "industrialist" and her Russian racecar-driving husband. Ati and her brother lived together in a $12 million house in Beverly Hills. There was a permanent staff of five to tend to their needs, but they hadn't seen their parents since Ati was nine years old. She had a yellow Ferrari Enzo; her brother drove a $1,700,000 Bugatti.

From Hyde, Kayla and Ati and their friends had gone to the bar at the Roosevelt, but it was a Sunday night and nothing was happening. They headed home around two thirty, which was okay even on a school night because Kayla went to New Roads—"one of those places where parents park their kids just to keep them out of trouble during high school," she told Leon. Her sister was the studious one in the family.

As for her parents, Kayla thought they were both FOB—Fresh off the Boat—"Persies" with a totally skewed view of themselves.

"They have this idea that we're this nice, respectable, normal family, like all those other Persians," she told Leon. Her cell phone vibrated in her hand every few seconds with a text or call, and she stopped to check the screen each time.

"They don't want me hanging out with my friends because it's bad for their *aabehroo*, bad for my reputation, bad for marriage, bad for my kids. Except, *Hello?* We don't *have* a reputation. Well, except a *shitty* one. People hate us. Even Americans who didn't lose money to my dad have read about him and hate us. Little kids at Jewish day schools are telling each other jokes about us."

She got up from the bed, fished a pack of Marlboro Lights from her bag, and lit up.

"Do you mind?" she asked Leon only after she had exhaled two long puffs.

"So I say fuck my dad. I don't give a shit what happened to him. He can be dead for all I care, he's a jerk and a bastard and he cheated all his friends and even cheated on my mom God knows how many times, and she knows it too and doesn't say anything, hasn't once stood up for herself or my sister because, what do you know, it's bad for our fucking nonexistent *aabehroo*."

That word, *aabehroo*, is one of those for which no equivalent exists in the English language. It alludes to the impression that others hold of an individual's virtue and respectability. To have *aabehroo* means that the world regards a person in high esteem. To lose it—or, more literally, to have it leave the person—means he will live in shame unless he somehow manages to get his *aabehroo* back. You may be born with *aabehroo* because of your family history, but holding on to it requires a great deal of restraint and self-sacrifice. It means making sure you do everything in compliance with society's idea of what is right, that you live honorably and protect the sanctity of your family's name and reputation. It means being capable of feeling deep, personal shame before an exacting, infinitely multitudinous jury.

You have to have lived in a place like Iran, Leon thought, grown up with a strong sense of propriety and shame, and feared the judgment of others, in order to understand such a word. You certainly can't imagine what it means, really, if you've lived most of your life in America. In this land of perpetual hope and endless good fortune, this country built on the promise of "life, liberty, and the pursuit of happiness"—where else in the world is happiness a right?—where even the dead look good and healthy, dressed up and painted and coiffed in the coffin as if on their wedding day, there's no awareness, perhaps no need, nor would there be any tolerance, of that kind of sacrifice.

Leon could see how Kayla, born and raised in Los Angeles, might throw the word around so carelessly or deride her parents for being concerned with the judgment of others. If not for his own Iranian past, he might share Kayla's scorn.

As it was, however, he had nothing but appreciation for this and other aspects of a culture that valued grace, harmony, and spiritual growth above all. Even this emphasis on *aabehroo*, while stifling if carried to an extreme, signaled the importance of individual righteousness to a society's well-being. Raphael's Son and his ilk were not representative of the Iranians Leon knew; they were unfortunate aberrations and as such, alas, stood out from the crowd.

Esperanza Guadalupe di Chiara Valencia had made such a spectacle of herself by the car that after taking her statement, Jose Montoya sent her to her room and asked another officer to stand guard until Leon was ready to talk to her. She had used that time to put on makeup and false eyelashes, and squeeze herself into a pair of faux 7 For All Mankind jeans. When Leon knocked on her door, she opened wearing a pair of sling-backs with four-inch heels.

"I wear these at home," she explained when she saw him looking at her shoes. "I can't do work too well in higher heels."

Esperanza was the kind of maid who engaged in housework only when all other options had been exhausted. She liked to inform people that she had her own "staff" in El Salvador, plus a car, a swimming pool, and two dogs, and that she was often told she resembled Jennifer Lopez—"only I have larger eyes." Sixty years old and pleasantly plump, she kept pictures of herself and J-Lo in her wallet. Her bedroom at the Soleyman residence was decorated entirely in peach and gold, and smelled of face powder and hair spray. She kept the curtains drawn and screwed a pink lightbulb into the ceiling light fixture so that her image, when she looked in the mirror, was forever cased in a pleasant, if eerily Blanche DuBois–esque, glow.

Esperanza told Leon she had worked for the Soleymans for three years and seven months. She previously had a rule of not working for immigrants, no matter what country they came from, because they were invariably more demanding and paid less than Americans, but she didn't mind Neda because she wasn't a nosy boss. Unlike other Iranians who employed many of Esperanza's friends, Neda didn't entertain seven nights a week, didn't have sixty people over every Shabbat. She was quiet and minded her own business, barely leaving her room when she was in the house for fear, Esperanza guessed, of running into Mister. The only person Neda saw regularly was Nadereh—the therapist/life coach/yoga teacher who charged $300 an hour and didn't make house calls.

Esperanza knew about Nadereh through the network of maids

who worked for other Iranian families on the West Side and who made sure nothing that went on in any house ever remained private. That's also how she knew that Neda's marriage to Raphael's Son had been the scandal of its time, prompted, some said, by an unfortunate pregnancy resulting in the birth of their first daughter, Nicole. Esperanza had seen for herself that the marriage had been a bad idea indeed. The only time the two didn't fight was when they weren't talking to each other.

"She cries and says, *Aabehroo, aabehroo,*" Esperanza summarized the interaction, "and he screams and says, *Talaagh beguir.*"

She was about to translate for Leon the meaning of that last phrase—get a divorce—when a uniform knocked on her door.

There might be a witness—of sorts—who claimed he had seen everything, but he wasn't willing to say what "everything" meant. He wasn't going to talk to "any Podunk street cop." The only person he would give a statement to was "the chief."

The witness—bald with sunburned scalp, a long, oval face, and a blind right eye—was George P. Carter III, a.k.a. the Altoid Man. Something of a West LA institution, he had appeared on the scene in the mid-2000s—a tall, slim, and elegant figure with a closed eye and an affinity for spotless white sweaters and crisply pressed tan or light-gray pants. At the time, he was a PhD student at UCLA, had a Culver City address, and a seven-day-a-week surfing habit in Paradise Cove in Malibu. Then one morning he showed up on the corner of Santa Monica Boulevard and Whittier Drive, across the street from the Beverly Hilton Hotel—the preferred venue for many a charity dinner, million-dollar bar mitzvah, and, throughout that decade, numerous Oscar luncheons—holding up a sign that read, *LAPD BLINDED MY EYE AND REFUSES TO APOLOGIZE OR PAY FOR IT.*

The sign's fine print described a weekend altercation between him and the police: he was driving in the area—the border between Beverly Hills and Century City—and the cops pulled him over for no reason; he objected, since "we don't live in North Korea," so they beat him, blinded his eye, and took him to jail. Afterward, they wouldn't even apologize.

He appeared so sophisticated and held the sign with such dogged earnestness, he managed to slow down the already-excruciating traffic on the corner.

Below the fine print, a larger-type font declared that George P. Carter III was not homeless or hungry, didn't want motorists' money or their expressions of pity. He wanted "justice" for himself, compensation for his eye, and an apology from the police chief, the mayor, and the president of the police commission.

He got a lot of curious stares, a few people honking their horns and giving him a thumbs-up, but no reaction from the police. So he returned the next day.

Monday through Friday for the next five or six years, the Altoid Man arrived at his post on the seven a.m. bus and stayed exactly twelve hours. Every ten minutes or so he would put the sign down, reach into his pocket, and retrieve a box of "original" Altoids, pop one in his mouth, and resume his stance. He took a half-hour lunch break at noon, and sat out the weekends when the traffic on his corner was light. Over the years his appearance showed signs of attrition. He grew increasingly thin and disheveled, his clothes became ragged and dirty, and his sign turned weather-beaten and nearly illegible—but he never gave up his Altoid habit or his steadfast demand for reparations from the LAPD.

In time, he and his sign faded like celluloid figures off a black-and-white reel; he became just another angry soul riding the buses and wandering the streets of LA, but he never stopped fighting the good fight. Just in case he was attacked by the police again, he carried a disposable camera in his pants pocket and pulled it out every time a cruiser slowed down or stopped near him.

He told Montoya that he had seen "everything" with his one eye, and could give a precise description. "But I'm not talking to you goons," he said. "Go get your boss and bring him over here to lick my ass."

By "boss" he meant the police chief, Charlie Beck, but since he wasn't available or on the premises, the Altoid Man had agreed to meet with Leon instead.

He told Leon he had been riding the 4 bus from downtown to the beach, which was what he always did, going back and forth all night to avoid sleeping on the street, where he'd be vulnerable to "more police brutality," or in a shelter, where the company was intolerable "since I don't drink, do drugs, or speak Spanish or Ebonics." He'd had to get off the bus at two a.m. to fulfill a pressing urge, "and I don't mean just pissing." He liked Mapleton for that purpose, he explained, because it was a nice street where "a man with his butt bare" wouldn't be attacked by "a bunch of faggots" or robbed by "bean-eating Mexicans," and because there was a large construction site not too far away from Sunset.

"Some fucking maharaja's been building here for ten years. Must have spent a hundred million on it and all it's good for is a half-decent shit."

From the construction site, the Altoid Man had noticed the gray car drive up to the gates of Raphael's Son's house, had seen "everything, I can give you minute-by-minute details, but fuck you if you think I'm gonna tell you a fucking thing without first getting my dues from the fucking LAPD."

Back in the house, Leon found Neda in the "functional" kitchen, smoking a cigarette at a large, round, marble table next to the window. An espresso, prepared by Esperanza on her favorite new Nespresso machine purchased at Williams-Sonoma, sat untouched before Neda.

At the counter, Esperanza had laid out a formal place setting—a tall glass of passion fruit iced tea, a small salad in a china bowl, a grilled vegetable sandwich with a side of quinoa and garbanzo beans in a lemon tahini sauce from Joan's on Third on a matching plate, and a black cloth napkin—and had just sat down to eat her lunch. Dessert was a cup of mixed berries from Whole Foods, sprinkled with sweet agave nectar from Trader Joe's.

Esperanza might have been unusually pampered, but all the housekeepers Neda hired had a way of connecting with their inner princess the minute they came to work for her. It was like they went to bed the first night at the job, felt the single pea beneath the mountain of mattresses laid out for them by Neda, and woke up queen-in-waiting. After that, it was just a question of how much Neda could put up with. As a rule, firing the help was never a good idea: one disgruntled domestic could do a great deal of damage to a former or current employer's *aabehroo* merely by disclosing certain personal information, true or not, about the family she had worked for.

Leon stopped by the counter and glanced at Esperanza's sandwich. "Looks good," he said. "You should make one for your boss."

In front of Neda on the table, next to a silver bowl filled with little pink and yellow packets of fake sugar, was a small collection of plastic pill bottles all bearing her name: Ambien, Xanax, Wellbutrin, Lexapro, Neurontin, Soma—anxiety, depression, migraines, smoking addiction, sleeplessness. One bottle contained only a razor blade, the kind purchased at a hardware store for a dollar a pack. It was used, Leon guessed, to cut some of the pills in half.

"How's your lovely sister?"

His question jarred Neda.

"Nilou and I were in the same grade in Beverly," he explained, then regretted having revealed anything about himself to the suspect. He pulled a chair out and sat down, unbuttoned his jacket, put his forearms on the edge of the table. "I remember you too," he added. "You were quiet."

Neda blushed purple.

"I understand she's a rocket scientist," he continued. "At the Jet Propulsion Laboratory. That's very impressive."

Neda was quiet, but Leon realized that Esperanza had taken a break from her health-fest to stare him down with contempt. She could tell he wanted to rattle Neda, and obviously didn't like it.

"I run into her from time to time."

That's how it was on LA's West Side; you could run into the same people year after year, especially if you had gone to Beverly High, and even more so if you were an Iranian Jew who had gone to Beverly High.

Leon's eyes wandered back to the razor blade on the table. Suddenly Neda placed her hands, palms up, on the table.

"The other officer already looked," she said flatly, but he could tell she was still smarting from the comparison to her sister. "And they took pictures."

The hands were clean, no cuts or nicks or any trace of a razor blade. Then again, Leon thought, who said that the blood in the car had come from a cut? Until a body was found, all Leon and O'Donnell really knew was that Neda had reported her husband missing.

Even this, as Angela S. rushed to point out on Tumblr at two p.m. that day, was probably a lie: "He's most likely sleeping in his bed as I write this. Really! Has anyone checked? Chances are, he's right there at the house he paid for with other people's money, counting the many, many ways in which he's outsmarted the cops already, laughing at the idiot detective looking for his body all around town."

The one thing you could say for Angela, although most people didn't, was that she had been honest enough about her motives in publicly denouncing Raphael's Son: it wasn't for the sake of the victims. Excepting young orphans and old widows, she thought they were all a bunch of cretins—to trust a man with his past with their money, no questions asked. She especially disliked many of the wealthier creditors who thought their losses—in the tens of millions—were more important than those inflicted upon the "small" creditors.

To the extent that it pertained to Raphael's Son, Angela's main purpose, she readily admitted, was revenge.

To those who might have pointed out, perhaps correctly, that she and Raphael's Son had this—the desire to harm another—in common, she would have retorted that whereas His Sleaziness had resorted to telling lies and more lies in order to destroy the Soleyman family and most of the rest of the Iranian community, Angela pursued the all-American ideal of "the truth, the whole truth, and nothing but the truth."

It just so happened that, with Raphael's Son, the most harmful device *was* the truth.

And besides, Angela had been writing the blog since 2008. His Sleaziness's vendetta dated back to before she was born, when the Soleyman family was the toast of Tehran's high society and Raphael's Son a bastard child whose mother claimed, impossibly, that he was the one and true heir to the Soleyman legacy.

People who knew him then talked about how he stood at the door of every shop on Ferdowsi Avenue in downtown Tehran, a portly young boy wearing gray wool pants in the dead of summer because that's all he owned, sweating from heat or shame or perhaps both, and listened to his mother tell strangers that she was the widow of Raphael Soleyman, the eldest of the Soleyman brothers and heir to their father's fortune; that she had been wrongly evicted from her house after her husband died, and that "this here boy" (she rattled him by the shoulder) had been denied his legacy by Raphael's unscrupulous brother.

The mother was old and withered and shrill. She had gone so far as to state on the boy's birth certificate that his first name was indeed "Raphael's Son." She talked like a charlatan and cursed like a whore, embarrassing even her son as she lingered eternally outside the Soleyman mansion on the Avenue of Tranquility and screamed to the heavens and to every blind beggar and hungry orphan who passed by that "this here boy, my son, Raphael's Son, is the real owner of *that* house." When they saw her coming down the street, shop owners closed their doors and turned their backs, pretending that they hadn't seen her or her son, that they couldn't hear her bang on the glass with her fists. Often, they gave her a few rials just so she would go away—"You're bad for business, sister, take your son home and put him to bed."

It would have taken an act of God, at the time, to convince Raphael's Wife to give up her claim, however questionable, to the Soleyman estate, and it might have taken a second act of God for Raphael's Son to find his way out of the dusty twilight of old Tehran into the company of the Aaron Spellings and Hugh Hefners of the world, but that is exactly what had happened to him and to so many other Iranians in America; one minute they were selling old bicycles, the next minute they had become Internet tycoons. Only Raphael's Son had never really left the servants' yards and narrow back alleys behind the houses where his mother took him begging, never let go of the promises she had made on his behalf—that he would someday rise to obliterate everyone who had stolen his birthright, denied him respect and recognition, laughed at him or turned him away because they thought he had no power and therefore no right—never stopped bleeding from the sharp edges of the neighbors' dismissal.

TEHRAN

1952

I t began—this much everyone agreed on—with Izikiel the Red, so called because of his fiery red hair and eyebrows, and for the pale white skin that turned amber when he became angry, which was often, and for the whites of his eyes that became crimson when he drank. Born in 1901 in the Tehran ghetto, he had lived in two rooms with his parents and nine siblings, worked in a bottle factory from age six, married in 1921, produced two sons, and became a widower in 1960. He made his fortune trading wool and other fine fabrics imported from Russia, which he sold for far less than any of his competitors. When Reza Shah came to power and ordained that every man and woman in the country must pick a surname, Izikiel chose Soleyman. In 1954, he built Bagh-e Yaas—a stately mansion that became a symbol of hard-earned prosperity and hard-fought triumph over adversity not only for him, but for all the Jews of Tehran.

Bagh-e Yaas had a main residence, two satellite houses, and a seven-acre garden where hundred-year-old maple trees spread their branches over beds of pink and white Muhammadi roses. The yard walls were covered with the most fragrant vines of poet's jasmine anywhere in Tehran. The brick pathways leading to the Big House wound past glittering pools and cascading fountains, and ended at the edge of tiled verandas with French doors that opened into vast salons and long hallways and a black granite staircase that spiraled up five floors until it ended at a ballroom with crystal chandeliers and bay windows from which the sound of music and laughter flowed into the moonlit streets and shady back alleys of the capital.

Izikiel's older son, Raphael, was a sleepwalker with an extraordinary appetite and the physical appearance of a famine survivor. He ate as much as three men, and was always hungry. The appetite and the sleepwalking were caused by intestinal worms, which were as common as they were insidious, and they should have been curable— were in fact curable for every other person affected by them in the country—but they refused to be dislodged from Raphael's insides no matter what remedy was applied. The doctors and faith healers and plant-and-powder physicians who had tried and failed to stamp out Raphael's worms were of the opinion that the vermin drew their resilience from a second, more mystifying source, this one peculiar to the Soleyman family and which Raphael had inherited—a condition that, for lack of a medical designation, was known to the Soleymans as "incandescence."

Raphael looked normal enough in daylight, but at night, or in dark places, his heart glowed a pulsating blue-white color that exposed all its veins and arteries, all its muscles and tendons and fluids, as if his chest were made of glass and his skin were transparent.

No one knew what caused incandescence, but it had run in the Soleyman bloodline for generations. Every decade or so, a child—usually a boy in the family—was born with a glowing heart. The parents, fearing social repercussions, did their best to hide the condition, though by most accounts the affected person suffered from no other symptoms and developed no particular ailments. Raphael too might have been spared a life of agony had he not been invaded in early childhood with the worms that, the doctors hypothesized without any rational basis, seemed to draw special strength and resilience from the light in his heart. As it was, his sleepwalking was so acute, he ended up lost on the streets at least once a week. For a time, his parents locked the door of the bedroom where he slept with his younger brother, but Raphael climbed through the window and went out. They sealed the window, so he broke the glass and crawled through it, bleeding, into the yard.

In the end, Izikiel decided to let him be, and so Raphael took to the streets every few nights, barefoot and dressed in white cotton pajamas, the light from his heart attracting every moth and firefly and nocturnal bird in the city, plus an entire horde of restless, insomniac ghosts who had been turned away from their homes by their living relatives, and half a dozen street urchins who were always on the look-out for an adventure. They followed Raphael wherever he went, and then trailed him back home and into the room where he slept with his brother, Aaron, so that in the morning, when the boys woke up, the air was teeming with flying creatures and the floor was littered with dead leaves and fresh dirt and whatever else the barefoot ghosts had dragged in from the streets. Then Aaron would open a window and let out the moths that had grown into butterflies, and the ghosts dissolved into the light.

By age sixteen, Raphael was written off as a lost cause by every physician and witch doctor in the country. By twenty, he was relegated to the ranks of madcap uncles and embarrassing siblings that most families tended to keep hidden from the world, until they grew old and died in some quiet corner of the house. He was not married and had no prospects, and he was not expected to do a full day's work for as long as he lived. As for his rights of inheritance, there was no question he had none, given the state of his health. It is true that upon a father's death, his eldest son conventionally inherited the entire estate. If the eldest son was no longer living, the next oldest son was second in line, followed by other male siblings.

But the state of Raphael's health ruled out the possibility of him managing anything at all, or of producing children. Instead, it was clear that the mantle would pass to Aaron. That's what Izikiel had determined and what everyone deemed just and reasonable, and everything would have been just fine, the family would have continued to live in peace and prosperity, had it not been blighted with the arrival of the Black Bitch of Bushehr, later known as Raphael's Wife.

She emerged out of the heat wave of 1950, during the endless summer that began in the south and spread northward, laying the country to waste with its relentless, desiccating breath. In the port city of Bushehr on the Persian Gulf, the heat boiled the fish in the sea and sent them to float on the surface—the sheen of their scales blinding against the sunlight on the horizon, hiding the green of the water in daytime, glowing silver in the moonlight. Around the harbor, the beach was littered with red and yellow and striped fish, young boys with brown skin and scraggy limbs lay in the shade of foreign ships—English and Norwegian, Russian and German and Italian. They were nearly naked, their feet wrapped in cloth or newspaper against the blistering sand. Before the heat, their fathers had worked as fishermen or smugglers, sailors or dockworkers. The boys had dived for pearls or sunken treasure, begged the foreigners who arrived on the ships for chewing gum and cigarettes. Now the water held nothing but jellyfish and seaweed, and the sailors barely left their ships for fear of heatstroke.

Raphael's Wife came from a family of palm readers and sorcerers and harem maids—Jews with Arab skin and Cimmerian eyes who inhabited the veiled and narrow edges of a diverse and idiosyncratic society. She was thirty years old, pitifully unappealing to the eye and woefully unaware of it, when she escaped her hoodlum father and eleven bandit brothers and left Bushehr in search of cooler climates and a kinder destiny. She headed north, for the capital. By her own account, the journey had taken eighteen months and eleven days; she rode on trains and on the backs of camels and mules, traversed the Great Central Desert without a guide—alone but for the lizards and scorpions and the occasional caravan. She had stolen a bedouin's headdress to guard against the sun, lifted a pair of severely used oxfords from a young Dutch tourist who had fallen asleep next to her on a bus, and she crossed the gates of the city of Tehran one morning in the winter of 1952 just as the song of the muezzin soared above the brick minarets and blue-tiled domes of every mosque in the city.

She asked for directions to the Square of the Pearl Cannon—the place of pilgrimage where, it was known around the country, the most outrageous prayers and undue wishes came true—and entered it just at the moment when Raphael, glowing heart and hungry ghosts and a cloud of moths and mosquitos and all, came in through the opposite gate. This, the Black Bitch of Bushehr would later insist, was an act of God—the first and only time in her life when an otherwise miserly Almighty opened His habitually clenched fist and threw a crumb or two in the old maid's direction. She attributed it to the hallowed nature of the grounds upon which she and Raphael had stood, and especially to the propitious powers of the blessed cannon itself.

The Square of the Pearl Cannon in South Tehran was a vast rectangle that served as an axis to many historic sites and celebrated areas of the capital. It was built in the sixteenth century as a gateway between the city and the barren lands beyond, with the inaugural name of Square of the Citadel, and had none of the allure and exaltedness that was bestowed upon it some three hundred years later, during the unfortunate reign of Fath-Ali Shah Qajar. An art-loving, wife-collecting, vain-even-for-a-king dandy of a monarch who had a habit of abdicating every battle before it had begun, Fath-Ali Shah embraced every monstrous treaty that was offered to him as the price of surrender. When he was not busy losing broad regions and major provinces of the country to foreign powers, he married 158 women (many of them princesses from other dynasties), and produced 260 children and 786 grandchildren. He also spruced up the Palace of Roses—a sixteenth-century relic that sat at one end of the Square of the Citadel—and hosted poets and artists and more than a few genteel foreign "advisors."

He might have been more suitably advised to spend his money on reining in the power of the Shia clergy in Iran, who were all but ruling the country along with the French and the British, or improving the state of his own army, which at the time was nothing more than an unfortunate assortment of unpaid, poorly fed, and often unarmed soldiers, but you couldn't tell a shah what he should or shouldn't spend money on—that was the job of the mullahs and the Europeans and they, it seemed, liked the army just as useless and ineffective as it was.

To defend the country against the ever-marching battalions of Russian soldiers intent on stealing every part of Iran, Fath-Ali Shah liked to wear his "Robes of Wrath" and sit on his Peacock Throne. The robes were entirely red, and he accessorized them with a crown of rubies, meant to incite the fear of God in the czar and his invading forces, because they signaled that the shah was angry—a condition that, within Iran itself, did imply that very bad things were about to happen to the subject of his wrath. He even asked his courtiers, as he sat on the throne, just how concerned—*very, very concerned, Your Majesty*—and how terrified—*extremely, inordinately terrified, Your Majesty*—the czar should be by news of the shah's donning of the robes. Only when he had lost to Imperial Russia the entire province of Georgia and a great fortune in monetary damages did he consider updating his army's weaponry.

Because the czar had cannons, Fath-Ali Shah commissioned a set of new state-of-the-art ones himself. The prototype for the cannons was made by a well-known forger in the city of Esfahan. Built at a stupendous cost and brought to Tehran with great fanfare, the cannon was unusually large and extremely heavy. It was installed on the grounds of the Square of the Citadel, next to a shallow pool of water that reflected its image, across from the shah's palace. For the unveiling, Fath-Ali Shah summoned his entire court as well as ministers from foreign nations, created the kind of spectacle usually reserved for long-awaited prophets, and promised to give the world a glimpse of Persia's transition from a tired, crumbling empire to a dynamic, modern state.

In the presence of the shah and his legions of guests, the cannon was armed, its barrel turned toward the desert that lay beyond the gates of the square, and fired. There was a deafening sound. The earth shook and the skies darkened and a rain of oily black particles fell on the guests as they ran every which way for cover, coughing riotously and bleeding from the ears and blinded by soot. The shah himself was blackened from royal head to sacred toe. When he inquired about the source of the disturbance, he was told that the cannon seemed to have a built-in idiosyncrasy: instead of projecting the ball through the mouth of the barrel as any ordinary cannon might, this one preferred to excrete it from the back. As a result the ball, which didn't have enough room to exit whole, imploded inside the cannon's belly, then spewed soot and gunpowder into the air.

Given its dismal performance, a less creative monarch might have ordered that the cannon be summarily destroyed, its builders sent to the gallows, and its existence erased from memory. But no one was going to accuse Fath-Ali Shah of lacking either vanity or imagination. Shortly after ascending to the throne in 1797, he had extended his royal title from King of Kings, Shadow of the Sun, Ruler of the Universe, to include Most Formidable Lord and Master of the *Encyclopaedia Britan-*

nica. Rather than admit failure with the first modern cannon, he gave the useless heap of metal a name—the Pearl Cannon—placed it on permanent display on an especially built platform outside the Palace of Roses, chained a ferocious lion and a truculent bear to each side of the platform to guard the cannon, and designated the area surrounding it as hallowed grounds. Just like in a place of worship, it would be recognized as a refuge for anyone who entered. In its shadow, every prayer would be answered and every wish would come true.

From that day on, the Pearl Cannon became a haven for petty thieves and ruthless murderers, exposed spies and failed coup leaders, escaped convicts and bankrupt merchants who were entirely safe from the reach of the law or their enemies for as long as they remained on the premises. Some of the refugees lasted a few days, then gave themselves up; others stayed for years, surviving on alms thrown at them by passersby and on food brought to them by young women in love, or parents of ailing children, or even old witches with dreams of holy matrimony who traveled for eighteen months and eleven days to rob the Soleyman family of a night's peaceful sleep.

It doesn't matter what's true, Raphael's Wife had learned during the days and months of pilgrimage, only what's believed.

She claimed she had fallen in love with Raphael on the spot. She said this from day one—to him and to his family members and to every friend and stranger with whom she happened to cross paths—and she said it again, through the next three decades, in good times and bad, in poverty and riches. No matter what preposterous lie she was busy defending or what harebrained scheme she applied herself to, the one assertion that remained constant was that she was, wholly and unreservedly and so very selflessly, in love with Raphael.

Never mind that she was an old woman with no family, no place to live, and certainly not a dime in her pocket; or that she had a face that was dark and furrowed and generally offensive to the eye. Never mind that she'd found Raphael when he was half-naked, sleepwalking, inhabited by vermin, and surrounded by ghosts. She said she saw him and thought he was an angel fallen from the sky, his glowing heart proof of his purity, his bare feet and skeletal figure evidence of his saintliness.

Either that or, as Izikiel the Red would conclude based on the facts on the ground, she was a lonely, penniless woman who found a sleeping rich boy and snared him before he had a chance to open his eyes.

That morning at the square, she took him by the hand and said she knew just what he needed to quell the bedlam in his bowels. She poured ground coal mixed with dried, pulverized crow's feet and seven drops of turpentine into a sheep's stomach and had him drink it all in one gulp, and a moment later he was vomiting heaps of slithery, agitated worms, some a hundred feet long, others as short as forty feet. After that, she took Raphael's head onto her lap and whispered to him until he fell asleep. When he woke up, hers was the first face he saw.

She walked him home that day, sat outside the house, and waited till dark when everyone was asleep and Raphael emerged in his nightclothes. She led him, still sleeping, back to the square, and there they remained on the edge of the pool reflecting the image of the cannon until the sun came up and the scribes and mullahs who conducted business at the site dragged themselves in with their fountain pens and worry beads. Raphael's Wife didn't ask the unsuspecting young man in her clutches if he was married, because she didn't want to know. Even if he were single, she figured that his parents would never consent to their twenty-two-year-old son marrying an older woman, much less one as poor and unattractive as she. But if a legitimate Jewish marriage was out of the question, a temporary Muslim one was not.

Islamic law allows a man to take four permanent wives at any one time. But it also provides for an unlimited number of "temporary" wives. The temporary marriage can last anywhere from an hour to ninety-nine years, depending on the terms specified at the outset. It can be performed by a mullah in a matter of minutes, no questions asked and no paperwork provided, and it expires automatically at the end of the contract's stated length.

Raphael's Wife later claimed that he had married her "temporarily" for a period of ninety-nine years. That might have been true, though Raphael told his brother, Aaron, privately that he thought the contract was for ninety-nine days, but there was no way to know for sure because the contract was verbal and did not require the presence of a witness. None of that mattered anyway because, legend has it, Izikiel the Red took one look at Raphael's Wife, then turned to his son and said, "*Ghomesh kon*"—lose her.

Later, Raphael's Wife would claim that the Soleyman family had her to thank for Bagh-e Yaas. By that she meant they had usurped her husband's right of ownership and that it was she who should be living there—a claim that was vehemently denied by the rest of the family. Still, there was no debating that her marriage to Raphael had been the catalyst for Izikiel to built Bagh-e Yaas: until Raphael brought home the Black Bitch of Bushehr, the family had lived on Sepah Street, not far from the Square of the Pearl Cannon. Raphael may not have been an ideal son, but he was obedient and undemanding. Then he went and fell under the witch's spell and suddenly found, first, the nerve to bring her home like the prize that she wasn't, then the audacity to refuse to "lose" her as Izikiel had ordered.

In a rage, Izikiel banished Raphael from the house, so he went back to the square and lived there with the Black Bitch for three consecutive months. His mother cried her eyes raw and begged Izikiel to show mercy on her sick child, and word spread around the city that Izikiel's eldest son was living on alms and scraps. Aaron was dispatched to bring sense to his brother—leave this whore and come home—and when he failed to convince Raphael, others volunteered or were conscripted to mediate between father and son. In the end, Izikiel caved.

It was his first and only defeat as the head of the family, and he blamed it entirely on Raphael's Wife. He let the two back into the house, with the proviso that he never have to lay eyes on Raphael's Wife. To make sure of that, and to mend the damage to his name and reputation as a result of the standoff, he built a house large enough for Raphael's Wife to be lost in.

Izikiel bought a four-and-a-half-acre parcel of land, shaped like a diamond, that was situated in what, at the time, was the northernmost part of Tehran. The Big House, where Izikiel would live with his wife, was at the top corner of the diamond, closest to the Elburz Mountains that constituted a changing backdrop—blue in daylight, shadows at night, snow-covered tips glowing silver at the first hint of dawn—against its golden brick shell. From there, the land sloped gently downward, widening at the center, becoming narrow again at the opposite end from the Big House. On the right and left sides of the diamond were metal gates that opened onto a narrow, covered walkway, like a private access road with a roof, and that eventually led to the back entrance of a small one-story house.

The two small houses were almost identical in shape and dimension, and could be accessed from the street so that the inhabitants could come and go without crossing paths with one another, which was exactly what Izikiel wanted—to keep Raphael under supervision without having to suffer the sight of his wife. In 1954, when construction was complete, he gave the house on the left to Raphael, and the one on the right to Aaron.

To everyone involved, and to impartial observers, this seemed like a fair and rational plan. Raphael, they thought, was lucky to receive anything at all from his father—given his defiance of him and the embarrassment he had caused the family by marrying the Black Bitch. He did not have the physical capacity to manage his own or the family's finances, and his health was deteriorating at an ever-faster pace. The worm colony that had nestled at first in his intestines had over time expanded into the entire landscape of his body, feeding not just on what he ate and drank, but also on his blood and bone marrow, rendering him brittle as a dry leaf in autumn, so that his skin cracked and his limbs broke at the slightest pressure, forcing him to lie in a bed of goose feathers. He slept days and sleepwalked at night, and he still glowed in the dark—a gentle, innocent luminosity that made him resemble a fading lantern and that broke his father's heart every time he set eyes on him.

The wife, meanwhile, washed and dressed and fed Raphael, bound his cuts, and reset his bones. Sometimes, she even followed him and his posse of ghosts around the city, to see that no harm came to him by the young boys and stray dogs who often chased him. She claimed she was motivated purely by love, but you didn't have to be especially cynical to discern an element of self-interest in her efforts to keep him alive: as long as Raphael was living, and as long as he refused to divorce her, Raphael's Wife could count on having a roof over her head and three square meals a day.

She managed to stay on the ride for a good ten years before it was interrupted.

One morning in the winter of 1962, Izikiel woke up and announced to his servant girl, a fourteen-year-old mute he had purchased two years earlier for a thousand tomans, that he was going to die that day. He was sixty-one years old and in perfect health. He wasn't contemplating suicide and didn't think he was going to be murdered. He just knew his time had come, and that he had till midnight to set his affairs in order.

He made a call to Aaron, who had been studying in France for four years, and told him to rush home and bring all his things, "because you won't be going back; I'm dying today and you'll have to take my place." He would have liked to say his other goodbyes in person, but they were in the midst of the first real snowstorm of the season. Roads were closed all over the city and roofs were caving in and glass cracked from the cold in window panes, so he sat in a pale blue armchair by the large bay windows in the main salon all day. He drank hot black tea sweetened with saffron-flavored rock candy, and wrote letters to everyone he could think of whose life would be affected by his death.

"My father is waiting for me at this side of midnight," he began each letter.

At nine o'clock in the evening he took a bath, put on a clean suit and a black tie, and lay in bed with his shoes on and his hat resting on the pillow next to him. He left the light on and his door unlocked, so that when he called for the servant girl, Manzel, at seven minutes to midnight, she heard him immediately in her own bedroom downstairs. It took her two minutes to put on her shoes and run upstairs. She found him lying supine in bed, still fully dressed. He asked for a glass of water. A moment later, he inhaled deeply, let out a long, slow sigh, turned over onto his left side, and died.

The undertakers were sent for at five a.m. and arrived an hour and a half later. They were let in by a weeping Manzel and shown to Izikiel's bedroom. In spite of the early hour, the house was already bustling with family members who had been alerted by the cook, and had rushed over to offer their sympathies and arrange for the burial and shivah. The undertakers sought permission to enter the bedroom and, once granted, went in with their heads bowed and their hands clasped in respect for the deceased. They found nothing—no body, dead or alive, no trace of Izikiel's clothes or shoes or hat, no footprints or other signs of retreat.

From the letters, and from Manzel's version of sign language, people came to the conclusion that Izikiel had not so much died as simply departed—in the company of his father and, as he had predicted, for good. They understood there would be no burial, because there was nothing left of the man to bury, but they did expect a shivah because that's what you do when you lose a person for good (when they die or disappear or marry outside the religion or, worst of all, willingly convert). Afterward, they assumed, Aaron would move into the Big House and take ownership of all of Izikiel's other assets, continue to support his sick brother as their father had done, marry a rich, beautiful girl, and have a few sons of his own.

It wasn't exactly "happily ever after," but a close-enough version, and one that any mortal man (save, perhaps, an American) would be exceedingly fortunate to live. Only an American would have the gall to want more than that, or to put happiness on the list of essentials.

The truth about Aaron is that he was at once blessed and cursed by a birthright he would never be able to escape. You could see it in his eyes—this awareness of the heft of the responsibility he had to bear. He was the offspring of a wealthy Jew who had, thanks to the kindness of the shah and his own outsize abilities, risen overnight from the hardships and deprivations of the ghetto into a world of privilege and excess, who remembered the past too well and was determined never to go back, or even to pause long enough to catch a glimpse of where they came from and how far he had traveled. His father had given Aaron every financial advantage a young person could reasonably aspire to, but he had also charged him with the backbreaking task of fulfilling, in his own life, every lofty ideal and impossible expectation, every foolhardy dream and failed ambition of all the generations of Jews who had lived and died in all the ghettos and back alleys over three thousand years of history in Iran.

That's important to remember, given what happened next and everything that followed from it—that the silver spoon Aaron was born with was also his shackle, that his good health and robust intellect in fact restrained his freedom, that the great wealth he came into entitled him to very little of his own.

It's different when you inherit not just money, but a legacy; when you embody not just your own dreams, but those of many.

Aaron had a boyish face, a taut, agile body, and an old man's eyes. They had that faded look—the pupils rimmed with a bleached halo, as if the color had been seeping slowly into the whites and turning them creamy. It was an unsettling disparity: a wise old man standing at the window of a young one's face, peering out at a world he's seen too many times before.

He was the only person in his family to attend high school. He finished at the top of his class and sat for the college entrance exam where he came in fifth nationally, but instead of letting him go to university in Iran, his father sent him to Paris to study medicine. Aaron left in September of 1958, shortly after his eighteenth birthday—a quiet, quick-witted boy with a suitcase full of starched white sheets and another packed with starched white shirts, all of them monogrammed by hand and folded with mathematical precision and attesting to the extreme fastidiousness that had ruled every fragment of his life since early childhood. Four years later, when he was summoned home, he was more self-assured but no less exacting, disappointed that he was not able to complete his studies and become a physician, but never—not once—questioning his duty.

His duty, as Aaron knew it, was above all to safeguard the good name and reputation of the Soleyman clan. This is what he tried to do that first week after he arrived in Tehran and sat shivah, and what he would continue to do for the rest of his life, regardless of the harm it might cause. He was not what people at the time referred to as "overly punctilious" and that psychologists now call "obsessive-compulsive." He wasn't driven by forces he could not tame. He was just a man who believed in doing things well and keeping his promises, and this was unfortunate because no sooner had he taken his father's place than Aaron found himself at war with the Black Bitch of Bushehr and her single-minded, fanatical quest to muddy the Soleyman name.

Thirty days after his father had passed, Raphael rose from his sickbed and went sleepwalking into the street. Opium Morad, the old addict who lived on the sidewalk a stone's throw from Bagh-e Yaas, saw him and thought he was going to catch his death of cold: it was the middle of the night, the temperature was well below zero, the ground frozen, and yet Raphael was barefoot and dressed only in his cotton nightshirt. How he managed to stay asleep in spite of the cold Morad couldn't fathom, but he did note that for once Raphael was walking alone. All the ghosts and birds and insects that normally followed him, Morad figured, had the good sense to stay indoors.

Morad himself was wrapped in a blanket he draped around the little brazier where he heated his opium. He asked Raphael where he was headed.

"To see my father," Raphael said, which was alarming, given Izikiel's recent relocation from the world of the living, but Raphael kept slogging away down the middle of the street and in the general direction of the Jewish cemetery that was many kilometers outside Tehran and accessible only through a narrow, dangerous road. The glow from his chest had dimmed to a languid flicker, Opium Morad noticed, and he never did appear to wake up or to open his eyes, never did see the mammoth truck that flew the green and black flags of mourning and the white satin signs displaying verses from the Koran—prayers for the dead in Arabic—the red and green lightbulbs that lined the outside of the cabin, the hand-painted exhortations to the Almighty, the Prophet Muhammad, and his disciples, Ali and Hussein; or maybe he saw the truck barreling down the street with its headlights flooding the darkness but without so much as a whisper—no sound from its massive engine, no noise from its gargantuan wheels, no reverberation from the rattle of windows or the jolting of metal or the piercing of still night air—like a ship sailing quietly but at breakneck speed through a dark channel, the wind from the truck's movement bending the trunks of trees and raising the water in the open gutters, churning the dust and dry leaves and bits of discarded newspapers from the sides of the road, tearing the veils off the heads of streetwalkers on their way home from the night's final encounter—a vision at once so terrifying and so beautiful that even the mangy stray dogs and crippled child beggars asleep on the sidewalk sat up to watch it with glazed eyes and open mouths, and the only person or entity, Opium Morad later insisted, who didn't pause or hesitate to walk toward it was scraggy and decrepit Raphael.

He looked, in fact, like a man bent on meeting his destiny, which is just what he did—"I realize you have trouble believing this, gentlemen, I do have a tendency to see things that don't exist, it's true that opium plays tricks on the mind, but this one, I assure you, was real, he kept walking straight toward the truck, and it didn't slow down or slam on the breaks or even sound its horn, it just rolled toward him and then onto and over him, the whole thing took less than half a second, I didn't even hear it hit poor Raphael, it just absorbed him, I thought, and then I looked up at the driver's-side window just as it passed by me, and I swear on the spirits of my dear mother and my revered father, the cabin was empty, there was no one in the driver's seat, no one at the wheel of that truck, I couldn't make that up if I smoked an entire poppy field's worth of opium."

Aaron sat shivah again and afterward allowed a decent interval before he moved to set his brother's affairs in order. There was the house Raphael and his wife had lived in, and the few thousand tomans she had managed to save from their allowance. And there was the wife herself, though she was not really a wife at all—just a woman with no marriage contract and not even a verbal promise of recompense (at the time of the temporary marriage or later) for the years she would spend with Raphael. She had brought nothing of monetary value to the union, so she was entitled to nothing in return. There were no children who might need her parenting services. Legally, Aaron owed her nothing but a safe return to her father's home. By custom, there was no chance of her being able to stay with the family once Raphael was gone. Still, Aaron realized that what's legal is not always right, and he was determined to do right by his brother's caretaker. Once they had passed the thirty-day mark, he sent Manzel the Mute to fetch Raphael's Wife.

The girl came back twenty minutes later looking bewildered, making gestures that were incomprehensible to Aaron. He called in another one of the maids to translate Manzel's signs, but the older woman couldn't make sense of them either so Aaron sent the second maid to Raphael's Wife.

This one too returned without an answer. Pallid and trembling, she kept reciting a prayer against blasphemy and hiding her face from Aaron as if in shame.

Exasperated by the drama, he trekked down to Raphael's house and knocked with his fist on the door. The Black Bitch opened almost instantly.

"You're not sending me away," she said. "I'm pregnant with your brother's son, and when he's born he'll be first in line to inherit all this."

It was a foolish move on her part, a scheme so swinish, it left Aaron little choice but to do just what she had warned against. He never believed, even for a moment, her claim about the child—a near miracle, she was willing to concede, given his illness and her old age, but just remember Abraham and Sarah—he was a hundred and she a young ninety when they conceived Isaac. Because of this, Aaron realized that she had intentions far more ambitious than what he was willing to allow. He decided that he must cut her out like a bad tooth before she became an all-consuming pain.

He counted 15,000 tomans—one thousand for each year she had spent with Raphael—added to it fifteen gold coins, and gave her thirty days' notice to vacate the house. He waited a month, and when she didn't leave he waited another month. Then he sent two policemen to force her out and padlock the door. She was allowed to take her own and Raphael's clothes, the 15,000 tomans, and the fifteen gold coins. Finally, to ensure that she realized her expulsion was permanent, he sold Raphael's house.

The new owners were a Jewish couple with an eight-year-old daughter and a pair of six-year-old twin boys. The husband was a former professor of mathematics at Tehran University; the wife was an obstetrician who specialized in difficult pregnancies. They had met in 1950 when they were both students at Tufts University in Boston, married, and returned to Iran. She had a thriving practice; he hadn't worked for six years because he was severely agoraphobic and could not bear to leave his room. He spent his time writing the math section of the concourt—the national college entrance exam—memorizing encyclopedias, and caring for the children.

The older daughter, Elizabeth (after the queen), was doe-eyed and fair, exceptionally bright, and eerily independent. Before she entered kindergarten, she could solve complex mathematical problems in her head and memorize a dozen pages of text after a single run-through. By age eight, she read science textbooks for entertainment, and was teaching herself English and Arabic while girls her age still played dress-up and begged their mothers for blonde, blue-eyed dolls. She weighed which university she should attend and what courses to take. That was her dream and her goal: to go to university. She was always dressed in her uniform, even on Fridays when there was no school, and she wore her voluminous hair in a ponytail with an enormous white bow that she starched and pressed every day. Her only friend in the world was a Muslim boy named Hussein Zemorrodi who was two years older and nearly as smart as Elizabeth. Their idea of fun was to recite from memory entire sections of the *Shahnameh*, the Persian equivalent of the *Odyssey*, all written in verse. Other than that, she had no relationships with anyone outside her immediate family: she was too weird for other children, too frighteningly bright for adults. And there was the smell.

For reasons that even her physician mother and professor father could not fathom, eight-year-old Elizabeth emitted a warm, sweet-and-salty-and-humid-as-the-sea-at-midnight scent that, depending on how you felt about fish and algae and sand crabs and the tide, could be exceedingly pleasant or plainly offensive but, either way, maddeningly persistent. The first whiff of it had seeped into the air when she was barely a cell inside her mother's womb, when Madame Doctor had burped after drinking an ice-cold bottle of Coca-Cola. She and the professor were on their honeymoon in the port city of Ramsar on the Caspian, and the marriage was already a fiasco because he had panicked at the prospect of being in a hall with a few hundred other people and therefore bailed out of their wedding reception, and now he refused to leave their room because he could not stand the thought of running into anyone he didn't know or anyone he did know. At any rate, there wasn't much point in leaving the room because they had come to the sea during the rainy season; it poured in Ramsar from the minute they arrived till long after they returned to Tehran, which might have made for a romantic setting—newlyweds together in a room with one big bed and nothing else to entertain themselves with—if only the bridegroom weren't so fainthearted and easily spooked.

Let's just say he made love like a man who writes math tests.

The story goes that Madame Doctor lay in the hotel bed thinking of the sea outside the window and let her insides fill with the humid, briny air where the professor came up short, listening to the rising tide and thinking of the fishermen on the tiny islands that dotted the sea, their sun-ravaged faces and ropy limbs and hail-Imam-Reza boats, and became thirstier by the minute until the deed was done and the frightened little mathematician had scurried into the bathroom and she could pick up the phone and order a Coke, *taggaree*—cold as hail—drinking it down in a single stream, then letting out a belch that, ominously, smelled like the sea.

Later, she kept farting and burping the smell of the sea as her stomach started to expand, and she even perspired it like an urgent fever, until at last her waters broke, Elizabeth slid out, and the nurses in the maternity ward abandoned their posts and ran for cover from what they could only deduce was a biblical flood that must have spilled out of the Caspian and traveled 350 kilometers south to Tehran.

For most Iranians, the Caspian Sea and its surrounding regions evoked either the striking beauty and unbounded peace of golden-green rice fields and near-mythical white tigers, or the heart-stopping terror of midnight suicides by drowning and in-broad-daylight invasions by blood-on-their-hands and human-flesh-at-the-tip-of-their-spears Russian soldiers. Not the safest choice of a scent to overwhelm one's surroundings with, but no amount of lemongrass and arrowroot oil, rosewater baths and coconut oil enemas, could rid the poor child of this birthmark. The only aspect of her that might have been considered charming was her complete lack of guile, a certain obliviousness that, if mistaken for stupidity, could count in her favor with men and save her from dying an old, grizzled virgin buried chin-high in books.

The dumb-as-a-donkey label, while perilously wide of the mark, did have a certain resonance in light of the intellectual shortcomings of Elizabeth's twin brothers. They were friendly and boisterous and always ready to embrace anyone, even strangers, or to walk off with them without the slightest hesitation, but they had trouble performing the simplest tasks, from holding a pencil correctly to tying their shoelaces to, alas, developing the capacity for speech. They could hear well enough, and they understood the meaning of things, but the part of their brain where words are created must have been left on the drafting table the day these two boys were formed because, strive as they might, neither their parents nor their doctors nor teachers nor any other well-meaning soul managed to get the twins to say, or even write, a single comprehensible word.

The closest they came to communicating was through a network of numbers developed by—who else?—Elizabeth and registered in a logbook for the benefit of Madame Doctor and the mathematician, a kind of sign language that appealed to her and was accessible to the boys because of its linear, one-dimensional, and free-of-nuances-and-subtleties quality.

People said that the twins' many "peculiarities" were caused by their mother's selfish pursuit of a medical degree, which must have put too much stress on her and the children. In her own defense, Madame Doctor pointed to her husband's own "peculiarities"—his agoraphobia, his obsession with memorizing every one of the twenty-three volumes plus the index of the 1956 edition of the *Encyclopaedia Britannica*—as evidence of a genetic malfunction that must have passed to the twins. She even regarded Elizabeth's advanced math skills, her extraordinary composure and unusual self-control, as cerebral kinks.

She said as much to Aaron the first time he invited the new family for Shabbat dinner. She arrived in her lab coat and with only Elizabeth in tow, explained that her husband "didn't go out" and that the twins "didn't do well in social settings," and that "this one"—she pointed with her head toward Elizabeth—"you won't even know is here." Then she announced that she was heading back to the hospital where a patient was in labor, left her daughter, and rushed off.

In her school uniform and pressing a spiral notebook to her chest, Elizabeth looked every bit the star student who has shown up for class only to find it's a holiday. For a minute or two after her mother had left, she stood steadfast and calm in the middle of the room, her face radiant with expectation and her hair reined into a single, lustrous braid. After that she went and sat—straight backed and with her feet dangling inches above the ground—in an armchair next to the window overlooking the garden.

She didn't seem bothered by the leaden stares of the other children, or the open conversation among the women about who she was and how strange her family had always been, why Aaron Soleyman had sold his brother's house to such peculiar people, and whether it was true, what the servants whispered, that Raphael's Wife had cursed the house and the new owners before she left. Nor was she in the least curious about Aaron himself, though she could sense, even without glancing up from her calculus problems, that everyone around her was fixated on him and his every gesture or word.

Look at him, he's a real prince, all handsome and elegant and speaking French, and now he owns all this, just thirty-two years old and he's the chairman of the board and the king of kings, I'll bet every mother in this town is paying a sorcerer to put a spell on him for her daughter, and every girl who crosses paths with him is pouring love powder into his wine, he's going to be snatched up and taken whole in no time, my dear, some people know how to catch a big fish, they have their ways, and, believe me, they're going to put it all to use for this one.

She sat through the first three hours of the evening without once making eye contact with anyone. At eleven p.m., when dinner was called, she searched around hesitantly, as if wondering what to do with herself, how to negotiate this next hurdle. She watched the older guests file languidly into the dining room, cigarettes in one hand and crystal glasses of Black Label on the rocks in the other; watched the children be corralled by servants from the garden and the patio and other parts of the house where they had dispersed to play, and she was still furtive and unsure when she felt a hand on her shoulder and glanced up.

An old man's eyes trapped inside a young face smiled at her.

"Aren't you hungry, little one?" he asked.

She went home and told her parents she had found her future husband. He was the man who lived in the Big House, she said, the one all the women wanted for their own daughters. He had called her "little one" because he didn't know her name, and he had not addressed her again or even appeared aware of her presence until she went up to him after midnight to take her leave. She extended her hand to him and said, "Thank you, sir. You honored me by this invitation," which seemed to have surprised him, she told her parents, because he had pulled his head back a little, narrowed his eyes, and examined her as if for the first time.

"Such big words for a little person," he had said, and only then did he take her hand and shake it. Letting go, he peered down at his palm, as if searching for the source of the scent, and then he turned to her again, this time with fascination.

"You smell like the north," he had said.

Her parents, then, might have tried to explain to Elizabeth the dangers of giving her heart so quickly and at such a young age, especially to man who, by her own testimony, took not the slightest bit of interest in her, but they were busy fighting the small flood that had poured out of a broken pipe somewhere underground and was spreading throughout the house with alarming speed. Unable to pinpoint the source of the water, they sat up all night and watched it rise around their feet and ankles and all the way up to their knees, so that the furniture was floating around in the rooms and the children had to be sent onto the roof to sleep. In the morning they called a plumber, then a contractor, then the original architect of the house, and when none of them managed to stop the water, they dug the ground to where the pipes came in from the street and filled them with cement.

That stopped the flood, and ushered in the drought.

For weeks, the family's furniture, their clothes and books and the children's toys, lay in the yard waiting to dry. Surprised by the incident and eager to defend the soundness of the house he had sold,

Aaron insisted on paying for all the damage and the cost of repair. He knew there was nothing wrong with the plumbing, and that he had no legal obligation to fix anything. But in a world where a man's word was his best asset, and where one's name and reputation outlived him for generations, it was essential that he make good on what he had represented in the sale. He ordered the old pipes dug up and new ones laid, replaced all the faucets, repaired the damage to the paint and the moldings and the floors. The day the furniture was moved back in, the new pipes went dry.

So began the Battle of the Pipes that would plague Raphael's house for as long as Elizabeth's family lived in it, and that mystified Aaron and the rest of the city. No matter what remedy was applied, the house was alternately flooded or without running water, the yard soggy or scorched. The storage tank was infested by the decomposing bodies of stray cats and giant, thirsty rats that managed to fall into it even with the hatch closed. Mold set into the damp walls and wooden furniture rotted, dishes piled up in the sink and clothes remained unwashed because the water had suddenly stopped flowing to the house, and it got so bad, caused so much disruption, it became the subject of constant chatter and ceaseless speculation around town.

Manzel the Mute was convinced it was the work of the ghosts and spirits that had gathered around Raphael for so much of his life. Left orphaned when he died, they must have crawled into the pipes or fallen into the well to escape the light, causing trouble every time they moved. Other people, more educated than the maid and therefore less given to ghost stories, speculated instead that the house had been cursed by Raphael's Wife when she was forced out of it, or that—this one enraged Aaron more than the rest—he was being punished by the Almighty for having sinned against an old woman by turning her out when she had nowhere to go.

Aaron hated superstition, and he was exceptionally sensitive to the suggestion that he might have done wrong to the Black Bitch. In part, this was because he was certain he had been more than fair to her. He also worried about the damage to the family name if people's perception was skewed in the witch's favor. But there was also that distant, nagging fear, the voice of his mother and grandmother and all the other women he had known as he was growing up and who often spoke of the hardships they had endured at the hands of their husbands and fathers. Those women spoke of something they called *aaheh zaneh beeveh*—the widow's sigh. They said it was a black wind that blew from the darkest corners of the universe to punish those who broke a widow's heart. It was, the women insisted, all that guarded the weak from the mighty, a cosmic justice that could strike anywhere, at any time—the righteous hand of destiny exacting revenge on those who transgressed the unwritten rules of mercy.

The scent Aaron had detected around Elizabeth, that he said reminded him of the north, hung in the air long after she had left that first Shabbat evening in her saddle shoes and gray, pleated skirt. It was all he would remember about her from that first meeting—that, and her oddly adult mannerisms and language. The rest he forgot the minute he turned from her to his other guests.

But at home on Saturday evening, he smelled the Caspian in the hallway leading from the main door to the kitchen, and for a moment remembered a pair of white kneesocks and a large satin bow. On Sunday, he noticed that the air outside the Big House was more humid than anywhere else in the garden, and after that he kept encountering that scent in odd parts of the house or around it, on a rug or a curtain and once even in the rice the cook had prepared especially for him. He called the cook into the dining room and complained—there's a limit to how much salt and fish you should put into the food—but the poor man had no idea how to explain the scent; he mumbled for a minute or two and finally promised it would not happen again.

He made the same promise the next time Aaron ate at home. The following occasion, he washed the rice seven times instead of the usual four, boiled the water once before pouring the rice into it to boil again, and handled every step of the making of the duck-and-pomegranate stew himself to make sure nothing would be contaminated. When Aaron sent the food back, complaining that it smelled like seawater, the cook finally marched into the dining room in his turmeric-and-saffron-stained shirt, rubbed his two-day-old stubble down with the front of his apron, and said, "I can't lie to you, *agha*—sir—it's that girl who snoops around here every day that brings the smell."

What Aaron didn't know was that Elizabeth had spent every weekday afternoon and all of Friday in his house, starting the day after his first invitation, and that she was planning to remain there for as long as it took to become of age, marry Aaron, and make the house her permanent home. She came straight from school with her book bag and stacks of loose paper, and she stayed in the kitchen where

Manzel, herself a lonely teenage girl with no real family, let her spread
her books and pencils and compasses and protractors on a small table
in the farthest corner from where the cook worked. The cook had let
her stay at first because she was polite and self-effacing and really no
trouble to anyone at all, but after a few days, when he realized that
her scent was permanent and overpowering, he had sent her home to
bathe "until you smell like a normal person." Still, she came back the
following afternoon dragging the sea behind her, content only to catch
a glimpse of Aaron, or hear his voice, before the cook shooed her away.

Aaron sent word to the professor to restrain his daughter, and the
poor man did all he could—sat her down and gave her the this-is-an-
embarrassment-for-your-mother-and-me, think-of-our-*aabehroo*-if-not-
your-own talk—but his feeble attempt at exercising his parental authority was interrupted by yet another explosion of the pipes and the
subsequent flooding which, they all knew by now, would engender a
drought.

By 1967, the Battle of the Pipes was in its fifth consecutive year and
raging as fiercely as ever. The uncertainty of what may happen next
and the bedlam caused by each eruption of the pipes had turned the
twins into a pair of agitated, faltering, forever distrustful creatures
who clung to their father unceasingly and sapped every bit of strength
from him. The father, in turn, was so perturbed by the constant traffic
of plumbers and bricklayers and painters and upholsterers who came
to restore the flow of water to the house or to clean up the debris once
it had started to flow, he had lost thirty kilos and taken to drink. Madame Doctor stayed at her clinic as much as possible, the twins were
increasingly unhinged, and Elizabeth had become a de facto resident
of the main kitchen in the Big House. He asked the gardener to trim all
the trees and uproot all the plants and flowers on the immediate pe-
riphery, and hired two men to scrub every wall and ceiling and floor,
every cabinet and dresser drawer, window and tabletop and mirror,
with white vinegar mixed with water. He had all the rugs taken outside and beaten with wooden sticks, then washed and left to dry; he
installed new curtains, changed the cotton stuffing of his own mattress and the down in his pillows.

When she wasn't doing homework or burning through college-
level math and science books for fun, Elizabeth helped Manzel with

her chores, then sat her down and insisted on teaching her to read and write. It was an extraordinary scene: the mute village girl in plastic flip-flops and old hand-me-downs sitting next to the teenage professor in the white dress shirt with rounded collars, both of them bent over a notebook with lined paper as if to unearth a secret. An illiterate and a prodigy, a Muslim who had been taught that Jews are ritually impure and a Jew who didn't have the first clue about her own religion but who could recite the entirety of the Muslim *namaz* in Arabic.

In spite of their differences, each was the other's only friend, the closest she would come to having a protector. Manzel was the one person in the world who made sure that Elizabeth had eaten breakfast or lunch each day, checked if she wore dry socks to school or put them on wet and moldy from the latest flood. Elizabeth used her pocket money to buy Manzel chewing gum and sour fruit rolls and other treats from street vendors that were not allowed in Bagh-e Yaas. She brought her children's books and glossy cutouts from women's magazines and pencils with white erasers attached at the end, made lesson plans and assigned homework and conducted each study session with utmost gravity.

In the end Elizabeth became so much a part of life in the Big House that it seemed she had been born there. Her parents gave up on trying to salvage her pride or good manners and retreated ever further into the background, and Aaron got used to the scent.

Then the Black Bitch of Bushehr came back to sully it all.

Raphael's Wife returned to Bagh-e Yaas in 1967, five years to the day after she had been evicted without ceremony, looking older and more withered and dragging by the hand a boy with a round face and round eyes and the faltering, disoriented expression of the nearsighted, who she declared, "Oh ye of little faith, this is the true and legitimate son of Raphael Soleyman."

As chance would have it, she arrived at the yard gates just as Elizabeth was walking through the pedestrian door at the end of the school day. Too polite to walk in ahead of an older person, even one with disintegrating clothes and parched skin, Elizabeth stood back to allow Raphael's Wife and the boy to pass first. Instead the woman stopped, inches away from Elizabeth, and bore into her with those angry, unforgiving eyes. She sized up the fair skin, the clean hands, the school clothes; this was no maid or maid's daughter, Raphael's Wife could see, and yet she had a key to the pedestrian gate that stood between Bagh-e Yaas and the street. Raphael's Wife glanced from Elizabeth toward Raphael's house and back. Then she said, "*Inshallah*—God willing— you'll be buried in its dirt."

Aaron was not home but the maids who saw Raphael's Wife mistook her for one of the many ghosts who, orphaned by Raphael's death, had been forced underground into the water wells and the pipes and the roots of trees, only to burst out every few weeks or months, shatter the plumbing, and flood the land and roam the garden without purpose—hollow, colorless creatures dressed in faded clothes and torn shoes, congregating in the shade or lying in the sun on the lawn, even climbing into the television box and staying there, black-and-white and grainy, until eleven o'clock when programming ended and the TV went dark.

It was only when she began to speak, laying forth the inconceivable story of the boy being Raphael's child, throwing expletives and curses and promises of eternal flames engulfing seven generations of Soleymans unless they recognized the child as legitimate, that anyone realized Raphael's Wife was alive in the flesh. She must have been nearly fifty though she looked decades older; her husband had been dead for five years and useless for at least a decade before that. The boy bore no resemblance to her or to Raphael or anyone else in the family. And yet, here he is, the once and future king of Bagh-e Yaas, accompanied by his mother, the dowager queen—go ahead and deck the halls, prostrate yourselves before him, and hand over the throne and scepter and, most important of all, the treasured family name.

There was nothing to do, really, but laugh at her audacity. A name, after all, defined not only the person, but dozens of generations of his grandchildren as well. It determined a family's status, occupation, and the limits of their aspirations, their chances of moving up through marriage or commercial alliances, the kinds of opportunities they would have access to, and even the manner in which they were viewed by the law. Raphael's Wife's demand that the Soleyman name be handed to this scrap of a boy she had dragged in from the street was lunacy. But it was also laced with the power of all the curses and evil wishes in her massive sorcerer's book.

She waited all afternoon for Aaron to come home. Without an invitation, she walked into the main salon and sat herself down in the chair that had been reserved for Izikiel when he was alive and that was now Aaron's. Reacting to the scent of the sea that permeated the air, she sniffed a few times, then opened a window. She ordered Manzel to bring her and her son tea and food, and more tea with dates, and when the boy grew restless, she had him stretch out on a wood-framed sofa, put a silk pillow under his head, and draped a cashmere throw over him so he could sleep. At nine o'clock, she was still waiting for Aaron when she peeked out the French doors overlooking the terrace and saw Elizabeth walking away from the Big House. Raphael's Wife jumped to her feet and opened the door.

"Where to?" she called in that shrill voice that made the skin crawl.

Elizabeth stopped, then began walking toward the terrace. She was too polite to yell an answer out to an older person. The closer she came, the more Raphael's Wife sniffled.

"I'm going home," Elizabeth said when she was close enough, "with your permission."

That last phrase, "with your permission"—*baa ehjazeh*—was merely an expression of respect, but Raphael's Wife seized on it nevertheless.

"You do not have my permission, you little seed of the devil, and you never will. You've stolen my son's house and occupied it without my blessing and that's going to cost you, just wait and see, it's going to cost a great deal, I'll make sure it does, I'll curse you and your thieving, swindling parents until you're all living on the street and begging my son for your dinner."

One thing you could say about Raphael's Wife: she didn't make empty promises.

Later, when the Soleyman family had splintered apart and Izikiel the Red's great fortune had vanished, when their children were wandering the world alone, and their women had been widowed or abandoned, and only a shadow remained of the good name and reputation they had once prized, Aaron Soleyman would wonder if it was Raphael's Wife's misfortune, her broken heart and acid tears—her "widow's sigh" in the aftermath of Raphael's disappearance—that had brought devastation upon them. But in the early years of his tenure as patriarch, when luck embraced him and opportunity lay prone at his feet, when Soleyman Enterprises was the largest and most successful concern of its kind in the country and Aaron was responsible for the well-being of hundreds of family members and associates and employees—he was still a man who believed in logic and reason and the blind indifference of the law. Back then, he would have cut off his right hand before he accepted into the family what he knew was an imposter with bad vision and overly plump thighs.

He said this to Raphael's Wife once, the morning after her first visit. She had waited for him in the Big House from the afternoon and into the night, and she was still there when he walked in at ten minutes past two the next day. He let himself in through the front door, turned on the light in the foyer and the staircase, and was halfway up the steps toward his second-floor bedroom when he noticed that the light was on in the main salon. He thought the servants had forgotten to shut it off and close the door, so he went back down and was about to go in when he saw the Black Bitch's shadow, like a volcanic cloud, stretched across the floor.

Aaron didn't know what stunned him more: that Raphael's Wife was back and standing in his house, or that the very sight of her evoked such revulsion in him. She was like an illness you thought you had recovered from that struck again, like a debt you thought was forgiven that came up for collection. Then she leapt into a tirade of threats and accusations, roused the boy from sleep by pulling him to his feet, and it was clear to Aaron that she had lost her mind and was feeding off delusion.

He remained standing in the doorway. "What is it you *really* want?" he asked.

It was a reasonable enough question, given that the demands she made were so entirely impossible to meet, but then he went inside and closed the door behind him so that the servants, who had awakened and felt obliged to eavesdrop, were not able to hear the rest of the conversation. All they knew was that within minutes the door burst open and Aaron stood with his fist clutching the doorknob till his knuckles were about to burst through his skin. Inside the salon, the boy let out a pitiful yelp but Raphael's Wife remained immobile until Aaron crossed back over to her, grabbed her arm, and started to drag her out. She scratched and clawed at him so he took hold of her other hand as well and tugged at her, then picked her up from around the waist like the sack of old bones that she was and carried her to the main entrance, the boy calling her name over her piercing cries. Aaron deposited her outside the front door on top of the steps leading up from the yard.

"Don't come back," he spat as he began to close the door, the boy barely squeezing through.

The minute Aaron let go of her, Raphael's Wife lunged back toward him with a howl, tripped, and fell facedown on her right forearm.

I f it's true that there are moments in a life that engender and seal a man's destiny, this was Raphael's Son's hour. Decades later, he would still recall the color of the sky that morning when he and his mother were thrown out of the Big House, the scent of the sea that had lingered in the hallway and followed them out. He remembered the way the door slammed behind them the moment they had cleared the threshold, how the sound of it felt like an explosion in his ears.

He remembered too his mother's right forearm and wrist appearing much longer and more twisted than the left, how she had cried in pain and asked for help because "he broke my arm, my working arm, he's made me a cripple!" It was her own hollow bones, the force with which they had landed on the ground, that had caused the damage. But the impact would not have been as harsh if Aaron hadn't slammed the door the way he did, if he hadn't thrust her out of the house and the family.

All his life Raphael's Son would carry in his head the sound of the door closing. He heard it in his sleep and woke up in a cold terror, heard it every time someone raised their voice at him, however briefly. He heard it all the years he lived in Iran, and later in America; all the time he spent in Los Angeles as an outsider trying to penetrate "society," and even after he was allowed in and accepted into people's homes and offices, but not—it is true—into their lives.

He never did manage to gain their genuine respect or admiration, but he evoked their envy. And he never did get rid of that sound in his head, but in time he made sure that every man and woman he crossed paths with would also tremble at the sound of that long-ago disgrace.

That night, Elizabeth dreamt that Madame Doctor had shed her perpetual lab coat and instead wore a ratty, patched-up dress and shoes of newspaper. Her husband and children were poor and hungry and had waited till dark for Madame Doctor to bring home a whole fish for supper. The fish, she said, was old and rotting and thrown into the garbage heap behind the fishmonger's stall, but when she laid it on a piece of wood and cut into its stomach with a knife, a stream of clean, clear water flowed out like a fragrant mountain spring, poured onto the carving board and Madame Doctor's hands, on her shoes and the floor and up around her and Elizabeth's ankles. The water was sparkling and cool. It slid under the door of the kitchen and into the neighboring room, and from there it spread slowly all through the house and rose up to knee level, so that Elizabeth's bed, when she awoke, was already floating amid the rest of the furniture and all her books and ledgers and school clothes, the curtains billowing with water and the windows and door caving in under the pressure of water seeking a way out, and the room resembled a fish tank that had been drizzled with blue ink—all the handwritten notes and loose sheets of paper that were washed clean—and then a glass shattered and water flooded the next room where the twins were sleeping innocently, lifting their beds and carrying them out into the parents' room, and then at once they were all floating away in their sweet slumber, pulling, as if with a giant, irresistible magnet, every movable and fixed object in the house, every rug and window pane and plastic doll and leather-bound encyclopedia, every shoe and plate and bicycle wheel and black-and-white and color picture—the parents' wedding, the children's birth—down across Bagh-e Yaas and through the back gates that yielded to the water without a fight, down into the wide tree-lined Avenue of Tranquility until there was nothing left but darkness and Elizabeth standing barefoot and soaked on the ground where Raphael's house had stood.

I n the morning, the gardener found her standing alone on a sodden patch of land. Her nightclothes were shredded as if by a storm, and she had the staggered expression of a creature who had gone to sleep in one universe and awoken in another. Around her the ground was covered with wood splinters and shards of glass, strands of hair and pieces of underground pipes and fallen antennae. In the midst of the ruin, Elizabeth had the air of a shipwreck survivor.

The hint of misfortune looming, that portent of loss and disappointment heretofore hidden from Aaron, had been released by the flood and remained, suspended, like a low, persistent fog.

She had escaped the flood because she had been awakened by the dream of the fish that brought the deluge. That's what she said, and there was no reason to doubt her since she alone had observed the events of the previous night and seen her family carried off. Throughout the day, accounts surfaced of four bodies, two adults and two children, caught in a flash flood and floating, faceup and peaceful as if in sleep, uphill and northbound toward the slopes of the Elburz Mountains and the Karaj River. When the waters ebbed, the earth was paved with hundreds of 4" x 4" black-and-white pictures with latticed edges that the professor had taken of his children and archived with obsessive accuracy in dozens of oversize albums, and that washed onto the branches of trees and the windshields of parked cars, into private mailboxes and the front windows of shops.

The bodies were picked up and brought to Bagh-e Yaas by Good Samaritans or military cops, and when all four had been identified, they were loaded onto a hearse and sent off to the Jewish cemetery to be washed and wrapped in shrouds for burial. After that, Elizabeth went out to recover the photos. She walked the trail of the flood, holding a flashlight and a messenger bag. She climbed fences and knocked on windows and jumped knee-deep into the gutters on the sides of the streets. By the time she was done she had counted 281 photographs, wiped them clean of mud and debris, and filed them carefully into her bag, and that's when she realized that it was nearly midnight, that she hadn't eaten since the day before and didn't have a change of clothes or any of her schoolbooks, but she knew she had a place to go back to.

She never doubted this—that Manzel would have a dry bed and plenty of food for her. In later years, when she spent hundreds of millions of dollars of her own money building hospitals and orphanages and homes for the sick and elderly, Elizabeth would still recognize Manzel's hospitality as the greatest act of kindness a person could commit. He who saves one soul, someone said in the Mishnah, saves the world.

What she didn't expect to find was a room arranged for her on the ground floor, with not only sheets and towels but three sets of school uniforms, three pairs of saddle shoes, white kneesocks, and an entire roll of white satin ribbon—all delivered to the house after hours on Aaron's orders. There was also a black dress she was to wear to the funeral the next day, and a book bag that would be filled by new books, and a promise, relayed to her by Manzel in her childish handwriting and flawed spelling, that she could stay in the Big House for a few more days until she found a new place to live with someone from her extended family.

An unmarried girl and a single man sleeping under one roof, no matter how large that roof, was a scandal in the making. But for the impropriety, Aaron would gladly have given Elizabeth safe harbor in Bagh-e Yaas for the rest of her life if she needed it. He saw no irony in tossing his brother's wife out, ignoring her so-called son, only to take in a stranger's daughter. To him, Raphael's Wife was an imposter who had insinuated herself into the family by taking advantage of her husband's illness; Elizabeth was an innocent child caught in a cross fire between the Black Bitch and Aaron.

It would be some time before the implication of this reasoning—that Elizabeth was the victim of Raphael's Wife's revenge against Aaron—made itself evident to him: if the flood was her doing, then there must be truth to the notion of the widow's sigh.

That's what she said when she came back the next morning to plant her flag in the swampy remains of Elizabeth's life and to promise Aaron there would be more where this came from. She rang the bell on the yard door at ten minutes to six, and when a maid answered, Raphael's Wife demanded to be let in because she had something of grave importance to share. She marched into the Big House dragging the boy by the arm and murmuring expletives, stood in the first-floor foyer, and called Aaron's name like the Angel of Death summoning his next victim.

He didn't respond, so she went on yelling that her prayers had been answered: "The scum-of-the-earth family you let into my son's house was washed away like the filth that they were, and this is just the beginning, you wait and see, it's going to make the seven plagues of Egypt look benign unless you do right by us and give my son his true name."

At this, a small, quiet shape appeared at the end of the hallway. It was Elizabeth in the black dress she had put on for the funeral. She had been awake all night, sitting on the edge of the bed in the room Aaron had assigned to her, and staring at the dress that hung in the open wardrobe. She had no idea what time the funeral was going to be or when she'd have to leave, had never been to a cemetery and didn't know what to expect, so she put the dress on at four in the morning and went into the kitchen to wait for Manzel. Now, in the dreadful hours when the house was still quiet, in the hollow middle of a world where every bit of certitude had been cored out for her, Elizabeth felt Raphael's Wife's curses reverberate through her with harrowing strength.

Through the interminable fall of 1968 and into the winter of 1969, Elizabeth shuffled from one family member's house to another. Everywhere, she was welcomed with sympathetic hugs and pitiful tears, told she could stay for as long as she wanted, but ushered out quietly at the end of a few days. Any longer than that, her hosts feared, would mean they would be stuck with her for good: she was an orphan girl nearing the age of marriage. She had no dowry, more than a few deficient genes, and rotten luck. The scent that emanated from her was heady and strange. It drifted from her hair and skin and filled every space she walked into; it was in her breath and urine, made any bed she slept in smell like the outer deck of a ship, turned her bathwater into a sap, and left a limpid, disquieting trace on anything she touched. It polluted the water that boiled in the samovar in her hosts' kitchens, and spoiled the ground saffron and cumin in their pantries.

After three weeks, she had exhausted her familial options and was standing at the gates of the school, her cheeks hollowed out from hunger and her legs blue from the cold above her knee-high stockings, when her friend, Hussein Zemorrodi, pulled up in his father's orange Paykan. Hussein's parents were working-class Muslims who had been fortunate and resourceful enough to grasp onto the opportunities afforded by rising oil prices and the shah's modernization efforts. The mother worked twelve-hour days sewing beads and crystals onto the ball gowns and wedding dresses of rich women, and the father drove a taxi, but their three sons went to high-class private schools on government scholarships and, with a little luck, would soon cross over from being the grandchildren of peasants and children of migrant slum-dwellers into the rapidly rising middle class.

Hussein had seen Elizabeth standing alone at the gates when his father came to pick him up in his cab. He knew she was there because she had nowhere to go. Without having discussed it with his parents or obtained anyone's permission, he took her hand and said, "Let's go."

* * *

The fifty-eight nights that Elizabeth spent at the Zemorrodis' house in South Tehran would influence every major decision she made in her life thereafter. There was the kindness of these strangers, the generosity with which they shared with her their earned-with-blood-and-sweat food. There was their complete dismissal of their mullahs' teachings—"All the Jews are the devil's children, they have tails growing out of their backs, they contaminate everything they touch and make it ritually impure"—and the unsullied faith that hard work and sacrifice was every man's destiny. But there was also the realization, on Elizabeth's part, that the distance between wealth and poverty, comfort and insecurity, is much smaller than most people realize, that the way back is long and bitter and strewn with the bodies of "also trieds," and that for her, trapped and waterlogged after the flood, there was no choice but to resort to drastic measures.

On the Persian New Year in March, Elizabeth packed her worldly belongings—a spare uniform, two pairs of socks, and schoolbooks all donated by the headmaster—kissed Mr. and Mrs. Zemorrodi's hands and Hussein's face, and headed out. It was four in the afternoon on an unseasonably cool spring day, and the streets were buzzing with holiday cheer. The last of the winter's snow, having only just melted, sat in puddles along the sides of the road. Elizabeth used the few tomans Hussein had given her to buy a pack of fruit-shaped miniature marzipan arranged in colorful rows in a clear plastic box, wrapped it in newspaper, and held it to her chest for the entire hour-and-a-half walk to Bagh-e Yaas. By the time she arrived, her white socks were splattered with mud and her white bow was coming undone, but the package of marzipan remained intact. She told Manzel she had come to see Mr. Soleyman.

In the main salon, Aaron sat with half a dozen men in suits and ties, their elegantly dressed wives, and exceptionally well-behaved children. The men sat with Aaron, smoking cigarettes and exchanging opinions about the latest dispute between the shah and the US government over a billion-dollar debt from oil revenues that American oil companies had failed to repay. The women converged into a circle of stiff beehives and exposed necklines, waving bejeweled hands and discussing just how and why the most eligible bachelor in Tehran's upper-class Jewish society—Aaron—had managed to escape the noose.

At nearly thirty, Aaron had outlasted most of his contemporaries in evading the many traps set by the families of eager young women. The other bachelors his age were either too poor to support a family or too flawed to attract the kinds of prospects they had in mind. One or two were rumored to place their friendship with another man above their duty to marry and procreate. A few had been hoodwinked by loose women they couldn't possibly be permitted to marry.

Elizabeth walked into the salon with her chin trembling slightly and hands balled into fists, having clearly grown out of the frayed uniform and saddle shoes she was in, and walked directly toward Aaron. She was fifteen years old, barely 5'2", flat-chested, and bereft of any womanly flair.

She put her offering of marzipan on the table before Aaron, took five steps back, and stood with her feet together and her hands stiff at her sides.

"Happy Nowruz," she said. "If you'll have me, I would like to be your wife."

The wedding was a small affair at the Darband restaurant in the foothills of the Elburz Mountains in the northern part of Tehran. Because she was a year shy of the legal age of marriage for women, Aaron had to obtain special permission from a family court judge. Instead of a gown, Elizabeth wore a white cotton dress with a pleated skirt and a belt that tied in a bow in front. She had shopped for the dress alone, refusing the many offers of assistance from all the aunts and uncles and cousins who had greeted her with welcoming smiles when she turned up at their doors but grown churlish and irritated after she had been their guest a few days, who thereafter quickly looked away and crossed to the other side when they saw her on the street—until they learned that she was to become Aaron Soleyman's wife, and suddenly they felt a renewed sense of kinship, reached out to her with invitations to luncheons and dinner parties and shopping trips and all-day visits to the hair salon.

She wasn't being vindictive in turning down the offers of support and companionship; she just didn't see the point of two people shopping for one dress, of spending an hour (much less a day) arranging one's hair when a ten-second comb-through and a simple braid would suffice. She had never done the things other women and young girls liked to do—the seven-hour fittings at the atelier of the seamstress of the moment, the early-afternoon trips to the movies, the once-a-week ritual of soaking their hair in beer, then wrapping it in curlers, unraveling the curls when the hair was completely dry and straightening it with a clothes iron.

She bought her dress at a small boutique on Persepolis Avenue without telling the owner what occasion it was for, and she used a fraction of the budget Aaron had allotted to pay for it. In the three weeks between the day she proposed to Aaron and the night of their wedding, she hardly left the Big House or answered the dozens of calls that came for her. News of her audacious (not to say immodest, presumptuous, and—who're we kidding?—downright shameless) offer had burst across Tehran in a matter of hours and made even the most disinterested individuals sit up and pay attention. From the scheming parents of eligible young women, to the disappointed wives who had "settled" in their choice of husband and subsequently wished they hadn't, to the most lethargic of old, opium-addicted servants in the homes of the well-to-do, everyone wanted to know just how such a thing was possible.

Why would a man with Aaron's resources and reputation, who could have his pick of any girl in the world—just say the word, my dear, and the parents will hand her to you on a gold platter—choose a teenage orphan whose greatest talent was solving mathematical problems no one else cared to tackle?

To the many inquiries directed at him—why, why, why would you do this?—Aaron responded with a smile and a quiet, "Why not?"

To Elizabeth, who appeared not a bit surprised when he accepted her proposal, he promised "affection, loyalty, and the willingness to forgive."

To himself, in the predawn hours when he awoke with a start from a restless sleep, he said he was doing his part in upholding the Soleyman family's good name.

It was all true. Then again, truth has many layers, some visible to the untrained eye and others not.

The year he left for Paris—1958—had been the best and the worst of Aaron's life. In April, he lost his virginity to the woman he had secretly loved since he was twelve and in middle school. In August, he made the mistake of confiding in his mother the identity of his lover. In September, only days before he was to start university in Tehran, he was picked up from Bagh-e Yaas in a company car and driven to the airport where he was handed an airline ticket and a visa to exile.

His parents told their friends that Aaron was in France to study medicine. That was true, and not unusual for the times. Many a child of well-to-do families was sent away to a Swiss finishing school or an English military academy. Some were as young as eight or ten years old, others had finished high school and failed to pass the college entrance exam in Iran, or simply sought a European education. Most obtained their degrees and returned, triumphant, to marry a girl of their parents' choosing, take over the family business, or establish themselves in their chosen professions. A few fell in love with the West, or with a Western girl, married against their parents' wishes, and faded into a quiet life in Europe or America.

So Aaron's departure, though unexpected, raised no questions. Nor did the fact that, unlike other students abroad, he never came home in the four years he was away: Izikiel was not the type to indulge frivolous activities such as taking a vacation. And Aaron was too serious a young man, too dedicated to his studies, to indulge homesickness or a longing for family. That other matter—the love affair that had so alarmed his parents that they had banished him to another continent and would have kept him there till he agreed to give up the woman—remained secret.

The woman—Fereshteh Ghareeb—was a doe-eyed, husky-voiced temptress fifteen years Aaron's senior and married, alas, to his maternal uncle. The first time Aaron set eyes on her she was ensconced in a hundred yards of white lace and sitting under a choopa in her soon-to-be-husband's home. Twenty-seven years old and a divorcée, she had pulled off the nearly impossible feat of finding a second husband who was neither a widower in search of an unpaid caretaker for his young children, nor too poor or sick to walk away with a "desirable" bride.

Fereshteh's first husband had divorced her because he felt he could not trust her to remain faithful. Depending on whom you believed, he was either a paranoiac who accused even stray cats of being flirtatious with other men, or simply astute enough to detect intention before it had translated into action.

The second husband, Jay Gatsby (formerly known as Jaaveed Ghareeb), was an Iranian Jew with a degree in English literature from Harvard and an affinity for silk scarves and tiepins and white suits with wide, padded shoulders. In high school, his flair and elegance had prompted some speculation as to his masculinity, and caused him a great deal of quiet suffering. To establish his bona fides as a man, he had taken the unusual step of voluntarily signing up for military service: although technically compulsory for all young men under the shah, the service was really for those who were too poor to bribe officials, too unmotivated to go to college instead, or too unconnected to call in a favor. Two years later, when he was honorably discharged, Jaaveed brought his weapon home and put it on display in his parents' living room. It wasn't an easy feat; the army did not like having civilians with guns in their homes, but it was important, Jaaveed felt, because it would dispel the ungainly rumors, make his mother a little less frantic to marry him off, and, if he was lucky, give Jaaveed some time and space to pursue his passion: to read novels and write poetry.

His favorite book of all time was an obscure little story about a North Dakota farm boy named James Gatz who had made fast money and moved to New York, then changed his name to Jay Gatsby. The book had been published in the United States in 1925 and was almost immediately forgotten. Jaaveed happened upon a copy of it in the school library. Almost from the first page, he felt he was reading his own and his people's story: there was the rags-to-riches trajectory, the tension between new and old money, the yearning for beauty (in time, though Jaaveed did not know it yet, there would also be forbidden love and marital infidelity). Before he graduated from Harvard and returned to Iran, he changed his name to Jay Gatsby.

* * *

Aaron's mother, when he confessed to her his love for her brother's wife, blamed Fereshteh Gatsby for being a brazen whore and a pedophile. His father blamed Jay for being a cuckolded milksop who couldn't control his wife. But to hear Aaron tell it, it was he who had fixated on Fereshteh the night of her wedding and thereafter, dreamt of her every night, and found every possible excuse to see her daily for six years until one night, when he was eighteen and she thirty-three, he had found her alone at home, then cried bitter tears and begged her to leave her husband, abandon her children, and run away with him.

He would dispute this vehemently, but the general consensus about Fereshteh Gatsby was that she wasn't that much to look at even in her youth, and certainly no great beauty by the time Aaron fell for her. What she did have was that amorphous quality Jews described as "being like a Muslim woman." That was a highly flattering characterization for any female, especially from a male point of view: it meant that she carried herself with just enough confidence to pose a challenge, but not so much as to be forbidding; that she knew how to dress and what color to paint her lips and what angle to cross her legs at to be welcoming but not easy; that she could dance before a roomful of men without losing her nerve, toss her hair around without looking like a shrew, conduct many an affair quietly and let her husband do the same without upsetting their social or domestic standing.

Fereshteh Gatsby must have been all that and more—*reckless* is a word that comes to mind—because instead of eloping with Aaron she arranged to meet him on odd nights, in her own home with her husband safely tucked away in his bedroom. They lived in a two-story house on Molavi Avenue, a short distance from the Razi Hospital. To believe Fereshteh, her husband had no interest in her except for the purpose of unsuccessfully attempting procreation; he was happier looking at pictures of the Marlboro Man, David Bowie, and Prince Charles of Britain than seeing her naked. Early in their marriage, he had declared he couldn't sleep well with another person in the room, and moved his own bed to a different part of the house.

Fereshteh and Aaron carried on this way for five months and could have done so for many more, maybe for the rest of their lives, had he not allowed his conscience to ruin his life. As much as he spent every minute of every week anticipating the brief hour of encounter with Fereshteh, he was also tortured by guilt and by the fear of scandal. He knew he would never have the strength to stop the affair as long as he remained under the same sky, so he spent the summer before college tearing out his heart in little bloody pieces and building up the courage to confess his sin to his parents. Before he left, he wrote Fereshteh the longest letter he would ever write and signed it, *Yours Truly, in life and thereafter*.

Aaron married Elizabeth because he had to take a wife sooner or later in order to produce heirs for the Soleyman bloodline; because she was too young, he thought, to sense his emotional absence and sexual indifference; because she herself was more of an onlooker than a participant in much of what went on around her. He knew her family's demise had something to do with his own feud with Raphael's Wife, and he was happy to give her a new home and family. He was fond enough of her to find her quirks amusing and her earnest affection for him endearing. And though he couldn't give her his love, he had every intention of giving her his complete fidelity.

It was a common enough practice to give children Western names, so no one was alarmed, or even made the connection, when Aaron named their first child Angela. In fact, he chose the name because Angela was the English translation of Fereshteh—*angel*. That was the only concession Aaron granted his own still-grieving heart—to be able to say Fereshteh's name as often as he wanted without raising suspicion—and the one conscious signal he gave her that she was still and forever his one great love. Not that you could tell, by the way he handled his personal and professional life, that anything was seriously wrong. Two years later, when Elizabeth bore a second daughter, he named her Noor—*light*. By then he had expanded Soleyman Enterprises into the largest concern of its kind in the country, established a reputation for dealing fairly with his employees and honestly with his partners. His wife adored him in her own dispassionate way, and the rest of Tehran's upper crust—Jewish, Muslim, and Baha'i—all appeared to like him, so Aaron thought this was it, he had achieved what he was expected to, fulfilled his responsibility as Izikiel's heir, and now just had to wake up every day and live and breathe and go through the motions of a man who has a pulse but no soul.

That's what happens, in the East, to people who suffer an irreversible loss: to survive, they trade their soul for the shell of a body.

It's only in America that what doesn't kill you makes you stronger.

They never had a chance to tell him this, but Aaron's children sensed his absence throughout their time together. Angela, who always did have a way with words, would later compare her own longing for an emotional connection with her father to "trying to ride a straw horse. You can mount it and whip and kick and command all you want, or you can feed it sugar and a bucketful of apples, but the hard thing is, you know even before you start that it's never going to move."

It didn't make it any easier for Angela that her mother, Elizabeth the "Ice Queen," was able to accept Aaron's emotional remoteness. Not even sixteen years old and without the benefit of an ordinary childhood to draw upon when they married, Elizabeth never fell into line with what constituted a normal life. She certainly had no idea how to live like the *aadam hessabis*—people of substance—whose ranks she had joined. The wife of an *aadam hessabi* would bear children but not raise them, leave them in the care of nursemaids and servants at first, and boarding schools in Europe later. She didn't breast-feed, bathe, or cook for the children. She was aware of what went on in the house without getting too bogged down in the details. Her job was to know the rules of high society and to insert herself into those ranks. She had to be well dressed and beautiful all the time, seen in the right places—an exclusive hair salon or tailor's shop, lunch at the new Russian restaurant, dinner at Darband—by the right people. She had to go to parties and host them as often as everyone else, look fresh and cheerful in front of the men. She had to dance beautifully, plan extravagant trips, buy the most exquisite jewelry. In this way she would ensure her family's standing, a good name for herself, and good marriages for her sons and daughters.

If held to those standards, Elizabeth would have failed. The ageless maturity she had displayed in childhood neither grew nor diminished with time. She had appeared no different at twelve than she would at eighteen, and she didn't seem to want much more either. The plain sheet dresses and flat shoes she went around in, whether at home or on the street running errands or even at the few parties she and Aaron attended, were barely distinguishable from her beloved school uniform. She didn't splurge for luxuries because she didn't see the point, continued to take her meals in the kitchen with Manzel the Mute, didn't have the slightest idea what use to make of the dolls and toy strollers and miniature tea sets that visitors brought as gifts for Angela and Noor.

Even the fact that she had only girls, that she hadn't produced a son, didn't seem to be of the least concern to her. When asked by well-meaning citizens why she wasn't in more of a hurry to give Aaron an heir, she appeared genuinely puzzled. When told that girls did not constitute an heir, she was even more stumped.

Maybe all those numbers and data and facts she had filled her head with as a child had left no room for good old-fashioned common sense.

Maybe she *was* trying to a have son, but wasn't able to. Maybe

Aaron had lost interest in her. Maybe she didn't want to take a chance at having yet another girl. One is bad enough; two is awful; but, really, three would be a calamity.

The truth was, neither Aaron nor Elizabeth longed for an heir or felt the need to expand their family. They had each lost too much— he, the love of his life; she, her family of origin; he, the ability to love again; she, her life's dream of going to university—to want more than the small piece of contentment they had managed to wring from fate and circumstance.

Only they didn't know, yet, that the less you ask of God, the more He'll begrudge what little He's let you have. He's good at that— poisoning the well just as it starts to run dry.

The poison in Bagh-e Yaas, whether Aaron chose to believe in it or not, was the widow's sigh.

Raphael's Wife came to the house every few weeks, and she dragged her so-called son along with her. At the gates, she held down the doorbell until someone answered, and the longer that took, the more she screamed curses and obscenities.

"Let me in, you whores and dog shits," she screamed at the gates. "Open up, you common thieves, you've stolen my son's inheritance and thrown us into the gutter, let me in or I'll curse your children so they'll be eaten alive by plague."

The neighbors and regular street vendors all knew her and her story; they either ignored the outbursts or yelled at her to shut up and take it elsewhere. Strangers passing through stopped and stared at her and the boy, asked questions, then shook their heads in disbelief and eyed her contemptuously, as if to say they knew she was lying. Anyone could see that Raphael's Wife was too thin and dark, much too unattractive for any man to copulate with, and much too old to have a son as young as the boy she claimed was Raphael's.

In her fist she clutched the neck of a filthy white plastic bag that smelled like the inside of a dead sheep and that she guarded vigilantly, as if fearing it would be stolen from her. As soon as she arrived, one of the maids would run to the door and let her in so as to cut short the scene she was making on the street. She marched ahead of the maid into the Big House and stationed herself in the main salon to wait for Aaron. If Elizabeth tried to speak with her, Raphael's Wife would spit in her direction and call her a "motherless tramp" and a "crazy man's daughter." If Manzel brought her a tray of food, Raphael's Wife would kick it to the floor and slap her son's hand if he so much as reached for it. She wanted to speak only with Aaron and she would wait, she threatened, wait all day and night if she had to—he wasn't going to avoid her, not for as long as she drew a breath or until he consented to give her son his father's name.

Aaron had no doubt—none whatsoever—that he owed nothing to

this woman and the boy. But he was not so coldhearted, or so unconcerned about others' judgment, as to remain oblivious to the holes in the widow's stockings, the mud caked on the boy's shoes, the smell of the outhouse that emanated from them because they lived without indoor plumbing or a septic tank. He gave her money for rent and food every time she came, and agreed to pay for the kid's schooling, which might have been generous if, as Raphael's Wife believed, it wasn't their own money he was giving back.

As he grew older, Raphael's Son began to understand that nothing came from those visits but disgrace and mortification. He resented his mother for this, for taking him around like a mark of shame, lugging the old plastic bag in which she kept her money and her keys and what little else she owned that was worth protecting. In her pocket, she carried his birth certificate which she took out a dozen times a day to show to any stranger willing to listen to her story.

There it was—she pointed to the place where his surname should be:

First name: Raphael's Son
Last name: None
Provenance: Bastard

She came to the house one afternoon in the summer of 1975, looking worn out and desperate and about to burst with rage. Next to her the boy, who would have been twelve if Raphael's Wife weren't lying about his blood and birth, seemed bereft of emotion. In the Big House, Raphael's Wife sat down on the edge of a sofa in front of Aaron, placed the bag on her lap without loosening her grip on it, then grabbed her son's arm and tried to make him sit as well. He remained standing, hands in his pockets and eyes sewn to the ground, a pillar of resentfulness.

"Are you sending him to school?" Aaron asked without introduction, referring to the boy as if he weren't present.

Raphael's Wife scoffed, "We barely have a roof over our heads. The food we eat isn't fit for a dog, we need new clothes, new eyeglasses, and you ask about school?"

In a tailored suit and monogrammed shirt, Aaron sat in an ice-blue armchair with silk upholstery and wooden legs painted with gold dust—a replica of a chair that was on display at the Topkapi Palace in Istanbul. Slowly, he reached for a cigarette, lit it and took a drag, exhaled the smoke.

"I've told you his school is paid for," he said without looking in her direction.

At this, Raphael's Wife dropped her plastic bag and dug her nails into her son's arm.

"You TOLD me?" she erupted at Aaron, shaking the boy who remained stunned and unable to react. "You TOLD me?" She let go of the arm and grabbed her son behind the neck, pushing his face forward as if it were separate from the rest of him. "Look here! He's nearly blind. I can't get him new glasses because I have no money."

She released the boy and picked up the plastic bag from the floor, turned it upside down above the table. Two dozen raw chicken feet, some a light pink, the rest a sickly yellow, poured onto the polished wood surface.

"This!" she screeched as the smell of rotting meat rose in the air. "This is our dinner. The butcher gives it to us for free because no one else wants it."

Aaron watched her dispassionately, then glanced at the boy who stood trembling without a sound. Aaron reached into his pocket and took out a wad of hundred-toman bills. He counted ten, then put them on the table before Raphael's Wife.

"Take this," he said coolly, "and understand you're never going to get from me what you want." For a minute, the two stared each other down. Then Aaron softened his tone, glanced once at the boy, and almost appealed to the mother.

"You must know this," he said, as if pleading for common sense to intervene. "No matter what you may want or how badly—you must understand that in this country, at this time, you and your kind don't hold a prayer against the likes of me."

It's strange how insignificant words can appear at the time they're uttered, how savagely latent their power can prove over time. What had been, to Aaron, a simple declaration of fact—practical advice, even, to Raphael's Wife, so she wouldn't spin her wheels and ruin her son's life chasing what he would never attain—became, for her, an invitation to war.

That night at the Big House, she glared at Aaron till her eyes began to water, then said, "Now you're going to see what my kind can do."

All those nights when, as a teenager, he had crawled in the dark through the doors that Fereshteh left unlocked for him, crept past the servants' bedrooms and up the steps, past her husband's, at times even her in-laws' rooms; all those nights when he had climbed, trembling with desire and ready to die if only from joy, into the narrow wooden bed where she waited, bare legs and eager breasts and unfettered hunger; all those nights when they thought they were alone in the world and safe from the judgment of others, Raphael's Wife had been there, in the tenebrous quiet of the yard in Jay Gatsby's house, watching.

"This name you hold so dear," she said, no longer desperate, "it would be less than dirt if I opened my mouth and told people what you did with that faggot's wife."

There's the harm you do to others in order to gain an advantage for yourself, and then there's the harm intended only to inflict pain upon the other. Raphael's Wife had tried the first tack with Aaron for many years, and failed. This time, she would try the other.

It was inevitable, she told Aaron at the Big House, that she would find out. She had been Raphael's caretaker, the person who stayed up all night when the glow inside him began to burn and the ghosts and night creatures drew him out of the house. Often, she had to run after Raphael into the streets, like a mother trailing a wayward child. Of course she would see Aaron stealing away from Bagh-e Yaas.

She realized now that she had only one hand to play. If she threatened Aaron with a public shaming and he didn't bend, her only other option would be to go through with her promise.

"Do you want a name that's smeared with shit," she asked, "or do you want your *aabehroo*?"

There was that scent again—sweet rain falling onto a lake at midnight—as if evoked by forces unseen in advance of some irreparable shift in the geography of lives. It swept through the room like the breeze at dawn that awakens sleeping infants and blushing brides, cleansed the air of the smell of putrid animal flesh and open wounds to the heart, and lay bare for Aaron the dimensions and shape of a future caged by Raphael's Wife.

She was staring him down, she thought, because their eyes had locked, but the light was too dim and she was too nearsighted to see that his gaze was vacant, his absence complete.

Slowly, word began to spread about a rumor so appalling and outrageous that even repeating it was a sin, concerning Aaron Soleyman and the wife of his maternal uncle. That crazy witch of a wife of Raphael, it seemed, was going around with her mutt (What did she do—find an orphan? Steal the kid from his parents? She certainly didn't give birth to him.), swearing on every holy book she could find that she saw with her own eyes, more than once . . . well, the rest is too odious to repeat.

That's what it was, at first: a rumor about a rumor. Repeated enough times, it became a very unlikely possibility that became a vexing doubt that morphed into a virulent suspicion that struck, with all the force of an imploding reputation, at Jay Gastby's soul. Suddenly, the old gossip about his staring too long at other boys and playing flirtatiously with the fringes of his silk scarves was revived and re-examined. Could it be that he had failed to satisfy his wife to such extent, people wondered, that she had sought relief elsewhere? Did he know about the affair and turn a blind eye? Did he not realize he had a houseguest some nights because he himself was busy entertaining?

Jay Gatsby had spent a lifetime and made many a sacrifice to keep his good name from being soiled by accusations of homosexuality. In a rage, he accused his wife of having behaved in such a way as to allow people to entertain such repugnant thoughts. That was bad enough. It never occurred to him that it could be any worse.

She could have apologized and promised to do better, let him burn with the shame of having a wife about whom untrue murmurs spread. Instead, she told him it was true; all of it, even the part about she and Aaron being lovers, sleeping in a bed together in a room next to her husband's. It was all true because he, Jay, was not a real man.

Years later, Elizabeth would still hear the sound of the phone ringing in the dark. It was Sunday, October 31, 1976. In Bagh-e Yaas, the girls were asleep; the servants had finished the day's work and retired to their own quarters. In the sitting area next to the master bedroom, Elizabeth was engrossed in an English-language engineering account, complete with blueprints, of the 1938 construction of the first US regeneratively cooled liquid-propelled rocket engine. The designer, James H. Wyld, had died in 1953 at the age of forty-one, but not before a later version of his engine had been used to break the sound barrier for the first time.

Elizabeth read science books and engineering accounts the way other women read romance magazines and weekly installments of translations of *Jane Eyre* and *Les Misérables*. Leaving school at age fifteen had derailed her presumed future, but it had made little difference in the ways in which she maintained a connection with the physical world. It was like the language of numbers she had invented for her drowned brothers, the words and sentences she had taught Manzel the Mute to write: what looked to others like a random cluster of digits or an impossible labyrinth of lines was, to Elizabeth, a poetry of meaning and attachment.

The phone rang twice, stopped, then started to ring again. Elizabeth, who had stood up from her chair to reach for the receiver, paused halfway and turned instead toward the window: the last time she had peered out, the sky had the luminous blue-black hue of fall in Tehran, when the air was dry and stars were scattered all the way to the edge of the horizon. Now, a thick film of humidity, like the soupy fog before a storm, coated the outside of the glass. Beyond it, where she couldn't see, a wave rolled forward though the dark, gathering height and becoming louder the longer the phone rang.

She took hold of the receiver and was about to lift it when she felt something akin to lightning burn her palm. She loosened her grip and pulled her hand away, but the ringing didn't stop.

"Answer it," commanded five-year-old Angela, barefoot in pajamas, from the doorway.

There were nine rings; twelve. The moment she picked up, Elizabeth knew, the tide would break against the walls of the house and bring them down, wash away everything in its path.

"Pick it up, already!" Angela ran to the phone. "It's probably—" She was going to say, *It's probably Dad*, but Elizabeth took the receiver out of her hand.

A man's unfamiliar voice, laced with a provincial accent, spilled into the line: "Is this the residence of the late Mr. Aaron Soleyman, God bless his soul?"

The shooting had occurred at seven thirty p.m., in Aaron's private office on the penthouse floor of the Soleyman Enterprises building on Pahlavi Avenue across from the park. From what the military police were later able to infer, Jay Gatsby had acted swiftly and with great precision: the first shot was heard less than sixty seconds after he had walked into Aaron's room. It took off half his face and left the rest unrecognizable. It also sent the secretary running down the hall and away from the sound, shrieking louder than a train's whistle till she had drawn all the male employees out of their offices and sent them rushing toward Aaron's door only to find that it had been locked from inside.

Before anyone could break in, Jay Gatsby's 6'3", 180-pound body, lean and smooth and disturbingly well tended, crashed through the penthouse window and dropped, backward and half-decapitated, seven floors down onto the sycamore-lined sidewalk. Having established his masculine credentials by shooting to death his wife's purported ex-lover, Gatsby must have wavered between shooting himself in the head and jumping to his death. Maybe his hand had trembled before he could pull the trigger with the gun in his mouth, or maybe the shot had been fired accidentally as he approached the window, but either way, he arrived onto Pahlavi Avenue with his neck blown out and his head attached to the rest of him by a few precariously hung ligaments.

Elizabeth listened to the man on the phone the night Aaron was shot. "Yes, this is Mr. Soleyman's residence . . . Yes, this is his widow speaking." Yes, she would start making funeral arrangements for him. Then she had hung up and stood at the side of her bed and stared down at the night table and the phone without moving a muscle or making a sound even as little Angela pulled at her hand and yelled out her name and asked, "Who was that?"

Angela would have screamed herself into hysterics and Elizabeth might have turned to salt and remained in place for good had Manzel the Mute not come to their rescue. She didn't have to be told the specifics to understand, from the hollowness in Elizabeth's stare, that she was, once again, entirely lost and alone.

She went out in the same clothes she had worn at home all day. It was the middle of the night, hours before a rabbi could be reached or an announcement made, but she knew exactly where to go because she had been there before, in another flood.

The cemetery was centuries old, unpaved, and stowed in a hillside far enough away from the city as to avoid polluting the ground beneath the feet of God-fearing Muslims. The Jews who, until the advent of Reza Shah, were banished to ghettos because they were ritually impure and risked contaminating Muslims with the merest touch, had never been allowed to expand the cemetery. Instead, they stacked the dead in the ground a dozen deep, which was helpful in preserving the integrity of the family but made for unpleasant accidents when, in trying to add a new arrival, the gravedigger's shovel stabbed an old parent or a dearly missed child. When the young boy asked her why she had come, Elizabeth said only, "I want to make sure you don't put him on top of the twins."

The mortician explained that graves were assigned by paternal lineage. Only married women and widows were buried with their husbands; everyone else got to decompose with his or her father.

"Go home and get ready for the shivah," the boy counseled, as much to help Elizabeth as to let himself get a few more hours of sleep.

She said nothing, just stood there next to the coffins, staring down at her feet as rain dripped from her hair and clothes like the tears of an immense, inconsolable whale.

The coroner signed the death certificates without mentioning either murder or suicide, and sent the bodies to Beheshtieh to be buried. Since both victims were men of status and some wealth, everyone understood that the official cause of their passing would be "unfortunate accident." "Suicide" would be mumbled only in a whisper, and "murder" banned from any conversation about them. It was another one of those secrets that was fiercely guarded because it was so universally known, and it would be easy enough to maintain, would have spared both families a whole lot of embarrassment and agony, if the rain would do everyone a favor and stop.

The sound Elizabeth had heard when the phone rang, which she thought was the ominous portend of a thousand-mile-an-hour tsunami, was in fact the ripping open of storm clouds that had come from nowhere, gathered over Bagh-e Yaas and the Avenue of Tranquility, up Pahlavi Avenue and every inch of the way between Elizabeth and her already dead husband, and that unleashed, even before she had heard the news, a murky brown downpour worthy of biblical mention.

For three days the rain did not relent. It fell against a dirty white atmosphere, opaque as seawater in a storm, that gummed up the daylight and made the night dark and heavy as the inside of a coffin. In Beheshtieh, the young mortician boy who had inherited his job from countless generations of his forefathers, like a curse by a jealous queen, took special care to wash the bodies with lye and wrapped them in extra layers of caftan, selected two of his least damaged coffins in which to carry the corpses to their resting place, and went outside to dig the graves.

No sooner had he made the smallest dent in the ground than the rain washed a shovelful of mud back in. By the end of the first day, the earth was too soft to even walk on without sinking knee-deep. On the second evening at sundown, headstones were floating in the marshy pits. On the morning of the third day, a mudslide had pulled enough dirt off the top of the graves as to expose the corpses and send them drifting downhill.

In the middle of all this the only sight more striking than the rotting shrouds and protruding skulls, freed from the earth and floating like happy fish, was that of Aaron's widow—the young, flighty genius who could draw the engine of a spaceship from memory but not give the cook instructions for the day's meal—standing watch in the grave-digger's shack in a plain wool sheet dress and a pair of saddle shoes, resembling something that had fallen off the side of a shipping boat, impervious to the elements and deaf to the poor boy's assurances that he would send for her the instant he was able to begin the burial.

On the fourth day Raab Yehuda, the chief rabbi of the country, sent in a small army of men to corral the stray bodies and runaway headstones, put them back in their places under a tarp weighed down by stones. They erected a tent around the Soleyman family grave, held the mud back with a makeshift dam, and slipped Aaron in before the rain had a chance to bring down the canvas and poles and ropes holding it all in place. They did the same for Gatsby, and then Raab Yehuda uttered the fastest prayers he had ever let a dead man get away with, lamented loudly the poor turnout at the burial of a "great man" like Aaron but said nothing about Gatsby, and brought the proceedings to a finish.

"Go home." He patted Elizabeth gently on the shoulder. "The dead don't come back."

He didn't have to say anything to Fereshteh Gatsby because she was nowhere near Jay's grave or even the cemetery. She was either holed up at home waiting out the rain, or she had gone into forced seclusion just to avoid showing her face, so bereft of any trace of *aabehroo*, to another person. If so, that was probably the best idea the foolish harlot had had in a few decades, and it may not have been such a bad one for Elizabeth either.

Raab Yehuda started to mumble his important, precious advice to her: "You're not exactly unsullied by scandal, my dear, what with your husband's dalliances and that other matter, the Black Bitch of Bushehr, I think she's called. It's time to put an end to this war, give her something to make her go away or shut up before she sighs again and this time, God forbid, takes your children."

Not that anyone asked, because there was no need to—the answer was so obvious, even the village idiot would have figured it out all on his own—but there was a reason why eight-year-old Elizabeth had homed in on Aaron from the first encounter and never let go, wasn't letting go even now, with him good and soggy. You didn't have to know Freud to see that Aaron embodied everything Elizabeth's father had lacked: confidence, power, good looks, the ability to make a quick exit if the house were on fire. Add to these qualities a more than impressive estate, across-the-board social charisma, and a name that inspired immediate deference, and you had your reason a thousandfold.

She was a child when she first set her heart on Aaron, an orphan when she offered herself up to him, and though she became a mother times two, though she went through the motion of matrimony and parenting as best she could, she never gave up her unqualified reliance on Aaron to stand in for her not only as an adult, but as a person able to engage with the world.

Slowly, while Raab Yehuda trekked down toward his car and the gravediggers hauled away the empty coffins and their wheelbarrows and shovels, the rain thinned out. Within the hour, just as Elizabeth finally abandoned her post, the fog lifted and sunlight revealed a hillside and a city that had retched its insides out and lay ragtag and disorderly and badly in need of a new plan.

The kinfolk had sat out the burial and later claimed they had no idea it had happened, but they took advantage of the first hours of dry weather to line up outside Bagh-e Yaas with their condolences and questions, their expressions of concern for Elizabeth and the girls and offers of advice and assistance because, you see, you're too young and naive to get this now but the world is full of charlatans and sharks, every other person in this town right now is angling for a piece of your husband's holdings and interests and what can you do? A woman with three daughters. And I'll bet he didn't write a will either, why would he? A young man like that. How was he supposed to know that Gatsby would lose his mind and pull a gun on him? This is one for the books, really, but you have to know your friends from your enemies or you're going to be turned out into the street with only the girls and not a penny to your name, just another widow crying foul in the wind.

That Aaron's widow and daughters could easily meet the same fate to which he had condemned Raphael's wife and son was not the subject of controversy. Nor was it viewed as particularly poignant, given how frequently it happened, or especially unfortunate, given that Elizabeth herself had snatched the goods from the legions of better, more qualified candidates for marriage to Aaron. What did concern everyone was the ferociousness with which distant relatives and new and old business partners began to attack one another even before Aaron was loaded into the coroner's truck, and the levelheaded, seemingly dispassionate reception they each received from Elizabeth.

She had gone home after the funeral and taken a pair of scissors to her hair, cut off the braid in one jagged snip, and put it, wrapped in newspaper, into a box. Later that day, she gave the hair to Chamehdooni, the strange little man who went around with a beat-up briefcase and who traded in women's hair for a living. He stole most of the hair from dead women—prostitutes and old widows and political prisoners whom no one dared claim—at the city morgue where he tipped the attendant to let him in at night, and he sold it to wigmakers in the posh, upscale salons of North Tehran. Elizabeth gave him the hair without explanation, but he didn't have to be clairvoyant to see what it meant for a young woman to give up such an essential part of her appearance, or why her face was suddenly carved with the laugh lines and crow's-feet of middle age.

She threw the dress and shoes she had worn at the cemetery in the trash, locked up the master bedroom and made a narrow bed for herself in Aaron's home office, and set about getting the house ready for the shivah. Within hours, the glass in the windows, mirrors, even on framed pictures was covered with black cloth. Music was forbidden and television was cut off and everyone—from Elizabeth to the maids to five-year-old Angela and three-year-old Noor—donned widow's black. By the time the first callers arrived, Elizabeth had grown up, grown old, and grown into the wife she had never expected to be.

This she owed to Raphael's Wife.

Elizabeth thanked the well-wishers for their good advice and offers of assistance with that same spectator-like expression she was so known for, but you got the feeling she didn't quite recognize anyone or remember how they were connected to Aaron. She certainly didn't give any indication that she intended to call or rely on any of them for either help or advice. The men were encouraged by this—her obvious cluelessness as to what awaited her—but the women, who know their own kind better, were alarmed. If she wasn't in a panic and already clawing at every chance to defend her daughters' inheritance against the wolves, it must be that she had a plan.

She wasn't religious and didn't know a word of Hebrew except the mourner's kaddish, which she had learned when her family drowned (though she wasn't allowed to say it because she was a girl), but she sat in the front row of the women's half of the room and trained her eyes directly on the pseudorabbi who had been brought in to pray from dawn till well after dark. He had a long dirty-white beard and chapped lips, stopped eating only when he had to relieve himself, and was loathe to make eye contact. He rocked back and forth slightly, mumbled ever so softly as he chewed, and was always staring at people's hands as if to inspire them to grow money and extend it to him. For all anyone knew, he was reciting the day's news or uttering obscenities through that forever-ruminating mouth of his, dissolving the last of his sugar-blighted, tobacco-stained teeth in a steady stream of sweetened black tea and plump, juicy dates, but he was one of those fixtures you could not do without at a time like this, and he seemed to hold a special fascination for Elizabeth anyway.

She said later that he reminded her of what could become of a person who settled.

Then again, not settling had its own perils. You had only to utter the name Raphael's Wife to win that argument, even if the woman herself was too blinded by ambition to understand. So many times, people who were tired of watching her self-destruct tried to reason with her that a fraction of something—which is what Aaron had been willing to give her—was better than all of nothing; that it was better for her son to be a comfortable bastard than a poor one; that she should have invented a story that made some sense, even if it didn't place her son at the epicenter of the Soleyman riches, instead of one that was impossible to believe.

But if there was ever a time when Raphael's Wife might have tired of her Sisyphus-like campaign on behalf of that pear-shaped, squinting, taciturn-as-a-retired-math-teacher excuse for a son, it was good and gone ten seconds after Jay Gatsby closed the door behind him in Aaron's office. Never mind the elation of seeing the enemy's demise, or the rapture of discovering the extent of her own power: with Aaron gone and his second-closest male heir a cousin twice removed, Raphael's Son was all but a shoe-in for the post.

Raphael's Wife had the good sense to stay out of the way during the week of the shivah, but she didn't plan to give Elizabeth a single day of rest after that. She all but stood on the street corner screaming to the world that it was she—the wronged widow—who had made "calamity" a household name among the Soleymans. She even went the extra mile, sent word to her own erstwhile family, the relatives she had been so eager to leave and with whom she had maintained no contact for over a decade, in Bushehr. She didn't have an address for them, didn't know what surname they had chosen for themselves since the local government began to enforce a law that every person must have a first and a last name.

"Ask for the kosher butcher," she told the young bus driver on the Tehran–Bushehr route as she shoved a few crumpled bills into his palm. "Tell them that any day now, the son of Raphael Soleyman's widow will be able to buy and sell all of them with the small change in his pockets."

She had a plan: Now that Aaron would no longer be there to stand in her way, she was going to apply to the Ministry of the Interior for a new birth certificate for her son. Before any of the other pretenders had a chance to make their move, she would file suit in court—something that would have been impossible while Aaron was alive and could use his influence—on her son's behalf. Ten years ago, she might have lost outright to a man—any man—who challenged Raphael's Son's entitlement, regardless of the truth or fairness of his claim. But Iran in the 1970s was a much kinder place to its women—at least on paper—than it had been even a decade earlier.

All this was perhaps a bit too ambitious for a woman who lived in South Tehran, in a rented room she shared with her son in one of those old-style houses with a sunken courtyard, one outhouse, and portable kerosene lamps for heat and cooking. The neighbors were mostly Muslim migrants from faraway provinces; they had abandoned the land they had farmed for generations, come to Tehran in search of better jobs and more pay, and found the big city and all of its cruelties and temptations overwhelming to say the least. Compared to these people, Raphael's wife and son were quite fortunate: she worked as a maid in the Razi Hospital, and had been saving her monthly handouts from Aaron, plus the occasional sums he paid just to rid himself of her shrieking in Bagh-e Yaas. There was also the school tuition and the money for uniforms and books that he sent directly to the principal at the Shah Reza Academy—to make sure it went toward the bastard's education instead of being put to other use by Raphael's Wife.

She might have had a happier life, raised a better human being for a son, had she accepted her limitations and let go of her aspirations. But Raphael's Wife, like Elizabeth Soleyman, wanted more than to simply subsist. She didn't compare herself to the hunchbacked grandmothers with black gums and hollow bones she saw all around her, didn't see her son as equal to the barefoot village boys and bewildered young men who thought they were lucky if they got a job laying bricks for some rich person's new mansion.

How Raphael's Wife came by the notion that she deserved more than what fate had parsed out for her is something no one figured out.

What is clear is that all the devastation that resulted from her campaign was the outcome of this inherent sense of entitlement, the perception, however false, that she was as worthy as any rich and happy person walking God's good earth.

That's how revolutions start.

She didn't have to wait long to have it out with Elizabeth. Raphael's Wife had geared up to launch her assault on the eighth day following Aaron's burial. On the seventh night, she smelled the sea and all of its living creatures, went outside to detect its source, and found Elizabeth at the door.

The only part of Elizabeth that hadn't changed since the last time Raphael's Wife had seen her were the moonstone-colored eyes and that whatever-it-takes reflection of inevitability.

Raphael's Wife was so shocked by Elizabeth's appearance she thought that she might have been ambushed, that she was about to receive some kind of payback for Aaron's demise. She glanced around furtively for a warning sign, turned instinctively toward the house, and called for her son. To her great dismay, Elizabeth picked out the fear.

"I mean no harm," she said respectfully. "I've come to make peace."

There was that earnestness again, that I-couldn't-lie-if-I-wanted-to simplicity in Elizabeth that made other women suspicious of her and drove Raphael's Wife mad. She felt her son come up from behind and stand next to her. She put a hand on his shoulder as if for balance, and spent a few seconds searching for the right tone. She decided on derision mixed with sarcasm.

"So that's what you people do," she said, a forced smile, like a grimace, splitting her face. "When all is lost, you sue for peace."

They were standing a few steps outside the front door of the rental house, on the edge of the narrow alley with the open gutters filled with garbage and the stench of stray animals' feces. Though it was dark, most of the neighbors were still outside, hiding from the quickly spreading mold and decomposing rugs and furniture, the wet plaster and lingering debris, the children's disintegrated schoolbooks and the carcasses of drowned cats that the three days of rain had brought. They had all seen Elizabeth arrive in her Mercedes, and now they were watching the exchange between her and Raphael's Wife.

Elizabeth, of course, did not get it.

"I did lose my husband," she began, but Raphael's Wife interrupted her.

"Huh! Your husband! He's the least you've lost." She sensed Elizabeth's mounting confusion. "You may not know it yet, because your donkey brain hasn't caught up, but you've lost it all! You're a widow with no sons and no one to show you the smallest bit of mercy. You're going to be thrown out of that house along with your litter just as I was in my time, and the person who's going to do it," she gripped her son's shoulder so tight, it made him wince, "the one who's going to do to you what your husband did to me," she shook him again until he pulled away, "is right here. Take a good look. If you never noticed him before, all those times I brought him to you, you're going to see him now."

She was breathless with rage, electric with satisfaction. Her excitement seemed to frighten her son and further puzzle Elizabeth.

"Look," Elizabeth said, still respectful despite Raphael's Wife's outburst. "I don't know what the truth of your fight with my husband is. I didn't start this and want no part of it."

It had been dark when Elizabeth first arrived, and it was even darker now, making the white of her car stand out more offensively against the grayness of an unpaved alley with no trees or streetlights. A dozen or more men and women, their faces lit only by the tips of burning cigarettes, watched intently.

"You want no part of it?" Raphael's Wife let out a shriek like someone had just driven a knife into her back.

Her cries brought the spectators closer as the crowd grew in the alley. That, in turn, made her son bristle with shame. He had retreated as far back from his mother as he could without going into the courtyard of the house and closing the door, and he was standing with his eyes narrowed to slits and his right leg stabbing the ground with the tip of his right shoe.

"I've come to make peace," Elizabeth said again. "I want to offer you whatever it takes."

Even Raphael's Wife was stunned by this. She mulled it over for thirty seconds, then ventured, "You have nothing to offer," just to see what, exactly, Elizabeth had in mind. Was she really going to decamp from Bagh-e Yaas willingly, take her daughters, and leave it all to the competition? Could she—could anyone—be that much of an imbecile?

"Well," Raphael's Wife continued tentatively, hoarse from the earlier screams and cautious not to walk into a trap, "you can start by hightailing it out of my son's house."

"I want to give you whatever it takes for you and your son to leave us be." Elizabeth paused, perhaps alarmed by the fire that was again rising in Raphael's Wife's eyes. "There's enough money . . . I'm sure . . . enough to provide—"

"So there it is," Raphael's Wife sneered, "that's the catch. You think you can buy peace from me. Give me enough to make me go away because you know, you have seen, what I can do to you all."

She knew she was right because the smell of the sea became stronger, more dense.

"You know I can take away not just your husband but everything you care about."

Who says revenge is not golden? Let them stand here, in this putrid alley with its half-crumbling walls and the tales of woe hanging from the clotheslines, and watch Miss Queen-of-the-World go pale and soft with fear.

Because Aaron sold her house to the professor and Madame Doctor, Raphael's Wife wished a flood that took away Elizabeth's parents and siblings and left her alone and impecunious at fifteen. Because Aaron refused the Soleyman name to her son, Raphael's Wife revealed a secret that took away Elizabeth's one great love and left her a widow at twenty.

And yet, when Elizabeth said the last word that night, there was no mistaking her message or resolve.

It wasn't a bargain she had sought or a fight she wished to join even now, but nor was she inclined to let her losses be in vain.

"You're right," she said. "I am afraid of you. I have come to buy peace. But I'm not going to give back to you that which you've made me pay for in blood."

Assuming his mother had told the truth—that he was conceived in the last days of Raphael's life and born in 1963, after a thirteen-month pregnancy that produced a twelve-pound baby who rolled over on his third day and sat up before his thirtieth—Raphael's Son was thirteen years old the night Elizabeth made her ill-fated attempt at reconciliation. The trouble was, his mother could not be telling the truth, or even a modified, adapted-for-popular-consumption version of the truth. The Soleymans knew this. So did everyone else who heard her story, even if they pretended to believe her just to end her monologue and make her shut up. And now, as he grew from a stricken little orphan into an awkward and edgy young man, so did Raphael's Son.

The indisputable, clear-as-daylight facts that he had bought into wholeheartedly as a child, because that's what children do—believe their parents until they don't—had become increasingly difficult to explain to other children when he was in elementary school. In middle school, he found that the only way to defend his story or establish his mother's honesty was to respond to every challenge with a string of expletives lobbed at the accuser. By the time he reached his teens, Rafael's Son had to resort to physical violence, which was unfortunate because he was too heavy and uncoordinated to land a punch, but he wasn't half bad as a target himself, so he came home every day with a new set of cuts and bruises that he tried very hard to hide, along with the added humiliation, telling himself this wasn't the last those boys would hear from him, there was more than one way to make a person pay for their actions. His mother was gone most of the time—cleaning at the hospital or pouring her heart out, along with his birth certificate, Raphael's forged will, and the rotting remains of long-dead animals she carried around, still in the same plastic bag, as evidence of the Soleymans' cruelty.

He felt sorry for her. He felt he had let her down by failing to be the crown prince she claimed he should be. He was grateful beyond measure for her unrelenting defense of his rights. And yet.

His earliest memories were of the times he and Raphael's Wife had stood outside Bagh-e Yaas while she screamed and cursed as passersby threw coins at her or slowed their pace just to say, "Give it up, sister, take your kid home and stop acting the fool." He remembered the terror he felt every time his mother dragged him onto the bus heading north toward the Avenue of Tranquility, how as a small boy he would squirm and squeeze past her and make a run for the door at every stop, hoping to get off before they arrived at the dreaded destination. He carried that terror—the way his skin nearly burned with shame as they waited outside the gates of the house, the way he stood inside the Big House when they were finally let in, and imagined that half his body had become invisible, leaving only his head and legs for others to see—he carried the acute awareness of being unwanted and unvalued to the end of his life.

Who to blame, though, for this agony?

So many times, after he was big enough to brave her beatings and defy her, he had screamed at his mother that she should let go, stop the begging that, only to her, appeared as "a legitimate demand for justice."

"I'll grow up and earn my own money," he had promised. "I'll make us richer than those Jews. I'll make them see we don't need them."

"And what does that make you?" Raphael's Wife challenged him every time. "A bastard with no name. Belonging nowhere and wanted by no one."

Raphael's Son didn't dare tell her, but he never did buy into his mother's cheerful certainty that "our time has come" just because Aaron had died. Nor did he believe for a moment that the rickety old woman with the bent spine and aching knees had the power to direct the universe to act in her own favor. He, more than anyone, recognized her uselessness not only in grand, cosmic affairs but also in the everyday struggle to stay alive and maintain one's dignity at the same time. What struck him the night of Elizabeth's visit was how pathetic his mother seemed compared to the younger woman, how small and old and unsightly she was as she made her threats and promises. He hated his mother for this, and hated Elizabeth even more. He hated her eyes that appeared to see everything and nothing at once. He hated the way the white paint on her expensive car glowed in the dark, how it reminded him and everyone else that she alone could get away from the squalor, the constant wanting, that trapped them.

Raphael's Wife, her son concluded that night, was no match for Elizabeth Soleyman. It would fall to him to arm himself properly and reduce her to the same torment she could so easily impose on others.

Throughout most of the 1970s, Iran was flush with oil wealth and booming with development projects. Tehran's expanding economy and an influx of tourists, foreign workers, and migrants from villages and small towns around the country, had created a heady and volatile sense of opportunity and danger, peril and promise, that was unprecedented. For a brief time, old and new, devout and blasphemous, rigid and lenient, commingled without coalescing. Shiny high-rise buildings tore through the ground next to ancient monuments; girls in hot pants and miniskirts rode the bus with women wrapped in black chadors from head to toe. Young men prayed at the mosque five times a day and gathered in underground cells at night to study Marx and Lenin; teenage girls listened to David Bowie and plotted revolution against the corruption of capitalism.

In Bagh-e Yaas, Elizabeth absorbed her grief and responsibilities with the kind of cool rationalism and logical determination that was implausible (some would say impossible) in a woman. Gone was the shy and unobtrusive almost-houseguest who, even after she had married Aaron and bore him children, felt more comfortable eating at Manzel the Mute's kitchen table than in the grand dining room. Gone too was the sensible little schoolgirl who, even as she clinched the title of mistress of Bagh-e Yaas, couldn't seem to understand its usefulness.

What emerged instead was a faithful and unfaltering guardian of the remains of a war that, though she was not a party to it, had cost her her life's dream: the name, the estate, and what was left of the Soleyman family. The first thing she did was turn up at her husband's office the day after the end of the shivah. By then, she had already morphed into an ageless, steel-faced creature who did not pay the slightest attention to the awkward smiles and sideways glances extended at her from every corner, had no problem cross-examining Aaron's secretary, assistant, and any one of the string of men who walked into his office that day without knocking, just to see with their own eyes what they had heard the widow was up to.

They found her sitting comfortably at his desk, reading letters and reviewing the papers that had piled up in his absence.

Her only ally, that first day and in all the subsequent months when she fought off every direct and disguised attempt at taking over the estate, was an immaculately dressed and scrubbed and shaved and combed and cologned "attorney with friends in the all the right places" who had advised Aaron on business affairs and, out of loyalty to him, felt allegiance to his widow. He told Elizabeth about a highly controversial and widely unpopular piece of legislation imposed by the shah in his effort to modernize Iran. The set of laws known as the Family Protection Act (FPA) had been introduced in 1967, but they were only enforced beginning in 1975. Among other provisions, they granted women the right of inheritance. Daughters were allowed half as much as sons; widows could inherit up to one-eighth of the husband's property. This was revolutionary enough, but the law also stipulated that for the purposes of dividing the estate, civil courts would have dominion over family and religious institutions.

The law's unpopularity stemmed as much from financial considerations by men as from the social implications of having women run around with money in their pockets. Worse yet was the outrage of allowing secular judges to meddle in affairs historically entrusted to mullahs and rabbis. Not that anyone believed the law would have real-world consequences in all but the most extreme eventualities. By far the majority of the country, especially its cloistered, uneducated, barely-allowed-to-leave-the-house-without-a-male-companion women, remained entirely ignorant of its existence on the books. Those who did know would nevertheless have to be cretins to think that either man or mosque would tolerate such anarchy in its realm. This was even more so among Jews who, traditionally, handled family affairs more privately than the larger Muslim community.

But then there's the one-in-a-million instance of a very rich man who goes and dies when he has no living father, brother, or nephews, leaves behind two young daughters and a wife who has no clue how a woman should act but can recite the entire text of the FPA the way her father could recite the *Encyclopaedia Britannica*, and what you get is a briefcase-toting, constitution-quoting lawyer in a double-breasted suit with a silk tie and matching pocket handkerchief filing briefs and serving notices on behalf of—what has this world come to when a widow can do more than sob and sigh?—Elizabeth Soleyman.

The great snowstorm of 1977 began on a Tuesday in February and lasted twenty-two days. By the fifth day, traffic in Tehran was at a standstill and schools had closed and the frozen bodies of stray dogs and street drunks were covered by piles of new snow that would turn to ice overnight and remain locked all winter. In Bagh-e Yaas, Elizabeth sat with her daughters in the midday twilight and rehearsed the multiplication table, assigned writing exercises, and practiced reading. Power was out and the phones were dead because the lines had caved under the weight of snow, and running water was scarce because the pipes had frozen and cracked.

On the night of February 24, Elizabeth put her daughters to bed at eight o'clock, locked all the doors, and went into Aaron's old study to work. At eleven, she looked in on them again, turned off the lights in the hallway and staircase, and went to bed. At seven a.m., she woke to Angela shaking her forcefully by the shoulder.

In spite of the hour, the sky was still dark. A cold wind, like the sting of a viper's tongue, cut through the air from the direction of the girls' rooms. Before she had cleared the darkness out of her eyes Elizabeth heard Angela say, "I can't find her."

Elizabeth bounded, barefoot, toward Noor's room. The door was open, the light on. The window, unlatched and loose on its hinges, flapped back and forth in the wind. Below it in the yard, the ground was covered with five inches of fresh powder, unblemished but for a single line of footprints that led from below Noor's window to the yard gates and, beyond them, a city of 4.5 million people.

They searched the house, then searched it again. Elizabeth called the military police and enlisted an army of officers and her own employees to comb the area around Bagh-e Yaas. She asked all of Aaron's old friends in high places to call their contacts in the shah's secret police. They put the word out to the legions of spies and informants in Tehran and its vicinity that a four-year-old girl with light-brown hair and a white nightdress had been snatched from her bed.

The footsteps in the yard looked like a man's. They led to the main yard gate closest to the Big House, and from there blended into a dozen others on the sidewalk along the Avenue of Tranquility. In the Big House, all the doors remained locked, and none of the servants had seen or heard an intruder.

Elizabeth's first impulse was to blame Raphael's Wife. If anyone hated the Soleymans enough to resort to stealing a child, she told the police, it was the bellicose widow and her truculent son. Her suspicion was echoed by Manzel and her husband, and by the other servants in the house, so the police descended on Raphael's Wife just as she arrived home after a night's work emptying bedpans and washing soiled linens at the Razi Hospital near Kennedy Street. Public transportation had come to a near halt because of the storm, so she had waited at the bus stop on Customs Square for over an hour in the early-morning freeze before deciding to brave the snow and walk home. She arrived cold and exhausted and covered in mud and slush to find three men in dark blue uniforms threatening to take Raphael's Son to jail if he didn't show them where his mother was hiding "Mrs. Soleyman's daughter."

"In a shroud, six feet underground, with a dog pissing on it all day long," is how Raphael's Wife answered the question for her son. "That's where I'll put them all one day soon."

Her ardent wish notwithstanding, she claimed she had no hand in Noor's disappearance.

"I was rubbing shit out of metal toilets all night," she said. "Go to Razi Hospital and ask for yourself."

Child abductions were rare but not unheard of in Iran. In nearly all the known cases, the kidnapped were not hurt. They were sold for profit or raised by an infertile couple, or they were held for ransom, or spirited away by Gypsies and put to work as beggars. In the old days when girls were married off as early as seven or eight years old, some ran away from home and surfaced in a nearby city. In more recent times a handful of women, having been divorced by their husbands and denied the right to see their children, stole them from the father's house.

For weeks, the servants in Bagh-e Yaas were interrogated by the police and private detectives. Neighbors, street vendors, beggars, and even teachers at the girls' school were questioned multiple times. Twice after the initial interview, Raphael's Wife was picked up in an army jeep and taken to the police station to answer questions. Her son was approached by ex-SAVAK agents turned private detectives and offered money in exchange for information.

Elizabeth had turned Aaron's office into a search-and-rescue workplace. She memorized every detail, however irrelevant, paid for every tip, sent Manzel's husband or drove herself to every location. She ran ads in every daily and weekly newspaper and magazine, promising a reward. She hired a government informant to watch Raphael's wife and son. She had a notebook in which she wrote the name and information of every person she knew or every stranger who had contacted her or the police about Noor. She didn't need the notes herself; she remembered every word, every digit, and every address without trying. She kept the written record for the police and the detectives, for Manzel and her husband, for Angela, even, in case it took that long—long enough for her to grow into adulthood—before Noor was found. In case Elizabeth died and left the task of finding the child to Manzel. In case the professionals gave up and new ones had to be hired.

A city teeming with new faces and multitudes of new immigrants every day; where more than half the female population was hidden under chadors; where a network of covered alleys and domed pathways connected old shops and houses thronged with occupants, and taxis and buses packed to double and triple capacity merged into and out of a maze of ancient streets and new highways. This was the torment of a woman at once incapable of delusion and unable to capitulate. She would never stop searching, yet she, more than anyone, was aware of the near-impossibility of finding Noor. She could be anywhere, invisible in plain sight; or she could be kingdoms and time zones away.

Years after the formal search for Noor had stopped and the mystery of her disappearance had morphed into an urban legend that haunted the children of Tehran's rich and beautiful, those who remembered Raphael's Wife still believed she had devoured the girl with the force of her widow's sigh.

People called every day—well-meaning people, mercenaries who demanded money in exchange for information, policemen looking to supplement their salaries, street sweepers and local beggar women and even a resourceful Gypsy. They had seen a child who fit Noor's description; they had seen a picture on a wall somewhere; they had heard of a barren woman suddenly coming into a toddler.

A few hours before the Persian New Year in March 1977, a night nurse at Razi Hospital in Tehran admitted a five-year-old boy with severe dehydration. The woman who had brought him in, a one-legged Gypsy who, at first, claimed she was the mother, told the nurse that the child had refused to eat or drink for many days; he had to be force-fed to stay alive, and even then he was yellow and listless and hadn't urinated in more than a day. He had a boy's name—Ahmad—and a shaved head, which was common, but when she removed the many layers of clothing he was wrapped in, the night nurse discovered that the patient was in fact a girl.

The night nurse had barely finished the call to the police when the one-legged Gypsy changed her story: the child was a friend's; the real mother was too fearful of being blamed for the girl's condition to bring her in. She might be five years old or she might older, or younger. She was being passed as a boy so she wouldn't be shoved aside or beaten by other kids begging on the street or selling cigarettes and lottery tickets. Still, the nurse insisted that the police come in and talk to the woman.

She placed the call at 2:15 on New Year's Day. The police captain on duty promised he would rush over but took his time, drinking hot tea with sugar and smoking his beloved Oshnoo cigarettes until the nurse called again at 5:15. He still hadn't arrived at eight when the nurse's shift was over, so she took it upon herself to call the number advertised in newspapers and on the radio for information about Noor. The one-legged Gypsy and her boy-girl patient were still there when the nurse left the second-floor, thirty-bed hall reserved for patients with noninfectious diseases. She called the police station one last time to warn that she was going to leave the hospital, instructed the other nurses to keep a close eye on the girl until Elizabeth or the police arrived.

At 8:40, no one on the floor recalled having seen a one-legged woman or a dehydrated child for some time.

That night, a man called on a crackling, staticky phone line. "Forgive me for calling so late," he said. "I've been in America and just learned about the catastrophe."

He introduced himself as Hussein, which meant nothing to Elizabeth under the circumstances, as she could think of two dozen strangers by the same name who had called her since Noor vanished, and a few more who had been stopped and questioned by the police, by her own men, even by her and Manzel's husband in the frenzied, desperate search the day before for the two fugitives from Razi Hospital.

"I would have called sooner, had I known, just to express my sympathy. I don't have children myself, you see, but I imagine it must be agony."

He sounded nervous, at once eager to explain and in a hurry to hang up.

"Who is this?" Elizabeth asked with the remains of all the strength she could muster.

The man paused. "Oh," he said after a moment. It was clear her question had surprised him. He must have been certain she would know who he was.

"It's Hussein," he said, disappointment spilling across the line. "Your old f—" he caught himself, "classmate." He paused again, still hoping he wouldn't have to say any more, then gave up. "Hussein Zemorrodi."

As if to console himself, or because he couldn't stand the silence that followed even that introduction, he added, "Of course I didn't expect you to remember. It's been some time. And you must be preoccupied."

Eight years had passed since Elizabeth took refuge with the Zemorrodi household when she had nowhere else to live. In the interim, he had finished high school, attended university in Iran, then transferred on a scholarship paid for by the shah's government to Cal Poly Pomona in California. For her, that was a lifetime during which she became a wife, mother, widow, and finally now a woman searching for her lost child.

"I wanted to say," he murmured, "beside my sympathies, that is. My mother . . . I called to wish my family a Happy New Year, you see. She told me the police were in the house, looking for a woman they thought had . . .

"At any rate, my parents are happy to help. They said the police went door-to-door all over the area."

"Is there something you wanted to tell me?" Elizabeth finally asked. Her voice was calm and steady and betrayed neither great anguish about Noor nor pleasure at speaking with her old friend.

Hussein considered the question.

"I was thinking. There must be a way to find people you lose. A better way than what we have. There must . . ."

He fell silent again, breathing fast and urgently as if to keep up with the rush of thoughts in his head.

"I tell you what," he finally announced. "Take down my address and phone number. I'll be working on this for a while, and I'll get back to you as soon as I'm able to explain, but in the meantime, feel free to . . ."

She memorized his information, never intending to call or write.

Toward the end of March, the weather finally thawed. All over Tehran, mounds of dirty snow that had been shoveled to the side of the road and remained frozen throughout the winter began to melt into muddy rivulets that streamed down the alleys and gathered in potholes and water storage tanks.

On April 1, 1977, a street sweeper came upon a child's white cotton nightgown, dirty and torn, in an overflowing gutter on the side of the street behind Razi Hospital. He tried to pull the gown onto the pile of garbage he was going to haul away, but he felt something heavy tug at it from inside the gutter. So he put his broom away and got out a shovel, dug up the dirt and stones and other bits of trash that must have been freed from some icy heap behind the hospital and dragged into the gutter, and found a child attached by the neck to the nightgown.

The body had been smashed to the bone with a rock or heavy object, then preserved, blood and flesh and hair and organs pushing through open wounds, in the ice. The gown looked like it had been soaked in blood, much of which had washed out in the stream, and pulled off the body and over the head, where the collar caught on the chin. The face was unrecognizable, but there was no mistaking the shaved head. The Gypsy woman, the police decided before they broke the news to Elizabeth, must have escaped through the hospital's back door. Fearing detection and arrest if she were caught with a stolen child, she had bashed Noor's head in, pummeled her body, then shoved it under the week-old mountain of hospital waste that had not been gathered and taken away because of the snow.

I t's not true, what they say about "what doesn't kill you." That's a myth invented by people who can't accept defeat, even as they're being dragged, with ball and chain, into the gallows of destiny. What doesn't kill you will nevertheless leave its mark, like those cracks you see after an earthquake in a house that just barely held itself together, that's still standing amid the devastation, a thousand little pieces separated by a hair's breadth but holding fast—for an hour, a year, maybe a decade—until the earth moves again, a tiny aftershock that registers nowhere but that—lo and behold!—levels the house.

To survive a tragedy with a hard shell and a broken inside does not mean one is stronger. To endure does not mean one has defeated the opponent. What it does mean—what it meant for Elizabeth when they brought her Noor's remains, when she took them to be buried on top of Aaron, came home to Angela and told her it was just the two of them, each was all the other had—is that you've learned to silence your pain, smother your longings, abandon your wishes, and accept.

Elizabeth did not grieve for Noor because she knew that once unleashed, the storm would never abate. She counted her losses, reckoned with the enemy—Raphael's Wife—and resolved to go on in spite of her. It didn't matter anymore that Elizabeth had had no part, bore no blame, in the fight that had been brought to her. For the rest of her life she would wake up every day to battle the pernicious sigh of the Black Bitch of Bushehr. Every night she would dream of Noor, alone and horror-stricken, her hands and feet blue with cold as she cried silently for Elizabeth and felt her way, hopelessly, in the dark.

The summer after Noor died, Tehran was in flames. Smoke rose from the charred carcasses of buildings and melted frames of cars and buses and from the burning piles of tires that coated the air with a viscous, oily film that traveled in the wind and lingered for days in the stomach and the lungs. Every day, news of arrests and shake-ups and decrees by the shah's government circulated amidst rumors of military coups, army crackdowns, foreign invasions. In August, 477 people were burned alive inside a movie theater in the southern city of Abadan. The cause was arson. All the exits had been sealed from the outside. The shah and his opponents blamed each other for the incident.

By September, when school started, nearly half of every class was empty—the children having gone abroad with their families, or sent alone to boarding schools, or staying with friends and relatives in the West while they waited out the "disturbances." Some of the teachers too had left the country; many others, sympathizing with the opposition to the shah, were on strike. That same month, army tanks and helicopters opened fire on protestors in Tehran's Jaleh Square. The army announced that eighty-eight had died; the opposition put the number in the tens of thousands.

In October, oil workers joined a national strike that had crippled the economy and brought daily life to a standstill. In November, Muhammad Reza Pahlavi, Shah of Shahs, Shadow of the Sun and Ruler of the Universe, went on television to admit that "mistakes were made" and ask for a second chance.

In Bagh-e Yaas, the climate of anxiety and grief that had prevailed since Noor's kidnapping was exacerbated by a mounting sense of imminent ruin. Manzel the Mute kept warning Elizabeth not to trust any of the other servants, or to allow strangers into the house for any reason at all. She came to work every morning with teary eyes and trembling hands, having endured yet another bout of arguments scrawled on scraps of paper with her teenage son who, like so many other cretins those days, had discovered that God spoke to him through a mullah's mouth.

* * *

Manzel had been a child, a village girl from Chaloos, when her father enlisted her into service at Izikiel's house. She worked seven days a week for a small salary plus food and a place to sleep. Once a year she took a bus back to Chaloos where she stayed for two weeks. When she was fifteen years old, her father went to Tehran to ask her employer's permission to marry her off. A few months later, a young man with gleaming white teeth and a wooden leg knocked on Izikiel's door.

Manzel and her husband were sent to live in the servants' quarters behind the Big House in Bagh-e Yaas. He took driving lessons and, once he had obtained a license, started to work as a chauffeur at Soleyman Enterprises. When their family grew, they moved again from the servants' room to an annex built especially for them. Their children—four boys—were sent to a school paid for by Izikiel. The older ones eventually went to work for Aaron, got married, and moved out. The youngest, Mojtaba, was still living with his parents when Noor disappeared.

He was an angry boy, forever defying his parents and teachers and even his brothers who, because of the order of their birth, should have wielded a great deal of authority over him. They told him that he should be grateful for the work that the Soleymans gave his parents, and thank God for the opportunity to go to school, to know that he would always have enough to eat, that he would not be separated from his family as a child and sent away to live with strangers just to earn a living. Mojtaba didn't see these things—a sated stomach, a roof over his head—as a blessing; he saw them as an injustice that must be corrected.

He had grown up watching his parents serve the Soleymans as if heeding a law of nature—as if some people were born to be masters and others to be slaves. He was eleven years old when Noor was born, and after that he felt he had lost his mother, who spent seven days a week caring for those two girls as if they were her own, even slept on the floor of their room on nights when Elizabeth or Aaron were away. Manzel dressed her sons in each other's hand-me-downs, but spent hours starching the lace on the girls' collars, bleaching the smallest stain out of their white socks. When her own children defied her or talked back, she beat them with a stick till they fell in line. When Noor screamed and demanded attention, Manzel lavished her with kisses and sang her to sleep.

Manzel was alarmed by the intensity of her son's ill will toward the Soleymans. She thought it was the fault of that mullah he had been going to see of late, at the mosque where she and her husband went on Muslim holy days. When he was younger, they had tried to convince Mojtaba to take Koran lessons and go to Friday prayers, but he had never shown an interest until the old mullah was sidelined by a young new arrival. This man had a way of speaking to Mojtaba and the others boys that excited them. They went to see him every Friday, then during the week after school. They studied Arabic and learned to read the Koran, but mostly they sat cross-legged on a dirty rug and listened to the mullah talk.

By thirteen, Mojtaba had become a devout Muslim who criticized his mother for wearing her chador too casually, and swore under his breath every time he saw a revealing photo of a woman in a magazine or on a billboard. He insisted that his parents and brothers should not be working for Jews, that Manzel should not eat at a Jew's house. At fifteen, he dropped out of school rather than sing the national anthem and swear allegiance to the shah every morning before class. In the weeks before Noor disappeared, he started to warn his father against driving unveiled women in the company car, or skipping his five-times-a-day prayers because they conflicted with his work schedule, or referring to the late Aaron as *agha*—sir.

"There's only one *agha*," he said, meaning the grandest of all grand mullahs, the Ayatollah Ruhollah Khomeini, who had sworn to bring down the shah and restore the kingdom of Islam on earth. He was in exile in Iraq, smuggling audiotapes of his sermons into Iran and distributing them through the network of mosques around the country. Rumor had it that on a clear night, his silhouette could be seen on the surface of the moon.

For over a year, Mojtaba pressured his mother to stop working for "Jews and monarchists." In December, he came to Bagh-e Yaas with four other young men and threatened to beat up or kill her boss unless Manzel quit work right then. She left sobbing and apologizing, Angela hanging on to her until she was wrenched away by Mojtaba.

At the headquarters of Soleyman Enterprises, all but a few dozen employees were either on strike or showing up to work only to spend the day discussing the sacredness of the ayatollah's dicta against the monarchy. Managers who dared remind the staff of their duties were branded as enemies of the revolution and marked for future reckoning.

Like other religious minorities in the country, the Jews were deeply loyal to the shah. To him they owed their recent freedom, literacy, civil rights, and wealth; the end of 1,400 years of ghetto life, massacres, and forced conversions; the license to proclaim themselves "real" Persians. Without him, there was no telling what would become of them and other minorities, if they would be imprisoned or killed as often as in Iran's Shia past, or expelled at gunpoint from the country as in nearly every Arab country since 1948. Many started to liquidate what assets they could, and went abroad to wait out the troubles. Elizabeth, however, had no such intention. She had a child and husband buried somewhere in that vast and turbulent country. With or without the shah, her only interest was loyalty to her departed family.

Twice in January, Manzel snuck away from Mojtaba's grip and rushed to Bagh-e Yaas to warn Elizabeth of what was coming. The mullahs and their posse, she said, had drawn up extensive lists of Zionist and imperialist Iranians, all of them wealthy and prominent and, by extension, corrupt and godless. Any day now, the forces of Islam would crush the fist of tyranny, the shah's soldiers would stand down, and the army of God would exact just punishment upon the sinners. When that time came, anyone connected to Soleyman Enterprises would be a target.

Later that month, the shah and his wife left the country. In February, Khomeini returned to Iran after twelve years in exile. In March, Habib Elghanian, one of the leaders of the Iranian Jewish community, was imprisoned for the crime of Zionism. In April, a national referendum was held whereby 82 percent of voters approved the establishment of an Islamic Republic in Iran. On Wednesday, May 9, Elghanian became the first Iranian Jew to be executed because of "corruption," "contacts with Israel," and "friendship with the enemies of God."

News of Elghanian's arrest stunned the Jewish community in Iran and abroad. In the days that followed, other Jews were arrested and held on charges of Zionism. Prisoners had no right to an attorney or to a trial; often, their whereabouts were unclear and anyone who tried to contact them would himself be imprisoned. At this rate, it would be a matter of time before Elizabeth fell into the mullahs' hands.

Do you know, miss, what they do to women in those jails?

On July 22, Elizabeth's name was printed in the afternoon paper on a list of Zionist spies and enemies of God. That night and the next morning, state-controlled radio and television ordered her and the others to turn themselves in. At two p.m. on July 23, a truckload of armed men with dark beards poured into the main offices of Soleyman Enterprises to arrest Elizabeth. Their leader, Seyyed Mojtaba (the title *seyyed* having been conferred upon him by a mullah in recognition of his service to the revolution), announced that they had come to "wipe a stain off the face of the republic."

With his gun drawn and an automatic rifle slung on his shoulder, Mojtaba led the men as they tore through the quiet hallways and mostly vacant offices, past terrified employees who did their best to avoid being seen, and stunned onlookers who had observed the men enter the building and followed them to satisfy their curiosity, the ragtag militia kicking open doors and smashing glass partitions as they called out Elizabeth's name until they had searched all seven floors and the garage as well and came up empty-handed. Then Mojtaba ordered everyone back into the truck and directed the driver toward Bagh-e Yaas.

She had left in the dead of night. On July 21, she had walked out of her second-floor bedroom with the lights off and Angela asleep in her arms, down the black granite staircase with their shoes in her hands so as not to awaken the servants. In the yard, the poet's jasmine was in full bloom, glowing on the vines in the light of a full moon, emitting a scent so sweet and viscous, it made the lizards slow and lazy as they emerged from the cracks in the yard wall.

Earlier that day, during the hour of the siesta, Elizabeth had packed a suitcase each for herself and Angela, hiding them in the trunk of her car. In the evening, she had waited till the servants had locked the house and gone to bed. She had hoped for a cloudy night, but the sky was a deep, limpid indigo gleaming with the electric silver light of the moon. Beneath it the garden—the ancient maple trees, the rose beds, the redbrick pathways winding through grass lawns and freshwater pools—looked like a fairy-tale kingdom asleep under a thousand-year spell.

The metal gates screeched when Elizabeth opened them. Beyond them the alley was empty, its cracked and uneven asphalt surface glowing dark and bare in the moonlight. Rather than turn the engine on, Elizabeth put the car in neutral and let it slide backward until it had cleared the metal doors. Then she sat there, behind the wheel, and stared through the still-open gates at the enchanted forest and the tall, darkened castle of her childhood and early youth. She saw the eight-year-old schoolgirl who went alone to her first Shabbat dinner, and the young man with the transparent eyes who called her "little one." She saw Madame Doctor waving as she pulled away in her car to go to the office, and the professor wading through knee-deep water, grasping at books and toys, cooking utensils and picture frames that had been set afloat, yet again, by the ghosts who lived in the pipes. She saw Noor asleep in her bed that last night, and the footprints in the snow leading away from the house. Then she got out of the car and closed the gates.

* * *

On a dirt road off Vanak Avenue in North Tehran, Manzel's husband waited for them in the beat-up taxi he had started driving since Mojtaba forced him to leave his job with the Soleymans. Elizabeth left her car and slipped into the cab with Angela. They drove for three hours, toward Manzel's hometown of Rasht. All the way there, Manzel's husband prayed to the Imam Zaman—the Prophet Muhammad's twelfth disciple, who had fallen into a well and from there into occultation—to help them at the crossing. On the last stretch of the trip, Elizabeth fell asleep in the car and dreamed of the Big House. It was still night but the servants, who had remained at their job only to spy on her and the girls, were awake. Elizabeth's bed was unmade, still warm from her body. Her clothes were still in the closet. Everything was exactly as it had been only hours ago except that she—Elizabeth—had been erased from the picture.

They would have to traverse a thousand miles in hiding. From Tehran to the city of Van in Turkey, the journey was fraught with danger. If they avoided the military police and border guards in both countries and survived the gruesome conditions, they could rest in Van, then take a bus another five hundred miles to Istanbul. That's all Elizabeth knew.

It was dawn when they arrived in Rasht on the Caspian. The July air was heavy and humid, but sweet. The Caspian Sea was in fact an immense lake, its water devoid of the saltiness that would otherwise seep into the air and blow in the breeze. The house they had come to sat across the street from a harbor, backed by a softly rolling, emerald-green hillside. There were two rooms, an outhouse, and a lopsided addition with a ceiling too low for an adult to pass below without bending. Outside, a woman sat on her knees next to a hole in the ground. She rolled pieces of fresh dough into a ball, beat it with the flat of her hand, and slapped it on the inside wall of the hole. Minutes later, she reached in again with her bare hand and peeled the bread off with bits of coal and blackened stone stuck to it from the wall. These she picked off with her fingers even as they still glowed hot.

A little girl, younger than Angela, with braided pigtails and a sheer yellow head scarf, brought tea and bread. Just then Manzel's husband came in with another man.

"My cousin will drive you to Zanjan," he said. "There, you'll change drivers to Tabriz. I don't know them but they're safe." He put his hand gently on the cousin's shoulder and nodded. "My cousins know you're precious to us. They wouldn't give you over to bad people."

He rubbed his hands together and peered down at his shoes.

"You must forgive me, *khanum*. I'm your servant and so is Ahmad," he turned to his cousin again, "but the rest of the way," his voice almost broke with embarrassment, "I don't know how to say this, it reflects badly on Manzel and me, I know." His head hung even lower now and he wouldn't look up, so Ahmad came to his rescue.

"*Khanum*, it's dangerous work. They hang anyone they catch smuggling people, and you—your excellency—"

"I'm on the list," Elizabeth finished his sentence.

Elizabeth guessed what the two men were getting at.

"I don't expect anyone to do this for free," she said. She reached into her handbag and took out a stack of American dollars. Every Iranian of means knew to stash dollars at home and in bank safe-deposit boxes in case of an economic or political meltdown. The smarter ones had also opened savings accounts and bought property in the United States. "There's $3,000 here," she said. "It's all I have."

It was decided that the smugglers on the Iranian side of the border would be paid $1,000, and that the Turks would take the same amount. The Turks had been known to take the payment, then turn the refugees over to border guards, so Elizabeth was instructed to pay half at the start of the journey and the rest at the end, when she and Angela were safely in the city of Van.

They sewed the money into the inside of Elizabeth's dress, then sewed her watch and wedding ring into Angela's undergarments. Manzel's husband promised he would go to Bagh-e Yaas and take what valuables he could, sell them on the black market, and, once Elizabeth was settled in Turkey, send her the money.

"That's dangerous," she said. "If your son finds out, or the other servants report you . . ."

At this, Manzel's husband broke into tears. Over and over, he apologized for his son's wickedness, swore he would never have had a child had he known what God intended it to be.

"You must write to us so we know you're safe," he pleaded with Elizabeth, "or Manzel will never sleep again. You must let us send money to you as soon as you arrive in Turkey."

He kissed her hand and caressed Angela's hair, followed them to the car with a bowl of water to pour on the ground for good tidings. When the car pulled away, Elizabeth peered back through the rear window: he stood there crying, waving vigorously, until they merged onto the highway and he vanished.

They spent the night at a small hotel in Tabriz. The driver signed them in and walked them to the room, then snuck out when the attendant was away answering a call.

"Good luck to you," he said with what Elizabeth thought was great sincerity. "*Salaam-eh mara beh-reh-soo-need*—give my regards." To whom, it was not clear.

Elizabeth and Angela were hungry, but Angela was afraid to leave the room and Elizabeth decided it was best not to draw attention to herself by going out, so they sat on the lone bed and ate the stale bread and cheese they had brought for the road from Rasht. Elizabeth tore a piece of the bread with her hands, rolled it around a bit of cheese and half a walnut, and handed it to Angela. She poured tap water into the glass by the sink and brought it to her.

"Eat this," Elizabeth said quietly.

Angela sat there, cross-legged on the rough blanket, ignoring the sandwich in her hand. After a moment, her knees started to shake.

Elizabeth was tired. "It's okay," she muttered, unconvinced.

At this, Angela began to sob. She had been quiet since they left Bagh-e Yaas, remained stoic and done exactly as she was told, but now she was loud and inconsolable. She had no idea what to make of all this; she wanted to go home, but she understood that "wanted by the regime" was a bad thing. She had seen the front-page pictures of rows of naked men lying in pools of blood with bullet holes in their heads and chests, heard the names of the wanted and the dead announced every hour on the radio.

They slept in their clothes, woke up at three in the morning, and went downstairs. Across the street from the hotel, a man stood smoking by a dented brown Volvo. When he saw them approach with their suitcases, he threw the cigarette on the ground and shook his head.

"Wear whatever you can and leave the rest," he said. He walked to the front of the car and turned his back to them. "Hurry up. It gets cold in the mountains at night."

Elizabeth carried a suitcase in each hand. Instead of following the man's instructions, she remained in place, staring at the back of his head as if searching for the answer to some puzzle, until Angela tugged at her.

"We can't leave them," Angela said, grasping a handle with both palms, forcing it out of her mother's hand. "We can't leave our things."

The driver was one of those weathered-and-sick-of-it-all Middle Eastern men who go straight from childhood to old age. One minute they're playing soccer barefoot with a plastic bottle for a ball on the street, the next minute they're working sixteen-hour days to make a pittance with which to support their parents and siblings. Their skin is dark and scarred from too much sun and their voices are coarse from too many cigarettes and their muscles twitch with anxiety and impatience because any minute now the sky might fall, because it always does for people like them.

He came over to Angela, put one knee to the ground, and said softly, "Daughter, where you're going there's no room for luggage." He glanced up at Elizabeth. "They told you you'll be on horses?"

They hadn't.

"It's either that, through our parts, or in a shipping crate over the gulf," he said, standing up. He sounded sorry for them.

"This is not as bad as being locked up in a crate on one those smuggling ships, but you can only take what you carry on yourself."

In the suitcase she had packed for Angela, Elizabeth had brought some of her and Noor's clothes and favorite books. In her own suitcase, she had mostly pictures: all the faded black-and-white and waterlogged images she had collected on the wet and muddy trail of the flood the day her parents and siblings drowned, all the professional portraits of Aaron and the children on special occasions that she tore out of albums at the last minute, Angela's first- and second-grade report cards, the children's birth certificates, Noor's nameplate.

She slipped the nameplate into her coat pocket. Though it was the middle of summer, she ordered Angela to put on all the warm clothes she could manage. Then she knelt next to the pile of pictures that lay inside the gaping suitcase, picked up a portrait of herself and Aaron from their wedding and two of Noor. She stuffed them inside her coat pocket, then took out the notebook that contained all the tips about

Noor's whereabouts, and set it away from the suitcase on the ground.

The driver was hovering over her impatiently, glancing toward the road, but Elizabeth remained mesmerized, as if unaware of danger. She drew a shallow breath and looked up at the driver.

Silently, she raised her hand, palm up and open, and held it toward him till he understood, fished his Bic lighter out of his pocket, and gave it to her. Here was her life—what remained of it, what she had chosen to save. She flicked the lighter and held the flame to the corner of a picture, then put it down in the open suitcase and watched it catch.

From Tabriz the road wound into the mountains, northwest toward Lake Urmia and beyond it the borderlands with Turkey. Late in the afternoon, they crossed the bridge and landed firmly in Kurdish territory. The driver took them to a mud hut in a village of fewer than a hundred people. The minute they got out of the car, they were surrounded by young Kurdish boys with aqueous eyes and knowing expressions who began to ask Angela questions she didn't understand. They spoke a mixture of Kurdish and Persian, then tried Turkish, Kurmanji, and finally the broken English they had picked up by watching pirated American movies on smuggled VHS cassettes.

"This is where it's going to get difficult," the driver told Elizabeth. "You're lucky it's not winter." He hesitated, as if measuring their chances. "You'll be fine. Just don't talk to anyone but your guides. Don't ask questions. And don't pay the Turks until you're safely in Van."

They spent the night in the safe house. In the morning, the smugglers put Elizabeth on one horse, Angela on another. A teenage boy with a long stick in one hand and a rifle slung over his shoulder rode in front; a tall, silent man, also armed, followed them. Neither would answer Elizabeth's questions about how long the journey would take or how the smugglers planned to avoid running into border guards along the way.

They took a circuitous route developed over decades of clandestine commerce, climbing ever higher into the mountains which hung more than five miles above the valley. The road was unpaved, barely wider than the horse, forever at risk of being blocked by one of the many boulders that hung precariously over it.

They paused around midday, sat in the shade of a rock, and ate more bread and cheese with dried walnuts. The sun set early that afternoon and the darkness was absolute. They stopped at a clay hut built into the side of the mountain. The boy boiled water over a kerosene lamp and made tea. The quiet one chain-smoked Marlboros.

"If we die here," Angela whispered to her mother as they lay on a coarse blanket on the floor, "if these men kill us or we are eaten by wolves, no one would know we ever existed."

Elizabeth was lying faceup. She rose on one elbow toward Angela. "That's why we're not going to die or let anyone kill us," she said, stroking her daughter's face. "Whatever it takes, we're going to make sure they know we existed."

They traveled on horseback for nine days with two different sets of guides. To avoid detection, they crossed into Turkey at night, still on horseback and across mountain roads. The border wasn't marked but the guides kept riding until they were met by three other Kurds in a creaky minivan filled with used auto parts. They ordered Elizabeth and Angela to crouch in the back of the van, covered them with a tarp, and stacked the load of metal to block them from view. Like unscrupulous guides, Turkish police often turned refugees over to Iranian border guards in exchange for a bribe. Sometimes, they sold young women to brothel owners or wealthy men.

In Turkey, they stayed in a rundown boardinghouse crowded with other Iranian refugees.

Having never fathomed the predicament in which they found themselves, the refugees were at a loss for the most basic information: how and where to rent an apartment by the month, where to shop for towels and groceries, how to mail a letter and where to pay the phone bill and how to find a mohel to circumcise a newborn son. Two and three generations of anxious and disoriented men and women milled around in cheap hotels and dingy boardinghouses, reassured each other and the children that all would be well again soon, that it wouldn't be long now before the CIA took action, invaded Iran, and restored the shah to his throne.

In the meantime, they followed the relentless stream of bad news from Iran, waited for calls that never came, stood in line for buses that never arrived. They spent entire days standing in the waiting rooms of embassies, notaries, attorneys—anyone who might approve their status as political refugees and give them a visa to somewhere else.

"Where to?"

Elizabeth had no idea.

* * *

From newer arrivals she learned that the Soleyman estate—the land-holdings, the businesses, the bank accounts and jewels and even their Persian rugs and antique furniture and expensive clothes—had become the subject of a grab-now-and-prove-ownership-later campaign by Seyyed Mojtaba. He had moved into the Big House with his two wives and three children, and announced he was turning the place into a religious school. He was going around dressed like Fidel Castro and with an equally plush beard, arresting people for crimes against humanity or for wearing nail polish, sending the men before Islamic tribunals set up in various parts of town and presided over by mullahs. The trials took from three to fifteen minutes; defendants did not have a right to an attorney. Afterward, the men were taken onto the roof of the building and shot; the women were sent to jail to be raped—because Islam forbids the killing of a virgin—before being put to death.

In the midst of all this, Raphael's Wife screamed in the wind and filed petition after petition with the Council for the Protection of the Innocent and Impoverished, wagging her faded documents and hurling insults and curses as she tried to establish ownership of all former Soleyman properties, including Bagh-e Yaas.

"Where to?"

In the second half of 1979, a struggle broke out between the various revolutionary factions in Iran—the nationalists and democrats and Communists and Islamic Marxists who, earlier, had joined forces to bring down the shah's regime. In a fool's gamble that none of the parties would later be able to justify, each plotted secretly to "use" Islam as a rallying cry to overthrow the shah before they took over.

They should have known better.

For a while, the factions fought each other and the mullahs for control of the country. But any hope that the more moderate forces would prevail upon the clergy and allow the exiles to safely go back were quashed when the mullahs won a referendum on the future shape of the government and conferred upon Khomeini the title of *Vali-ye faqih*—Supreme Leader and Custodian of the People. In much the same way as a group of cardinals elect a new pope who, by virtue of the title, is suddenly imbued with celestial qualities, a band of

Muslim clerics had anointed one of their own with divine authority and unleashed him on the world.

Khomeini's ascent to the holy throne was finalized and set in stone. "Where to?"

In December, Elizabeth called the number Hussein Zemorrodi had given her. She reached a restaurant in Hollywood.

The first three people who came to the phone did not know a Hussein of any kind; the fourth one, a man who introduced himself as John Vain, laughed out loud when he understood the source of the confusion.

"Of course he works here," he said. He spoke with a heavy American accent, but he switched to Persian after the initial exchange.

"He's just such a loner," John Vain said of Hussein. "No one knows his real name. They call him Hal . . . like in the film *Space Odyssey* . . . the mechanical brain . . . Did you see the film?"

Was Elizabeth Hal's wife or girlfriend? Was she in Iran, or had she made it out already? Did she have a visa, a plan? Was she short for money?

"Call back in a few hours," he finally said. "Hal should be here by then. We'll make sure we get you over here ASAP."

ahanshah Varasteh (a.k.a. John Vain) was an Iranian Jew who owned a restaurant on the corner of Sunset Boulevard and Crescent Heights, just outside Beverly Hills at the western tip of Hollywood. He was 6'4" and lanky, all taut nerves and tense vivacity, and had a fondness for wearing cowboy boots that he bought during yearly trips to a shop in Austin, Texas. The shop was owned by an Irishman; the workers were all Mexican. They had trouble pronouncing his Iranian name, so after his sixth or seventh visit they started to call him John Vain for convenience. Jahanshah wasn't a big movie buff but he could see the advantage of having a name that was easy to spell and remember, so he adjusted it to fit his initials.

Even before Iranians started to move to LA en masse, John Vain had a reputation for being extraordinarily kind to people in need. He was as generous with his time and goodwill as with his money—a full-service support system for every down-and-out friend or stranger who happened upon his path. After the revolution he was the first of the old-timers—the handful of families that had immigrated to Los Angeles in the early '70s—to help the newcomers settle. For nearly two years he opened his house to every helpless mother or frightened teenager who showed up at his door, let the men use his restaurant as a makeshift office from which to conduct their business, and sat through the interminable string of stories every new arrival felt duty-bound to share.

John Vain told people he did all this for his own benefit—the pleasure of getting to know those he might otherwise never cross paths with, the peace of mind of feeling he had done what he could to make a life easier. It didn't even bother him that most of the time he was giving away money he didn't really have: Lucky 99 was always full, often with B-list actors (John Vain insisted they were "B+") and their half-dressed hangers-on, but it had never turned a profit because John Vain picked up more checks than he collected. His house in Trousdale Estates was worth nearly $200,000 dollars even before all the Iranians moved there and drove up the prices, but it was mortgaged for twice its value. His black limited-edition Cadillac Seville Gucci, complete with interlocking designer G's on the vinyl top, headrests, and wheel covers, and the personalized plate *ALAMRCN*—All-American—was a special-order piece built for an Arab prince who drove it around for one summer and sold it to John Vain for much more than it had cost.

On the face of it, Hussein Zemorrodi was just another one of John Vain's charity cases, hired because he needed to eat while he pursued his more lofty ambitions. He was a young man with dusky skin and prematurely gray hair, no practical skills whatsoever, and no idea how to get along with regular people. He had answered an ad in the *LA Times* for an "electrical engineer able to modernize a spectacular dining establishment." He turned up carrying a small suitcase that he held between his right arm and hip because the handle was broken, volunteered that he knew less than nothing about the job for which he had applied, "But really, sir, my life's mission is to invent things no one else has thought of." Then he put his suitcase on John Vain's desk and began to sort through a mess of papers and charts, looking exasperated and harried and apologizing as he searched for whatever it was that would help John Vain understand.

Hussein had been sleeping in his car, showering at the Y, working in the library, and eating what he could afford. Of course he would accept a job as "kitchen helper" at Lucky 99 if it meant he could work nights and have the days to draw on his graph papers, get all his meals for free, and sleep in the storage room. He even drew a salary in cash for doing things like taking out the trash and stacking cans and boxes, cleaning out the freezer, and picking up tablecloths from the laundry. Never mind he had a tendency to become sidetracked and take half a day to complete a job that should require a half hour. He was polite and harmless and extremely grateful to John Vain.

John Vain's accountant and the restaurant's manager knew better than to exercise their throats trying to explain that, far from earning his keep, Hal was likely to end up on a seventy-two-hour hold in some county hospital, that he was just taking up space and collecting a salary for work that should be part of other employees' responsibility. John Vain just didn't believe that helping others in need was a bad idea, no matter what the cost to himself. More importantly, he didn't believe that anything he did, no matter how reckless, could ever result in serious harm.

Years ago when he was a small boy in Iran, he had met a woman who sold him ninety-nine years of good fortune for ninety-nine tomans. He'd used up a handful of the years in Iran, but he brought most of them to America.

The hardest part of being an exile, the Iranians would soon learn, was the vanishing—not of the self, but of its likeness in the eyes of others.

You see yourself, to begin with, as a reflection in a parent's eyes. You learn who you are, what you are, by looking at that picture day after day until your world begins to expand and you find the image in many sets of eyes, and before you know it you've become real—a whole, separate person, carved and cast and endowed with life out of the idea that others hold of you. Everything you know about yourself is either an affirmation or a deviation from that idea. Everything you do, anything you become, is either in fulfillment or thwarting of that concept.

Then all at once the mirror breaks and the world goes dark. You're forced out or flee for your life. Your home becomes a gallows, your people, executioners. The fourteen-year-old who is saved by the Hebrew Immigrant Aid Society (HIAS) and becomes the ward of Chabad because he has no family, the ten-year-old who is sent to live with an older sibling or an aunt, and who won't see her parents again for thirty years. The poet who forsakes the language in which he writes, the writer who becomes uncomprehending and incomprehensible in the new country. What do they find, in their place of refuge, in the eyes of their neighbors, but a blank slate? A pencil sketch of a person with no name, no past, no way to define himself without the colors and hues in which he had been painted before.

There is a part of this obscurity that unshackles and liberates, that allows one to reimagine and reinvent herself, to start again, unfettered. And there's a part that lessens and devalues. For most, it turns "I am" into "I used to be."

That's why immigrants congregate in communities—so they can hold on to what remains of themselves in the memories of others—why so many Iranians settled in New York and California in the aftermath of the revolution. The moment they arrived on either coast they called another Iranian—a sibling, an old colleague, a friend of a friend.

They gathered in each other's hotel rooms and in the Westwood Manor apartments, and waited for the news that the shah had suppressed the "disturbances" and that it was safe to go home. They sat all night by the large windows of Ship's coffee shop in Westwood, drank hot tea, and told each other that the mayhem in Iran would soon be over; the shah would not fall; the West would not let him. They searched for the few Iranians who had come to America before them, asked for advice on how to rent furniture and where to go if they were sick. For most, this connection was enough to create a new footing.

But what of a family like Elizabeth's, already disengaged from the community and diminished through tragedy, who have nothing but memories with which to sustain themselves? A family of one and a half women, say—a mother in her midtwenties, an almost eight-year-old daughter—who have had to abandon the graves of the ones they lost. The first thing they learn in the new place is that, as difficult as it is to find themselves in the eyes of others, it's nearly impossible to find any trace of those left behind.

The dead and missing cannot cross borders; their exile is our forgetting.

Elizabeth landed in Los Angeles in May 1979, nearly a year after she and Angela had escaped from the country that promised to become their prison. She had no college education, not even a high school diploma, and no work experience. She could read and write English well enough, but she had trouble understanding or speaking "American" because her teachers in Iran (usually the spouses of diplomats or oil company executives on assignment in the country) had been mostly British. She had used up nearly all her cash while awaiting the visa that John Vain arranged for her and Angela, and she was already in debt to him for the attorney's fees and other charges relating to her application as a political refugee. More than anything, she was alone.

Unlike most other Iranians who quickly joined extended family and old friends upon arrival in LA, Elizabeth had only John Vain's number in her pocket and no material possessions. She wasn't the first young mother with a small child to have turned to John Vain for help. Other families had been divided in this way. Some husbands sent the wife and kids abroad but stayed in Iran to protect their belongings; others were under investigation and forbidden to leave. A good number were lingering in jail or had been executed.

The wives, however, had been raised to think as little as possible, concern themselves only with domestic matters, and take no initiative whatsoever. If they were lucky or had any sense, they had gone from their father's house straight into a husband's in their late teens or early twenties. They had never traveled alone, couldn't go from one city in Iran to another without written permission from their spouse. Suddenly they had to make every decision not only for themselves, but also for their children. They could recite poetry and sew, but they had to learn how to open a bank account and write a check; they could orchestrate the most extravagant meals for a hundred people at once, but they had to be told what to pack their children for lunch every day. That they rose to the occasion as well and as quickly as they did was, in John Vain's mind, proof of an inherent ability that had, for centuries, been suppressed by the laws and traditions of the East. To get there, however, they needed a hand to keep them steady.

He was waiting for Elizabeth and Angela outside customs at LAX. He had come instead of Hal because you could never quite trust the man's punctuality—he had the best intentions but he might show up on a Tuesday instead of a Thursday, or at eight in the morning instead of the evening. "And besides," John Vain had told Hal, "the sight of you may scare the poor woman right back to Turkey."

By the time Elizabeth and Angela emerged from the terminal, they had been traveling for more than two days. They were sleepy and disoriented and smelling of airports and anxiety, hesitant to look anyone in the eye or smile back at all the strangers' faces. Yet to John Vain, they looked like the family he had always wished he had.

The last time John Vain saw his father, in 1960 when he was eight years old, they were in the city of Gonbad-e Kavus near the Caspian coast. He had gone there with his parents because his father, who was due to take a long journey abroad, wanted their small family to spend time together. For a week, they drove up and down the shoreline, visiting major towns and small villages. In Gonbad, John Vain's father took him to see the monument after which the city was named.

In the eleventh century AD, a king had built himself a mausoleum in the shape of a two-hundred-foot tower made entirely of bricks. Upon his death, his body was to be placed in a glass coffin that hung from the top of the tower, away from human hands where he could see the sun rise every day.

"That's the difference between a man who becomes king and one who remains a slave," John Vain's father had told him. "The slave recognizes his limits; the king reaches for the sun even in the darkness of death."

Years later, John Vain would understand that the parable had been intended more as an apology than a life lesson by his father. Traveling west after their "field trip," John Vain and his mother woke up in a motel room in Ramsar to find a hundred-toman bill next to each of their pillows. They assumed the father had gone out for an early-morning walk. Then they assumed he was out buying lunch; on a day-long boat trip; on a fishing voyage out in the open sea; kidnapped by smugglers; arrested and imprisoned by evil Soviet border guards; tortured and killed and fed to wild dogs; or maybe—maybe he had gone to reach for the sun, alone and unencumbered.

Two weeks later, heartbroken after waiting endlessly for his father's return, John Vain left his crying mother and walked into the small town. Dusk was settling in, bringing with it the smell of the sea at nighttime. Here and there, the small, yellowish flickers of gas lamps illuminated the leathery dark faces of fishermen, red flares from coal burning inside braziers reflected back from the eyes of teenage boys squatting on the sidewalk to grill chicken liver and kidneys on metal skewers. Little girls in chintz skirts and gold hoop earrings ran barefoot ahead of older sisters or young mothers, all curly hair and giggles.

Just when he thought he should head back to the motel, he heard someone whisper, "You, there!"

The woman had dark hair and narrow eyebrows. "Do you have any money?"

She wore a transparent white chador that had slipped from her head onto her bare shoulders, exposing big white earrings and rows of white pearls.

"What for?" John Vain asked.

"Depends on how much money you have."

"What are you selling?"

"What do you want?"

He gave her the hundred-toman bill and said he wanted his father back.

"How long has he been gone?"

She laughed when he told her.

"And you're still waiting?" She stuffed the bill in between her breasts and pulled out one toman. She put the coin in John Vain's hand, then folded his fingers around it and brought his little fist to her chest.

"I'll give you something much better than your father. Close your eyes and count to ninety-nine." She held his hand against her heart. "I'm going to give you ninety-nine years of good luck."

He had only to inhale Elizabeth's scent, close his eyes, and remember the flare of magic that had lit up the night that time in Ramsar, to know that she had traveled twenty-two years and 7,500 miles to belong to him. He shook hands with her and Angela, explained that he had volunteered to pick them up because his time wasn't nearly as precious as Hal's. "He's a genius; I'm just a short-order cook."

He was so exhilarated by Elizabeth's presence, so enlivened by the awareness of the blessing he had received, he forgot to ask where she wanted to go or whether she had plans for where to stay.

"Hal tells me you're the smartest person he knows," he said as he pulled out of the parking lot and onto Century Boulevard toward the freeway. "Which is scary, because he's the smartest person I've ever met. Either that, or he's just nuts."

He talked all the way to within minutes of his house. At the light on Sunset and Foothill he fell silent, as if deflated by the sudden appreciation of the circumstances: he hadn't told Elizabeth where he was taking her and Angela, and they hadn't asked. They sat together in the passenger seat, the child asleep on her mother's lap, her head resting in the nook of Elizabeth's neck, the mother still and stoic.

When the light turned green, he put the gear in park and shifted in his seat to face Elizabeth. It was the first time he had really looked at her. She seemed ageless, like a very old painting of a young woman.

"I thought I had an eventful life until Hal told me your story."

He dropped his eyes when he said this because he couldn't bear the intensity of her gaze.

"I was lucky enough to have come here, to this town, some time ago. I've helped a few people and I'd like to do what I can for you."

He realized he sounded like he was reciting a prepared monologue, and blushed.

"I have a largish house." He turned to the side window, hoping to hide the redness in his face. Behind them cars were honking madly. "You're welcome to stay as my guest."

The light had turned red and green again, and drivers were yelling at him from open windows, so he put on the hazard lights and waited for Elizabeth to say something.

"It's just . . ." he searched desperately for the right thing to say. "It's just a . . ." He stopped, then started again. "You wouldn't owe me anything. Not now. Not ever."

John Vain was fourteen years old and poor as an honest banker when his mother sent him to America to make money. That he spoke only a few words of English, had a total of thirty dollars in his pocket when he boarded the plane at Mehrabad Airport, and no idea what to do once he landed in New York, was of little concern at the time: their next-door neighbor in Tehran had shipped her own twelve-year-old son to England a few years earlier with even less than what Jahanshah took away, and he—the neighbor's son—was sending a fortune home every month. Jahanshah's mother had considered England first, but his high school teacher had suggested otherwise: he wasn't a good student and didn't have the best manners or discipline. The teacher had said that "boys like him go to America," which wasn't a compliment to either the person or to the country, but it sounded reasonable enough to the mother.

He landed in New York on July 1, 1960. He spent the first three nights at the airport, walking the terminals and looking out the windows at the tarmac and wondering if this was all there was to New York City. When he finally got the courage to step outside, it was to follow a Pakistani doctor he had met in the washroom who had offered him a ride into Manhattan. From what Jahanshah could understand of the doctor's English, he too had come to America broke and without a friend. "I slept on subway trains and ate at a church," he had said, or that's what Jahanshah would recall later.

For weeks he rode the subway into and around Manhattan and Queens and Brooklyn, studying the maps and barely stepping out of the tunnels for fear of getting lost on the street. He lived on donuts and coffee from underground shops, and the occasional hot dog from a street vendor right above the subway entrance. It was midsummer and the heat and humidity were oppressive. By September, broke, he had gained enough courage to venture into a small radius around the Port Authority terminal on 40th and Eighth.

His first job was as a dishwasher in a diner one block from the terminal. He worked twelve hours a day, starting at nine in the evening, for $150 a month. He was paid in cash and allowed two meals per shift. For a while, he rented a cheap room in a sleazy motel on 41st; then he discovered a church on Tenth and 39th with a separate staircase that led from the street up into an attic where, on any given night, a dozen or more men made their beds on the floor. By the time Jahanshah arrived in the morning, the night tenants had cleared out and the room, plus a toilet with a sink and a mirror, could be rented for three dollars a day.

It was not an easy existence, but something about the dirty air, the grease-stained clothes, the neon lights and linoleum counters of the diner, the hours he spent working with gruff, disappointed older men or bright-eyed, eager young ones from places as far away and diverse as Bombay and San Juan and Tripoli and Accra, thrilled and elated Jahanshah. After a few weeks, he was promoted to busboy, which was the same thing as waiter since only two people worked the night shift, but it meant he could talk with the patrons and pour endless coffee refills and look the other way when they spiked it with something wrapped in brown paper. By Christmas, he was friends with all the employees and the regular customers at the diner. He knew the shop owners and bums and hookers and cops in the area, spent his lunch and coffee breaks smoking cigarettes and exchanging war stories about difficult customers with the cab drivers from the taxi stand across from the Port Authority.

A week after New Year's, his boss, an aging Latvian Jew who had sat behind the cash register of the diner every day for thirty-seven years without once staying home sick or going on vacation, lost his wife. He took a week off to sit shivah, then came to work and announced that he was going to sell the diner and go to LA to live with his daughter. He had a brand-new Continental he wanted to drive across the country, but he didn't want to travel alone because he was afraid of all the "bums and killers" who lay in wait for him "in places like Kansas." Only a year earlier, the Clutter family had been murdered in their bedrooms by a pair of convicts released from the Kansas State Penitentiary. The Latvian, who didn't fancy meeting the same fate, offered Jahanshah a free ride to LA.

To most people in LA, Elizabeth and Angela cut a mystifying figure—at once pitiable in their worn-out clothes and daunting in their air of self-sufficiency. They looked nothing alike, yet you'd never see one without the other. Elizabeth was small, quiet, much too demure for her age; Angela was feisty and boisterous and too assertive for her own good. To anyone who knew their story, they were sad reminders of what can happen when civil war breaks out within a family. To strangers, they were that increasingly common sight in LA—a new type of refugee that could not be easily classified.

But to John Vain, from that first night when he dropped them off at his house, showed them the kitchen and the guest bedroom, then left to go back to the restaurant, Elizabeth and Angela were a sign from the universe that every good thing he had ever wished for would someday be his.

"I'm going to marry your friend," he announced the minute he saw Hal in the back room of Lucky 99 that night, "and you are going to be my best man."

To which poor Hal, who had temporarily forgotten Elizabeth, responded, "I don't have any friends."

Later that week, John Vain helped Elizabeth rent an apartment on Olympic and Spalding on the farthest edge of Beverly Hills. He chose the location because the school system was one of the best in the country, and the building far away enough from the swanky parts of the city to make the rent affordable. He bought them beds and dishes and furniture, enrolled Elizabeth in driving school and adult English classes at Roxbury Park, showed her how to take the bus from her apartment to Angela's new school. At night, he drove them to Lucky 99, planted them at the best table in the house, introduced every one of his regulars to them, and boasted of Elizabeth's intelligence and pedigree.

Angela was thrilled at the great food and beautiful company, but for Elizabeth those were torturous evenings. She was still exhausted

from being on the run and the anxiety of not knowing what to antici-
pate next. She felt a wakefulness, a blurry, constant disquiet, that had
begun with Aaron's shooting and only grown deeper over time. She
had no idea how to make small talk or feign interest in strangers in
high heels and silk suits.

She tried, in her own polite Iranian way, to pass up John Vain's invitations without offending him. It would have been anathema for her
to admit a lack of enthusiasm or dearth of energy to take advantage
of his hospitality. On the other hand, all her protestations of "we've
already imposed on you far too much" did nothing to mitigate John
Vain's fervor for having her close at all times. He had been in America
too long to remember the hidden meaning in some terms or be able
to distinguish between their literal meaning and what they implied.
He went right on showing up at Elizabeth's door every night at seven,
bearing gifts and good cheer and promises of great things about to happen, drove them to Lucky 99, and ordered Hal, relieved of kitchen duty,
to keep them company while John Vain tended to the other guests.

Hal was glad—so very glad—to see his old friend again; he had such fond memories of their childhood together, of the math games they played during recess, the two months she had lived with him and his parents. He was honored to make Angela's acquaintance—she was clearly as smart as her mother and equally erudite. Children mature so much faster in the East, he told her. There's more expected of them earlier, the world around them is older and more demanding; they are taught about duty, practicality, industry—it's only here, in America, where even death is not quite real; do you know they lay the corpse in a satin-lined coffin, dress it up, and do hair and makeup like it's going to a fancy ball instead of the grave? And damn if you're not looked down upon if you mourn too much or for too long, if you don't declare, before the headstone has been installed, that you're going to pick up a cause, create a foundation, make lemonade.

He spoke with his chin tilted slightly toward his chest so as to avoid insulting Elizabeth by staring directly at her. His hands, fingers interlaced, rested on the table in front of him as if in prayer. He even made an effort to appear presentable, wearing a Salvation Army tie over a white short-sleeved tennis shirt he had fished out of the lost-and-found bin at the Y. He had longish hair and a narrow jaw, a hint of gray in his week-old stubble, a permanent tick that pulsated in his left eye every few seconds.

Like any good scientist or engineer, Hal Zemorrodi suffered from undiagnosed obsessive-compulsive disorder. That's what enabled him to pursue one goal at the expense of all else. Unlike good scientists and engineers, however, he was so determined to realize his vision, he failed to see the inherent flaws in his plans.

A device that can track people from great distances, in darkness or light, by detecting the heat emitted by their bodies: that was his pipe dream and he felt he was close, he had it almost all figured out, yet every time he thought he was ready to create a prototype, something went awry and the entire edifice crumbled. He had been grappling with the same problem for so long he was ready to shred all his papers and stick a wire hanger into a light socket till his brain was good and fried.

Whenever John Vain summoned him to sit with Elizabeth and Angela, he came to the table with all his charts and blueprints, his reams of notes, his 307 reasons why the world was waiting for his heat-detecting radar and didn't even know it. As soon as he had dispensed with the formalities, he pushed the plates and glasses out of the way and spread his papers before Elizabeth, launched into a very polite but urgent explanation of what everything meant, and didn't stop even after their food had been served. He continued as if convinced that Elizabeth had as much interest in the subject as he, kept apologizing to Angela for "boring you with all this," but never contemplated stopping. By ten, when the place was buzzing and the noise level at its highest, Angela would be asleep with her head on her mother's lap, and Elizabeth would be more pallid and exhausted than ever, but poor Hal was nowhere near done with his presentation.

Finally, one night, Elizabeth interrupted.

"It's wrong."

Either because he hadn't heard her, or because what she said made no sense, Hal kept speaking. She listened for a full minute before she repeated herself.

Irritated, Hal shook his head, as if to discourage a persistent fly, and started again. She reached toward him, put her hand, palm down, on the chart he was referring to, and said, "Hussein! Your numbers don't add up."

She might as well have told him that his entire life amounted to nothing. He stared at her blankly, took a deep breath, then dropped his eyes to the graph on the table.

"You have no way of knowing that." He sounded so wounded, it made Elizabeth wish she hadn't said anything. "You haven't studied the numbers," he muttered without lifting his eyes to meet hers.

Three years ago, she would have had no hesitation in responding, "I don't need to have the numbers in front of me to study them, I remember every last one and I know you're mistaken, my friend, they don't add up no matter how badly you want them to."

Three years ago, she still believed in the inviolability of some truths and the necessity—the unqualified importance—of telling it like it is. She didn't know yet that truth can kill you as easily as it can set you free; that there's such a thing as one too many facts. That numbers can represent too many losses, too much time gone by, too little hope for miracles.

"You're right," she said so softly her voice was nearly drowned out by the din around them. "I may be mistaken."

The next night, Hal did not show up for work or for dinner with Elizabeth. The night after that he went into the kitchen through the back door but hid every time John Vain went in to look for him. He spoke to no one, not even to answer a question or acknowledge a command, and slept in his car instead of in the storage room. He spent all of the next day poring over his files. In the evening, he was waiting for Elizabeth when she and Angela came in with John Vain.

"There!" He slammed his suitcase on the table as soon as they sat. He was clearly daring someone; you just couldn't tell if it was her, or himself.

Hal wiped his palms on the frayed lapels of his jacket, then popped the locks of his suitcase. The top burst open, shooting up sheets of scribbled and crumpled lined paper. Grunting under his breath, he gathered the papers, forced a smile, and handed them to Elizabeth with the expression of a man who's entrusting his sick child to the only doctor in the world who might save it.

That first year after the revolution, local Angelenos didn't know what to make of the thousands of Iranians who suddenly populated the city. In the wealthier parts of town, residents who for decades had been accustomed to a certain kind of immigrant—working-class, non-English-speaking, skin-of-their-teeth types, mostly from South America and Southeast Asia—suddenly found a population of highly educated, worldly Iranians inhabiting large swaths of Westwood, Santa Monica, and Beverly Hills. They shopped at Saks and I. Magnin on Wilshire Boulevard, ate at Chasen's and Perino's and the Luau on Rodeo, and fought vehemently over the check because everyone wanted to pay for the others. The men wore suits and ties even to the park on Sunday afternoons; the women walked around as if surrounded by a royal retinue. They went everywhere in groups, sat around at Ship's coffee shop on Wilshire and Westwood half the night, or at Clifton's in the Century City mall on Saturdays, as if they owned the rights to the land. They went to each other's hotel rooms and apartments every day, ate dinner at ten on weeknights, later on weekends.

In the schools, American parents were alarmed by the sight of so many dark-eyed, dark-haired children suddenly sitting next to their blond kids. Librarians couldn't convey the concept of "no talking" well enough. Teachers, who didn't know that parents in Iran are not allowed to interfere in the school's business, complained that Iranian parents lacked the volunteer spirit, that, following Middle Eastern custom, they would arrive an hour late for a twenty-minute parent-teacher conference and fail to understand what they had done wrong. Once the hostage crisis broke out and wild-eyed young men badly in need of a shave screamed "Death to America!" at every television camera broadcasting from Iran, American-born children, blond and blue-eyed, long-legged and beaming with confidence, tormented the dark kids and called them hostage-takers.

In neighborhoods with a large influx of Iranian residents, homeowners suspected a hostile takeover by these unruly strangers who turned off the air-conditioning in their homes and instead hosed down the yard twice a day (never mind the drought) in order to fight the summer heat, haggled for everything because where they came from the "asking price" was only a place from which to start negotiations. In Beverly Hills, white flight became a serious threat; those who stayed did so mostly out of a sense of patriotism, a Florida-style "stand your ground" mentality that pitted old Eastern European and South American immigrants of fifty years ago against the Iranians of the day.

And yet there was also this: the laws of the United States and the spirit of generosity upon which it was founded assured a level of tolerance and opportunity rarely available anywhere else in the world.

Elizabeth had to find work, but she had no idea how to go about doing this or what she was even qualified to do. Every morning she woke up in the dark, made Angela a breakfast of white toast with Smucker's jelly, then they both took the bus down Olympic to Rexford. From there, they walked the twelve blocks to the Hawthorne School where Angela had started midyear in third grade. She had been a top student at her school in Iran and she had no trouble speaking and understanding both English and French, but here she was identified as an ESL student and automatically assigned to the "slow" track. She was angry about this—about the way her well-meaning teachers spoke to her too loudly and enunciated too slowly, the way the white kids avoided the Iranians and the Iranian kids banded together and showed no interest in befriending the whites. She had discovered that the Iranian children all knew each other from some other place or time, that their parents had known each other in Iran and were friends in LA, that many of them seemed to be privy to every part of the Soleyman history.

"They know everything about you and Dad and your parents and Bagh-e Yaas," she told Elizabeth. "They ask me if we ever found Noor, or if you found out who stole her, or how she was killed. How come you don't know them?"

How to explain to a nine-year-old that you can be in exile even while at home; that Elizabeth had neither sought nor missed the sense of belonging that was so crucial to so many; that her self-sufficiency, her independence, would at once liberate and shut out both her and Angela.

* * *

From the school, Elizabeth walked up to the library next to city hall, sat on a bench outside, and read every single help wanted ad in the *LA Times*. She had no idea what a "résumé" was and wouldn't have anything to include in it, so she only inquired after the jobs that didn't require one. The few times she used the public phone outside the library to call the numbers listed, she found herself stuttering and incoherent, too intimidated by the questions and too mortified by having to say, "No, I don't have a college degree, not even a high school diploma, I've never worked 'outside the house' before, I don't have a car, I don't know how to 'greet' customers in a retail store." But she had no trouble finding her way around or remembering the routes, numbers, and times of the bus schedule; she had only to study those things once to have near total recall. So she started to show up at the addresses listed in "apply in person" ads, even planned to stop at random offices or shops and offer to work.

They looked at her—thin, pallid, much too serious for a woman her age—and didn't know what to think. She seemed too well off, too sophisticated to work as an assistant in a day-care center, or as a grocery clerk, but she was too inexperienced to be trusted with the care of the children or the cash register. She couldn't start work till after eight and had to leave by two because she had a child, didn't know shorthand or how to type or operate a switchboard, but she insisted she could do a full day's paperwork on time, learn anything she was shown once. For the first time in her life, Elizabeth's intellect was neither recognized nor deemed especially useful.

And there was the scent.

It must be a perfume she wore, people thought, something foreign and extravagant that evoked long-forgotten memories—a story they had heard in childhood, a day they had spent by the sea, an outlandish hope, a first kiss. It preceded her into every room and hallway, onto the bus, into the staircase and elevator, drew curious stares and tentative questions—what is that you're wearing, what flower or plant is it extracted from, what country was it made in?

Embarrassed, Elizabeth would offer a quiet, "I don't recall the name, it was a gift," and look down, waiting for the moment to pass. The sense of bewilderment would cast a pall over the conversation and she felt, more than ever, that she could neither explain nor evade her birthright.

It had been different in Iran. She rarely went out, hardly met new people. Nearly everyone she came into contact with was either accustomed to or aware of her strange smell.

"And do you plan to wear this perfume at work? Are you willing to use less of it? It's not unpleasant—no—but it's distinct and unmistakable, heady even, it makes a person want to lie down and look at the clouds."

She was in her third week of job hunting, eating carrots and celery for breakfast and lunch so she could save her remaining money, when John Vain discovered what she was up to during the day. He still called or stopped by every evening to take her and Angela to Lucky 99 for dinner, but he was disarmed by talk of homework and school early the next day, had to swallow his disappointment, and, as he confessed to Hal, "take it like a man." He had been away from Iran for so long, he had no idea how inappropriate all this was—a man lending a single woman money and buying her things when he was not a spouse or directly related to her by blood, his presence in her house when no one else was there to chaperone, even his addressing her by the more informal, intimate *tow*—you—instead of *shomaa*.

He could sense her shyness, the hesitancy with which she accepted his offerings, but he attributed them to her pride. And he was tactful enough not to shout his eagerness to be with her every second of the day from every rooftop; she was, after all, still a recent widow. But time had a way of folding in on itself whenever he was near her, so that an hour became a minute, painfully precious and maddeningly short, then stretched monstrously when she was absent. So he came up with ever more innovative reasons to "touch base," as he liked to say, which meant daily visits, albeit for just a few minutes, with or without an invitation.

This—being impulsive and impetuous and "all-in"—was genuine John Vain. Even before he made the deal of the century and bought himself eternal good luck, when he was just a fatherless boy walking barefoot on a musty sidewalk in a little coastal town, he had not an ounce of caution or a grain of distrust to slow him down. He was what people in Iran called "large"—as in a person with largesse. He knew what he wanted the moment he saw it and he was always sure he would get it one way or another, no matter what the obstacles or how much he had to sacrifice. He was a promise, constant and unwavering, that the road through darkness would eventually, inevitably, lead to light.

One Sunday he rang Elizabeth's doorbell holding a bagful of brunch items, having dragged Hal in tow "for appearance's sake, so I don't come off as a mad stalker," and found Angela alone at home.

"She's gone to the look for work," the girl explained, trying hard not to sound either hopeful or angry. They needed the money, but Angela also needed her mother.

"She'll probably come back and say no one would hire her."

John Vain put the bag down on the three-foot-long kitchen counter, considered Angela's statement to make sure he had understood, and silently blessed the strange woman who, long ago in a time of utter hopelessness, had for a pittance sold him ninety-nine years of good luck.

Elizabeth had responded to a recurring ad by a "domestic agency." She knew "domestic" referred to family, home, and household, so she took three buses to Sherman Oaks, walked for twenty minutes from the corner of Ventura and Sepulveda to Van Nuys, then up two flights of stairs in a strip mall to the address listed in the ad.

The door was open. Inside, two dozen women sat on metal folding chairs, handbags on their laps, speaking Spanish and seeming quite at home. The room was dark, with only a small window that appeared to have been painted shut. In the far corner, a middle-aged woman with drawn-on eyebrows and false eyelashes sat behind a metal desk, staring at the phone as if to will it to ring.

"Good morning," she said, motioning with her hand for Elizabeth to come in. The other women fell silent, glared at her from head to toe and back up, then started to talk to each other in Spanish. Elizabeth forced a smile and nodded at them, said good morning in English, slowly made her way to the desk.

"Live in or out?" the woman with the eyelashes asked in Spanish. When she saw Elizabeth's reaction, she asked, still in Spanish, "Don't you speak Spanish?"

A moment later she repeated the question in English. "Live in or live out? It's a hundred dollars cash either way when you sign up, fifty a week for four weeks once you've found something. Do you have papers?"

It dawned on Elizabeth that she had misunderstood the meaning of the word "domestic." She didn't want to offend the eyelashes by admitting she wasn't looking to clean houses—not yet, anyway, though if it came to that, if she found nothing else, she would do whatever she had to. And she was too ashamed to admit she didn't know this other meaning of "domestic." She would have filled out an application just to be courteous, but she couldn't spare the money. She told the woman this, as quietly as she could because she was aware that everyone was still eyeing her from behind.

"Don't bullshit me," the woman snapped. She motioned with her chin toward Elizabeth, as if to use her as evidence against herself. "You look like you have a lot more than a hundred bucks."

Back at the apartment, she found Angela sitting crossed-legged at the base of the couch with a book in her lap. John Vain was washing dishes. Hal sat at the two-person dining table where Elizabeth had organized the masses of files and papers related to his invention into neat piles. She hadn't had a chance to study them yet, as she had offered, but she could tell the moment she opened the door and saw the expression on Hal's face that he was holding a wake of some kind, watching the years of hard work and mountains of dreams slowly wither before his eyes, forcing himself to learn to let go.

Angela jumped to her feet when she saw Elizabeth. "Did you get it?" she cried, too hopefully. She was holding the book open against her right thigh, pressing down on it as if to keep her legs from running to the door. "Did they give you a job?"

Elizabeth wouldn't take a handout from John Vain, and she was too smart not to realize the "position" he was offering—financial advisor and business affairs coordinator—was created for her alone. Her first reaction, therefore, was to thank him sincerely but decline.

"I can't let you do any more for us than you already have," she told him on Monday morning, when he called at seven to make sure he caught her before she and Angela had left for school.

Never mind she was no accountant: "Hal says you're good at math."

Never mind she couldn't work evenings because she had to be home with Angela: "You can come and go as you like."

She turned John Vain down again that night when he stopped by to ask if they would accompany him to Lucky 99 for dinner, and she intended to stick by it, to remain proud but poor for the rest of her life if she had to because those things matter, you see—things like honor and dignity and knowing when to stop taking advantage of another's kindness, the small footprints that remain when we're gone, the traces of ourselves we leave upon the world.

She tried to explain this to Angela, who had been watching Elizabeth that morning as she talked to John Vain on the phone.

"Why did you say no?"

Angela had light skin and long legs and an explosion of shiny brown curls that had a way of escaping any restraint, so that at any given time part of her hair was pulled back and the rest hovered around her face. The growth spurt that would leave her taller and bigger than most other Iranian women in adulthood wouldn't occur for another year or two, and the know-it-all attitude wouldn't set in for another decade, but she was already brave and obstinate and, yes, a little angry.

"I thought you said you can't even get hired as a maid."

On Tuesday morning, when the phone rang again at a few minutes past seven, Angela threw herself on the receiver before her mother could reach for it.

"You have to say yes," she warned, her little hands wrapped around the phone as it kept ringing, her voice breaking midsentence. Her eyes, dark and alert and forever vigilant, were clouded with fear. "You can't decide everything the way you want to."

Later, Elizabeth would claim this was the moment she realized her daughter had become American.

The first thing Elizabeth discovered in John Vain's books was that he shouldn't have hired her or half the workforce at the restaurant because he didn't have the funds, hadn't had them for a long time, maybe ever—he was paying for things with borrowed money that he couldn't pay back anytime soon. She was alarmed by this, but not nearly as much as by his reaction to her report.

"Don't worry about that," he said when she gave him the bad news. He had this expansive, nothing's-ever-gonna-go-wrong manner that was reassuring and endearing to a great many people, but didn't convince Elizabeth. "I've always been poor."

He would have followed that with a confession he was dying to make: that he didn't care what she found in his accounts as long as he could sit there and watch her go through them.

He would have told her this, gotten down on one knee and proposed marriage, if he didn't think it indecent to make a move on a woman when she was in such vulnerable circumstances. He was, of course, aware of his own limitations: here he was, a street kid with barely an education, before the genius widow of an upper-class gentleman whose name people still uttered with deference. Then again, he had half a century of good luck to draw from, and at least as much patience. And he had the restaurant.

The Lucky 99 Grill, at the intersection of Sunset and Crescent Heights, was built on a one-acre lot situated on a hilltop. A rambling structure with high-beamed ceilings and large windows and open verandas overlooking Los Angeles, it had a parking lot in the back and a row of limousines and Rolls-Royces in the front. The cars were rented, along with their spiffy drivers in black Armani suits, at the (discounted) rate of three hundred dollars a day, to transport wealthy patrons and out-of-town friends to the restaurant and back. The rides were complimentary, as was the bottle of Veuve Clicquot that arrived at every VIP's table as soon as guests were seated, along with the daily amuse-bouche from the chef and a bowl of Caspian beluga caviar from John Vain.

He had opened the restaurant with the help of a loan officer at a small regional bank—Bank United of California—where a friendly clerk with a growing family helped small entrepreneurs "establish" credit. Brady McPherson was a Pentecostal Christian from Echo Park, a grandnephew by marriage of the Canadian revivalist preacher Aimee Semple McPherson, founder of the International Church of the Foursquare Gospel. Though Sister Aimee and her children had profited handsomely from the Lord's bounty over the years, members of their extended family had been left to struggle like ordinary folk.

Early in his career, Brady had used his aunt's connections to sustain his loan brokerage firm called the Foursquare Loan Corporation where, for over a decade, he had obtained special "Lord's Loans" for church members: in exchange for a 10 percent commission, handed to him in cash, he doctored loan applications for good, God-fearing folk who would never have qualified without the benefit of Brady's powers of amplification. By the time the banks caught on and the federal government stepped in, he had made millions of dollars and was married with three children. He went to jail for twenty-seven months and emerged penniless, divorced, and owing child support. So he made up a new résumé, leaving out the little matter of his sojourn in the state's equivalent of a bed-and-breakfast—because that's all it was, really, a minimum-security prison with wide-open grounds and fresh country air—and soon enough, he was back to making magic with loan applications. He got John Vain an $800,000 loan and a $200,000 line of credit at 11.25 percent interest. That was in April 1972. By 1980, he had added another $700,000 to the original amount.

John Vain never knew what McPherson wrote on the loan applications that he filled out and only put in front of John Vain to sign, but he was sure it was the kind of information the bank liked to see. Still, it wasn't until Elizabeth began to examine his books that he learned just how rich and successful the bank thought he was. The loan documents showed him flush with assets and enjoying a more than considerable income—which was fine with John Vain, and fine also with McPherson and his bosses at the bank.

The only spoiler in the bunch, once she accepted the position he had created for her and actually took it seriously, was Elizabeth. Although new to the country, she had a sense that exaggerating the value of one's assets, or inventing them outright on what seemed like official papers, was wrong. To make her happy, John Vain checked with McPherson and came back to report that the bank was free to verify every statement that had been made. If it didn't attempt to verify, it was because the responsible parties were satisfied with the terms and conditions. He explained this was the way business was done in America, the reason money grew so fast here and everyone prospered. You have to have faith that the loan officers know what to write on the forms and the banks know how much money they should lend and that the holes between what is and what should be will somehow be filled over time. That's how everyone gets rich in this country, he said: with a lot of loans and a great deal of optimism.

Elizabeth, though, didn't see the wisdom of going so deeply into debt. She understood that John Vain wasn't as interested in making money as he was in spending it, but she couldn't accept his kind of recklessness. She didn't believe numbers lied or could be wished away. She suggested he trim his overhead by keeping a smaller staff. He said he couldn't imagine ever laying off the Latino busboys he had hired illegally, because they didn't have papers and were underage, and whom he paid three times the minimum wage and sent home every night at ten so they could get a good night's sleep before heading to school in the morning, whose "guardian" he served as so that the school called him instead of the parents when they had been tardy or cut class, and whose report cards he checked—because he had been there, done that, he would tell them, he'd hired them because they needed money but only as long as they stayed in school.

So what if he was spending much more at Lucky 99 than he earned? He told Elizabeth that the champagne and caviar were an investment in the restaurant's long-term success—a way to attract celebrities who wanted everything free but whose presence, in turn, drew regular paying customers. In LA, he said, you had to look rich to become rich, and anyway, being rich had never been a priority to John Vain. Neither in his youth in New York, when he slept on the floor of the church attic amidst the stench and muck of wet army blankets and open footsores in wintertime and unwashed bodies and rotting garbage in summer, nor later, in the air-conditioned lobbies of five-star hotels or near the crystalline waters of private swimming pools, did he enjoy holding on to his earnings. In the beginning, when he had just arrived, he sent nearly all his money home to his mother. Then she died of pneumonia and no one told him, so he kept sending money that her relatives picked up and spent, until one day he called her house and a neighbor told him she couldn't be reached because she was long dead and buried.

Instead of making him more careful with his spending, the relatives' betrayal caused John Vain to try harder to make new friends and help people. As for the loans, by late 1982 Brady McPherson had been promoted to vice president, and Bank United of California was just about to grow from one branch to three.

$$\sum_{k=1}^{n} I_k = 0$$

One of the two fundamental laws of electrical engineering: *The algebraic sum of all currents entering and leaving a node must equal zero.* So basic, you can't move on or build from this unless you got it right. Unless you were a mathematical genius with a rapacious imagination and an inexhaustible drive, a poor son of working-class parents from South Tehran who knew no home or country, no language or religion, followed no pathway other than the one illuminated with numbers.

Out of Cyrus Street and placing first in the national college entrance exams in Iran, selected as one of the three most promising engineering students by the shah's government and dispatched on a full scholarship to Cal Poly, jettisoned by the old country and enraptured by this notion, this awareness of something essential and transformative that was waiting to be given physical shape, Hal could see his heat-detecting radar more precisely than he could see his own hands. He left Cal Poly in 1979 so he could devote all his time to his invention. He was so beset by the certainty that it could be done, so possessed by the understanding of how it could be done, he all but willed the machine into existence, made the equations work out, the problems solve themselves. Time and again, he calculated and mapped and charted his way from beginning to near the end, rammed into failure, worked backward through every single step, every problem, looking for the flaw, the place where he had taken a wrong turn. His teeth whittled down to tiny stubs because he ground them so fiercely while he worked and his hair turned prematurely gray, his gut began to bleed every time he ate and his body twitched every which way—and still he couldn't detect a single mistake.

For an engineer, Kirchhoff's current law is the equivalent of the first stone utilized in the building of the Great Wall of China. Hal Zemorrodi could see the wall, every tiny piece of it, every crack and curve and angle of it. He weighed and measured and removed and replaced every piece hundreds of times. But it never occurred to him to go back to that first stone, crack it open, and see the hollow middle upon which his entire world was balanced.

Elizabeth had spent months grappling with the shock of Hal's miscalculation, agonizing over how to break the news to him when the implications were inevitable. His idea didn't materialize because it didn't exist—it wasn't even in the realm of the possible. Hal had created it based on a false assumption, like a whole garden out of a single dead seed. She finally decided it would be easier to tell him on neutral ground—not his car, which was his domicile, or her apartment, but at Lucky 99 where, at the very least, they were assured of John Vain's positive intervention.

It was in the middle of summer, one of those rare evenings in LA when the heat wouldn't relent. To help control his mounting debt, she had convinced John Vain to shutter the restaurant on Monday nights when the turnout was low even among the nonpaying patrons.

She found Hal in the storage room, aimlessly shuffling cans and boxes in an attempt to "earn" his salary, though nothing he could do would have justified the amount he was paid or the "housing" benefits (a rollaway bed, an elegant bathroom, and a standing offer to use the shower in John Vain's house in Trousdale instead of the Y). When he heard Elizabeth behind him by the door, he stopped working but didn't turn around.

"I have some thoughts about your numbers," she said softly. "I wanted to show you."

They were a pair of elementary school children, he in patched-up gray pants and hand-me-down boots from the children of the family whose house his mother cleaned, she in her starched and ironed uniform and a white satin bow in her hair; the son of a cab driver and a maid, the daughter of a professor and a physician.

Hussein Zemorrodi stood quietly through Elizabeth's explanation. When she was done, he kept glancing at the papers as if to extract more punishment, and when that didn't happen he started to nod ever so gently, up and down like one of those dogs people like to put in their car window, and he nodded for so long that it began to worry

Elizabeth, so she then took the unusual step of touching him on the shoulder—Iranian men and women did not touch randomly in those days—and that must have awakened him from his catatonia because he stopped nodding, turned directly to her, and smiled.

He seemed to regress in time, not to the very beginning but to the early years when he, mechanical brain or not, was still the son of servants, knew his place, and acted accordingly, so he suddenly bolted upright before Elizabeth, bowed deeply, and said, without making eye contact, "*Khanum*, madame, I'm very grateful to you."

The last time anyone saw Hal Zemorrodi he was driving down Hollywood Boulevard in his yellow jalopy, headed for I-101 with the headlights off.

It needn't have been such a calamity.

Just because Hal's one approach to creating the radar was flawed didn't mean he couldn't find another. He was certainly smart enough and he had the imagination to think of another way, or come up with a new invention altogether. It's true that he was ashamed—to have spent so many years on an impossibility; to have overlooked such an obvious error—but he could have lived through that. He wasn't so proud, not nearly so vain, as to believe himself unerring. The thing that really took it out of Hal was the realization of what this experience truly meant: he might know a thing or two about the way machines worked; he might have fooled a few people about his native abilities; but at the end of the day, he wasn't the real deal.

It's like that when you're the son of working-class, illiterate parents from a place where boundaries are drawn in blood. No matter how many of them you cross, part of you will always feel like a fraud.

A few months after Hal's disappearance, a woman showed up at Lucky 99 with two young girls and a handwritten note bearing his signature. It was scrawled across the back of a Pan Am plane ticket and bore only John Vain's name, the restaurant's address, and Hal's initials—*H.Z.*—scribbled in pencil. The woman, Zeeba Raiis, claimed she was given the note by an Iranian cab driver with no teeth and not a single strand of hair—not even an eyelash. He had picked her and the girls up from her granduncle's apartment in Queens and driven them to JFK.

Zeeba Raiis told John Vain that she had been traveling for nearly two years. Her husband was hiding from the mullahs in Iran but she and her daughters had managed to escape by land through the Pakistan border. They had spent eleven months at a refugee camp in Peshawar, and only got out through the good graces of the International Red Cross. The first country that had given them a visa was Italy, so she went there with the girls and waited for the next opportunity to get to the United States. She and her husband were both Muslim, but her great-grandfather had been Jewish. At twenty-one, he had fallen in love with a mullah's daughter, converted to Islam, and married her.

Zeeba Raiis, therefore, took a chance on appealing to HIAS for help. She was sponsored by Chabad and flown to Maryland. She was grateful for the assistance and hospitality, but she couldn't hack it as a Jew, or at least as a Chabad kind of Jew. Her granduncle, son of the convert and the mullah's daughter, was in New York with his children. She had begged them for help a dozen times since she escaped Iran and was ignored every time, but she took a chance and showed up at their door with her two daughters and three suitcases. They let her stay for ten days, then suggested a trip to LA. The climate was much more agreeable, and apartments were larger, more suitable for accommodating uninvited, unwelcome houseguests.

"Go to Westwood," they had said, "and just shout a word in Persian. Every head on the street is going to turn."

This was Zeeba's only plan when she got into Iranian man's taxi in Queens. She told him she was going to Los Angeles where she knew some Iranians from the glory days in Tehran, but that she had no idea how to find anyone or whether she could rely on them for help. The cabbie wrote down John Vain's name and address.

She folded the note and put it in her bag as Option B, and she didn't think about it much on the flight to LA. They landed at night and slept in an airport hotel; the next morning, their cab driver was, again, Iranian. On a lark, she asked him if he'd heard of a restaurant owner in Hollywood named John Vain.

"Of course," the driver announced. "I must have dropped two hundred people at his door over the years."

Zeeba Raiis was one of those I-didn't-sign-up-for-this women who believed herself the subject of a great cosmic hoax: she had married one man and woken up next to another. The person she married was the smart, highly educated son of privilege whose father hosted a lavish wedding for Dr. Raiis and Zeeba, and gave them a house to live in. Dr. Raiis was young and handsome and idealistic—one of those boutique intellectuals (in LA, he would have been called a Neiman Marxist) whose idea of a good time was to drink a glass of Bordeaux as he read Jean-Paul Sartre in the shade of a maple tree on one of Tehran's famously narrow alleys. When he married Zeeba, he already had lofty ideas of serving God and country by giving freely of his medical expertise. Soon after, he founded a medical corps of young doctors and nurses willing to forge through vastly underserved provinces and out-of-reach villages to prevent such common calamities as blindness from trachoma and paralysis from polio. For a while in the late '60s, this was both laudable and practical: with only a young wife and no children to pay for, he could play Florence Nightingale and still earn enough to keep Zeeba happy.

But then the children came, and Zeeba's friends and siblings moved from their first houses into larger, more lavish dwellings, and what had been a nice pastime for Dr. Raiis started to become a hindrance for the family. Zeeba began to press him to stop being *saadeh*—a polite term for stupid—and put matters of personal honor and professional duty where they belonged: in words, not deeds, and by looking after his own family's needs instead of those of perfect strangers.

Dr. Raiis would always deny this, but his wife was convinced that he was motivated more by vanity than principle: he treated the poor even though they couldn't pay because he liked their expressions of gratitude, saw himself as a scholar rather than a businessman because he thrived on the veneration accorded to men of letters and science. That the same people who admired his public service would not be caught dead choosing it over making money in their own lives remained ungrasped by Dr. Raiis. The more Zeeba complained that he wasn't making a good enough living because he was too busy giving away his "assets," the more Dr. Raiis tried to prove that he was secure in his decision.

Zeeba, in the meantime, kept a running tally of every social and financial advantage her husband's obstinacy cost her and the children. She kept the books on the income and assets of every other family so she could report to her children just how much money their father was giving up every day on their behalf. She said that Dr. Raiis had a natural aversion to being rich the way some people feared rats or snakes, that he was selfish because he continued to treat poor children for free and, as a result, had to deny his own kids "basic luxuries" such as monthlong shopping trips to Europe. Because of him, their daughters were going to have to settle for a bad marriage or none at all.

There was no telling how many of Zeeba's dire predictions would come to pass, but no one ever lost money by betting on calamity in Iran. Dr. Raiis and his wife fought about his work for the first ten years of their marriage, then broke new ground when, in 1978, chaos and violence erupted on the streets of Tehran. Zeeba wanted him to follow the advice of "those who know better," open a bank account in London, Switzerland, or New York, and wire their savings out of the country. She thought they should convert their valuables to jewelry, which could be transported easily, pack it up along with the children, and go abroad for the summer. She would have done all this on her own if she could, but even under the shah, when things were as good as they'd ever get, women could not travel or take their children out of the country or open foreign bank accounts without written permission from a male "guardian."

For his part, Dr. Raiis did not believe that the army would fold, the United States would withdraw its support, and the shah would fall. Even if the unthinkable came to pass, he told Zeeba, he had nothing to fear from a new regime because he had done nothing wrong. His conscience was clear; his sleep, except for when Zeeba woke him up to vent, peaceful. Just look at that medal of honor he had received in 1976 from Her Majesty, Empress Farah Pahlavi, for selfless service to the country.

The medal was made of eighteen-karat gold and hung from a velvet band in the red, white, and green colors of the Pahlavi flag—a testament to his personal integrity and professional service to humanity. While the shah was in power, it was framed and hanging most prominently above the mantelpiece in the Raiises' living room. Afterward, Dr. Raiis had to relent to Zeeba's entreaties to take it down and hide it because "any minute now, one of the servants or neighbors will report us to the mullahs for being friends of the royal family—and you know what that means—it'll be the end of you, at least, if not both of us." She left with the girls three weeks before he was identified by the regime as a *taaghooti*—corrupt on earth—and ordered to report to Evin Prison.

That night, Dr. Raiis gathered all his honorary degrees and commendations, as well as the medal, and buried them in a fireproof safe in the backyard. He held a flashlight against his chest, and a soup spoon in his right hand. It was two in the morning and the temperature was at least ten below freezing. Dr. Raiis's hands and body shivered from the cold and from fear, but his insides felt hot, and his hair was wet with perspiration. The flashlight kept slipping from its tenuous cradle and the neck of the spoon bent a little more every time he tried to break the ice with it. He realized he should be using a shovel, but that would have raised too much suspicion on the part of the servants. They were always watching him, sifting through the trash, eavesdropping on his conversations, and reporting even the most banal details to the local *komiteh*. He had snuck the spoon into his pocket the day before when the cook was taking his afternoon nap, and so was digging in the dark.

"It doesn't matter what's true," Zeeba had told him a thousand times before he woke up, bloody and beaten and strapped naked to a chair in the basement of the Evin Prison, "only what's believed."

Dr. Raiis had bet his whole life on a single truth, and lost.

Zeeba Raiis needed a place in which to live and Elizabeth couldn't afford the rent on her own apartment without help from John Vain, so she invited Zeeba to share the one-bedroom in Beverly Hills. She and her daughters took the sofa bed in the living room; Elizabeth and Angela slept on a twin-size mattress in the bedroom. The close quarters—barely eight hundred square feet—would have been unimaginable in Tehran, but in Los Angeles the apartment became a source of comfort for everyone living in it.

The two older girls, Angela and Nilou, became fast friends. Nilou—*blue petal*—was a beautiful creature with exuberant charm and a solid mind. Angela was bold and outspoken and already able to debate any issue to her opponent's death. Next to them, Zeeba's younger daughter, Neda, had as much personality as a dying slug on a burning sidewalk in August.

She was such an oddity at school, so unable to make friends or even get a pity invitation to any of the dozens of gatherings and parties that took place every weekend, she might go entire days without exchanging more than a handful of words with anyone but Nilou or Angela. If anyone did notice Neda, they would see that she studied through every moment of every day: during recess and lunch at school, at home in the afternoon, even Friday nights. Her social life consisted of hanging back in a corner of the room when Nilou and Angela had friends over. The only phone calls she received were from kids who wanted to know what the homework was or what test they had to prepare for.

During the school year, she took the bus home every afternoon and stayed in till the morning. On weekends and holidays she studied or walked to Roxbury Park to hit tennis balls against the wall by herself. She chewed her nails and bit her lips till they bled, never spoke in class unless she was called upon by a teacher, and then, though she knew her lessons inside out, often mumbled the wrong answer.

She was so insipid and slow, so quavering even before her own shadow, that Angela declared her an "endangered species, like the

ones that can't survive on their own. You have to keep her in a pro-
tected place and watch so she doesn't get torn up or shot by humans."
Even at that age, Angela had a way with words.

Angela's old classmates from elementary school in Iran would later
attribute her hard edges to the French education she had received at
the Lycée Razi in Tehran. Her teachers were all French and so were
many of the students, which meant no one had time for subtlety or
tripe or the nonsense known as "sparing another's feelings." They
were permanently out of sorts because they had once "owned" Persia
but lost it to the Russians and the English and finally the Americans;
they thought their language was the most beautiful in the world and
their culture the most refined, but they fell in that battle to the English
and the Americans as well. As a result, they were forever eager to tell
the world just what was wrong with it. Every other sentence they uttered began with, *"Je vais vous parler franchement"*—I'm going to be frank
with you—which meant that what followed was going to be hurtful
or offensive or worse, and that there was no room for disagreement or
negotiation.

In time, Angela herself would attribute her combative attitude to
"a genetic inability to roll over and play dead." That didn't mean, as
some people believed, that she actively relished fighting. It was just
that life had presented her with a choice between bowing her head
and taking the blows, or charging out of the gate every day, ready
for a fight. In middle school in LA, when the other girls excluded her
from games at recess, she would confront them—one against a dozen—
and demand a place. When the boys pointed at her overly developed
breasts and called her "dairy cow," she would shove them and stand
her ground until she was bloodied and bruised and sent off to the principal's office. In high school, when the American kids laughed at her
matronly clothes and geeky glasses, called her "rag-head" and asked if
people in Tehran still rode to school and work on camels and donkeys,
when strangers stopped her on the street to tell her to go home, called
her "sand-nigger" and "hostage-taker," she yelled back and told them
just how ignorant and misguided she thought they were, how empty
their lives must be.

Her resilience helped Angela endure the unpredictability and dis-
location of the first few years of exile. Her single-mindedness helped

her overcome language and financial barriers, resist the hungry pull of inertia and hopelessness that could otherwise have consumed her when she lost her father, sister, and home, all within a three-year span.

But there was also this: it wasn't all up to her. Where she fit in wasn't entirely a matter of choice.

Once, two years after they had arrived in Los Angeles, an elderly American woman she had met only minutes earlier gave Elizabeth a compliment on her watch. They were at Lucky 99; the woman was a patron; the watch was a wedding gift from Aaron.

"I like your watch," the woman said. "It's so art deco."

Elizabeth had no idea what art deco was, but she knew the proper response to an older woman's expression of flattery. She took the watch off and held it out to the American. "It's not worthy of your excellence," she said, presenting it to her as an offering.

That was a *taarof*—the only civil way to respond. It was done every minute of every day in every corner of Iran and among Iranians in America. Upon getting passengers to their destination, a cab driver with any class would refuse to accept payment. Store owners declined to charge for merchandise. Diners invited strangers to share their food.

But *taarof* worked both ways. The person receiving the offer was certain to reject it. The only people who were exempt from this were members of the royal families dating back many hundreds of years. They were the true owners of everything—people as well as things—in the country; everyone else was just a caretaker. The royals didn't have to ask, and certainly didn't have to pay for what was theirs in the first place; they just had to "admire" something—a house, a farm, a beautiful woman—and it would be offered to them on the spot, under the implied penalty of death. Mere mortals, on the other hand, wouldn't dream of accepting a *taarof*.

Sadly for Elizabeth, the American woman at Lucky 99 didn't have a clue what *taarof* was. She took the watch. "My goodness!" she cooed. "How very generous of you."

She slipped off her own watch, put it into her purse, and wore Elizabeth's instead.

"Thank you." She sounded suspicious, as if the thing may explode any minute. Then she started to walk away.

When she saw this, Angela, who was old enough to understand

what had just happened but not too old to not express herself freely, pulled at Elizabeth's arm and said, loudly, "Why did you do that?"

Elizabeth was mortified that the woman might hear Angela's objection. She tried to shush her, but that only incited Angela more.

"Get it back!" she yelled.

Elizabeth pulled Angela out of the woman's earshot. "Stop that," she said. "It's unseemly."

Angela hated that phrase. "It's unseemly"—*bah-deh*—was an ax that fell in a Persian household dozens of times a day.

To renege on an offer that had been made and accepted would mean you weren't as good as your word, and that you cared more about material possessions than your *aabehroo*.

"But it's not the same with Americans!" Angela pleaded. "They don't know you were *taarof*-ing. It's not unseemly to ask for it back."

As they walked past the woman's table to leave the restaurant, Elizabeth and Angela heard her say to her companions, "These rich A-rabs don't know what to do with all that oil money."

The oil money, of course, was flowing anywhere but into the pockets of Iranian Jews in exile. It belonged strictly to the mullahs and the army of thugs and cutthroats they called Sepah-e Pasdaran. If it wasn't used to round up and torture and kill their political opponents, it was stowed away in bank accounts in Switzerland, the Caymans, and the United States. The vast majority of Iranians who took refuge in the West after the revolution escaped with barely more than their lives. It is true that most were more educated than the average immigrant, that centuries of French, English, and American influence in Iran had made them conversant not only in the language but also in the culture of the West. In this regard they had more in common with immigrants from Western nations than with others, but just like all immigrants, they worked hard and paid dearly for their success. The storybook life, of palatial homes and red Ferraris and shopping trips to Neiman Marcus, belonged to only a sliver of the Iranian immigrant population.

Zeeba told Elizabeth what she knew of the fate of the Soleyman holdings in Iran: it was based mostly on rumors, Zeeba said, and a few notices in the newspaper or on the radio while she was still in the country. Bagh-e Yaas, she said, had become the private residence of Seyyed Mojtaba, his two wives, young children, and many relatives. Soleyman Enterprises and its assets had been "nationalized" immediately upon Elizabeth's escape, which meant a handful of mullahs had become very rich.

Elizabeth had heard the same reports from a number of other recent refugees, and she gleaned as much from the few phone conversations she'd had with Manzel's husband recently. She had not called or written to them for over a year after she left Iran because all the mail was monitored—opened and reviewed before being delivered—and the phone calls were listened to. In the case of Manzel's family, things were even more difficult because they shared a phone line with eight other households. Her neighbors knew she had worked for Elizabeth who was now a fugitive. Like most believers in those early days of the revolution, they trusted the mullahs' good intentions and pure motives. Every day on the radio and television, the mullahs said that America, Israel, and the *taaghooti*—the corrupt on earth—had conspired to crush the movement and return the monarchy to Iran. The shah may be dead, but his two sons and many siblings were alive and scheming. To prevent their takeover of the country, every citizen had a duty to spy on all others. Mother against child, student against teacher, brother against sister—no matter how close the ties, the sanctity of a person's faith superseded the relationship.

Manzel's neighbors eavesdropped on each other and listened in on the phone. They would not have hesitated to report her to the Pasdaran—the mullahs' private army—or to complain to Mojtaba about her sedition.

Things became easier once war broke out between Iran and Iraq and the regime had to direct its resources to the effort. Elizabeth wrote to Manzel and her husband under a false name and they wrote back. Their other sons, they reported, had taken care of them until the war, but now they had all been drafted and sent away. As for Mojtaba, Manzel and her husband cursed him every day and night for bringing disgrace to their name, and they were aided in their wishes by the Black Bitch of Bushehr who, having believed herself within reach of her dream, had seen it snatched yet again—this time by Mojtaba.

For Raphael's Wife, the year of bloodshed that led to the ruination of the old upper class was a time of rebirth and empowerment. She relished the sight of cars burning and store windows being smashed, the news of the shah's departure from Iran and the subsequent saga of his shuttling from country to country, unable to gain entry into any one, even the same United States whose interests he had represented so faithfully for thirty years. She loved the middle-of-the-night raids by street thugs now called Revolutionary Guards, the dragging of secular nationalist ministers and military leaders before revolutionary courts where the trials lasted three minutes and were followed by summary executions on the roof, the pictures of the naked and bullet-ridden bodies of dead rich men—killed because they were rich—pasted on the front pages of the evening newspapers. For her, each one of those men was Aaron Soleyman, every one of those soldiers and bankers and politicians a pillar that had buttressed his advantage.

Where was he now to hiss in that cold voice, "In this country, at this time, you and your kind don't hold a prayer against the likes of me?"

Raphael's Wife was so busy celebrating the Soleymans' demise, she forgot she was a Jew—at least in name—and this, an Islamic revolution. She forgot that the mullahs had been the Jews' biggest persecutors for a thousand years, that the only reason they wanted the shah gone was so they could take his place. The first chance she got, she rushed out to the Interior Ministry of the Islamic Republic of Iran where, she must have thought, the new rulers were holding a fire sale on fairness and equity. She stood in line for a day and a half, her ever-present plastic bag filled with real and forged documents, and when her turn finally came, she emptied the contents of the bag onto the desk of some unwashed and unshaven clerk in combat fatigues stolen from God only knows which army depot, and said, "I've come for my son's name."

You had to feel sorry for the woman. She was either insane or stupid to think that the mullahs would spend a hundred years in virtual exile, then make the biggest comeback of the century, only to hand over the country's riches to anyone who asked.

The clerk gave her sixty seconds to tell her story, then asked if her claim was on the estate of the same Aaron Soleyman who had been declared *taaghooti* and whose widow was on the run from the regime.

It was.

And was the house, Bagh-e Yaas, the mansion on the Avenue of Tranquility?

It was.

The same that belonged to Seyyed Mojtaba?

Raphael's Wife never recovered from the stab wound to the heart where the revolution had promised her relief.

The first thing she learned as she stood by, helpless once again, and watched Mojtaba move into Bagh-e Yaas with his wives and children, was that there were two kinds of *mos-tah-zah-fin*—oppressed and exploited—in Iran: the kind that would remain oppressed, and the kind that would go on to become the new oppressors. The second thing she learned was that everything that was bad under the old regime only became worse under the new one.

The old regime might have trampled the weak and only thrown crumbs at the people; this new one slaughtered man and beast and stole the skin off their backs. Raphael's Wife learned this when she appealed to the Ministry of the Oppressed for help against Mojtaba, and was rewarded with a two-day-long interrogation, followed by a beating that left her permanently incontinent and with a broken hip. Her son learned this when he applied for a new birth certificate as *Soleyman, Son of Raphael*, and was summarily arrested, flogged, and forced to confess to being a Zionist because of his "ties" to Aaron Soleyman.

Once it became evident that the mullahs would outshine any dictator, alive or dead, in greed, duplicity, and willingness to kill, Raphael's Wife, at least, had the moral rectitude to accept responsibility for having bet on the devil to save her from God's cruelty. The rest of the "dispossessed," the million of Iranians who had marched in the street with their fists in the air, demanding Khomeini's return, now cried foul and appealed for help to the same "international community" whose interference in the country's affairs they had condemned a year or two earlier. The more honest among them would later admit that they had been either mad—to repeat history hoping to reach a different result—or stupid. The rest complained that the revolution had been "stolen" from them.

Can you complain of being robbed if you invite the thief into your house, hand him the keys, and ask that he please take charge?

Raphael's Son was eighteen years old when he was arrested by a truckful of young street thugs in military fatigues bearing automatic weapons. No longer the helpless if reticent boy in a man's woolen pants with the cuffs rolled up, being dragged around by his mother on a mendicant's pilgrimage through upscale neighborhoods and luxury stores and high-rise offices that were forbidden to the likes of him, he had a street urchin's manners and a farmhand's education, no charm or good looks, and no money. In their place was a yawning, bottomless gash carved into him by every bit of indignity and embarrassment he had suffered by "those rich Jews," and a single-minded resolve to pay them all back.

He had studied them his whole life, understood their weaknesses and vulnerabilities. He knew all about vulnerability—this bastard son of a woman who had made a career of being wronged and slighted. He hated the perpetrators, yes, but hated his mother just as much for being maligned. Appeal to the hangman's sense of justice is what she had done. Curse the executioner just as the ax fell upon her time after time. Trample her own and her son's pride into a reeking mess of raw animal innards that she held up as proof of her impotence to the enemy she hoped to defeat.

Even before he was old enough to do the math, see his mother for the grasping old woman that she was and the story of his conception for the fool's gospel she preached, Raphael's Son had understood that weakness was no defense against the mighty. He suffered not so much from his circumstances as from the shame, the public humiliation, the utter dismissal by people who seemed to know much more about him than he knew about himself. He could have tolerated his poverty, his fatherlessness, the insanity, even, of a mother who made a profession of being evil; the nearly intolerable aspect was being pointed at as if he didn't exist, talked about as if he didn't matter, told day after day that he simply, fundamentally, wasn't.

So he retreated into himself and, from the vantage point of the invisible, studied the sources of his torment. Years later, in America, he would still remember the sound of the doorbell at Bagh-e Yaas, the shade of the paint on the metal gates, every square centimeter of the parts of the yard and the house where he and his mother were allowed. Without admitting it to himself, he would paint the walls of his house the same colors, pick the same kind of furniture. He would despise smart, outspoken women who, he imagined, had resembled Angela as a child, loathe "career women" whom he viewed as replicas of Elizabeth. Even at his most successful, he couldn't enter a roomful of his peers without hearing the long-ago laughter of the boys every morning when the teacher took roll. She called everyone else by their first and last name. She called him "Raphael's Son None."

It was a fraught and painful predicament to be in—this wanting to belong to a world that punished you, to be accepted by people who laughed at you. It would have been easier, less internally divisive, if all he had to do was to get away from the cause of his suffering. But to long to be embraced by the same individuals whose very name made you cringe?

He knew he wasn't what or who his mother claimed; he could see that he bore no resemblance to any of the Soleymans, that Raphael's Wife was older than most grandmothers. He knew no human could be pregnant for thirteen months. But it's one thing to know, and something else to believe.

Believe that you have no one but a mother you detest. That you're wanted by no one, recognized and valued by no one.

So he had no choice but to think he should have been accepted and welcomed, embraced and feared, by the community, the family, that had rejected him.

And then, just as he was strong enough to fend off his mother and mature enough to plan his own war, just when the revolution leveled the playing field for the haves and have-nots, the Muslims he knew turned against him for being a Jew and the Jews he wanted to be recognized by abandoned the fight and stole off for the West. They took with them the boldness of the once-untouchable ghetto dweller who, overnight, became part of the master class in Iran, the greenness of the carpetbagger who believes he can carry an entire civilization in his slight, battered suitcase.

The gilded castle Raphael's Son yearned to be admitted to, the elusive universe of legends and actuality, desires and dissent, that had rejected him—Elizabeth Soleyman and her surviving daughter—had gone elsewhere and, by so doing, made him once again invisible.

t took four months and a whole lot of scars and broken bones for Raphael's Son to convince his captors that he did not qualify either as a Zionist or as a *taaghooti*. By the time he was released, he had realized there was no advantage in being a son of a felled and fallen dynasty, no matter what his rights of inheritance. On his way home from prison after the months of captivity, he recited under his breath, "*Ash-shadu an laa ill-laaha illa-lah*"—"I testify there is no God but God." This is all that was required of anyone who wished to convert to Islam; he didn't need to go to a mosque or study or answer questions in order to become Muhammad "Jadid al-Islam"—New Muslim.

His conversion was not so much an act of surrender of his rights or ambitions as it was a declaration of war by other means. For the first time in his life, being unknown and insignificant to the world became an asset: he grew a beard and went around in a white dress shirt buttoned around the neck but with no tie, a smart blazer over a pair of khaki pants, and combat-style Doc Martens looted from a distributor's warehouse and sold on a street corner for a quarter of the retail price. He commanded his mother to stay home and out of sight, picked up a string of worry beads, and started to say *namaz* five times a day where everyone could see him. He went to Friday prayers at the mosque and to nightly gatherings of self-appointed moral police in the district. He told the head of a local chapter of the Sepah-e Pasdaran that he knew of dozens of *taaghootis*—women as well as men—whose past and ongoing criminal deeds they should investigate. Once they were arrested and jailed, he sent word to their families that he might be able to arrange for their release through his contacts among the Pasdars.

It was a game of blackmail and extortion that everyone he targeted recognized and still had to play. The cash payments and deeds of trust, the ownership papers and promissory notes, the wedding rings and antique silver bowls and silk rugs and fur coats the prisoners' families provided in exchange for Raphael's Son's intervention would not guarantee their loved ones' release or safety. But the consequences of not paying were appallingly clear.

When the war started with Iraq and young men and teenage boys were called to the front, Raphael's Son extended his services to anyone who could afford to buy his way out. That was easy in the first half of the war, when the country was chock-full of unemployed, able-bodied men all too eager to offer up their earthly lives in exchange for a permanent seat in Khomeini's paradise, seventy-two virgins and eternally mild weather included. One phone call from Raphael's Son and 20 percent of his fee shared with his "people" in the Ministry of War was all it took to spare a thirteen-year-old from having to walk in front of tanks as a human minesweeper. But then the cemeteries were crammed full and new graves couldn't be dug fast enough, Saddam Hussein was having a field day with the mustard gas and other weapons of mass destruction he had made with help from the United States, and the dead men's families had worn themselves out with all the celebration and festivities in honor of their sons' and brothers' martyrdom. Raphael's Son had no choice but to raise his fees, and even then he could not guarantee that the waiver he obtained would be permanent.

In six years, he amassed nearly $3 million, much of it from "clients'" family members already living in the United States and Europe. By then, his mother was little more than a leaky, trembling bag of bones wrapped in a dark chador and cared for only begrudgingly by her son. A lifetime of pounding and clawing at doors she had failed to open for herself or him, of setting others to ruin without managing to build for herself, of using him—this is how he saw it—to make herself legitimate, had left her completely alone and entirely unwanted.

In the spring of 1986, Raphael's Son paid a distant maternal cousin, a kosher butcher's apprentice named Joshua Simcha, $5,000 to smuggle Raphael's Wife out of Iran. Free now and unencumbered by his mother, he turned his full attention to the task of avenging himself against the *taaghootis* and wrongdoers of his childhood. They might have forgotten him—those rich and educated Iranians who had left the country rather than face the truth that they were no longer relevant or respected; but he—Raphael's Son—remembered *them*.

LOS ANGELES

Tuesday, June 25, 2013

"I don't care what it looks like," Leon told O'Donnell in his office. "The wife might have helped him escape, but she didn't kill him."

There were only two chairs in O'Donnell's office—an ergonomic executive desk chair for him, and a metal-framed, no-seat-pad-or-armrests, sorry-excuse-for-a-seating-implement for guests. The latter was so narrow, it barely contained the entirety of Leon's frame.

"Couldn't you get something with armrests?" He asked the same question every time he sat in that chair. In response, O'Donnell always smiled and turned his hands palm-up, as if to say, *It's the best I could do*, which they both knew wasn't true. O'Donnell didn't like people coming into his office and lingering, bringing with them germs and viruses and the smell of cigarettes and garlic and whatever else clung to their skin and clothes. As it was, he had two air purifiers working overtime in a 25' x 30' space.

Leon wiggled on the chair until he felt semisteady, then assumed a "this is a teachable moment" tone and attempted to bring his boss up to date.

Forget, for a second, that Neda was half Raphael's Son's weight, with bird bones and not enough strength to lift a ten-pound dumbbell above her head at the gym; that even if surprised, Raphael's Son could have crushed her forearm with one hand. Forget, also, that she didn't have a single nick or cut on any of her fingers; that she had endured nearly eighteen years of living with Raphael's Son and had no special reason to want to be rid of him *now*. Or that, with him dead, she would have been poor by the standards to which she was accustomed: Raphael's Son had no life insurance, and had not kept written record of where his assets were hidden. And, of course, forget that there was no body and no weapon, no witnesses or other clues.

Leon wanted O'Donnell to understand that women like Neda never—not once, ever—made a decision of such importance on their own. Neda, especially, looked and acted like she couldn't order off a restaurant menu without getting an anxiety attack.

Leon's gut told him that Raphael's Son was not dead. He was just hiding somewhere with the money. He had staged the "accident" and coached Neda to report seeing him bloody and lifeless so he would be declared dead, the case against him abandoned, his creditors giving up on trying to recoup any of their assets, and he could go right on cheating helpless old widows into ripe old age. Even assuming he was dead, however, there was no chance—none at all—that Neda was the killer.

For the first time since he had become a detective, Leon felt that being Iranian gave him an advantage in solving a case.

"The fact is," he explained to O'Donnell, "Iranian Jewish women do not kill." Even if they did—and they don't—they would not kill their husband. Not violently, anyway, and not all at once. It's that simple and Neda, unaware as she was, had to have known that. Even Sabya—the legendary crazy woman of the old Tehran ghetto who, in time, was immortalized as an adjective—*sabya-esque* means frighteningly, uncontrollably, violently insane—never killed anyone. Once or twice, in the days when divorce was not an option, a wife might have poisoned the bastard slowly till you could see daylight through his liver, or she might have tempted him into a heart attack by turning on her feline charm, but even then there was no telling who exactly was to blame. Men did smoke a lot in those days, and most cigarettes were unfiltered. And besides, this is California, home of community property and no-fault divorce. You don't have to kill the guy to get rid of him.

It's true some things have changed for Iranian women since they came to the United States. Cheating on one's husband, which was rare to nearly nonexistent, is no longer out of the question. But having a nice, quiet affair with a friend's husband in Bel Air while your own spouse is off chasing hookers in Southeast Asia is not nearly the same thing as sending the man to his grave. The only time in thirty years any Iranian Jewish wife is known to have made an attempt on her husband's life was in the early '80s: they had been married for half a century and he still got on her nerves. It was soon after they had moved to America and all people talked about was how easy it is for one's children to become prostitutes and drug addicts, or to marry "foreigners," or to be killed on the way home from the library by some lunatic with a gun. People killed for pocket change, the wife had heard. So she asked her South American gardener if he would kill her husband for three hundred dollars; he agreed, if she also paid for the weapon. Then he went to the police and turned her in.

That one doesn't count because no one died, and the DA didn't even press charges against the wife because she was old and her husband needed her to come home and cook his meals. Since then, Iranian women have reached a milestone or two. They have become brain surgeons and CEOs, renowned artists and engineers and architects, but killers they were not and will never be.

"I would go on," Leon concluded his lecture, "but I see you're pressed for time."

O'Donnell had checked his watch three times in the last three minutes. He checked it again and said, "Well, that's the biggest bunch of bullshit I've heard all day."

O'Donnell was a native of South Carolina, openly gay, and planning to run for a seat on the city council in West Hollywood. He knew many Iranians and liked most of them, couldn't understand native Angelenos' resentment toward what he saw as a rather worldly, often well-dressed, happily ostentatious group of people. O'Donnell himself was always shaved and showered and smelling like he'd just stepped out of a cool, fragrant garden. Even at work, he had a fondness for pink Façonnable shirts and lime-green Donna Karan cardigans, Hermès belts and Gucci loafers. He ate egg whites and yogurt for breakfast, quinoa salad for lunch, chicken breast and arugula salad for dinner, but he'd been to a few Iranian parties over the years and he liked the mountains of food, decadent desserts, and cascading flow of alcohol that were the staple. In one house, he was told that the tropical waterfall was made with stones imported from the Iguazu Falls on the border of Brazil and Argentina. Gianni Versace, O'Donnell had thought then, would have liked these people.

Even before the coroner's report came back, it was clear to O'Donnell that—judging by the amount of blood in the car, and by Neda's cockamamie account—Raphael's Son was dead and his wife had killed him. It was also pretty clear that unless a body was found or a weapon could be linked to both the killer and the victim, Neda was going to walk.

That didn't bother O'Donnell all that much. According to Montoya, a door-to-door inquiry from the neighbors had revealed that most of them had no idea who Raphael's Son was, and the ones who did know him didn't have one good thing to say. That meant there weren't going to be any calls from powerful area residents to the mayor or the chief of police, bringing pressure on O'Donnell or the department to apprehend a killer. If anything, the homeowners would rather the cops go away and keep property values from slipping.

Neda herself didn't seem like the kind of person who'd kill again, or for the hell of it—meaning there wasn't that much urgency to putting her away.

As for O'Donnell, it was twenty minutes past one and he had a two o'clock Pilates appointment in Venice.

The last person to see Raphael's Son alive, assuming one believed Neda's story of having found him dead in his car, was his bookkeeper and personal slave, Edward Araxamian, in the Century City offices of Soleyman Enterprises on the evening of Monday, June 24, 2013. The building's security cameras and sign-in log showed him arriving at work that Tuesday morning at 9:40 a.m., and leaving nearly fourteen hours later, at 11:30 p.m. In between (this according to the hallway and elevator cameras), Araxamian had taken eight bathroom breaks (he had an overactive bladder fueled by a constant stream of Turkish coffee which he made on a camping stove in the office kitchen), thirteen cigarette breaks (he also had a long-standing death wish that became more urgent the longer he worked for Raphael's Son), and one lunch break (he bought a stale bagel from the Starbucks in the building lobby, took three bites, threw it away, and smoked two Marlboros instead). His key card had been scanned in the building's parking structure at 11:34, and his image had been captured behind the wheel of the ancient blue Volvo station wagon he had bought in Orange County from a beautiful middle-aged woman named Marilyn; she had told him she was a poet and introduced him to her cat, and then she had voluntarily knocked off $1,000 from the asking price of the car "because I sense you're under pressure." She was right, if "under pressure" means wanting to set himself or someone else on fire several times a day.

From the outside, the apartment building where Eddy lived appeared condemned and uninhabited. There were no balconies, and the windows had to remain closed to keep out the noise and pollution of the freeway, and because the frames would bend and stick too often. The intercom was left over from the '70s. There were no names or apartment numbers next to the rows of buttons, probably because most of the tenants were in the country illegally and did not wish to be found.

Leon parked his car at the 7-Eleven across from the building and dialed Eddy's number. The phone was turned off, probably to avoid

the rush of callers fishing for information about the case, his voicemail
full. But the Bengali who owned the 7-Eleven told Leon that Eddy
was home. The Bengali's wife was Eddy's mother's emergency contact: bedridden and barely able to use the phone, the mother spent
the entire day alone while Eddy was at work. The 7-Eleven was open
twenty-four hours, and Eddy checked in with the Bengalis every time
he left or returned home.

"I'm very worried," the husband told Leon when he inquired
about Eddy. "He's never missed work before."

In the front vestibule, the elevator, such as it was, had been broken since the day it was installed, so Leon climbed up three flights.
He had to knock three times before a man's voice invited him to "get
lost." Then he had to identify himself and threaten to keep knocking
till the door fell open.

Edward Araxamian, a.k.a. Eddy Arax, Caucasian male, 5'11" and 143
pounds, suffering from high blood pressure, arrhythmia, major depression, and post-traumatic stress disorder, lived with his sixty-eight-
year-old, ailing, legally blind mother in a one-bedroom apartment
in a three-story gray cement building one block down from the San
Fernando Road exit off Route 134 in Glendale. His was not the Glendale of the twenty-first century, with its megamalls and overpriced
sushi bars, Armenian-owned Persian bakeries with rows of marzipan
in forty-two colors displayed in the window, and the original kebob
place—an outdoor restaurant owned by an Armenian named Raffi that
served only rice and kebob, none of the "Royal Persian Cuisine" of
Westwood and Beverly Hills. Where Eddy lived, the landlord was an
Armenian from the former Soviet Union (not to be confused with Armenians from Iran, since there's a lot of bad blood between the two
factions: the Iranians are gentle, law-abiding citizens; they'll tell you
that Soviet Armenians are thieves and cutthroats who give their people
a bad name). Rent was collected every two weeks, in cash, and never
claimed on a tax return. City inspectors—Latinos, for the most part,
who depended on the generosity of the landlord to afford luxury cars
for their wives—vouched for the safety of the building sight unseen.

Eddy was a good and honest man with an astonishing memory,
but he had no high school or college degree, and wasn't trained to do
anything except smoke and drink Turkish coffee. He was also adept at

dodging bombs and sidestepping land mines, which he had learned by "serving" the Islamic Republic for three long years in the Iran-Iraq War until he nearly died from the effects of one of Saddam's dirty bombs and received a medical discharge; but Los Angeles wasn't exactly rife with demand for such skills. He spoke Persian with a heavy Armenian accent, and his English was elementary at best. He did, however, have command of a good number of words in Bengali.

These language issues aside, Eddy was in the United States on a tourist visa that had expired six years earlier. Back then, he had spent a year looking for a bookkeeping job, but no American with two pennies in his corporate account was willing to trust a person who, when asked where he obtained his license, named a school that did not exist. The Iranian business owners he approached for jobs did not hold his immigration status against him; they were, after all, recent refugees themselves. What kept them from hiring him was that they couldn't bear to look at his face.

Thanks to Saddam's dirty bomb, Eddy's face, neck, and hands were a patchwork of light skin mottled with large yellowish-brown blotches. On the right side, his upper jawbone had crumbled, so that the flesh of his cheek hung limply between his nose and ear, like plastic that had melted and cooled. On the left, his cheek had caved in because he had lost all his molars. The skin on his forehead was crumpled, and the front part of his scalp was all scar tissue. The only part of the face that had remained intact were his eyes, and these, anyone who looked at him long enough would see, were bottomless holes of sadness.

It was the sadness, and the fact that he couldn't read or write English, didn't have a driver's license, and radiated cigarette smoke, that prevented other Iranians from hiring him for an accounting job. They did, however, want very much to help Eddy, so they handed him "a small offering"—a hundred dollar bill, maybe, for his troubles. They might as well have spat on his father's grave.

The apartment was small, and smelled like laundry detergent and fabric softener. An ugly brown leather couch doubled as Eddy's bed. A round glass table, the kind sold in the small Korean-owned stores up and down Venice and Robertson Boulevards, functioned as dining table and desk. There was an ancient TV perched atop the arms of a dining chair, and a three-drawer plywood dresser, painted a faint pink with white plastic knobs, that leaned against the part of the wall closest to the kitchen area. The dresser looked like it had been salvaged from a little girl's room and purchased in a yard sale. The kitchen consisted of a two-burner portable stove, a narrow refrigerator, and a washer and dryer all crammed into an alcove with a sink. The stove and a carving board sat on top of the washer and dryer; the top of the dresser served as storage space for cooking utensils and condiments. Eddy himself looked like he had had one Turkish coffee too many that day.

"So what's going on?" Leon said as he searched around for a place to sit. "Where're you hiding him?"

Eddy was not amused. "I already talked to the American cop."

"Who? O'Donnell?"

"Whatever his name is. And some Armenian woman called too, but I told her to fuck off."

"But you don't mind if we talk," Leon said, apparently without irony. That showed what a lousy detective he was: you had only to see the way Eddy cringed at the very sight of Leon to realize just how much he did mind.

In the bedroom behind Eddy, a woman moaned pitifully every few seconds.

"Go ahead," Leon nodded toward the door. "I'll wait."

Instead, Eddy headed to the "kitchen."

"So is he dead or not?" he asked with obviously feigned indifference.

The lab had determined that there was only one person's blood in the car, and that it was Raphael's Son's. The coroner had decided there was too much of it for Raphael's Son to have survived without an immediate and extensive transfusion. The forensic team had yet to find a single trace of the man anywhere outside the car.

"What do you think?" Leon tested.

There was the moan again. Eddy sighed and rubbed his left eye with his fist.

"What the fuck do I know?"

"If he's dead, and you were the last to see him, I'd say you may know a great deal."

Eddy's face flared with rage. "I hope he burns in hell, is what I know."

The rawness of the statement sent a shiver up Leon's spine. He tried hard not to look away from Eddy.

Eddy started to mash a cooked apple with the flat side of a fork. Cautiously, because it appeared too old and unstable to support his weight, Leon sat down on the arm of Eddy's sofa bed.

"So you do believe he's dead."

Eddy opened a twelve-section, seven-layer pill container and took out a capsule, opened it, and poured the contents over the mashed apple.

"This thing tastes like poison," he said, mixing the powder much too forcefully and making sure he looked only at the plate. He added some sugar and what looked to Leon like chocolate powder, crushed the paste some more, then finally picked up the plate and a teaspoon.

"I have to feed her this," he said as he walked past Leon. Two steps later he stopped, let out what sounded like an ironic laugh, and peered back at Leon.

"I don't know if he's alive or dead," he said, "but if he's dead, I'm willing to swear the Riffraff did it."

The Riffraff Brigade—all verminous twenty-seven of them, plus their dull-witted spouses, innumerable children, woebegone in-laws, and ill-treated maids—had told the police they had spent the weekend at their recently acquired family estate in Rancho Mirage. They had left Los Angeles Friday at noon, in time to be safely out of their cars and ready for Shabbat before sundown, and planned to return on Tuesday morning.

The occasion for the trip was to celebrate the purchase—$12 million plus change, all cash, thirty-day escrow—of the house that would henceforth serve as proof, to themselves if to no one else, of the Riffraff family pedigree and their old-money identity. That they had bought the house for less than it had cost to build was, of course, an advantage. That it was paid for by other people's money was, to the Riffraff, just the sweet flavor of success.

All this was noted in the report filed by Jackie Kevorkian, a detective with a fondness for black eyeshadow and long acrylic nails with square corners and red polish, who was always in a bad mood because she couldn't get through one day without being asked, at least once, in jest or seriousness, if she was indeed related to Jack Kevorkian of the assisted-suicide fame. She wasn't.

The Riffraff's weekend getaway, of course, could well be a foil: surrounded by a golf course, two waterfalls, two swimming pools, and four tennis courts, the estate was easy to enter and exit without detection. Because so many people would stay at the house at once, the temporary absence of one or two could have gone unnoticed by the rest. Because they were all liars and thieves and more putrid, even, than Raphael's Son (he, at least, had the excuse of having suffered as a child), not one of them was above bearing false witness.

Add to that the very relevant fact, well known in the community but not something the Riffraff would have volunteered to the cops, that the family's ancestral trade, stretching back three hundred years and two ghettos, plus Cyrus Street in Tehran, was *shechita*—the kosher method of killing animals for human consumption—and you might have yourself some viable suspects.

Shechita necessitates the use of a smooth, razor-sharp blade, a quick and continuous motion that severs the animal's jugular vein, arteries, trachea, and esophagus at once, and the draining of the carcass's blood.

You didn't have to be a Talmudic scholar to know this, or especially paranoid to buy into the theory that animals, like humans, have a soul; that *shechita* frees the soul and leaves only the flesh to consume; that animals killed any other way carry their soul in their flesh, from the slaughterhouse to the butcher shop and onto a man's dinner table and, upon consumption, into the human frame where it—the beast's unhappy, restless soul—will remain. But you did have to know the Riffraff well enough to realize that not one among them was brave enough to risk running into Raphael's Son's soul postslaughter—hence, one could argue, the single, smooth, and efficient cut to the throat, and the gallon of blood drained in the car before the body was taken away.

Leon knew the Riffraff well enough. As far as he was concerned, they were to Iranian Jews what the Oklahoma City Bomber was to the rank and file of the United States Armed Forces: a painful and tragic aberration. But perfidy alone wasn't proof of homicide.

"They thought he was going to throw them under the bus," Eddy explained at the apartment. He stood above the hot plate where he had started to make a fresh pot of Turkish coffee.

"They *thought*?"

Eddy stirred the dark, viscous liquid.

"Who gave them that idea?" Leon continued.

Eddy shrugged, and kept stirring. After a minute he picked the pot off the hot plate and turned toward Leon. "His lawyers wanted to quit. He wasn't giving them anything to work with and they said he was going to jail for twenty years and it would be bad for their reputation."

Without asking, Eddy poured the coffee into two small cups, put one on top of the TV for Leon, and picked up the other for himself. Leon ignored the coffee.

"So he gave them his cousins?"

Eddy downed his coffee like a shot of tequila, then felt in his shirt pocket for his cigarettes. "I have to go outside for a minute."

He couldn't smoke in the apartment and couldn't be around his mother with his hair and clothes smelling of tobacco. So he went downstairs every hour or so, inhaled two or sometimes three cigarettes at once, then came up and changed his shirt, washed his hands, and wet his hair before he tended to her again.

"Wouldn't it be easier to quit?" Leon asked rhetorically, as he followed Eddy down the staircase.

On the sidewalk, Leon waited till Eddy had lit up and sucked down a good lungful of smoke. "Okay. Come on," he pressed.

Eddy took another drag. His hands were shaking and his chest was so bony, Leon expected to see cigarette smoke flowing out of his torso. He was one of those people who seem to be perpetually on the verge of having a heart attack or a stroke, but who somehow pull through year after year, then finally die when no one's looking.

"I've been thinking this day would come," he said, and inhaled another cigarette.

In response to an invitation from Leon, the Riffraff sent three delegates, each representing one aspect of the whole, to the station on Monday afternoon: The brains, Joshua Simcha, was five feet tall in dress shoes. At sixty-three, he had hands the size of a child's, round spectacles, a mouth shaped like a wide beak, and the nervous, thin musculature of a bird. The brawn, Daniel Simcha—thirty-two, a six-foot-two block of solid, swollen muscle, with a full head of hair and a tinny, nasal voice completely incongruous with the rest of him. The beauty, Hadassah Simcha, forty-nine, resembled a hybrid gone bad: she had Joshua's beak and his bad eyes, Daniel's stature and pectorals, and it went downhill thereafter. She arrived wearing a white skirt suit—purchased at Ross Dress for Less on Westwood Boulevard and first worn at her eldest daughter's bat mitzvah some ten years earlier. Under the jacket she sported a black cotton dress shirt she had bought from Saks Fifth Avenue in Beverly Hills on the day of the historic "everything must go" sale in 2009 when, according to eyewitness and police reports, fully grown women from one of the wealthiest neighborhoods in the world had broken into fistfights over $5,000 Chanel purses at 50 percent off.

Hadassah had a firm handshake that bordered on aggressive. Daniel looked everywhere but in Leon's eyes, twitched and rocked and shook to release tension from his muscles like a basketball player before a game. Joshua wore a *kippah* and carried a box of Persian nougat he had just bought from one of the half dozen Iranian grocery stores on Westwood Boulevard south of Wilshire. He put the box on Leon's desk and sat down in one of two lightweight aluminum chairs without armrests.

The bearing of a gift, usually nougat or pistachio nuts, was one of those gestures that had been de rigueur in Iran: you never called on another person, or asked a favor, without bringing an offering of sweets, or a bundle of flowers, or, if dealing with government officials, cops, or the police and military, a paper bag stuffed with cash. In the early years after the revolution, white people in America and Europe received more boxes of nougat and packets of pistachios than they could have consumed over an entire lifetime. Everyone from the bank teller to the hairdresser to the traffic court judge in areas with large concentrations of Iranians had a stack of brown and yellow boxes of *gaz-e Esfahan*—nougat from Esfahan—on their desk. The whites had no idea what to make of these offerings, and they were too polite to ask. The Iranians, in turn, sensed the white people's discomfort and were embarrassed, but couldn't understand why. It took a year or two for most to realize that offering *gaz-e Esfahan* to a police detective in the midst of an investigation could be construed as a cheap and ill-advised attempt at a bribe. Three decades later, the Simchas still hadn't received the memo.

Joshua Simcha told Leon that he and his siblings were second cousins by marriage to Raphael's Son. Their father, thanks to Hashem, was a big landowner in Iran, and he had provided the seed money for their many investments in America.

"We did okay, thank God." He adjusted his *kippah* in hopes of drawing Leon's attention to it. "Lately, we've been hurting because of my cousin who ripped us off."

Like the handful of other Iranian Jews who had embraced orthodoxy in America as a business decision—good networking possibilities, and a general assumption that people of faith were more honest than others—the Simchas played the religion card whenever possible. They told Leon that they too had been victims of Raphael's Son's Ponzi scheme, only they had been singled out and blamed by the other creditors because of their family ties with him.

With Hashem as their witness, every last one of them had stayed in Palm Desert the entire weekend, plus Monday, and were nowhere within fifty miles of Holmby Hills.

They had no idea who could have committed such a heinous crime, only Hashem decides when and how we die. What they knew for sure was that the killer couldn't have been an Iranian Jew, and that's because, simply put, Iranian Jews did not kill.

You could go back three thousand years, study the entire history of the tribe, and, with the exception of those who had served in the army and fought in wars, you would not find a single instance—not one—of an Iranian Jew committing murder. Once every decade or so there might be a blow to the head or (more recently, in America) a shooting, but they all involved mentally ill people who avoided being medicated for fear of losing *aabehroo*. And there might have been a few suicides, but we'll never know for sure because the families would never admit to that, again because of their *aabehroo*.

Here, the three Simchas took a break from their narrative, exchanged a few pregnant looks, mumbled to each other in Persian, and finally came to a consensus.

"If I were you," Joshua reached over and put his own child-size hand on Leon's, "I'd look outside ourselves for the culprit." He was whispering—in Persian—and glancing to his right and left from the corners of his eyes for anyone within hearing range who might understand the language. "God forbid I should commit the sin of *lashon hara*, but you know, Mr. Soleyman had some dealings with that gangster, Jimmy Lorecchio."

Jimmy Lorecchio was a half bald, grossly overweight, never-learned-how-to-button-up-his-pants, sixty-nine-year-old alcoholic with only a high school diploma and a red, bloated face marked with pus-filled red boils oozing teenage acne. Barely anyone outside city hall had heard of him or would have recognized his Buddha-like figure with the much-too-small head where, in a futile attempt at vanity, he dyed what little was left of his hair a greenish blond. He would have been better advised to work on his teeth, or whatever internal fumes caused the intense sulfuric smell that lapped out of him every time he so much as opened his mouth as he sat at his desk, already at work on his Wild Turkey, by three every afternoon.

By five p.m. he would be on the phone, yelling obscenities at any and every person foolish enough to take his call at that hour, and by seven he was passed out on the couch in his office, or behind his desk. His wife had divorced him and obtained a restraining order two decades before, his children had changed their names and moved away, and his only living relative, a sister in Florida, hadn't reached out to him or returned his calls since Christmas 2001.

And yet, in spite of his atrocious physique and unsparing halitosis, Jimmy Lorecchio held the mayor, the fifteen members of the city council, the five county supervisors, and every other elected official in LA in a permanent state of terror. As head of the largest and most powerful union in the city, the International Brotherhood of City Workers, he could single-handedly swing any election by ordering his workers to vote a certain way. He traded on his reputation, well deserved, of being pathologically vindictive, unreasonable, and interested only in showing anyone who dared challenge him who held the ultimate authority in the city.

For years, there had been speculation that Lorecchio resorted to more than the plain old bullying of politicians to keep his fiefdom in check. Employees who left before they were fired often found themselves unable to find another job anywhere in the city; managers who so much as questioned a single decision he made were accused of everything from unethical behavior to flat-out madness, and summarily fired. Rumors abounded about unexplained house fires, illegal electronic surveillance, and accidental falls from the roofs of twenty-story buildings. No one—not the police, nor the district attorney, nor even private business owners who needed Lorecchio's support to obtain city contracts or advance their agenda before the city council—dared mention the rumors aloud, much less try to verify their accuracy. Even the mainstream press, struggling to survive the electronic age and weary of the possibility of a union strike, bent over to avoid offending the boss.

"Jimmy Lorecchio had some dealings with Mr. Soleyman," Hadassah Simcha said, joining her brother in not committing *lashon hara*.

Leon knew where she was going with this, but wasn't about to make it easy for her.

"That is," she said, "they knew each other through Lorecchio's deputy, that guy everyone calls Snake."

Luci's right-hand man was a ninety-year-old professional grifter known, not at all affectionately around city hall, as the Rat in the Hat. "Rat" was for his protruding yellow husk-like front teeth, and for his shifty, disloyal character; "Hat" was for the greasy, fraying, ill-fitting cowboy hat he wore day and night, indoors and out. The other was a dark-skinned chauffeur-turned-spy from East Asia who reeked of incense and bore an uncanny resemblance to a Bengali water buffalo. His name was Naji, but he was so openly devious, habitually deceitful, and instinctively mean, most people referred to him as "That Fucking Snake." Together, they carried out the unsavory tasks Luci did not wish to be linked to directly.

Hadassah was still waiting for Leon to exhibit a sign of recognition. Next to her, the younger brother had gone back to contemplating his knuckles, and Joshua remained still, mouth half open and eyes darting behind the glasses.

"You know that missing $30 million they wrote about in the papers awhile ago?"

Leon nodded.

For years, Jimmy Lorecchio had had singular jurisdiction over the union's funds and other holdings. He spent as he pleased, to support candidates he could control when they assumed office or to prompt

other unions to back his own stance on issues, and God only knows
what else, legal or not, because no one from the union, the press, or
the city was going to risk alienating him by demanding an accounting. Among his many expenses was a special fund set up in the year
2000 to "help facilitate greater understanding between labor and
business." At the time of its establishment, Lorecchio transferred $30
million from the union's coffers into the fund. After that, no one heard
about the fund for thirteen years.

In 2013 a *Los Angeles Times* reporter asked about the fund and was
told that it was empty. He asked what the money had been spent on
and did not get an answer. Normally, that was as far as the matter
would go, given Luci's sway. But courage comes from the most unlikely places. The paper pursued the question throughout the year. In
2014, a new city comptroller—apparently not angling for reelection—
committed blasphemy by asking the courts to order Luci to open the
fund's books or otherwise report on the fate of the $30 million. The
last anyone knew, Luci was accusing the comptroller of union busting
and had called for a citywide strike.

"Well," Hadassah sighed, as if truly saddened to have to break
such news, "I'll bet you can guess what happened to that money once
Mr. Soleyman declared bankruptcy."

According to Hadassah Simcha and her two brothers, Raphael's Son
had enticed Lorecchio to entrust him with the fund's money. They
had met in 1998, when Raphael's Son wanted to buy a piece of land
that belonged to the union. Technically, the property wasn't officially
for sale, so Raphael's Son followed the informal protocol of reaching
out to That Fucking Snake with an offer to be taken to the boss. The
land was purchased for $10 million, well below market value. Luci's
permission to sell the land was purchased for $2 million, deposited by
Eddy Arax in a numbered account in the Caymans. To Raphael's Son,
this was just the beginning of a long and fruitful relationship.

He prevailed upon That Snake to arrange a meeting with the Rat
in the Hat. He, in turn, carried a message to Lucifer. At a time when
banks offered an interest rate of 3.5 percent on a CD, Raphael's Son
guaranteed a 10 percent return. From that profit, he suggested, Luci
could reimburse the union its 3.5 percent and keep the difference for
himself.

They started with smaller deposits—a few hundred thousand dollars at a time. Once a month, the Rat would bring a stack of cash and hand it to Eddy, pick up the interest payment on the existing deposit in cash, and be gone. But Luci got bolder. The deposits became larger. The fund was established. Thirty million dollars was transferred into its coffers, then promptly handed over to Eddy Arax.

"But you see, Mr. Pulitzer," Hadassah offered her best Goldie Hawn smile, "you don't cross Jimmy Lorecchio and expect to get away unharmed."

And besides, Leon carried the thought to its logical conclusion, who knew what Raphael's Son would be willing to reveal in order to buy himself immunity from prosecution or enter a plea deal if the trial wasn't going his way?

To see if he could learn any more about either the Riffraff or Lorecchio, Leon paid a visit to the court-appointed bankruptcy trustee.

Not the most popular person on the block, the trustee and his army of lawyers, forensic accountants, and sundry other experts had so far collected close to $80 million by suing every investor who ever withdrew money (whether capital or interest) from the pool. They had also billed the account and received close to $80 million in fees.

In return for their services, they had managed to unearth the following facts: a) that Raphael's Son had lost or misplaced $500 million of "investors'" money; b) that he had kept no written record of how or why the money was lost; and c) that the trustee suspected most of the money was misplaced in overseas accounts, and the rest of it in the accounts of twenty-seven of his family members.

Many a page of the *Pearl Cannon* had been devoted by Angela to the simple observation that the trustee's $80 million worth of "discovery" could have been related, to any judge with an IQ of ten or above, by any one of Raphael's Son's victims. That the only people benefitting from the trustee's investigation were the trustee and his crew. That the victims should stop fighting each other and trying to make nice with the trustee so he wouldn't sue them again, and instead band together and demand that the judge who appointed the person rein him in.

Five years later, the trustee's divide-and-conquer tactics were still paying off (for him), and the judge still took no interest.

The office was on the twenty-fourth floor of a tower in Century City, across the street from where Raphael's Son had been. The ground floor and half a dozen others were occupied by the Creative Artists Agency, hence the frenetic energy in the lobby and the throngs of attractive young men and women, all dressed like Ralph Lauren models, carrying cups of coffee or lugging laundry bags. Like everyone else in LA with a pulse, Leon thought of CAA as a near-mythological place run by diabolical madmen and more difficult to penetrate than the inner bowels of the Pentagon. Before they moved their headquarters from Beverly Hills to Century City, Leon had tried twice to get a close-up glimpse of America's Forbidden City. Even with a detective's badge, trying to approach the agency's gatekeepers had been an exercise in humiliation. This time he did his best not to look toward the (was it really bulletproof glass?) door, but in the short distance from the street to the elevators he caught himself fantasizing that one of the agents who specialized in selling books for film adaptation had intercepted him and was asking him—Leon—for a meeting.

In his office, the trustee sat across from Leon with his elbows resting on a glass desk and his hands touching at the fingertips. He seemed more like a bad therapist, Leon thought, than a good lawyer. He wore a loose white cotton dress shirt over loose black pants, the obligatory two-tone Rolex, the kind of expensive eyeglasses television news anchors were modeling of late because they thought it made them more credible.

He told Leon that, as far as "the trust" had been able to establish, Raphael's Son had maintained 113 corporations, most of them unregistered, over a twenty-year period. He moved money around from one to the other until it was untraceable, and he didn't keep written records of the most important ones because he and Eddy were both products of the Iranian education system where memorization was king.

"I'm told that over there kids have to memorize entire books, first word to last, including punctuation, to get through school. To pass the college entrance exam they have to retain ten thousand math problems and be able to spew them out instantaneously. They don't need Quicken to keep track of their money."

It was true, Leon knew. Especially for someone as bright as Raphael's Son. Then again, what a waste it had been—all that work so he could be the human equivalent of some kind of bookkeeping software designed to steal from orphans and widows.

"The bookkeeper maintained a log." The trustee raised an eyebrow to emphasize how much contempt he had for this manner of record keeping. "Written by hand. In pencil. And good luck making sense of it."

Leon asked about a relationship with Lorecchio.

The trustee smiled mechanically. "I don't know anything about that."

Leon asked if the trustee had obtained records of a $30 million deposit, circa 2003.

"Compared to some others, that's chump change." The trustee touched his fingertips again.

"This is a wealthy community." He said this as if being rich was an automatic sign of corruption.

"This is a wealthy town." Leon challenged the implied criticism of Iranians for being successful. "You wouldn't hold it against the people?"

The trustee smiled. He didn't say no, or yes. For Leon, that was the last straw.

"In fact, I'm told you've become quite wealthy from this one assignment alone," he spat, then stood up.

He was almost at the door when the trustee said, "I wouldn't cross Lorecchio over this."

Leon turned with his most indignant look to the trustee. Was it not his job, for $80 million, to look into the provenance and fate of creditors' assets?

"You know, Mr. Pulitzer, the Iranians ask me why the Madoff trustee wrapped up that investigation in three years, and mine is still ongoing."

Leon waited.

"I tell you what I tell them: because Madoff's plan wasn't nearly as complicated."

Before he joined the academy Leon had changed his surname from Pooldar to Pulitzer because he thought other cops would take him more seriously if they didn't know he was Iranian. He also felt it did a better job of defining him as a person, since *pooldar* means "one who has a lot of money"; Leon had been close to broke at the time.

He had come to the United States when he was fourteen, part of a group of Jewish boys spirited out of Iran with the help of the Hebrew Immigrant Aid Society to save them from being used as minesweepers on the battlefront with Iraq. Some of the boys were sent to live with relatives in Israel or America; others, who didn't have family or friends outside Iran, were placed in Ashkenazi homes. That's when everyone began to notice the great cultural divide between the Mizrahi Jews of the East and their Western counterparts.

Leon's host family found him polite and shy and grateful for their hospitality. His English was grammatically correct, but his pronunciation and accent made them laugh. He had a habit of standing up, as if at attention, every time an adult walked into or out of a room. He did this in school whenever the teacher came in. The first time his host family took him to see a movie, he asked when the national anthem would play and when the audience would stand up to salute the image of the president. At home, he didn't laugh at any of the jokes on television, didn't understand why Archie Bunker was so unhappy about having his daughter and son-in-law live with him and Edith. He said all his prayers in the wrong rhythm and often in incorrect Hebrew, turned beet-red and hung his head anytime an older person addressed him.

The host family set out to teach Leon how to properly "integrate" into American society, and they did a good job of it, so much so that by the time he went off to the University of Baltimore hardly anyone asked him where he was from anymore.

His choice of law enforcement as a career was unusual for an Iranian Jew. Because he was a man, his aspiration to be a crime writer was even more unusual: while writing seemed to be the weapon of choice for every bored Iranian housewife in New York and Los Angeles, it was not the kind of work self-respecting men willingly engaged in. The housewives could afford to write because they had husbands who paid the bills, and friends who could be co-opted into buying the book and even praising it. The men, on the other hand, risked being laughed out of town if they confused writing with work. Work, for a man, was something that produced a paycheck.

Leon needed a paycheck not just to support himself, but also to care for his parents and sister. They had moved to the United States in 1997, thirteen years after they sent Leon away. They went to live with him in his two-bedroom house on Vanowen Street in Van Nuys. Leon had bought the house as an "investment property" when he still believed he was going to sell a screenplay a year and reach a Hollywood-type pay scale. Now, he slept in the smaller bedroom and had his shirts made by his mother, who had been a seamstress in Iran.

His father was one of the many thousands of Iranian men who had had to choose between living in fear at home or running to safe obsolescence in the West, between being alone in Iran because all their family had moved away, or moving to America to be with his son and, without a job, having to depend on him entirely. He woke up every day and dressed in a suit and tie even though he had nowhere to go. In the afternoon, he took the bus to the Orthodox Iranian shul that was held in a room on the second floor of a strip mall. Then he strolled down to the Persian grocery store on the ground level and spent half an hour selecting the slimmest, crispiest Persian cucumbers.

On his way home every afternoon, Leon's father sat in the rear of the bus and cried quietly for his wasted life and ravaged pride.

On his way out of Century City, Leon took stock of his growing list of possible suspects: There was the wife, Neda; the indentured servant, Eddy Arax; the greedy cousins, the Riffraff. There was the angry gardener, Gerardo; the union boss, Lorecchio; and the random angry creditor. This last category was large and varied. At one end was the example of Raphael's Son's father-in-law, Dr. Raiis, a seventy-nine-year-old Iranian pediatrician who had once tried to run over Raphael's Son with his ancient Volvo and missed. At the opposite end was Mrs. Scheinbaum, an eighty-four-year-old Ashkenazi woman from the Pico-Robertson area who had handed over her entire life savings to Raphael's Son because she had met him at an Orthodox shul and was impressed by his apparent piety. When she realized that he had "misplaced" her money and was not going to return her calls, and that she was not going to live long enough to see him punished, she opted for the fast track.

One Monday afternoon she put on her nice coat and comfortable shoes, and took the bus downtown. She got off at the Staples Center exit and stood on the sidewalk for a long time, waiting for someone who looked like a murderer-for-hire. When she did see such individuals, however, she was too frightened to approach them. Then, at last, she saw a black man in a dress shirt and jeans get out of a Lexus across the street. He was middle-aged and not very threatening-looking, but he had the other necessary qualifications, so she made her way over to him and asked if he needed "work."

The black man with the Lexus was the third-highest-ranking administrator at USC. He put little old Mrs. Sheinbaum in his car and drove her home, then told her landlord to keep an eye on her in case she ventures out to look for another assassin. That—through the landlord—is how the entire Pico-Robertson district learned of Mrs. Sheinbaum's downtown adventure, and why Raphael's Son sent Eddy Arax to file a police report against her. Two months later, Mrs. Sheinbaum was shopping for spring onions at Benny Produce, the Persian kosher grocery store on Pico and Oakhurst, when she felt a sharp pain in her temples, and dropped dead of a stroke.

From a detective's point of view, this was a case from hell: too many people with motive, no body, witness, or weapon, and many an interested party still convinced that the victim was not dead at all, just a fugitive. Leon knew he had been assigned the case because he was Iranian, and that was okay. He knew he could pick up and interpret bits of information that would have taken an outsider a lifetime to understand. You had to know the community, how every person's story stretched back a few generations, how the past steered the course of events in the present, to figure out where to look or even what questions to ask. You couldn't apply the same investigative methods to the average Californian—born elsewhere, here temporarily, sees the family once a year for one meal on Thanksgiving and spends six months dreading it; has cousins he doesn't know about or has never seen; knows nothing about the personal lives of his neighbors or coworkers, and only what his friends choose to reveal about themselves—that you would to people whose lives had been entangled together, their fate dependent on each others', for three thousand years. With the Iranians, significant facts might remain concealed simply because the person you were asking didn't think it was news, or was afraid he would be accused by others in the community as having had ulterior motives for sharing them with the police. Or he'll know something but keep it to himself because he thinks it's bad karma—enough people have been hurt already, why extend the suffering just to exact punishment?

There was all this, Leon knew, and there was also the fact that, had he deemed the case important enough, O'Donnell would have assigned a higher-ranking detective to oversee Leon's work. Instead, he had left Leon alone, with only Kevorkian to help muddle through.

As if summoned by his thoughts, Kevorkian rang Leon at that very moment. For once, she sounded upbeat and pleased with herself.

"You're gonna like this," she announced. "Methinks the wife has a lover."

According to phone records Jackie Kevorkian had dug up, Neda owned two cell phones, with two different service providers. One of the phones had been purchased on June 2, 2013, and was used to call only one number—a 7-Eleven on Brand Avenue in Glendale. Neda had called the place nearly every day since that date. In all, Kevorkian had counted twenty-eight calls in a three-week period in June.

The calls Neda placed to the 7-Eleven were always under a minute long. But she had also received calls, three in total, all from the same number. Those had lasted twenty minutes or more. The final call, made by Neda at 3:21 on the afternoon of June 25, had gone unreturned.

Eddy Arax lived on Brand Avenue in Glendale.

LOS ANGELES

1987

The first confirmed sighting of Raphael's Son in Los Angeles occurred in October 1987, in Attari—the Persian grocery store/café on the corner of Westwood Boulevard and Wilkins Avenue. He came in at eleven a.m., sat at table in the courtyard, and summoned the middle-aged Iranian man behind the food counter inside.

"Come here, boy!" he yelled through the doorway. "Bring a couple of Cokes. Make sure they're *taggaree*—ice cold."

The few patrons who were sitting at nearby tables eyed him with disapproval. Even the owner, a petite woman with well-tended hands and a clearly *taaghooti* demeanor, emerged from her back office to see for herself the person who had called a man in his fifties "boy."

Nearly eight years into life outside Iran, the social makeup of the community remained largely static. You could still tell a person's religious and ethnic background, and certainly their former economic and social status, just by their speech and manners, the way they walked and moved and carried themselves. Upper-class Muslims were exceedingly polite, humble, and conscious of the rules of noblesse oblige. Upper-class Jews largely resembled the Muslims. Upper-class Baha'is, who had been either Muslim or Jewish in their preconversion life, still bore their original markings. Upper-class Armenians stayed in Glendale and made sure they couldn't be mistaken for anyone else.

As for the rest—the other 90 percent of Iranian immigrants who, contrary to the prevailing perception among the natives, were well-educated but not rich—the Jews among them went to work alongside Korean and Latino immigrants in LA's Ragtown, the Muslims drove cabs and became bank-tellers and minimum-wage employees at small businesses, and the Armenians stayed in Glendale and made sure they couldn't be mistaken for anyone else.

If there were working-class Baha'is, no one knew where they could be found.

What all these groups of Iranian immigrants had in common was an awareness of the importance and necessity of maintaining the social graces that, for over two thousand years, had cemented a wildly diverse group of people into a single nation. In this context, a younger man addressing an elder as "boy" was not only offensive but an unmistakable act of aggression.

Attari's owner pegged Raphael's Son as an Islami—the exile community's term for a regime operative sent abroad to assassinate potential threats or invest the funds the mullahs had stolen from the country's oil revenues and hidden safely in American and Swiss banks. She had a good mind to tell him off, but then she remembered that a Persian restaurant a block away had burned to the ground the previous week. The cause was arson, but the perpetrator and his motive remained a subject of great speculation. The owner was ruled out as a suspect because his place wasn't insured; he claimed his competitors up and down Westwood Boulevard were to blame. Many of his customers, who knew he refused to serve Islamis no matter the consequences, thought he had finally angered one too many of them.

Raphael's Son downed two cans of Coke and two tongue sandwiches in ten minutes, smoked a cigarette, then ordered another Coke. When the older man brought it to him, Raphael's Son asked, "Been here long?"

The man kept his eyes on the table he was wiping. "Few years," he said. He had the worn-out look of someone who has fought for too long and finally given in, the three-day-old stubble and much too sunken eyes of so many Iranian men stripped of their jobs and titles by exile.

"Where from?"

"Shiraz." He turned to leave, hesitated, then faced Raphael's Son again. "I was a civil engineer." His voice ached. "We built highways."

Raphael's Son measured the man head-to-toe with his eyes. "And look at you now," he delivered the coup de grâce, "wiping tables in *Aamreekah*."

For the first year and a half after he set up shop in Westwood, barely anyone knocked on Raphael's Son's door. He had gone to court and legally changed his name from Muhammad Jadid al-Islam to Raphael S. Soleyman. He had rented an office on the seventeenth floor of a high-rise on the corner of Wilshire and Westwood, in a building erected by some Iranian Jews on the old site of Ship's coffee shop. He received a great many calls, but they were all spurred by the name. The first question people asked was whether this was Aaron Soleyman's office, which was stupid given the fate he was known to have met, but it infuriated Raphael's Son anyway.

"It's Soleyman all right," he responded coldly. "R.S. Soleyman."

He could never figure out if the silence at the other end, followed by a quiet "Oh!" and more silence, was a sign of the caller's confusion or an expression of disbelief. Some of the callers went on to inquire what R.S. stood for, and when he told them, there was more silence, followed by a halfhearted "good luck to you," before they hung up.

In those days, every chambermaid and seventh cousin thrice removed from the royal family was going around claiming they were a prince or princess. They started by introducing themselves as such to the natives in Europe and America, who didn't know better, and after a while they came to believe it themselves and would repeat it to other Iranians. Some of them wrote books about their presumed aristocratic families; the less brazen simply enumerated the many towns and villages, jeweled crowns and stolen scepters, they had to give up when they escaped Iran.

These new royals were not alone in taking advantage of Westerners' fascination with the monarchy. An absurd number of former conscripts from the Iranian armed forces suddenly seemed to have been "personal pilot to the shah." Every other homeowner seemed to grieve the loss of a seaside mansion. Every disappointed wife recalled an earlier suitor who would have given his life—and a very substantial fortune—to marry her.

How much of the fablemaking was intentionally deceptive and how much of it was simply a result of idealizing the past, no one could say. So while the natives in LA were quick to believe every tale of aristocratic lineage or heroic status, the Iranians became especially distrustful of strangers. In the case of Raphael's Son there was the added disadvantage of an ignominious childhood followed by a criminal youth, so that a person could be forgiven for wondering just what the young man thought he would achieve by reaching out to the people least likely to trust him.

Then again, one had to reckon, he hadn't made it as far as Westwood Boulevard in Los Angeles by being a complete imbecile.

Early on he discovered that unlike in Iran, where being Jewish was a social and commercial disadvantage, in LA he was better off as a Jew than just about anything else he might be expected to pass for. So he shaved the three-day-old beard and shed the buttoned-up dress shirts with no tie, stopped boasting about his influential friends in the regime, put the jewels he had bought with the blood of innocents in a safe-deposit box, and denied his own earlier claims of having left the country with a staggering amount of cash. In Westwood Village near UCLA, he discovered young Jewish men from Chabad offering to tie a *tefillin* or give the blessing of the *lulab* to students. It was the first time he had come across Jews who did not know him and did not care who he was, didn't ask his name or his origins, and seemed eager to welcome him into their midst. It occurred to him that taking up religion might help rehabilitate his image in the community, so he joined the Chabad shul in West LA and, within a few months, picked up two clients. He realized that the more observant he appeared, the more people seemed to like him, so he decided he would be Modern Orthodox. It worked well enough with the Ashkenazis, but with the Iranians . . .

The Iranians still cared about a man's name and *aabehroo*. To them, a family's history remained their best collateral, more important than any legal document, more effective than any ruling by a court. It didn't matter how often the younger-generation Iranians tried to explain to the parents that here, in the land of second chances, every person has a right to more than one life, that in America a name is just a layer of skin you can shed as many times as you need to, to keep moving forward.

Shed the skin all you want, the parents said. It's what's underneath that counts and *that*, my dear, doesn't change no matter what packaging you choose.

To these Iranians, the person who introduced himself as R.S. Soleyman was an unknown young man with more money than he could have earned honestly. His earlier incarnation, Muhammad Jadid al-Islam, was an extortionist who had sent scores of innocents to be tortured and killed. His original person, Raphael's Son, was a bastard boy picked off a street corner by the Black Bitch of Bushehr.

For a while, Raphael's Son prayed for patience. Sooner or later, he had to believe, the voices of those he had maligned were bound to fade, the image of Jadid al-Islam with his beard and buttoned-up shirt would be blacked out by the spectacle of the observant Jew in *kippah* and *tallith*, and a day would come—it had to come—when Raphael's Son's wealth and power would overshadow the memory of his earlier disgrace.

So he told himself it didn't matter what the family said, he *was* Izikiel the Red's real heir and would therefore act like it. He started to drop Elizabeth's and Aaron's names into every conversation, to refer to the family as "we" and "our." He pretended not to notice the skeptical looks and sarcastic smiles, willed his pulse to slow down and his skin to stop perspiring from anger every time someone asked, "So they finally accepted you?" innocently or otherwise.

With every dismissive smile and every quiet snub, every invitation extended to others that was denied him and every raised eyebrow when he was seen—awkward and alone, it is true, but wasn't his money as good as everyone else's?—in a fancy store or elegant restaurant, Raphael's Son became more intent on "showing them all."

At night, in his second-floor apartment above the Persian-language bookstore in Westwood, he sat alone and plotted and planned the next day's meetings, practiced his tone and body language, his handshake. Every Saturday morning he walked eight blocks to Wilshire and Beverly Glen and sat in on the Sinai Temple shul just to watch all the Iranians who converged upon the place like an ancestral homeland. Following old-country practices, they came late and lingered in groups. The men prayed earnestly; the women socialized and sized up each other's marriage-age sons and daughters. They spoke Persian in

the lobby and the hallways, threw candy at the bar and bat mitzvah
kids, announced a wedding for eight p.m. and expected the rabbi to
still be there, waiting patiently and in good humor, when at ten the
bride and groom hadn't yet made their arrival.

Raphael's Son spent the entire three-and-a-half-hour service
standing at the back by the entrance to the main sanctuary, doing his
best to appear austere and authoritative, like someone from within the
inner circles of the synagogue's leadership who had been infused with
the power to vet newcomers for significance and suitability. He ignored the inquisitive looks and invitations to take a seat from the temple's real proctors, all of whom were Ashkenazi and therefore unable
to distinguish between one Iranian Jew and the next. He took stock
of all the Iranians who recognized him and pretended they hadn't so
they wouldn't have to shake his hand, the ones who didn't know him
and didn't want to, and those who, out of ignorance or pity or plain
old courtesy, smiled and nodded every time they walked past him. He
despised this last group at least as much as he did the others; they reminded him of everything he had always refused to be—powerless, servile, accepting of limitations. If the rich and well connected deserved
to be destroyed for their sense of entitlement and their indifference
to justice, these others, who showed respect just because, should be
stepped on like the undiscerning cretins they were.

His biggest wish was to run into Elizabeth at one of these shuls. It had been easy enough to track her down in LA and learn her *jareeyan*—her current plight. He knew where she lived, had driven dozens of times past the gray two-story building with the cottage-cheese roofs and old plumbing where she and Zeeba Raiis were still roommates. He knew that she worked for John Vain, that he had arranged for her to do the bookkeeping for a few other restaurant owners. They paid little because she was not an actual CPA, but they swore by her abilities, insisted she was "smarter and more honest, more organized, even, than the Filipinos," which was as high a compliment as you could give. Raphael's Son rejoiced at the news of Elizabeth's travails. She may not be poor, or desperate, or physically decimated like Raphael's Wife had been back in Iran, he thought, but nor did she any longer have the power she had waved so easily over Raphael's Son and his mother.

In this country, at this time, he wanted to say to her, you and your kind don't have a prayer . . .

He figured his best chance at finding her in a temple was on the high holy days, and that she would go to Sinai Temple because that's where John Vain must go. Both these assumptions were wrong—John Vain did not belong to any shul, and Elizabeth would not step inside Sinai Temple for many years still. Nevertheless, Raphael's Son put on his best black suit and, on Yom Kippur Eve in 1990, set out for the corner of Wilshire and Beverly Glen. He had been to Sinai many times before without any trouble, but this time, a security guard at the entrance asked to see "the ticket."

"I'm not going to a movie," Raphael's Son snickered as he tried to walk past the man. Next to him, a second guard was tearing off a portion of other people's tickets before they were let in. He looked like an Israeli paratrooper who should be guarding the gold vault at the Federal Reserve.

"Only members with tickets tonight," the first guard said.

Raphael's Son had never heard of a temple that required membership. As far as he had ever known, synagogues, like mosques and churches, were built by philanthropists and community leaders, out of sheer benevolence or to fulfill a personal agenda. They were maintained through fund-raising efforts that spanned the entire year and culminated in the practice of "buying" Torahs on the high holy days. What you bought was a chance to hold the scrolls and walk through the congregation, and it cost you as much as the rabbi knew you could afford.

The security guards were big Israeli men without much interest in social niceties or patience for explaining the concept of membership to yet another Jewish immigrant. Raphael's Son took their rudeness personally and refused to leave, at first because he didn't believe their "you must have a ticket to get in; yes, it's just like going to the movies, only more expensive" pretext, and then because he demanded an apology that wasn't forthcoming. Before he knew it, two dozen Iranians were watching him get yelled at by an Israeli twice his height. One Iranian declared that it was people like this who gave "all of us" a bad name, and another volunteered to serve as translator, lest the misunderstanding be language related.

Raphael's Son sucked in his breath and muttered a few expletives in English, then turned around and headed down Wilshire toward his apartment in Westwood.

At Midvale outside the Avco theater, a woman sat behind the wheel of an ancient Honda, waiting for the light to change. Next to her in the passenger seat was a heavyset child with bulky glasses and wavy brown hair. It was dusk then, and though the car's headlights were on, he could still see in through the windshield.

Raphael's Son stepped off the curb and in front of the car, glanced to his left at the woman, and wondered if he had seen her before or if she just reminded him of someone. He stopped for a second, gazed harder at the pale face, the high cheekbones, that air of intense concentration on something visible only to her, and moved on.

On Broxton by Diddy Riese, he felt his chest tighten and had to stop. The sidewalk pulsed with sound and movement and the headlights of cars. For a moment, Raphael's Son feared he would be devoured by the crowd, erased and forgotten like the child trawling the streets of Tehran behind his mother. He took his glasses off and closed his eyes, dropped his head and pressed his thumb and forefinger into his tear ducts.

Something hard and heavy slammed into him, causing him to stumble sideways before regaining his balance. It was a chubby young woman wearing strawberry-scented lip gloss; she looked like she had been pushed by one of the boys she was with, and who was now laughing. Raphael's Son was never so intimidated as when he found himself facing young American kids. Compared to their counterparts elsewhere in the world, they were overly confident—insolent, even. They were not expected to show adults the kind of deference a younger person normally would, but they were forgiven every misdeed on grounds that they were "still children."

All the way through the village and down Veteran he felt a piercing ache in his temples, but it wasn't until he had put the key in his door and was about to turn it in the lock that he felt his hand go limp and a cold wave of terror rise in his stomach: He had seen Elizabeth. He had even walked in front of her, paused, and peered at her face without recognizing her.

The Elizabeth he had known as a child and had been chasing ever since was much older, bigger, more fearsome and detestable than this other woman in the Honda.

For the first time since Raphael's Son became Muhammad Jadid al-Islam, he began to doubt his own potential. He hadn't recognized Elizabeth, it was true, but nor had she recognized him. She had seen him—he was sure of this. She had stared right at him as he peered through the windshield of her car.

It occurred to him that she may not be as aware of his existence, or as fearful of it, as he had wanted to believe. That she may not be lying awake at night thinking about the damage Raphael's Wife had done to her, mourning the dead husband and missing child, knowing she was being punished for her own and her family's cruelty.

He decided to take the fight to her. He wasn't going to run into her at temple and he didn't want to risk the humiliation of showing up at her home only to have the door close in his face, so he resolved to look for her at Lucky 99. One Saturday morning he stopped at Bernini, the men's clothing store on Rodeo Drive that catered mostly to Arab men with money to burn, and bought a suit, dress shirt, and tie. Then he went across the street and bought a pair of Ferragamo loafers. The suit needed alteration, and he was shocked to learn that, unlike in Iran where tailors were on hand to get the work done within the hour, he would have to wait five business days before he could get the suit back. In the end, he decided to wear it as is.

He had made a reservation for nine thirty, but when he arrived, the hostess ignored him for a full five minutes, then asked his name and said, without bothering to look at him, "It'll be forty minutes." He objected that he had a reservation; she gave him a condescending smile and said, "So does everyone else. You're welcome to have a drink at the bar."

For the next half hour, Raphael's Son watched as the hostess, a classic California blonde, planted a kiss on every newcomer's face and walked them past Raphael's Son to a table. He finally went up and asked why he wasn't getting a table when there were so many still vacant.

"Because everything's spoken for," she said.

He pointed out again that he had a reservation.

"So does everyone else," she repeated with a smirk.

But what about the empty tables?

"They're being held."

He objected that she had seated patrons who clearly did not have a reservation.

She rolled her eyes. "They don't need a reservation."

Raphael's Son was sweating in his too-large, brand-new suit. The more he snapped at the hostess, the more disdainful she became. He asked to speak with the manager.

"I'm the manager," she said. "You can wait for the owner to come in if you want. It'll be a couple of hours."

Behind him, a tall bald man with a disastrous face-lift and too much foundation whispered to his companion, "You'd think he's in the industry."

It would be years before Raphael's Son learned that in LA, "the industry" meant the film business, and that it ruled hearts and minds above and beyond all else. In a rage, he turned to the face-lift and said, too loudly, "I can buy and sell this place with you in it three times in one day if I want to."

Then he marched out, the man's laughter trailing him.

The night of Angela and Nilou's high school graduation, John Vain hosted a dinner in their honor at Lucky 99. It was June 1990, and he invited ninety-nine guests. He closed the restaurant to the public, printed menus on scrolls of parchment paper painted like diplomas, had a string quartet play music in the background. "Invite all your friends," he had urged the girls and their mothers. Zeeba and Nilou each had a dozen guests. Angela came up with three, and Neda and Elizabeth had no one. At the last minute, to avoid the embarrassment of having a party with so few in attendance, John Vain made some phone calls and filled the place. He even invited a date for himself.

In the nearly ten years since he had met and, in his own heart, married Elizabeth, John Vain took fewer than a dozen women out to lunch or dinner or a movie. All things being equal, he would have much preferred to spend even those times with what he called, only half jokingly, "my real family." If he gave in to pressure from women who courted him or friends who insisted he should "get out" every once in a while, it was only to avoid making an even bigger spectacle of his devotion to the Soleymans. Not that anyone who knew him even casually could have missed the extent of his infatuation with Elizabeth or fondness for Angela. He had practically turned them into celebrities without their consent or participation. He had even taken Zeeba Raiis and her daughters under his wings. But he was much too kind, perhaps much too love-struck, to ever take a chance on declaring his feelings to Elizabeth herself. *She'd turn me down, and it'd be over.*

He was right about this—that Elizabeth did not reciprocate his ardor, would never have agreed to marry him or become more than friends. To Angela, who loved John Vain and yearned to recreate the family she had lost in Iran, her mother's tacit rejection of the man who had done so much for them only validated the Ice Queen hypothesis.

To hear Angela say it, the last time Elizabeth had made a display of emotion was when she went into the girls' room and found that Noor was missing. After that, through every ordeal, she had looked stricken but not lost; when they brought her Noor's body, when she watched the little corpse, like a headless doll, be washed and wrapped at the morgue, when she threw the first fistful of dust on the grave—all that time and forever after, Elizabeth displayed more determination than grief.

At the dinner, John Vain served champagne and toasted the girls with as much delight and appreciation as any father might have shown. He had written his speech and practiced it half a dozen times in front of a mirror, asked his "date"-to-be, an attractive Iranian woman with a fast-ticking biological clock, to correct any mistakes and substitute "better" words for the ones he had used. He had been doing this—trying to better himself—consistently since he met Elizabeth. He read books on etiquette and biographies of "great men," dressed more formally, even replaced the cowboy boots for lace-up oxfords much of the time. He knew there was no way to catch up with her in sophistication or ancestry, but he wanted to be as good as he could become. Most of the time, this meant spending large sums of money.

"I thank God and the ayatollah," he said in his speech to Angela and Nilou, "for sending you to me."

He teared up, paused to swallow, and tried to memorize the scene—the faces of the two girls beaming with joy and excitement, the color of Elizabeth's eyes in the yellow mist of candlelight, the certainty, within him, that he had managed to make something grand and meaningful with his life after all. Then he said, "Whatever happens from here on, I will know that I was blessed."

The dinner ended at midnight.

John Vain left the restaurant at one thirty.

The staff locked up at three.

At six a.m., the police called.

He headed down Loma Vista and onto Foothill with his eyes half closed from sleep, decided he shouldn't drive in that state, and drove back home to call a cab. The driver was a shaggy-haired, "I'm an artist, this job is beneath me, my mother was related to the last king of Hungary though I forget his name" type, who called himself Laszlo de Varga and had driven John Vain many times before and been treated to more than a meal and a bottle of Veuve Clicquot at the restaurant. John Vain called a taxi whenever he drank, and he was such a good tipper, drivers argued with dispatch over who should be sent to pick him up. Laszlo de Varga usually won, though he was often half-drunk himself, even at lunchtime.

That day, he had a fierce hangover and was in a confessional mood. As they drove east on Sunset, he started to tell John Vain that he—Laszlo—wasn't related to a royal as he had previously claimed; in fact, he was an orphan and didn't know his mother, and the so-called relation to the king was a story he had invented to help him get better tips because, let's face it, "people want to impress royals, they think we deserve more than regular folk." The "de" in de Varga was something his wife had suggested he throw in when he applied for his license just to emphasize his noble background.

They had driven as far east as Vermont when they realized they had gone way too far, and doubled back. This time, they went through the light at Crescent Heights and still didn't see the restaurant, so they made another U-turn and stopped behind the fire trucks.

The cop who called John Vain said there had been a fire at the restaurant, but there was no fire here. Nor was there a restaurant.

John Vain circled the trucks and looked up and down the intersection. All he saw was an empty lot, the charred remains of cars, and a heap of smoldering wood and metal.

He stood there, mouth agape. The air was cool but he could feel perspiration drip from his neck onto his back. Someone in a heavy jacket came up and asked if he was the owner.

"Your insurance company's going to want to send their detectives over; you should call them right away."

John Vain didn't answer. This was the second time that week he had heard the word "insurance." The first was when Elizabeth told him that the policy on Lucky 99 had lapsed and should be reinstated.

"Stop worrying so much," John Vain had reassured her. "Insurance is for unlucky people."

He went home and opened the safe where he kept his $5,000 "earthquake" fund. It was something all LA residents were advised to do: keep cash on hand in case the Big One hits and all the banks are shuttered and you have to live like in one of those apocalyptic films, where the entire world has crumbled around you and you alone are the key to the survival of the human race, and one gallon of gas, if you can find it, costs $5,000.

It occurred to him as he was taking the money out of the safe that he must have seen a devastating earthquake as a more likely prospect than a flood or fire. That was because earthquakes happened to everyone in an entire region; a flood or fire was reserved for the afflicted—which he was not.

He took out $4,000 and went back to the site of the restaurant in time for the afternoon shift to arrive. One by one he hugged the employees—the busboys, the chef, the doorman, the waiters and waitresses and bartenders. He divided the $4,000 among them equally and apologized for leaving them "on furlough" without notice. He was going to take a few weeks to straighten out his finances, then rebuild on the site, and he would hire back every one of them if they wanted to return, with a raise, plus back pay for the months they were out of work. He might have lost a great deal of money in the fire, but he had other significant assets, not the least of which was an infinite line of credit at Bank United.

For years, John Vain had relied on Brady McPherson to bankroll his extravagances and raise money for his friends. At last count, he owed the bank $1.8 million, which had alarmed Elizabeth to no end and, in John Vain's opinion, needlessly.

"If ever the bank wants its money back," he told her every time he borrowed more, "I have the house and the restaurant."

McPherson had told John Vain that to qualify for a loan, the applicant's assets must be as significant as the amount of money he borrowed. He had also said that, in his capacity as manager of the loan department, McPherson could see to it that the verification process was quick and unintrusive. Taking his cue from this, John Vain had let his imagination fill not only his own but also his friends' lists of assets. In the early '80s, when most Iranians were totally unfamiliar with the concept of borrowing in order to fund purchases, because every transaction in Iran was done entirely in cash, John Vain had the applicants sign blank forms and let McPherson fill them out.

Later, when Elizabeth warned him that making false claims to a bank to qualify for a loan was called mortgage fraud, that it was against the law, punishable by up to thirty years of imprisonment, he reasoned with utter sincerity that "whatever it's called, it's good for everyone: the bank gets its unholy interest, Brady makes his commission, and the rest of us invest the money and watch it grow."

Many did invest, but John Vain only spent. This worked out well enough until the fire eliminated part of the collateral against which John Vain had borrowed, and brought attention to his entire portfolio. Suddenly, higher-ups in Bank United's headquarters wanted to see proof of all the riches McPherson had so creatively dreamed of and which John Vain so assuredly swore by.

Alarmed by the prospect of being found out by the bank for his loose lending standards, McPherson cut off the line of credit and asked for repayment of the principal.

"Borrow hard money," he urged. "Sell your house. Whatever it takes, before I lose my license and you go to jail."

John Vain wasn't ready to believe the inventory of doom and gloom that McPherson laid out for him. Nor did he think for a moment that all the heretofore affable and deferential bank employees who had dined free at Lucky 99 and enjoyed a thousand other tokens of John Vain's generosity would suddenly stop answering his calls. It's true he wanted to pay the bank, but it wasn't fear that motivated him to honor his debts as much as shame—the possibility that anyone might doubt his integrity or ethics, or that Elizabeth might see him as less than a successful businessman, that she might lose respect for him, tire of their friendship.

He took every pain to keep the extent of his financial troubles hidden from her; he scrambled to borrow from one bank to pay another and found that the rules had become much more stringent. He tried to borrow from all the friends to whom he had lent or given money over the years, and found most of them unable or unwilling. He put his house on the market and sold it for less than the original purchase price. He sold all his rugs and furniture, his car, his collection of gold watches. He paid the bank as quickly as he could but the total of what he owed never seemed to shrink.

"And it's not just you!" McPherson yelled on the phone till his voice broke. "It's all the loans you brought in, all those forms you had people sign and me fill out. If you default, we're all fucked—you, me, your friends who borrowed from me, all because you were too stupid to have insurance."

Until the recession of 1992, the "old money" people in the exile community expected and received the kind of deference and admiration, the they're-special-because-they-deserve-to-be aura, they had possessed in Iran. Everyone else—the professional and working classes—scurried about to make a living. They were blessed in that they had no public image to conserve, no pretensions to justify. The rich didn't have it so good.

Whether they had left Iran with no money at all, or managed to save some of their assets, the *taaghootis* of yesteryear still had the burden of keeping their *aabehroo* which, in their case, was defined largely by their wealth. The aristocrat who had never worked a day in his life, the child of the ghetto who, under the shah, had worked and sacrificed and risen to unimagined heights, the men and women who had married into money and quickly forgotten that it was someone else's riches they were boasting about—all had the burden, in America, to prove they were still worthy of popular worship.

Before they had established a source of income, many *taaghootis* bought expensive houses and rented penthouse offices. To one-up the competition or keep up with it, they bought second homes and weekend cars, threw lavish parties, sent their kids to private schools and universities. They paid for everything the only way they knew—all cash. And they conducted business the old way as well: on a handshake, or merely by trust, with the other person's *aabehroo* as the main guarantee.

Later, when their cash began to run low, American bankers introduced them to the magic trick called "credit" that enabled them to spend money they didn't have. While the *taaghootis* borrowed and spent and borrowed more, those other Iranians, the middle- and working-class types who had started with little or no capital, who saved and invested like the proverbial bird in winter, emerged as a cash-rich, if not yet socially savvy, outwardly cultured and urbane group.

Among the *taaghootis*, the general impression was that "people you never heard of, whom you would not have trusted to shine your shoes in Iran, have somehow struck gold." In reality, the "gold" was nothing more than the ability to adapt to difficult circumstances, to sacrifice and be patient, expect a great deal of themselves and their children, earn first and spend no more than what you can afford.

So the old money consoled itself with its good name, and learned to reckon with, if not entirely embrace, the new arrivals. Family pedigree or personal reputation be damned, the banks want their money back or they'll foreclose on your house, who cares what the guy did in Iran? That world has died and is not coming back.

This is what Raphael's Son had been waiting for.

Later, when she gave up a promising career in law for the sake of exposing Raphael's Son's perfidy in her supposed book, Angela claimed that the start of the Ponzi scheme dated back to July 1992, two years after the fire at Lucky 99. That is when Raphael's Son, having followed the trajectory of John Vain's misfortune (though some might say he had it coming), hired the first and only employee of R.S. Soleyman Enterprises, with the explicit intent (so Angela believed) of making him a scapegoat for the fraud of the millennium.

When Raphael's Son found him, Eddy Arax had been in the United States for six years, working in gas stations and greasy burger joints and dry-cleaning stores and anywhere that would hire an illegal with his background. A few scuffles a year with random clerks at government offices aside, Eddy was a law-abiding citizen. His extended stay in the country was justified, he believed, because by any reasonable measure, the INS should have given him political asylum and a green card instead of a tourist visa: the wreckage that was Eddy's face was a gift from Saddam Hussein, in one of the many chemical attacks he launched against Iranian soldiers as well as citizens, during the decadelong Iran-Iraq War. Those weapons, the world would later learn, were developed with help from the United States where President Reagan, eager for Iraq to defeat Iran, did not deem the attacks "a matter of strategic concern." If Reagan's government could help Saddam kill a hundred thousand people with mustard gas, Eddy figured, it could also hand out a green card or two to the surviving victims.

He was not a bad tenant of his place of exile, but he was desperate for a white-collar job with regular hours, even if—especially if—he could do the work from home while caring for his mother. And yet, when he received his first and only offer of such a job, Eddy's immediate reaction was to declare that he would rather die with grease stains on his hands than spend an hour working for—Yes sir, some things are not easily overcome, even in America—Muhammad Jadid al-Islam.

They had run into each other at Raffi's—the Persian restaurant in Glendale where Eddy was a busboy and Raphael's Son a very unpopular patron. To be ambushed (as Eddy saw it) by old acquaintances, people who had known him in Iran where he had a respected family and a normal face, was what Eddy dreaded most in LA. To be discovered by someone he had wanted to avoid even in Iran, while he scurried about with piles of dirty dishes in his hands and tomato and kebob stains on his apron, was about as painful an incident as he could fathom.

But to have that same creature offer him a job he needed urgently, and to know this was the only game in town, no one else would hire Eddy, which is why Raphael's Son wanted him—they both knew this . . . Well, sometimes a man must eat the land mine if only to spare himself the agony of living one more day with the fear of his next step being his last.

Raphael's Son had been a thorn in Eddy's side since they were both in elementary school in Tehran and competing for the top prize in the annual exams. Some years, he beat Raphael's Son by half a point in the tests; other years, Raphael's Son robbed Eddy by just as small an advantage. On those occasions Eddy was convinced that the school's administration had granted Raphael's Son a point or two that he didn't deserve, because he was a bastard and the principal felt sorry for him, and also because Eddy was Armenian.

Eddy's father, Rasmik Araxamian, was a bookkeeper for the Metropole Hotel on Vanak Avenue from the day it opened till it closed in the weeks leading up to the revolution in 1979. Rasmik had written all the checks and collected all the revenue, paid off the tax men and the bureaucrats, caught the cheaters and the thieves within the company. In the United States, his position would come with the title of CFO—chief financial officer—and a handsome compensation; in Iran, Rasmik was a lowly *hessab-dar*—keeper of the accounts—a designation that applied to anyone who could use an abacus (and, much later, a basic calculator) and take note of simple financial transactions.

The fact that Rasmik could beat any old calculator in speed and accuracy up to six figures did not afford him the kinds of advantages some take for granted in the West. Nor did it result in an impressive salary. Rasmik's wages never quite kept up with the rate of inflation. Like any white-collar employee with a long history of honest service, he collected certain benefits: the gift of a house when he was ready to get married; a wedding reception paid for by the boss; his children's private school tuition. Still, the real source of glory for a man like Rasmik was not financial: it was in the fact that he had crossed over from his working-class background to the ranks of *daftaris*—office workers—that he presided over a major financial concern, and, most of all, that he was known for his honesty and trustworthiness.

Integrity and honor, Eddy always thought, were the crumbs that remained after the rich had gorged themselves at the feast of prosperity. These, they threw at the help.

* * *

It wasn't just the few fractions of a point that Raphael's Son got un-fairly that Eddy held against him. Over time, the bastard's advantage had come into play in much more significant ways.

In the established social hierarchy of Iran over the centuries, Arme-nians, though considered infidels and outsiders, were ranked slightly higher than Jews but far lower than any Muslim. Then came the shah and the oil money and the Zionist whatever-it-was, and suddenly the Jews who until yesterday had been "untouchable" were lording it over the Armenians. The shah liked them and they adored him in return. They also liked to study, which meant they became doctors and ar-chitects and all those things that a developing country needs and is willing to pay for. Unlike the Armenians, who had a homeland before they were chased out of it, and a language that they insisted on keep-ing alive, the Jews thought of themselves as Iranian. They had been in Persia—and, when the name changed, Iran—for 2,700 years and did not intend to leave. The minute they were given the chance, they were all in a hurry to shed the ghetto and become "integrated" within the larger Iranian society. The Armenians, on the other hand, kept right on counting the days till someone, somehow, gave them back their beloved Armenia.

When the war with Iraq began, the Jews who wished to avoid go-ing to the front had places to escape to—Israel, Europe, the United States. Either that, or they could afford to bribe officials and get their young children off the list of conscripts. The Armenians had to choose between Iran under the mullahs and Armenia in the Soviet Union.

As far as Eddy knew, Raphael's Son had remained Jewish in Iran until the shah fell and most of the rich and powerful Jews took off for the West. The minute power shifted to the mullahs, he dropped the Jewish thing and became a *seyyed*.

Eddy, on the other hand, was given the choice of going to the front or to Evin Prison. When he came back, disfigured and damaged from the war, his father took one look at him and dropped dead on the spot from grief.

At Raffi's that day, Raphael's Son let Eddy have his say, then smirked and threw one of his business cards on the table next to the now-empty plate of kebob and white saffron rice with sumac powder.

"I remember you have a good memory," he said, as if Eddy had not declined the offer. "I'd need you to keep the numbers in your head."

Five months later, having lost his busboy position at Raffi's after one too many altercations with the patrons and the rest of the staff, Eddy called the number on Raphael's Son's business card.

"I figure the only thing worse than working for you is to be homeless and starving with my sick old mother," he said by way of accepting the job offer.

Six dollars an hour, which Raphael's Son explained was really minimum wage if you factored out the taxes Eddy would have had to pay if he were legal. Eddy could work from home "until I find a bigger office. The catch is, I keep the written records; you memorize what I tell you."

Right then, Eddy knew he should back out, hang up the phone, and make a *Will work for food* sign out of a piece of cardboard and go stand on a street corner in Beverly Hills, where the average daily income of panhandlers, a newspaper had recently announced, was $120. He knew he should run away then, and he knew every day for the next two decades, but that's how great mistakes are made, one day at a time.

"So you know," he told Raphael's Son, "I'll let you fuck me in the ass because I don't have a choice, but I won't be a part of anyone else getting raped if I can help it."

His first assignment was to call John Vain.

Raphael's Son was sitting at his desk with his shoes off and his shirt collar unbuttoned when he glanced up and saw a tall man in cowboy boots standing in the doorway. It was nine a.m. on a Wednesday. The Iranian stores on Westwood Boulevard south of Wilshire were just opening, but the restaurants and bookstores and hair and nail salons were still closed. Raphael's Son had come to the office because he had been up since five and feeling restless in his tiny apartment, but he didn't expect visitors. He had the radio on a weather and traffic station and was working on a crossword puzzle in a Persian-language newspaper he had bought at the rose-water-and-pistachio-nut ice cream place down the street. He had left the door open for air, so his first thought was that the cowboy must be looking for some other office. Then the man walked in, extended a hand, and said, "Mr. Soleyman? I'm John Vain," and Raphael's Son thought, *This is how fate comes calling.*

He had heard about John Vain's troubles at the Iranian Orthodox (never mind the term was an oxymoron) temple recently founded by one of the many ambitious young rabbis competing for souls and pocketbooks on the West Side. This rabbi, the son of a well-known gambling and drinking man, had chosen to forget that Iranians were not Hasidic. He went around in a big black hat and long black coat, preached about the sin of drinking nonkosher bottled water during Passover, and had already fathered eleven children and was nowhere near done. Raphael's Son had started to attend his temple after the fiasco at Sinai Temple, and he discovered that the congregation was much more accepting and inclusive. All he had to do was show up at the shul, and even though he clearly had no idea what was going on or how to read the Torah, they liked thinking that a Conservative Jew (you might as well say gentile) had seen the light and was eager to become one of them. They were also much easier to please: a hundred-dollar contribution, scoffed at and disdained in the fancy temples, was appreciated in this storefront-with-plastic-chairs establishment.

Since the fire, John Vain's fortunes had been the subject of much speculation among the more religious Jews who (let's face it, the man never said no to anyone) were concerned that an easy and fertile source of fund-raising might have dried up. The first time he overheard two men talking about it, Raphael's Son blurted out, *"Hagh-eh sheh"*—"He deserves it." When he saw the men's puzzled faces he was tempted to explain, then thought better of it. To admit he had been ridiculed and humiliated by the staff and patrons of Lucky 99, he realized, would only diminish him in the eyes of his new acquaintances. This is what Raphael's Son had learned while his mother dragged him from door to door in search of empathy and justice. For years, he had tried to open her eyes to what was so patent to him—that people liked to identify with the victor; they may feel pity for the wronged, but if given the choice, they would choose to belong to the winning side.

So he didn't explain the cause of his animosity toward John Vain, and thereafter made sure he kept his mouth closed every time he heard mention of him, but privately, he relished the talk of financial ruin and possible prosecution. He even drove by the site of the restaurant a few times, in daylight and at night, just to see the devastation and imagine the hurt it must cause John Vain and, he imagined by extension, Elizabeth. That's why he had Eddy call John Vain.

Raphael's Son was nothing if not a shrewd businessman, and he had spent the better part of his life charting the path to revenge and riches, but it wasn't until he shook John Vain's hand and felt it tremble ever so subtly that day in his office that he knew he could finally put his money to good use.

"I'll lend you any amount you need," he promised John Vain, "and I won't charge more than the banks."

There was only one condition.

She arrived in the midst of a February rainstorm, walked toward him under a slate sky in her faded dress and scuffed shoes, an umbrella mangled by the wind and useless against the rain in her right hand and a manila folder wrapped in a white plastic bag in the left, and for a minute Raphael's Son thought he was going to break down and cry, fall to his knees and thank whatever god had created this moment, let him live long enough and come far enough to see his own and his mother's every prayer answered: the evil young queen of yesterday reduced to a mere supplicant; the irony of the white grocery bag apparently lost on her; the need—her need—to beg for money if only for a friend. But then Elizabeth finished crossing the street and stepped onto the sidewalk that was paved with purple bougainvilleas torn from the vines by the storm, threw the umbrella into a trash can and flung the wet hair away from her face, and by the time her eyes caught his, he knew that the balance of power had not shifted at all; no matter how changed the circumstances, she was still the lord of the castle and he, the tramp at the gates.

It shocked him that he still felt so small before her, that he had spent a lifetime musing about this scene—right here, in front of him, he standing under the awning of the building's entrance and she still in the rain—only to find that the scale had not shifted at all.

She had been to see him once before, barely two hours after he had met with John Vain, just as Raphael's Son was closing the window and getting ready to leave the office. He happened to glance at the street as she fed the meter, and he was so overcome with anxiety, he had to grab on to the frame so he wouldn't keel over. Then he pounced toward the door and locked it from inside, turned the lights off, and pressed himself, barely breathing, against the wall while she knocked for close to three minutes.

Afterward, he told himself he had hidden from her just to prolong her ignominy, make her go back a second time, but he knew that it was fear, old and rusted but embedded in him still, that had made him avoid Elizabeth. He didn't go to the office for the rest of the week, just called the answering machine a few times to check for messages. There weren't any, which disappointed him, if only because he would have liked to know that John Vain and Elizabeth were looking for him.

On Monday morning he decided he had made them wait long enough. As always, he parked his car in the alley behind the building, walked across the street to buy coffee at the 7-Eleven, then doubled back to the office. Under the front awning, he closed and shook his umbrella. He was trying the wipe the paper flowers that lined the sidewalk off the soles of his shoes when he felt a familiar sense of dread, turned, and saw her.

"I'm Elizabeth Soleyman," she said in Persian, as if he didn't know. Her hand was wet from the rain, but she extended it anyway and they shook. She was still in the downpour, soaked to the bone, he imagined, but he couldn't force his body to get out of the way so she could come into the lobby. She waited a few seconds, then squeezed around him and through the door. She threw her hair back again, wiped her dripping face with wet hands.

"I've tried to catch you a few times," she said, still shaking water off. "I thought if I came early enough today . . ." She stopped, gave him a knowing look, and smiled.

Upstairs he unlocked the office, turned on the lights, and invited her in. He might have offered her a towel if he had one, or he might have let her sit there wet and shivering, but she said something about the bathroom and disappeared down the hall. When she came back her face was dry and her hair and dress were damp but not dripping. She sat down in the armchair on the other side of the desk. He still hadn't said a word.

"You wanted to speak to me."

Suddenly, he didn't know why he ever thought he could make her beg. He may be rich now, much richer than she. He may have managed to get her to come begging, albeit for someone else. But he could see that for her, it wasn't a matter trading money for dignity. She wasn't asking for acceptance or legitimacy or love. That's why she had been so quick to respond when Raphael's Son sent word with John Vain: he'd lend the money if Elizabeth asked.

Now she was here and smiling at him, and in a minute she would ask for the money and then it would be over, Raphael's Son would have played out the only hand he ever had.

"I didn't invite you here to talk about money," he heard himself say. He realized that the phone was ringing, had been ringing for some time, but he ignored it till the machine picked up. He lifted a pencil from the desk, turned it over in his hands and examined it, then said, "I have something I believe you'd like to know."

She frowned slightly and narrowed her eyes, cocked her head to the side as if to understand him better. He turned the pencil like a windmill between his index and middle fingers, but his eyes didn't leave her face.

"I believe it's important to you."

Suddenly, her face went pale. Her eyes, so neutral, like yellow glass, darkened with what he hoped was anxiety.

Raphael's Son swallowed the bile that had filled his mouth. If he couldn't get the satisfaction of watching her debase herself, he was going to make sure she didn't leave unharmed.

He threw the pencil onto the desk, pushed back in his chair with his fingertips on the edge, and said, "You wanna know how your kid died?"

The young maid they had recently hired, a girl from Manzel's hometown, had let Raphael's Wife into the house.

Elizabeth remembered the girl—fifteen years old according to her birth certificate, though there was no telling whether the information was correct. She had light-green eyes against white skin—a beautiful face if you saw it wrapped in a chador—which is why Manzel had chosen her as a bride for her oldest son, paid the milk-money and bought the bus ticket to have her sent to Tehran. Manzel and her husband might be lowly servants in the capital, but in the eyes of their townspeople up north they were nothing short of aristocracy: they had a house and a car and two sons who went to university and worked in offices.

The girl's family had been more than eager for the union to take place. They married remotely—a mullah performing the ceremony on her end—and Manzel rented a one-bedroom apartment for them on the Avenue of the Tulips.

At the bus depot in her white chintz chador, the bride was just as ravishing as everyone expected. She was also very shy; she didn't make eye contact and wouldn't let a strand of hair or a millimeter of skin show except her face, which was a good sign; it meant she was pure and obedient and easily trained. When they arrived at Manzel's house for the family's first meal together, she kept her chador on even in the women's room. Later, when it was just she and the groom, he insisted on seeing her unveiled, even took off the first layer of her clothes to examine her more closely, but there was no convincing her to let him see her hair—she had worn a head scarf under the chador, and this she wasn't willing to shed.

For two days, Manzel's daughter-in-law kept her head covered. On her third night in Tehran, she took off the scarf and stood before her husband and his mother—green-eyed and fair-complexioned and entirely, unmistakably, bald.

The marriage was automatically annulled because the bride's family had misrepresented her qualifications. Manzel's son wanted to ship the girl back to her parents but she begged to be allowed to stay. She would rather die on a street in Tehran than endure the humiliation before her family and their neighbors. They were all seething with envy over her union, she said as she threw herself at Manzel's feet, counting the minutes till the groom saw just how defective she was and chucked her out.

Manzel *khanum* knew what it was like to be fundamentally defective and beyond repair. She too had married a man who had no idea she was mute and didn't find out for nearly a week. But for the fact that Manzel had a stable job and that her employers had agreed to hire him as well, her own husband would have returned her and asked for a refund the minute her secret was revealed.

She didn't have the heart to send the bald girl back, so she took her to Bagh-e Yaas instead.

"I'll be happy to work just for food and a place to sleep," the girl begged, but Elizabeth wasn't interested in taking on a slave. She gave the girl Manzel's old room and a salary, sent her to school, and insisted that she complete her homework before tending to household chores.

"I don't know how my mother got her to help," Raphael's Son answered the question he could see dawning in Elizabeth's eyes. "I don't think the girl hated you. I think she wanted to hit back at Manzel."

He thought for a moment, then laughed bitterly.

"Isn't it stupid? To think you can hurt a servant by taking away the spoiled little runt she has to care for instead of her own kids?"

They were sitting at eye level on either side of the desk. Without seeing Elizabeth's hands, Raphael's Son could tell that they were shaking on her lap and that her knees were trembling too, that between anger and anticipation, hatred and elation, her soul was stretched and tormented to the limit.

"Because of you," he told her, "my mother had to work nights in a hospital. She washed floors and emptied chamber pots, and when she came home she smelled of blood and shit and illness. Every once in a while, she'd see women in the maternity ward whose child was stillborn or died soon after birth. She couldn't get over how devastated these women were, like it was the worst thing that could happen to a person."

He paused, then added, "Or so they thought. I guess there are worse things," he chuckled, "like not knowing if the kid's dead or alive.

"One night, a mother and child were brought in after an accident. They'd been on the sidewalk outside their house, down near Telegraph Avenue, and some rich kid in a lime-green BMW drove right into them. He was barely eighteen years old, didn't have a driver's license—but since when does that stop anyone from driving?—and when he saw what he'd done, he backed up and tried to escape but people blocked his way forward and back, dragged him out of the car. He'd had a fight with his dad, he said. He was driving fast to blow off steam.

"They called the cops to come arrest the brat, but his father arrived with some colonel or sergeant or other piece of filth from the army, and they just took the kid away and had his car towed and that was it. The woman he'd hit survived, but her child died of her injuries. The driver's parents sent him away." Raphael's Son chuckled again. "He's probably right here, in LA. Maybe he's a doctor. His family sent a messenger to the hospital with a bagful of cash—a gift, the guy said, for the woman's 'troubles.'"

To his astonishment, he saw that Elizabeth was crying. She must know how this story ends, he thought.

"My mother would clean after the woman every night. She asked her how she'd like to make up for her dead daughter. One rich asshole had taken the kid from her; why not have another rich asshole," he stopped, tipped his head toward Elizabeth, "that would be you—pay with her own child's life?"

He felt a surge of wild, brutal emotion about to blow his chest open. He trained his eyes on the newspaper on the desk, tried to slow his heartbeat and quiet the pain in his temples.

"*You* made her into this," he mumbled. Then he stood up and leaned forward over the desk, let out a howl that stunned them both. "You!"

He saw Elizabeth then and realized he had gotten his wish: hit at the weakest spot and made her splinter and bleed.

"The bald maid unlocked the door after you went to sleep. My mother wasn't going to kill your little shit. She was supposed to fill in for the dead kid. But she choked on the rag, so they threw her away."

Only a handful of years earlier, they might have been able to verify at least parts of the story. Elizabeth or Angela could have called Manzel and her husband, asked them to go back to the hospital where Raphael's Wife had worked and see if anyone remembered an accident victim who lost a child. She would have been noted not so much because of her injuries as the cause of them: the son of a prominent family, a lime-green BMW. Of course the driver would evade justice. In this country, at this time . . . If they hadn't been killed by the mullahs, the driver and his family would be living in the West, stripped of their titles and status and the unstated law that the mighty are held accountable only to those more powerful than they. Most likely, they wouldn't own up to the truth even if Elizabeth found them.

For three years after she left Iran, Elizabeth had wired money to Manzel every month. The Iranian rial had crashed so badly that a few dollars went a long way—even with all the shortages of food and gas and other basic commodities. Then the bombing of Tehran began, entire swaths of the city were leveled, and families were dislocated for good. Children were dragged off from behind their desks at school, put on buses headed for the front, and chained together as human shields. Some escaped the country by land and vanished outside its borders. Most ended up in one of the makeshift martyrs' cemeteries that had become commonplace in Tehran, lying full of holes or in pieces under colored lights, green and black Islamic banners, and handwritten signs congratulating their parents.

One day Elizabeth realized that the money she wired was not being claimed at the other end. Someone who knew someone who had heard of Seyyed Mojtaba seemed to recall that he had fallen victim to the internal struggle for power within the clergy, sided with the wrong faction, and been stripped of his rank in the Sepah-e Pasdaran. He had had to evacuate Bagh-e Yaas, and move in with one of his wives' families. He slept with a dozen machine guns and a cache of explosives under his bed, and was convinced that his old comrades were coming to kill him on some mullah's orders. He was last seen naked in a mortuary near Yazd, his body riddled with bullets and his neck broken by a former ally's boot. His parents could not claim his body or have him buried for fear of being identified as equally seditious.

That's the last Elizabeth and Angela heard about Manzel and her family. Without them to investigate Raphael's Son's claims, Elizabeth had only her instincts and common sense to draw from. She decided the story was ugly enough, Raphael's Son's delivery of it bitter enough, for it all to be true.

aphael's Son never took John Vain's calls or agreed to see him after the encounter with Elizabeth. He told her as much before she left—that he had no intention of helping any friend of hers—though he wasn't sure she heard him or cared.

He made a point of walking behind her down the narrow, dark staircase. Outside, the rain had thickened, and now there was a low fog, so that he couldn't see from the edge of the sidewalk past the double yellow lines in the middle of the street. He wondered if Elizabeth might get hit by a car as she tried to navigate the crosswalk. He hoped she wouldn't, that she would have time to feel the full impact of what he had told her.

Without the loan Raphael's Son had promised, John Vain scrambled to find a new source of income. At first, he tried to persuade his old pals and patrons to enter into a partnership ("You put up the money, I'll do all the work, you get 70 percent") for a new restaurant. As chagrined as they were by the change in his circumstances, and as much as they wished him well and hoped he would recapture the old glory so they, too, could bask in its light, these people knew better than anyone just what a lousy businessman John Vain really was. They had been the beneficiaries of his famous generosity for too long to believe it would ever change or yield a different consequence.

He took a job as a maître d' at Jimmy's in Beverly Hills, but he was too proud to accept tips and therefore made nothing beyond minimum wage. He had been staying at the Chateau Marmont on a monthly rate, but now he couldn't make ends meet so he moved into a ground-floor apartment off Los Feliz Boulevard near Western. All around him were XXX movie theaters and seedy bars and male and female prostitutes—the down-and-outs of Los Angeles with whom John Vain had always felt at home. He had just started as a barback at Musso and Frank when McPherson called with news: he had made a deal with the feds, given up his mortgage broker's license, and agreed to pay $500,000 in fines. He was moving to Tennessee, where he had

family and taxes were low. He was thinking he'd go into the God business and become a preacher like his famous kin, the evangelist Aimee
Semple McPherson.

"As for you, my friend," Brady told John Vain in a voice that already suggested Father knows best, we must bend to His will, "you're
about to be sued for fraud by Bank United, the FDIC, and the FBI."

On January 2, 1994, John Vain was sentenced to thirteen years at the federal prison in Lompoc. Before he turned himself in, he wrote a letter to Elizabeth and Angela. In it, he said that for him, the hardest part of what had happened would be "to know that I have let you down. I proved myself unworthy of your friendship, and for this I'm sorry beyond words." Then he made a promise and a request.

The promise was that he would take himself as completely out of their lives as possible, "so that my shortcomings will not smear your good name."

The request was that "should you be tempted, out of pity or graciousness, to visit me in my soon-to-be surroundings, you spare me this final humiliation."

Elizabeth understood. She never tried to see John Vain in prison, but she wrote to him every Saturday for as long as he was incarcerated and signed each letter, *Hoping we'll see each other soon. Your friend, Elizabeth.*

Angela, who was away at Princeton, felt betrayed.

She was already angry at John Vain for his recklessness, and she also blamed Elizabeth for not leaning harder on him to insure the restaurant and set his financial affairs in order. That's what he had hired her to do, after all, even if it was a pity hiring. He trusted her and relied on her and all she gave him in return were a few (okay, more than a few) warnings. She should have pressed the point till he took action. Instead, she wrote notes and gave verbal reports, copied relevant sections of the small print on the back of loan applications from Bank United and left them, circled, on John Vain's desk, brought it up when he came by for a social visit, which, to Angela, "basically means you dropped the ball."

Even then, Angela thought she knew better than everyone else.

She had flown in from New Jersey for John Vain's sentencing, and she decided after ten minutes that the public defender who represented him was incompetent and uncaring. She was a senior in college, majoring in English because she wanted to be a reporter for CNN, "a Jewish Christiane Amanpour with a better haircut," she explained to Nilou. Amanpour had achieved international stardom three years earlier because of her coverage of the first Gulf War when Saddam invaded Kuwait. Physically, she bore a definite resemblance to Angela: they were both tall and big-boned, with booming voices that were a few notches too loud. And they both spoke with a great deal of authority on subjects in which they had no real expertise.

Angela had already done a three-month internship at CNN in Atlanta at the end of her junior year, and she was prepared to go back and work for below living wages if they'd have her, but she was so outraged by the shabby representation John Vain received from his court-appointed attorney, so certain after that experience that the legal system was skewed in favor of the rich, she went back to Princeton and signed up for the LSAT. She had had a full scholarship for Princeton; for law school, she took out a loan.

She would remind people of this later, when Elizabeth became the wealthiest individual (as opposed to family) among Iranian Jews, and people forgot that she had not always been rich, that she and Angela had struggled for years, bought groceries from Lebanese- and Iranian-owned shops because the prices were lower, and clothes from Goodwill or National Council of Jewish Women's thrift stores; that Angela and Nilou shared all their textbooks, then passed them down to Neda; that Zeeba and Elizabeth shared a car. But that wasn't the hard part of being poor.

After the first couple of years when she depended on John Vain's generosity and good references for an income, Elizabeth had taken a job with a Korean import business in Toy Town on 5th Street. She worked twelve-hour days as warehouse supervisor, keeping track of every ten-cent fire truck and twenty-five-cent princess gown and tiara from the moment it arrived from overseas till it was sold and delivered to the retail shops up and down the district. The warehouse was dusty and windowless and without heating or air-conditioning. She only took breaks if there was time, and ate standing up most days, but she kept the job because her bosses realized she did three people's work for the price of one. She took no vacations, and asked for a half-day off only when she had to go to Angela's school for parent-teacher conferences.

The hard part of being poor, Angela would later remind people if they tried to suggest that she had had it easy growing up, was the time she spent away from Elizabeth while she worked in Toy Town. It was having to turn to Zeeba, not her own mother, for the kinds of emotional comfort most children get from a parent.

Even harder than that was having to lose John Vain without being able to do a thing about it, because neither she nor Elizabeth had money to lend to him or with which to hire a private attorney for him.

"We let him down," she told Elizabeth, "and now, he's abandoned us."

N o sooner had John Vain disappeared from their lives than Zeeba Raiis got her husband back.

In 1982, Dr. Raiis had been spared a summary execution through the interference of Muhammad Jadid al-Islam, who took $50,000 from Zeeba's brothers in Iran to arrange Dr. Raiis's release, then reneged and asked for an additional $30,000. He waited ten days after the doctor was freed, then went to the authorities and pointed him out as one who had gotten away. Many a broken rib and $120,000 later, Dr. Raiis was returned to the empty apartment where he would linger for the next five years.

He had to wait until 1989, when the war with Iraq ended and the regime, reeling from its losses, turned its attention inward and away from so-called antirevolution, anti-Islam, anti-God-and-country *taaghootis*, to be allowed to leave the country on a thirty-day visa. Even then, he didn't go to Los Angeles because he couldn't face his family. Emotionally ravaged and physically impoverished, he didn't think he would survive the first hour with Zeeba, or the encounter with his children. He knew that Zeeba worked part-time as a teacher's aide in a Santa Monica preschool, that the children had weekend and after-school jobs, that they all lived in a rundown apartment on the edge of Beverly Hills so the kids could go to the schools, and that they had no health insurance.

What did he—the man, the provider, the head of the family—have to say by way of justifying the decisions he had made and that had brought them all to this point?

His best friend from medical school, who had left Iran in 1978, was chief of surgery at Emory Hospital in Atlanta; the friend's wife, also Iranian, was a professor at the university. Together they had promised they would do everything in their power to help Dr. Raiis start a practice or find work in the medical field. He went to them first.

He failed the board licensing exam twice in Atlanta, then followed another friend to New York and failed there. He failed the exam in Baltimore, Ann Arbor, and Chicago—all cities where his former colleagues had reestablished themselves in major hospitals and research centers while he—recipient of the medal of honor from Her Majesty, Empress Farah Pahlavi, for selfless service to the country—couldn't get so much as a license to practice. In Iran, he had been the top of his class every year, recognized as the smartest and the most deserving of success. In America, he was only as good as a test score.

Take away a man's faith in what he has known to be true, Dr. Raiis's friends whispered outside of his earshot, and what you'll have is a cold clod of earth where no new life will grow.

In 1994 he arrived in Los Angeles played out and defeated. Like so many other men who were forced into early retirement by the revolution, who became strangers to their children through cultural displacement and dependent on their wives for their livelihood, he might have shrunk physically and emotionally a little more every day, become a fixture that his family would step around on their way out the door.

But this was America—home of second acts, never mind it hadn't turned out that way for Dr. Raiis. He was damned if he'd let himself become a burden on anyone.

He took a job at Benny Produce, a hole-in-the-wall Iranian grocery store next to Pico Cleaners (environmentally friendly, delivery available seven days a week, and the owners speak Persian, French, and Italian). His coworkers were a pair of teenage boys from El Salvador who didn't know a word of English but got by just fine in Persian. Dr. Raiis made a point of greeting them every day with utmost respect and formality. He did the same with the customers who knew him from Iran, shaking hands and inquiring about the health of their children, and explaining—though no one asked—that he was here because the barriers to entry into the medical profession were impossibly high, and the system was slanted toward the young and the native English speaker, even if they didn't have a tenth of his experience or expertise, and had never even heard of, much less diagnosed or treated, the kinds of illnesses he had identified and cured over the course of his own career. He was here, at Benny Produce, because he wasn't ashamed of hard work, wasn't about to become a liability to his wife and daughters.

Customers who remembered the days when Dr. Raiis had saved

children's lives and received royal commendations tried very hard to disguise their shock and pity every time they ran into him at Benny. Old friends who saw him waiting for the bus pulled over in their expensive German cars and pretended this was all very normal—a brilliant physician in a formal suit taking the bus to a small strip mall where he would spend the day stacking boxes of fresh coriander and fenugreek. Who says only the down-and-out take the bus in LA?

They would drop him off at his destination and drive away, still pretending there was nothing wrong with this picture until he had disappeared in their rearview mirrors and they could let out a sigh, weigh the extent of the tragedy, and know that, but for the grace of God, this could have been their own fate.

Even the prison guards, who had seen a strange person or two in their time, couldn't stop staring at Hal Zemorrodi when he came to visit John Vain. He arrived in the shape of a tall, skinny man with olive skin, loose dentures, and not a strand of hair visible on his face or body. His eyeglasses were so smeared with fingerprints that it was a wonder he could see through them at all. He addressed everyone as sir and ma'am as if at a White House diplomatic dinner, carried himself like a physics professor who happened to have submerged his hands in motor oil for a decade or two. He told the guard who accompanied him to the visiting room that he had driven for six days straight all the way from New York, sleeping only three hours a night, just to see "one of my two oldest and dearest friends." While he waited for John Vain in the visiting room, he sat with his knees crossed and his jacket buttoned up, staring at the metal door through which the prisoners walked in. When he finally saw John Vain emerge, he sprang up so that the chair toppled over behind him, took three long steps with his arms wide open, wrapped them around John Vain, and started to sob like a grieving mother.

"I should never have left you," he kept saying through the cascade of tears and saliva. "It's my fault you're here."

The night he left Lucky 99 for good, Hal drove to the first freeway on-ramp he came upon, and kept driving till he ran out of gas. The next morning he sold his car to the owner of a gas station and used the money to buy a bus ticket that would take him across the country till he ran out of land.

He was desperate to forget not only his failed invention but everything he had ever known about science and engineering and all the lies he had been taught in school or had told himself since.

"I wanted so much to lose the ambition, and instead aspire to what I'm capable of reaching," he confessed to John Vain. "I think I might have done it, accepted my limitations, at least in part, enough to be able to sleep through a night without waking up to go through the numbers in my head."

Then he paused, sucked his lips into his mouth, and scrutinized John Vain's face. He had lost weight—at least twenty pounds—since they last saw each other. He seemed like a man who'd been stripped of his soul and handed something ill-fitting and defective. But he still had the old kindness, the extraordinary empathy, the fatal innocence.

"I can tell you this because I know you'll understand," Hal said, measuring each word. He threw a surreptitious look at the guard who had been watching him since he arrived, leaned a few inches forward, and lowered his voice. "She wouldn't let me."

They were sitting in a bare, badly lit room with cement walls and bulletproof windows, in a gray building in the middle of a compound built of concrete and metal, surrounded by a vast, empty plain and, beyond it, long, empty highways. They were there because they had believed, each in his own way, too much in their own fantasies. Yet like a mechanical brain in a science fiction film, Hal had chased John Vain to Lompoc, only to share with him yet another tall tale: "she" was Elizabeth.

There he was, in 1982, asleep in a sweaty, unwashed Amtrak car through Texas, when the entire cabin was inundated by the smell of the sea as if Elizabeth herself had walked in. It was a rainy night and Hal had been dreaming of his charts, so he told himself he had imagined the scent and went back to sleep.

There he was again, in Colorado, Philadelphia, Maryland, when every rain brought with it the scent of Elizabeth. Not as though she was chasing him or even reaching out; she was just there, like a fixture on the landscape of his consciousness, at once removed and immovable—a slight, quiet silhouette that nevertheless reflected all that Hal had first cherished and was now trying to leave. It reminded him of his childhood home that had been demolished in the war, his parents who had died without seeing him one more time, his youthful friendship with the strange Jewish girl no one else understood, the nights of flowers and caviar and beautiful women who tossed their hair back when they laughed in Lucky 99, the dream of creation.

The farther he went, the more present the scent became.

In the visitation room at Lompoc, the guards stared at John Vain and

Hal as if expecting an unpleasant surprise. The youngest one, who had walked Hal in from the check-in desk, put a hand on the holster of his gun and looked ready to pounce on the two men in case one of them moved to detonate a hidden bomb or throw a teargas grenade. It's true that, it being a minimum-security prison, the guards at Lompoc were starved for action. Still, while neither Hal nor John Vain would have struck any reasonable person as the break-out-of-Alcatraz type, there was something unusually charged and frenetic about Hal's speech and movements, like a person who has seen Mary, mother of Christ, walk off a billboard on Sunset Strip and cross the street dressed only in a halo.

John Vain himself had encountered quite a few of those types at Lucky 99. They usually turned up around one a.m. on Saturdays and often had to be sent home in a cab because they didn't remember where they had left their car or if they even had one. Most of them had drifted out of some club—the Rainbow, or Whiskey—after snorting one too many lines of powder in the bathroom. A few were genuine lunatics who could afford their fantasies thanks to generous trust funds. One or two really had seen a naked woman crossing the street and mistaken her for the Holy Mother.

John Vain had made sure that the "visionary" strays who turned to him for refuge were well fed and sufficiently hydrated. Sometimes, he drove them to an emergency room for a quick detox or a seventy-two-hour hold; at other times, he paid for the taxi ride. The way he saw it, a man was entitled to his delusions no matter what the reality. Maybe that's why he believed Hal's story now.

For years after Hal disappeared, Elizabeth had struggled alone with the blueprints for his heat-detecting radar. She told John Vain she blamed herself for depriving Hal of his one great love. She had thought she was helping him find the way; she had not expected him to abandon the project and his life in LA altogether. In the beginning, she wanted to keep the idea alive for when Hal came back to reclaim it. After a few months, when he couldn't be found and the police wouldn't classify him as a missing person and therefore initiate a real search, she felt she owed it to Hal's legacy if he were dead or to his memory if he were alive to make something of his life's work. Before she knew it, she was sucked in and entangled in the task of solving the puzzle just because it was there.

One day in 1989, she had called John Vain much too early in the morning and announced, in that bright voice of hers that made him quiver every time he heard it, "Hal was right; it can be done."

John Vain wanted to tell Hal that he knew about that scent because it haunted him as well, swept into his 8' x 10' cell with every rain, and filled him, once again, with joy. Instead, he dropped his hands between his legs and hunched over as if in pain, tried to keep his voice from breaking, and said, "She's been waiting for you. She has something you'll want to see."

Neda was nineteen years old, a freshman at Berkeley, when Raphael's Son picked her out from a pool of unfortunates who might become his wife.

He had been thinking about marriage for some time, not because he particularly wanted a family or cared about becoming a father, but because it—marriage—would be a good way for him to make inroads into the community. He did like women, especially tall, flat-chested ones, which ruled out most Iranian girls and, in LA (home of DDD bra sizes courtesy of some silicone manufacturer) also ruled out most Americans. In the beginning, when he had just arrived and was living in Westwood, he had neither the courage nor the social skills to approach any female. His mouth went dry and his heart shrank every time he walked by an attractive woman or even saw one on TV. Often, he would go into department stores at the Century City mall and just linger on the cosmetics or jewelry floors, pretending to look for a gift when all he wanted was to stand close to the painted and perfumed sales girls.

He got a much warmer reception from them than he did from their mostly gay, cruelly disapproving male counterparts in the men's section. He realized women liked a man who shopped for gifts; they judged him by how fondly he spoke of his fictional girlfriend or how eagerly he spent his money. Still, he had no idea how to express interest in any of them or what he would do when they rejected him. The truth was, the only women he had ever had sex with or even kissed were professionals who made the first move and were happy to offer as many compliments and as much affirmation as he paid for. In Iran, he had started with the prostitutes in Shahr-eh No—New Town—and graduated to more mainstream types after the revolution when all the hookers became "temporary wives." He never "married" anyone for longer than two hours, and never contemplated taking a permanent wife who might be an encumbrance in America.

But the loneliness began to get him.

It was one thing, in 1987 when he was twenty-four and recently off the boat, overwhelmed with just the effort of getting his bearings in the United States and enlivened by the prospect of launching his campaign of vengeance against Elizabeth. Back then, when he went entire days without really speaking to anyone, ate all his meals alone, and stared at the phone till his eyes watered, he told himself that the isolation was temporary. In the early '90s, when he still had no friends, he decided to impress people into liking him by making a bigger show of his wealth. He bought a two-bedroom house on Burk Place in Trousdale, joined Sinai Temple, and made the rounds at the Bistro Garden every Friday for lunch and Morton's every Saturday night.

He might as well have been the Invisible Man.

It wasn't just women who reacted to him as if he had a *Do Not Approach* sign on his forehead, not just Iranians who looked right through him without blinking. It didn't matter how generously he tipped the waiter, how warmly he greeted his next-door neighbor. He remained as irrelevant as he had been in childhood.

He gave up the office in Westwood and rented a much nicer one in Century City, began to insist that Eddy Arax show up to work "like a real employee" every day. He went to every public function in the community, handed out business cards like Halloween candy. He would suggest lunch or dinner to near strangers; joined the Sports Club LA on Sepulveda. Still, he found himself standing alone in movie lines, asking for tables for one at restaurants, being locked out and overlooked. He had blown past thirty and was watching his hairline recede and his waistline expand. So he undertook the two most effective, albeit costly measures available to a man of means who wishes to be liked: give to charity and get married.

He figured Neda was unpopular enough to have to settle for whomever would have her. And that she was dumb enough not to question his decisions for their life together. She came from a family with a great deal of *aabehroo* but no money, so it would be an even exchange—Raphael's Son would get the benefit of their good name, and the Raiises would see their daughter live comfortably.

He found Neda when she was alone and out of the range of her family's influence. It was January 1996, and she had just driven back from LA to start her second semester at school. In Berkeley she went into Langer's, the coffee shop where all the students gathered, bought a cup of coffee and a bagel for lunch. The place was nearly empty but she sat in the farthest corner anyway, at a small table next to the wall, away from the window and the traffic of customers. She had been at school for nearly four months without making a single friend. She felt exposed when she was out in public alone, so she made herself busy by balancing her checkbook.

A man walked toward her. She kept her eyes glued to the table in hopes that he would walk past her.

"I heard you were going to school here."

She sensed danger, didn't know if she should peer up or pretend she hadn't heard him, so she kept busy with the checkbook.

"I was hoping we'd run into each other."

For an instant, she thought she knew the voice.

"Soleyman," he extended a puffy hand. "R.S. Soleyman."

He smiled when she shook his hand—a soft, quiet smile, not threatening or invasive. He wore wire-rimmed glasses and a dress shirt with the two top buttons open, a leather jacket that tried very much to be elegant, and he was holding a small man-purse in his left hand.

"It's a pleasure."

Out of nowhere, he brought her hand to his lips and kissed the backs of her fingers.

Neda felt herself turn ice-cold from head to toe. She watched as he pulled a chair from a neighboring table and sat down, turned to the girl behind the counter, and said, "Hot tea," like he was in a teahouse in Tehran. He must not know he has to order and pay at the counter, Neda thought.

"I've been hoping to meet you," he said as if was the most natural thing in the world. "You're prettier than I had heard."

She looked down to hide her eyes. Her mind was blank and her heart felt like it was about to pump its last drop of blood and it was all she could do to stop herself from pushing the table back and running away.

She knew who he was. She recognized the name as soon as he said it, remembered all the talk, at home and outside, about his doings. She was almost sure he was the man who had extorted money from her family to help get Dr. Raiis out of prison alive, after he—Raphael's Son—had put him there. But these were all stories she had heard about a person she didn't know and a place—a country and a time—she had no active memory of.

For a long time, only he spoke. He talked about LA and San Francisco, his drive up there, his travels through California in search of property and land to buy. He was smart enough to be able to hide his lack of education for a time, but then he slipped and said something about Berkeley being a two-year college, like that other one in Santa Monica, and she realized he didn't know the difference, so when he asked why she had chosen Berkeley over SMC, she shrugged and said she wasn't sure. She did that to avoid embarrassing him, but he would hate her for it anyway some months later, when she had to explain to him that only a four-year college, as opposed to two-year community colleges, conferred bachelor degrees.

She didn't know what time it was when they finally left the café, but it was dark out and she didn't have a coat, so he took off his jacket and put it around her despite her protestations. The parking meter had run out and she had gotten a ticket even though it was technically a holiday. He took the ticket and said that he'd take care of it, that it was his fault she forgot to feed the meter. He asked where she was headed.

"My dorm."

He studied her face.

"Let me take you to dinner."

She was nineteen years old and thought she was going to be alone forever.

He was staying at the St. Francis hotel in the city. They had dinner in the formal dining room. He ordered wine, got up when she stood to go to the bathroom, told her she looked cute in her "hippie student clothes." He asked if she wanted to see his room.

Afterward, he asked if she'd like him to leave so she could have privacy and she said yes, she thought that would be best. She was still half dressed and her legs were stained with blood and so was the bedcover, which she dragged into the bathroom and washed by hand in the tub. She washed everything, washed herself, then sat on the soft armchair and held her knees and stared at CNN on the television all night. In the morning, she left at the first light. She couldn't face him again and didn't want to be reminded of what had happened.

She hadn't given him her phone number but he found it anyway and called three times in one day. She didn't pick up.

"I want to see you, my dear," he said in the first two messages. In the third one, he left his phone number in LA.

In the evening, a giant flower arrangement was delivered to the dorm lobby. It was so large, Neda couldn't carry it to her room and wouldn't have had the space for it anyway, so it stayed in the lobby where everyone who passed through stopped to look at it. She called to thank him; they stayed on the phone for an hour and twenty minutes.

He called her every night after that, sent her expensive gifts, letters and cards and stuffed animals bearing sweet messages. He never once mentioned the family connection or appeared in the least bit hostile.

"What do you want more than anything else in the world?" he asked one night, and she said, "I want children who love me."

The first time she missed her period she told herself that intercourse must have disturbed her cycle. She ignored the headaches and the sleepiness, the increased appetite. The second time she missed her period, she waited two weeks then went to the clinic on campus. She started to sob when the nurse gave her the news. Yes, yes, she wanted to have an abortion. She made an appointment for two days later, went back to her dorm, and crawled into bed. She knew there was no way she could tell her parents. She thought about calling Nilou or Angela, but didn't have the heart. She wasn't close to her roommate and wouldn't ordinarily have confided in her, but she was terrified and confused so she asked the girl if she'd ever had an abortion.

"No, because I'm not stupid enough to get pregnant."

That night when he called, Neda broke into tears and told him.

There was never a question, for Neda, of them getting married. She didn't tell him about the pregnancy so much as about the intended abortion, how she hated herself for the violence she felt she was about to commit, how ashamed she was of her own mindlessness.

The night at the St. Francis, she hadn't been overcome by lust or passion so much as found herself in a situation she didn't know how to get out of. She had liked the attention he gave her at Langer's and over dinner, and she even felt a small thrill when they rode up in the elevator together and he put his hand under her T-shirt and touched her breast. Then it was a matter of civility, of showing gratitude for his advances and feeling she might offend him or make him angry if she asked him to stop.

He could have been anyone—a total stranger or her family's best friend—and she still wouldn't have felt anything but flattered by his phone calls and gifts. As much as she abhorred the thought of ending a pregnancy, it never occurred to her that there was a choice.

So when he showed up the next morning in the lobby of her dorm with two dozen red roses and a permanent grin across the bottom half of his face, Neda had the sense that something calamitous was about to take place.

"I got into my car and started driving the minute we hung up," he said, breathless with enthusiasm. "I'm going to take you out and buy the biggest diamond in any store you choose."

She didn't want a diamond. Or the roses. Or Raphael's Son's gallantry. She was going to have the abortion and stay in school, keep away from him and other men, make something of herself the way Angela and Nilou were determined to do.

They argued. He pleaded with her. She cried. They were sitting in his car outside the Amoeba Music store on Telegraph Avenue. A steady stream of young people went in and out the doors. Neda couldn't hear what they said to each other but she could see they were holding hands, excitedly examining the CD covers they had just bought. All but a handful of them must have been her age or older, yet she found herself envying their youth.

She wasn't ready, she told him, to give up the dream of being one of those people. It was her last word, she said. Her decision was made.

Behind the wheel, Raphael's Son stared at the dashboard as if entranced by the red and white glow-in-the-dark hands on the dial.

"Marry me," he said from a thousand miles away, "or I'll tell everyone in LA what happened between us and leave you no shred of *aabehroo.*"

The year 1996 was not a time for pregnant brides, unwed mothers, and divorced wives in the Iranian community. The old societal rules might have been altered or amended to some extent, but they had not been savaged or ignored—yet—by the unrooted and unbelieving. That would come later, in the late 2000s and thereafter. Women would leave their husbands, demand half his money, primary custody, and generous child support. Sons would out themselves to parents, even marry lovers, and expect to be embraced and honored. Daughters would refuse to marry just to avoid becoming old maids; if they wanted children, they went to a sperm bank. Respect would be something that old people owed the young; obedience would mean enslavement. And while a few men and women—mostly women— would celebrate the wanton decadence as "progress," many others would take refuge from it in religious orthodoxy. Suddenly, Mizrahi Jews who had worshipped a certain way would take on the habits and beliefs of Ashkenazim. Iranian Jewish women would don wigs and stop wearing pants, refuse to eat even at their parents' house because the food wasn't kosher enough, insist that their daughter marry right out of high school and start having children. The men would wear black hats and long black coats, grow beards, and even refrain from shaking hands with their grandmothers. None of that, however, was visible on the horizon in 1996.

Neda went home and told her parents she was pregnant and was going to marry the father. Zeeba cried and swore she wouldn't survive one more disappointment. Dr. Raiis dropped his head and went into their bedroom, to cry alone. Only then did they ask who the father might be.

Muhammad Jadid al-Islam, the same man who had blackmailed and betrayed Dr. Raiis, bled him dry of money and caused him to endure torture. R.S. Soleyman, who had broken Elizabeth's heart by telling her how Noor died, later boasted of having led John Vain to water, then kicked him in the balls. Raphael's Son, who had begged and demanded and tried to steal respectability and was finally going to get a measure of it by leaching off the one good thing—the name—that life had allowed Dr. Raiis to keep.

He told Neda they could skip the traditional commitment party at which the bride's parents formally promise her to the groom by handing him a bowl of sweets, and that he would even forgo an engagement party because "these are affairs that must be hosted by the bride's parents, and yours are impecunious; I'd be embarrassed if my guests saw their house, or knew that my wife's father is a clerk at a grocery store." But he wasn't about to let go of the opportunity to announce his victory to the public.

He rented the main ballroom at the Beverly Hilton Hotel (capacity 1,200; home of the Academy Awards, the Golden Globes, Grammys, and the Carousel of Hope ball) for a Thursday night, drew up a list of everyone he knew in Los Angeles, Tehran, and Tel Aviv, and a wrote a script: "Mr. R.S. Soleyman, son of the late Mr. and Mrs. Raphael Soleyman, requests the honor of your presence at the celebration of his marriage to Miss Neda Raiis, daughter of Dr. and Mrs. Raiis."

He handed the script to Eddy Arax along with 1,100 names, and told him to start calling.

The problem was that half the people on the list didn't know who Raphael's Son was, and the other half, who did know him, wouldn't dream of slumming it at any function he hosted. It didn't help that Eddy Arax read from the script with all the conviction and exuberance of a pharmacy clerk reciting the scare sheet from a box of experimental pills. Or that, when asked about "the lucky bride," he answered in all earnestness, "I'd say she'd be luckier to run into a cement truck." Then there were other questions Eddy had no time or inclination to entertain: Why have a big affair like this on a Thursday night? Why had no one heard about this union earlier? When did the happy couple get engaged? Why the rush to get married? To this last one Eddy said, "Because she may come to her senses and bail."

It irritated Eddy that people always chuckled and dismissed his expressions of unqualified hostility toward Raphael's Son. Surely, they assumed, no employee would dare launch even one such attack on the boss seriously, or be allowed to return to work the day after he had done so. What they didn't realize was that Raphael's Son relished seeing Eddy have no choice but to show up to work every day no matter how badly he hated himself and Raphael's Son for it.

At the end of his first round of calls, Eddy had confirmed 180 people. About eighty of those were Raphael's Son's maternal cousins who, having gotten wind of his ill-gotten riches in Iran, fell over themselves to show support for his jackpot of a marriage. The rest were representatives of the various Jewish charities to which Raphael's Son had started to contribute, or, Eddy guessed, from the way they responded to him, "losers who can't do any better."

As for Neda, she had her parents and Nilou. She hadn't even considered inviting Elizabeth or Angela.

"You'd better get a smaller room," Eddy advised his boss with relish. "This is gonna be the most expensive party no one showed up to."

There was a line in a book Angela loved in high school, during those weekends when she secretly prayed that a call would come from someone other than Nilou or Neda, a potential new friend or (this, she hardly dared wish for) a boy who might ask her out. Elizabeth would be engrossed in her work and Nilou would be fielding half a dozen possible dates and there was only Angela and Neda, studying for tests and writing papers and doing their best "I don't have time for boys, they're all dorks and geeks" act. As a rule, Angela scoffed at the idea of young women feeling despondent over boys or trapped in their own loneliness. This wasn't how she saw herself or intended to become; she would have rather died fighting than spend a night crying into her pillow. But every once in a while she couldn't resist the tug of melancholy, the resonance of the lyrics to Janis Ian's "At Seventeen," or the emotional devastation in the words uttered by the young woman protagonist in Marguerite Duras's *The Lover*.

The day Nilou called to tell her Neda was going to marry Raphael's Son, Angela thought of that line: "Very early in my life, it was already too late."

Faced with certain humiliation by the low turnout at the wedding, Raphael's Son cancelled the festivities and blamed it on the Raiises' humble social profile. After the day outside the record store when he blackmailed Neda into marrying him, he had dropped all pretense of civility and proceeded to plant his flag on Dr. Raiis's name and *aabehroo* without so much as a "May I?" Not for him, the usual formalities of asking the father for permission to marry the girl, inviting the family for Sunday lunches and Shabbat dinners, taking day trips with the future in-laws to Santa Barbara for brunch at the Biltmore.

He met them for the first time the day he married Neda. It was a Saturday morning in city hall on Cesar Chavez Avenue downtown. Raphael's Son had come alone; Neda was with her parents and Nilou.

The Raiises were so ashamed of the union, so worried that Elizabeth would take it as a personal betrayal, they had waited till the last minute to break the news to her. Zeeba cried on the phone.

She cried again at city hall, and later, at the Ivy on Robertson where Raphael's Son treated the family to his version of a celebratory lunch. He insisted on a table on the patio because he wanted to be seen not only by the other patrons, but also the paparazzi that gathered outside the restaurant as a matter of course. Before they sat down, he tossed a look at Neda—thin, ashen, resembling a fish that knows it will never find its way out of the net—and said, "You might have fixed yourself up."

He took the seat facing the street, put Neda on his left and Dr. Raiis on the right. When Zeeba wouldn't stop tearing up, he handed her a cloth napkin and suggested, "You take yourself to the ladies' room and clean up." He ordered champagne and asked the waiter to bring a chef's selection of appetizers, made small talk with Dr. Raiis who had a hard time—anyone could see this—looking Raphael's Son in the face. He asked Nilou about school.

Even in a city that drew the most beautiful women from around the world, Nilou turned heads with her unusually good looks. This, combined with the fact that she was exceedingly smart and utterly guileless, made it difficult for most women to like her. Angela was a rare exception.

She hadn't been invited to the lunch, but she showed up anyway, forty minutes into the agony, when everyone had run out of things to force themselves to say and Neda had yet to take a bite of the chef's selection.

Angela had come from the East Coast without telling anyone, even her mother, only called Nilou that morning to ask where and what time "Neda's last supper" would be held.

"I'd go to city hall with you if I thought I could keep from throwing up," she had said with her usual empathy.

Once Angela got to the lunch, she went around the table and kissed the Raiises on the cheeks, hugged Nilou, and patted Neda on the shoulder. "You could've called me."

To Raphael's Son she said, "You're beneath contempt."

LOS ANGELES

Wednesday, June 26, 2013

When Leon went back to Mapleton at 8:30 Wednesday morning, Neda denied having ever heard of Eddy Arax.

She was sitting in the "breakfast kitchen" when Leon arrived. Esperanza had led him there in her gym clothes—sports bra, bare midriff consisting of three layers of fat, yoga pants from the Lululemon store on Beverly Drive; she was going out for a jog. Neda was having her fourth espresso of the morning. She wore a smart black dress and black pumps with four-inch heels, light makeup, beige nail polish. The quivers of the previous days and the expression of stupefaction were replaced by an almost appealing sadness that is usually seen on the faces of politicians' widows when they know they're being photographed.

Leon asked Neda if she knew a certain Edward Araxamian.

She didn't.

He informed her that Eddy was one of her husband's employees.

Her husband never talked to Neda about his work or employees.

Even one who'd been with him for more than twenty years?

Neda shrugged.

Was she sure? Because Leon had reason to believe that Eddy might be involved in Raphael's Son's death.

She held Leon's eyes for what felt like a whole minute.

She was sure.

Was she really so dumb, Leon wondered, to tell a lie that could be so easily exposed? And why was she not even trying to feign grief? The only tears Leon had seen so far were Esperanza's, and she appeared to have recovered magnificently from the previous day. Neda, on the other hand, hadn't once asked if the police had found any trace of the body, or wondered aloud if "the killer" might come back for the family.

A white person walking in from the outside might have mistaken this total absence of emotion with the kind of Western stoicism that equates grieving with weakness, and insists that every setback is an opportunity—the "what doesn't kill me makes me stronger" and "making lemonade out of lemons" philosophy that inspires some peo-ple to celebrate the life of a loved one instead of mourning his death. But where Neda was from, grief and joy were two halves of the same poisoned fruit—it was sweet and bitter, but in the end it would kill you all the same. People were born not, as in the West, to conquer and prevail and become president, but to learn patience and forbear-ance and resilience in the face of what life would throw at them. Their parents' losses became theirs and their losses became their children's and that's how they knew, better than any Westerner ever could, how to mourn.

From his car, Leon tried Eddy's cell phone a few times, rang the apartment once, and when he still didn't answer, Leon sent a text: *Pick up the damn phone or I'll be at your door in twenty minutes.*

He was in the two-hour-free parking lot on Brighton near Rodeo. Women with fake hair, lips, cheeks, and breasts drove along in their matrimonial sports cars, hiked down to the street on top of their ten-inch, crystal-studded heels, and went off like pilgrims to seek love and approval from the ten-dollar-an-hour salespeople at Gucci and Valentino.

Eddy picked up.

"What are you doing with Neda?"

Leon could tell Eddy stopped breathing for several seconds.

"Don't play games, Eddy. You knew we'd would find out. Don't act like you're surprised."

Eddy's voice, grainy and rough from all the caffeine and tobacco, sounded almost like static on the phone.

"I'm not playing," he said, clearly resigned. "Just tired."

Leon waited.

"She had problems with her husband."

Leon was still waiting.

"It was nothing like that," Eddy sighed. Leon's silence must have been more irritating than any open accusation, because after a moment Eddy said again, "I tell you, it wasn't anything."

"Why does she deny knowing you?"

Leon heard Eddy swallow (was it air? bile? more smoke?) at the other end. He was clearly thrown off by that last revelation.

"I asked her if she's ever heard of you, and she said no," Leon pressed. "Why would she say—"

"Because she's a fucking moron," Eddy breathed fire into the phone. "That's why."

A long-exploited, desperately dependent employee. A wronged and unhappy wife. A story with too many holes. Maybe O'Donnell wasn't wrong after all.

"You're just wasting your time with this one," Eddy said, more quietly. "You wanna find some real evidence, find Lorecchio's lapdog."

That Fucking Snake agreed to meet with Leon, but he was too fearful of being seen or recorded anywhere near a cop. He was adamant that Luci had spies in every corner of every city street and public building across LA County; he also had cameras installed in streetlights, hearing devices hidden inside electrical boxes, and unmarked cruisers just looking for potential sources of trouble. That's how, the Rat had explained, Luci managed to stay boss and get away with "everything he's done" for eighteen years.

The first two dozen places Leon suggested for a meeting, including his own apartment, were out of the question. The second set of locations Leon suggested—an empty parking lot at two a.m. in Lancaster, a bench in Forest Lawn Memorial Park in the Hollywood Hills, a desolate hiking lane in the Santa Monica Mountains—were too much out of the way and would provide excellent opportunities for any of Luci's hit men. In the end, they agreed to meet in the main lobby of Harbor-UCLA Medical Center in Torrance where, on any given day, a few hundred uninsured individuals milled around with their families, waiting to be seen by an emergency room doctor.

Though he claimed he was fifty-one, That Fucking Snake easily resembled a seventy-year-old with failing health. His enormous head and bulging eyes sat firmly over his torso through a too-short, too-wide neck, but the rest of him was narrow and angular and reeking of spicy cologne. His medical file would have had him dead and decomposed years ago from any one of the injuries or illnesses he reported having suffered while at work, and his psychiatrist had lost count of the number of antidepressant medications he had prescribed over time.

That Fucking Snake attributed all his physical and emotional troubles to the pressure of working for the Rat and Lorecchio. He also blamed them for the fact that he had not talked to his wife for twelve years running, two of his daughters were over thirty and unmarried, one was divorced with children, and his only son, well, the son came out as gay because his mother—That Snake's wife—encouraged and even accepted it.

"My ulcer started to bleed again the other night and I almost died," he confided to Leon at Harbor-UCLA. "My daughter showed me a Facebook picture of my son with his 'fiancé,' Mark."

The bleeding ulcer, Leon guessed, had as much to do with the gay son's decision to marry his partner as with the army of lawyers and accountants that the city comptroller and city attorney had unleashed on Luci, the Rat, and That Snake. When all his resistance and subversion did not make the matter of the $30 million go away, Luci testified before the city council that he had recently discovered that his associate, the Rat, had invested the money with what turned out to be an unscrupulous individual running a Ponzi. Upon learning this "just last week," Luci had fired the Rat on the spot, and promised his own full cooperation as he sat back and let the union pay for his very expensive defense. The Rat, fearing the worst—dying in jail—had taken the first flight to Doha in Qatar, where he knew he would have a home for at least the next decade while the case made its way through bureaucratic channels. This left That Snake to fend for himself or leave his family and escape to Bangladesh. Hence, the meeting with Leon.

"I may be hard to reach for a while," That Snake explained, "but I want to clear my conscience and come clean about a few things."

That conscience, Leon thought, could only be cleaned with industrial-strength fluoroantimonic acid. This man had come to inflict on Luci or the Rat whatever damage he was able to before he skipped town.

In early June 2013, Joshua and Hadassah Simcha had invited Luci to lunch at Shiloh's, their favorite kosher "dining establishment" (as opposed to any old restaurant) in Pico-Robertson. Luci, of course, would not be caught dead in that kind of company, but he sent the Rat, who, "by the way, is one of those Jews who're only Jewish when it suits them." Soon after that meeting, That Fucking Snake was instructed to deliver, orally and without keeping any record of the encounter, a certain phone number to Hadassah Simcha. He had met Hadassah at the Union 76 gas station next to the old Robinson's store on Wilshire and Whittier that had been empty and unused for a decade. While they pumped gas at either side of the same self-serve station, he had whispered to her a phone number.

That Fucking Snake had no idea whose number he had passed to Hadassah. He also made clear that, though he was happy to share this information with Leon "because of our friendship, I would not make a reliable witness in any court, given some issues in my past," and would therefore not be willing to give a formal statement. All he could tell Leon was that he sometimes made "referrals" of this sort "on the Rat's behalf."

"I'm not saying Luci knew a thing about this," That Snake emphasized. "But just think: Soleyman was laying low and overly cautious in those last days. He comes home in the middle of the night. The gate won't open. If he saw a stranger stroll up to the car he would never roll down his window."

He might do that, however, if it was a woman he knew who emerged from the bushes.

"I think one of the Simcha women baited him, and the Rat's man did the killing. That's the only thing that makes sense, given the way it went down. And don't forget, if anyone has the capability to transport a body and make it disappear, it's Luci."

Esperanza was in the "decorative kitchen," yelling at the pool man on the phone. It seemed he didn't show up when he was supposed to, and the pool—not the one at Raphael's Son's house; Esperanza's own pool, at her own house in Tarzana—was gathering algae.

She waved when she saw Leon come in, but didn't hang up until she had finished chewing out her employee.

"I swear to you I can't understand what he says," she told Leon. "He's Chinese. Terrible accent."

She took a sip from a bottle of VitaminWater.

"Would you like an espresso? We can go to the kitchen."

She meant the "functional kitchen."

"Where's Mrs. Soleyman?"

Esperanza looked slightly offended that Leon wasn't there only to see her.

"Miss Neda is not home," she said. "Did you have an appointment?"

"Where did she go?"

"Wednesdays she has yoga with Miss Azita. Private studio."

Leon heard a sound behind him and turned to see Neda's older daughter, Nicole, standing in the doorway. Her eyes were puffy and red from tears.

"You're looking for my mom?"

The way she said that, so sadly, with such resignation, embarrassed Leon.

"I had some questions," he said. "I'll wait for her, if that's okay." He sat down.

Nicole didn't object, but didn't offer her blessing either.

"No school today?" he asked, then immediately regretted it. It was the end of June; of course there was no school.

"We get done early," Nicole offered politely.

It occurred to Leon that she may want him to be there, may even have something to say to him. He turned to Esperanza, who was hovering over the table like a demanding maître d'. "Can I take you up on that espresso?" Then, to Nicole: "Want one?"

She shook her head, but inched toward the table, then slid shyly into a chair.

"Is it terrible?" Leon asked. He was trying to make her trust him, yes, but he also really wanted to know. She teared up.

"Do you think he's dead, like my mom says?"

Leon nodded. "I'm afraid so." He felt like he had just kicked a puppy in the gut. If he ever had a child, he thought right then, he hoped it would be a girl, like this one, only happier. "I'm sorry."

She lowered her head to hide her tears, but he saw one fall onto her leg. She was sitting with her hands tucked under thighs. Her hair, long and straight with only a single wave, reached her knees.

Esperanza shifted a few inches away, but did not leave.

Something about this girl—how sweet she was, how vulnerable and shy and obviously lonely she seemed—made Leon want to exonerate Neda.

"Did you see what happened?" he asked.

Nicole shook her head.

"They should never have married."

Did Nicole know, Leon wondered, that it was her conception Raphael's Son had used to get Neda to marry him?

"She was pregnant with me," she said. "She wouldn't have done it otherwise."

Who would tell a girl such a thing?

"I'm sure neither regrets having you," Leon offered.

Nicole still hadn't looked up.

"That's okay. I regret it enough for all of us."

Esperanza was still in the kitchen. It was clear she didn't plan to miss a single detail of her employers' saga or—worse—have to hear it from some other maid in the Latin American Housekeepers' Cabal.

Nicole didn't seem to notice her.

"She lied when she said she doesn't know Eddy."

Leon held his breath.

"We all know him," Nicole went on. "He called here all the time."

A voice inside Leon screamed that he had no right to this information, that this girl may have come to him for help, that she may be giving him the burden of her trust and not expect that he would betray it. The thought flashed in his mind that anything she said would not be admissible anyway, because she was underage and he didn't have the mother's permission to talk to her.

He saw that Esperanza was all ears and not even pretending otherwise. He thought about asking her to leave but decided it might spook Nicole.

"Did he call a lot these past few weeks?" Would he hate himself more for doing his job? Or for giving in to compassion and walking away from this?

He felt something shift within Nicole. Maybe she realized what he was up to—that he wasn't there as a friend; that talking to him was a bad idea. He was almost relieved by this, almost waiting for her to get up and leave and save him from being an asshole.

"She found out my dad had a kid."

She said this so softly, Leon wasn't sure he had heard right.

"Eddy told her my dad has another kid. That's why she kept calling him. He was the only one who knew—besides my dad, I guess—and he told my mom and that's why they were talking so much."

The inside of Leon's mouth felt like it had been filled with sand, scraped, and emptied again. Without thinking, he got up and went to the sink, realized he needed a glass, and started opening cabinets.

"They're in the one to the right of the stove," Nicole told him. Then, as if completing the same thought, "She never would have told you, you know. She'd rather you think she killed someone."

Leon took two glasses, filled them with water, and came back to the table. He drank his halfway; Nicole didn't touch hers.

"When?" he asked.

"When did he have the kid?" she replied.

"That too. But when did Eddy tell her?"

For once, Eddy Arax was relieved to see Leon.

He was pacing the block outside his apartment building, feverishly inhaling a cigarette, when Leon pulled up. In the glare of sunlight his face resembled a mask made of stiff rubber.

Before they went into the apartment Eddy took off his smoking shirt, hung it on a hook outside the door, and put on a clean T-shirt. The sofa bed was made this time, so he gestured toward it and went into the kitchen to wash his hands and face. He even ran his wet fingers through his hair, trying to get out the smell of the smoke for his mother's sake. Then Eddy wiped his face with a kitchen towel, dumped it in the sink, and started to make his Turkish coffee.

Raphael's Son had met the boy's mother in 2006, during one of his then-weekly trips to Las Vegas and back through Barstow. All he told Eddy about her was that she had schemed to have a child so she could live off the support money.

"Can you imagine someone pulling one off on him?" Eddy smirked.

Once a month, Raphael's Son instructed Eddy to wire $2,000 in child support through Western Union. As far as Eddy knew, that was all the contact Raphael's Son had ever had with the boy.

"How do you know it's a boy?" Leon asked.

Eddy gave him a look that said there's more to this than meets the eye, then went around and fell onto the couch.

"All of a sudden this guy shows up at the office one day—this black guy with one of those Jew hats. He says he's half black, half Jewish, and he's a rabbi—but he's got tattoos and wears jeans and a chain like he runs with gangs. He's an ex-con, he says, but now he's a social worker, and I know he doesn't know Raphael's Son because he asked if I'm him and I said yes—because we got served with shit all the time, you know, lawsuits and stuff, so I was supposed to say yes if anyone came to the door and asked. That way he hadn't really been served, you know?"

Leon knew.

"So I said yes, and next thing I know this guy's saying they've had the kid in foster care, the mother died in some accident in '08, and they found the kid in the car, or in the car seat in a riverbed or something—who knows what these religious types come up with to make you feel sorry for them. He says the social services in whatever hellhole the kid was in were just gonna park him somewhere in foster care for good, but this ex-con black guy took an interest, he says, because the kid is something special, and he—the black guy—looks around and finds out the father is a Jew, and he finds out our address, and he wants me—because he thinks I'm him, you know, Raphael's Son—to go see the kid."

They sat—Leon and Eddy and the shadow of Raphael's Son—with the weight of the story between them. A bastard child who abandons his own.

"How long ago was this?" Leon finally asked.

Eddy blushed a sickly red. "I don't know. A couple years. Maybe three?"

"Did he have the kid with him?"

"Who? The rabbi?" Eddy looked annoyed. "No. In case the father didn't cooperate, you know? I guess that's what he was thinking."

Leon studied Eddy. "So you've known for years about this child, and you've kept mum, and then all of a sudden, before the trial—"

"Fuck you!" Eddy yelled, spit flying from his mouth. "I'm not the kid's parent. It's not my fucking responsibility to look after him."

In the bedroom behind them, the mother let out a long, urgent moan.

Eddy yelled something in Armenian at the closed door, then stood up and started to pace the room. "I'm sorry," he mumbled. "Didn't mean to get excited."

Leon nodded. "Don't worry about it."

"You know," Eddy continued, "it gets to a point, you see someone do so much harm and you think it's not your business and you let him keep doing it and at some point, if you keep your mouth shut one more time, you're the guilty one."

True.

"So, you see," Eddy paced furiously, "I think to myself, fuck the bastard, he's already shortchanging the kid times a hundred, giving him $2,000 a month when, really, he should be giving a lot more, and if he finds out the mother's dead and the kid's in some foster place, he's gonna stop sending any money at all—"

"How do we know it's his kid anyway?" Leon interrupted.

Eddy stopped pacing, threw a sideways glance at Leon, rolled his one good eye, and started to pace again.

"So I take the money every month, you see, and instead of sending it to the mother, I make a 'charitable donation' to the child services whatever-it-is where they keep these kinds of kids." He stopped and looked at Leon, as if expecting disapproval.

"Until he found out," Leon guessed.

Eddy went to the hot stove and scooped more coffee into the Turkish coffee pot.

"A few months ago, April maybe, the black guy comes back, I don't even know why, maybe to ask for more money, maybe to see if Son of Satan will grow a heart and visit the place where the kid lives. Next thing I know, the shit is calling me names and threatening to throw me in jail for embezzlement, the fuck. He's got half a billion of other people's money stashed away with those shit slimy cousins of his, and he's gonna throw me in jail for sending a few thousand dollars to a bunch of orphan kids."

He put the pot on the burner, then turned to face Eddy full on.

"So you told the wife."

They stared each other down for a moment, Eddy challenging Leon to condemn him, and when that didn't happen, Eddy said quietly, "So I told the wife."

The mother's name was Jenna Rose Robbins and, yes, she was all of fifteen years old, penniless, and without a real family when Jonah was conceived. She had a boyfriend of sorts—a much older man who belonged to one of Barstow's original motorcycle gangs, but they weren't exclusive and he never gave Jenna Rose money. Her father was long gone and her mother tended bar all night at the San Manuel Indian Casino in Highland, which meant Jenna Rose grew up like a desert weed. She worked the four-to-midnight shift, as cashier, at the Shell station on Del Rosa down the street from the casino. She had already seen Raphael's Son's car when he came in to buy a pack of chewing gum and a bottle of water that first time, and she knew just what he meant when he eyed her and asked, "Is there a decent steak house around here?"

She was pretty but pale, thin in the way of young people who live on junk food, cigarettes, and beer. It was nearly midnight, the end of her shift, so he waited for her in the car and afterward they drove to the casino and she ordered the most expensive steak on the menu. She made sure they sat at a table close to the bar because she wanted her mother to see them and their steaks, which she did; she even saw the twenty-dollar tip he threw into the cocktail waitress's tray when she brought him a scotch and a beer for Jenna Rose. He hardly said a word to her the whole time they sat there, just complained that the place stank of body odor and rednecks, and that the steak was inedible, the leather in his shoes was more tender. The minute she was finished eating, he got up and walked to the registration desk, paid for the room in cash, and took her upstairs. When they were done, he gave her a hundred dollars. Buy yourself some decent meat.

Jenna Rose's mother was underwhelmed by Raphael's Son's supposed generosity. "That one can afford a lot more than this," she said.

Barstow was exactly halfway between Los Angeles and Las Vegas—forty thousand square miles of desert that had been settled in the 1840s as part of the Mormon Corridor. More recently, it was simply a point of convergence for three major highways, and the Union Pacific and BNSF railroads. There was a Marine Corps logistics base and the Fort Irwin Military Reservation, a drive-in movie theater, a Popeyes, a Panda Express, a "Railroad Museum" that was really an Amtrak station, and a pair of factory outlet malls where weekend travelers from Los Angeles stopped on their way home from Las Vegas.

Early 2005 was still a boom time for Vegas land speculation, and Raphael's Son traveled there at least once a month. He didn't stop to see Jenna Rose on every occasion; when he did, he told her nothing about himself, not even what country he was from. She guessed he was a contractor for one of the many companies that, in the days before the meltdown, couldn't build condos and spec houses fast enough, but it never occurred to her that he may own the company because she never thought of herself as someone who would know a person of such means.

He paid cash for everything, even when he took her to the shops in the casino and bought her things she liked. He never gave her a phone number or left the glove box of his car unlocked. Still, while Jenna Rose might have been young, she wasn't stupid: she made a note of the license plate on his car and had her boyfriend dig up the registration through a friend at the DMV. She even rode down to LA on the boyfriend's motorcycle one day and went into the lobby of the office building on Century Park East. That's when she realized Raphael's Son had real money. It's why, when she found out she was pregnant, she decided to keep the baby.

She wasn't sure Raphael's Son was the father, but she told him he was anyway. It was one in the morning and they had just finished their meal at the casino when the mother came and sat down at their table. Until then, Raphael's Son had no idea who she was or that she even knew Jenna Rose. But he could see the resemblance, however faded, between the two women, and he could sense an ambush.

He didn't flinch or frown, didn't do the usual,. *So what's it got to do with me and how do I know it's mine?* He offered to pay for the abortion, plus $1,500 "pocket money." She was about to accept, but the mother interrupted in a scratchy voice befitting an old man.

"That's a lot less than you'll have to pay over eighteen years for child support."

Anger lit up Raphael's Son's eyes. To hide it, he glanced down at the table, then flicked a bread crumb with his thumb and forefinger. He stretched the silence until he could feel sweat breaking through his shirt.

"You're picking on the wrong guy," he told the mother.

After that, he ignored the mother entirely and told Jenna Rose this was his best offer, she had three minutes to make up her mind, and if she stalled, he'd leave and not give a damn what became of her or her purported pregnancy. He threw a hundred-dollar bill on the table and stood up, raised his left hand to chest level, and looked at his watch.

"Starting now," he announced.

The mother called him an "A-rab piece of shit" and started back toward her place behind the bar. With her face turned away from them both she said to Jenna Rose, "Fuck him. He's bluffin'."

Three minutes later, Raphael's Son was walking out of the casino.

Jenna Rose said later that she had waited too long for Raphael's Son to come back. Her mother had told her there was no way a man like that—rich, middle-aged, probably married though he didn't wear a wedding band, A-rab or Eye-ray-nian or Jew—would take a chance on a girl surprising his family with a kid. Jenna Rose didn't know how pregnant she was and how much time she had to wait for Raphael's Son to cave in. It didn't occur to her that he might not have believed she was pregnant at all, for all he knew she was lying, she'd keep the abortion money and the bonus for herself. And he didn't know, either, if the thing was really his; she saw him once a month, saw the boyfriend much more frequently. He wasn't stupid enough to have sex without protection and what are the chances, really, that one accident would result in a pregnancy? But this way of thinking—putting oneself in the other's shoe and trying to see the world as he would—did not come easily to a girl of Jenna Rose's age; nor did the awareness that with some matters, taking a chance may result in some very permanent consequences. Jenna Rose was still waiting for Raphael's Son to come back with a better offer even after her stomach swelled through her Old Navy tank top and Salvation Army jeans.

A lawyer her mother knew from the bar wrote a letter threatening to file a paternity suit. Tellingly, the lawyer did not ask Raphael's Son to submit to a blood test. He had only to commit to paying Jenna Rose's medical expenses, plus $2,000 a month in child support.

Two thousand dollars a month was much more money than Jenna Rose had ever seen or that any child of hers would be able to use, but it was a great deal less than Raphael's Son could afford or was spending on his other children. On any other matter, he would have stonewalled and countersued and driven the other side into the ground by outspending them. But in this case, he was smart enough to understand that the potential danger of fighting far outweighed the cost of surrender.

Jenna Rose lost the biker boyfriend as a result of her pregnancy, but she otherwise didn't mind having a baby. She enjoyed the attention she got from coworkers and strangers, the questions from the customers about when she was due and what names she had in mind. Her mother left work early to take her to the hospital for the delivery, but she smoked all the way in the car no matter how much Jenna Rose asked her not to, so they got into an argument and her mom dropped her off at the emergency entrance and drove away.

No one at the hospital noticed the tiny spot of light behind Jonah's belly button. A nurse showed Jenna Rose how to diaper and feed and swaddle him, and then she was on her own, back to the smoke-filled trailer where her mother, who slept in the daytime, flew into a rage every time the baby cried. Once the child support money started to come in, Jenna Rose moved right out of the trailer and into a Roadway Inn where she lived like a queen for sixty dollars a night and felt safe enough to leave Jonah asleep for a couple of hours at a time while she ran errands or stopped at the Home Depot where a boy she had started to see worked a forklift. Her first brush with Child Protective Services came when Jonah was ten months old and already walking. She had been gone less than an hour when the motel's owner, a sour-faced Vietnamese woman who only understood English when she wanted to, called the police. A cruiser came by that afternoon, the cops spoke to Jenna Rose for a good ten minutes and filed a report with the county, but it would be a full seven weeks before a social worker stopped at the motel to look in on Jonah, and by then mother and child had moved on and were living with her boyfriend from Home Depot.

At thirteen months, Jonah broke his arm when he fell off the bed in which he slept with Jenna Rose and her boyfriend. The ER doctors examined him for signs of physical abuse and noted the glow in his stomach. They saw the same light on the X-rays and the MRI, and they all agreed they'd never seen anything like it, but the waiting room was packed with seriously injured people and the gurneys inside the treatment area were all occupied with trauma patients and there was no time to dwell on the mystery of the little boy's luminescence. The ER doctor recommended that Jonah be seen by his pediatrician in the morning, and a social worker gave Jenna Rose the phone number of the San Bernardino County Children and Family Services, where free lessons were offered in parenting and child safety. There was no pediatrician, and Jonah wasn't sick. Even with his arm in a cast he was overactive and exhausting.

In 2008, the Home Depot boyfriend decided to move back to his parents' house in Arizona. He wanted Jenna Rose to go with him, but Jonah was another story—he took up too much room and had too many demands, so why not send him back to his "Jew-ass father"?

Because Jenna Rose loved her baby, and because the three of them were living on the child-support payments. That's why. So it's her and Jonah or neither; Home Depot could go to Arizona alone for all she cared.

They packed Jonah in the car and headed east on the I-40, but Jonah cried and fussed and wet his pants one too many times. In Needles, Home Depot rented a room at the Rio Del Sol Inn. He and Jenna Rose argued all night. In the morning, they drove to Riverside and checked into another motel where Home Depot got drunk and fell asleep. Jenna Rose took Jonah and the car keys and headed right back to Barstow.

Ten miles out, the rain started and she realized the windshield wipers didn't work. She braved it for a while, but the rain was coming down hard and the inside of the car smelled like a thousand seashells and there were flash flood warnings on the radio, so she pulled off the freeway and drove toward a gas station in the distance.

The fire department pulled her out of the car after she had been dead for at least an hour. They found the baby's car seat, with Jonah still in it, trapped between two poles of the short metal railing on the side of the road. They guessed that the mother had released the seat and pushed it out the car door before it was completely submerged.

At twenty-seven minutes past two the next morning, Leon watched from his car as the 4 bus stopped on the corner of Sunset and Mapleton, and George P. Carter III, a.k.a. the Altoid Man, lumbered down to the street. He went straight toward the construction site. Leon met him on the sidewalk outside the gate.

"What do you want?" the Altoid Man said, not bothering to stop or even slow down.

Leon put his arm up to block the opening in the fence.

"For starters, I wanna know why you said you'd seen the murder the other night when there's no way you could've."

The Altoid Man examined Leon up and down, then reached into his pocket and took out the dirty box of mints. "You got something for me?" he asked.

"I don't believe you know anything," Leon said. "I also think you made up the story about your eye."

Even in the darkness, he could see the Altoid Man turn purple with rage.

"But I'm gonna help you out anyway," Leon said. "You give me something useful, I mean really useful about what went on over there," he nodded toward the dented gate of Raphael's Son's house, "and I give you my word that I'll do my best to help you get your case reopened and investigated. That's all I can do. I can't get the police chief to apologize to you and I can't get the mayor to shake your hand, so if that's not good enough you can hold on to your bullshit story till you die because I promise you no one else is gonna give a shit."

They sized each other up. Then the Altoid Man pushed Leon's arm away, shuffled into the site, and dropped his pants.

"Chevy Impala," the Altoid Man sighed with relief.

Leon heard urine trickle down onto the ground.

"Rental," the Altoid Man announced. "Fake plates."

Leon reached into his pocket for his notebook. "How do you know that?"

There was the sound of feet shuffling, then the Altoid Man's voice rose from closer to the ground.

"I heard the guy's car pull up," he groaned.

"What guy?"

"The dead guy, you moron!"

"You heard him pull up in his car?"

"A minute later, he started honking like a bitch."

Leon wondered how a bitch would honk, but kept the question to himself.

"How do you know he was the one honking?"

"Because I held my crap and stuck my head out and saw everything."

"What did you see?"

"The Chevy must have been the getaway car. It wasn't there when I got off the bus."

Leon could just imagine a jury trying to make sense of this account. "So when did you see it?"

"When it drove away. You're a real idiot."

"What else did you see?"

The Altoid Man took his time pulling his pants up and kicking loose dirt over the feces.

"Where was the driver of the first car when the Chevy pulled away?"

"Still in there," the Altoid Man motioned toward the gate. He laughed. "Not honking anymore."

"You think he was dead?"

"I think you should go fuck yourself or give me a twenty."

Leon chose option number two.

"Did you see the plates on the Chevy?"

"I told you, they were fake."

"How could you tell?"

"Rental plates have that stupid frame with the name of the company. This one didn't."

Leon didn't even know why he was bothering with the conversation anymore. "So how do you know it was a rental?"

"I told you: it was green. Forest green. The only time you'll find a more or less new green car is a rental."

"Is that all?"

"The woman stayed for a while."

"The woman?" Leon was exasperated.

"Yeah. Like a wet mouse."

LOS ANGELES

1997

Elizabeth and Hal registered their company, Z Industries, on the eighteenth anniversary of Noor's kidnapping in 1977. Within a year, they had funding to create and test a prototype. Two years after that, they started to manufacture the radar. By the year 2000, they had patented or developed a dozen other devices and created an angel investment network from Palo Alto to Tel Aviv to Bangalore.

Their success was so complete, it erased from the collective memory all the years of struggle and hardship, the late-night prayers and early-morning despair, the time away from her daughter that cost Elizabeth her relationship with Angela and the absolute heartbreak that cost Hal his teeth and hair and every other trace of youth and vigor in a man his age. Forty years of studying and experimentation, the combined capacity of two extraordinary minds, the relentless drudgery of a pair of obsessives was reduced, in the mythology of Z, to a mere stroke of good luck, a bubble that grew during the tech boom and that kept growing, people assumed, thanks to the irrational exuberance of the late '90s. Only this bubble didn't burst because, depending on who was telling the story, Elizabeth was much too sharp-witted to make a bad investment, or Hal was much too smart not to stay one step ahead of the market. Both explanations were incorrect.

The reason Z Industries continued to thrive regardless of the fluctuations in the stock market was that its principals weren't chasing money. Neither Elizabeth nor Hal had ever had the slightest idea how to enjoy the good life like normal people. To them, money was something you exchanged for a chance to pursue that other, more distant path—the one that took them away from ordinary life and let them indulge in the quiet, forever-constant pattern of numbers.

Ten years after he had been featured on the front page of the *Wall Street Journal* as one of the most successful entrepreneurs of the twenty-first century, Hussein Zemorrodi still went around in mismatched suits and loose dentures. When he did make an attempt to appear presentable, he'd emerge from Barney's or Ralph Lauren dressed in various shades of some pastel color—blue or lime-green or, once, yellow; he didn't care because he was color-blind and didn't know it, and the salespeople in the stores weren't willing to offend a person with a black Amex card by pointing to flaws in his choice of ensemble. He never got married or had a girlfriend. He lived out of a single trunk in one hotel room or another, never had more than a few dollars' cash in his pocket, couldn't tell a Honda from a Lamborghini to save his life.

Elizabeth was much more astute in financial matters, but, like John Vain, she made up for that by conceiving of ever more innovative ways in which to give her money away. Before she had enough to buy a house or even a condo with, she created a foundation and hired John Vain's old girlfriend, a pencil-thin, forever-tanned attorney named Stephanie Dalal, to run it. That's when she stopped being Elizabeth Soleyman, the orphan widow, and became, in the local mythology, Elizabeth the Great.

Raphael's Son had decided to remodel the house on Burk Place, so he brought Neda to live in a condominium at the Wilshire Manning on the Corridor. In Angela's opinion, he did it because the building was inhabited mostly by Iranians, which meant he could show off his newest triumph and make sure the rest of the community learned about it faster than if he had taken out a full-page ad in the *Los Angeles Times*. It was also an occasion for him to establish his financial advantage in the real estate market: he had foreclosed on the condo when the previous owners, who owed him money, couldn't pay their debt.

Almost all their neighbors in the building knew or had heard of the Soleyman family and their enmity with Raphael's wife and son. Many knew of his Jadid al-Islam years in Iran; a few had even fallen victim to his extortion. In the lobby and the elevators, on the floor and in the garage, they stared at Neda with a mixture of puzzlement and indignation, whispered to each other about her rising belly and too-tight dress and how she was able to sleep at night knowing what she did about him and his mother, their ignominious beginnings, the fact that the condo he had brought her to live in had been snatched away from its real owners. Sometimes, the older women stopped Neda in the hallways just to remind her of her own father's good name and reputation, how important it was for children to uphold their parents' *aabehroo*.

Come to think of it, neighbors whispered amongst themselves, she did look extremely pregnant for a newlywed, and really, what can you expect of a girl raised in America? Kids here have no sense of responsibility, they feel no guilt or obligation toward their parents, don't you see it on all their TV shows? The children are always right, they're always telling the parents how to live and the parents end every episode of every sitcom by apologizing to the child or at least admitting that he knows best.

Until Nicole was born and Neda had someone to take care of, she kept her head down and let cement the impression that she was simply too stupid to know just what an embarrassment she was. After that, she focused all her attention on her daughter, used her as an excuse to avoid even family gatherings, to stay out of the way of Elizabeth and Angela and even her own parents. It was as if she had made her bargain with the devil and intended to uphold her end, had given herself to Raphael's Son in exchange for a chance at having children.

But if Neda hoped that distancing herself from the others would minimize the damage he was able to inflict upon her parents and Elizabeth, she was sadly mistaken. For them, the last years of the century were marked by a gradual coming apart of the bonds of friendship and trust that had sustained the two families in their most difficult times.

Angela stayed in New Haven to work even after she graduated law school; Nilou went off to Pomona to study rocket science. No matter how much the two reached out to her, Neda remained detached. Her parents, who could neither make peace with having Raphael's Son as a son-in-law nor separate themselves entirely from their daughter, made a few agonizing attempts at tolerating Raphael's Son's company before he declared he had no use for them and told Neda they weren't welcome in his house. She could see them on her own if she wanted to, even take the baby with her, "just don't bring them near me or I'll have to tell them how far up they should shove their third-rate, has-been, *taaghooti* pride."

Neda was as alone in her marriage as she had been before it. Only now she could no longer deceive herself that someday, somewhere, she was going to grow a personality, discover some pluck, overcome the uneasiness that made her so shy and awkward with just about everyone. She was a devoted mother, but even with the girls she doubted herself, second-guessed every act, and regretted every decision. Later, when driving them to school and picking them up every day, she never once had the courage to stand around and chat with the other parents. She would go alone to all the meetings with their teachers, all their performances and after-school games, because Raphael's Son was "too busy making money so you can maintain your fancy lifestyle." She would venture into luncheons and bar mitzvahs and school fundraisers, dressed in expensive clothes and loaded up with Xanax to help her overcome her social anxiety, sit in one spot the whole time, and smile mechanically and pretend to enjoy herself before crying in her car all the way home.

Then Raphael's Son went and stole everyone's money, and Neda got a taste of what it's really like to be unpopular.

The real culprit, to take the long view, was money itself.
There was too much of it in the '90s and early-to-mid 2000s,
and it came too easily to too many people. There was so much
of it, the average Angeleno couldn't go to a Shabbat dinner or a shul,
a parents' meeting at his child's school or a ladies' weekly card game,
without the conversation descending immediately into a pulsating,
inflated, and curiously detailed accounting of how much money "other
people" had made the previous week. It wasn't just the dot-com boom
or the rising values of real estate; not just the stock market, or the
ninety-nine-cent business, or electronics. These "other people" were
raking in millions merely by waking up in the morning, or having a
pulse, or, as with Elizabeth the Great, knowing what tiny start-up to
buy, and when to sell it.

It was so easy, it seemed, to make money, anyone who failed to
become outrageously wealthy was either dense or slow or just unmotivated. Doctors and attorneys, accountants and architects and
engineers—especially engineers—anyone who had squandered years
pursuing higher education, then paying off student loans by billing an
hourly rate for their work, was wasting time. Never mind that their
parents had made every sacrifice to send their kids to university, that
the kids had studied in high school and college till their eyes bled,
spent years on their degrees and their residencies, graduated at the
top of their classes—and now what? Now they worked twelve-hour
days making a hundred thousand dollars a year while their not-so-
bright classmates, the dropouts and the truants, bought a piece of land
in Las Vegas today, and sold it in a month's time for double the price.

As for the Iranians, they were finally making their peace with the
fact that in America a name isn't worth the paper it's written on. It
lives and dies with the individual; it can be changed for a mere few
dollars as a legal formality; and unless you're a Vanderbilt or a Kennedy
or some other outlaw-turned-statesman, your name says less about
you than your Social Security number or your zip code or your bank
account number.

This is what Iranians had found out in Atlanta and New York and Los Angeles and Palo Alto in the years after the revolution: that halo around the heads of the American rich is actually the zero that turns one dollar into ten; the more zeroes there are, the brighter the halo will shine. To most, it seemed that everyone around them was raking in the zeroes by the truckload. And that they alone had missed the memo, were left struggling to pay the rent or the mortgage, the lease payments on the car, the private school tuition, the obligatory bar mitzvah celebration.

Then Raphael's Son came along, with his nearsighted squint and penguin's gait and all those suitcases full of cash that he claimed was "family money," and when he popped open the cases and announced there was more where this came from, just come along and invest with me and you'll get it back in spades, all those Iranians who had been waiting for an opportunity to catch up in America's race to the riches, and all those who wished to multiply the millions they had already made in America, put aside common sense and simple reason, and turned over their life savings without, in most cases, so much as a receipt from Raphael's Son.

They did so—trust a man with tainted origins, a made-up pedigree, and, at best, questionable resources—because they liked what he promised, saw it happen all around them to twenty-year-old college students whose biggest achievement was tapping on their computer keyboard long enough to hit upon a decent idea and suddenly become billionaires.

Never mind that the "family money" he had carried out of Iran belonged to families other than his own; that he had extorted the cash and the precious stones, the antique rugs and thousand-year-old artifacts from the wives and daughters of wealthy men who had been jailed in the aftermath of the revolution, condemned to death, and released only after hefty "donations" had been made to a host of mosques and mullahs and "facilitators" such as Raphael's Son. Never mind, even, that his own bookkeeper, a sickly Armenian man with an unbridled death wish he did his best to fulfill by smoking four packs of Marlboro Reds a day, was always warning the older and less wealthy "investors" against giving their money to Raphael's Son. The guy had started with nothing and made a fortune, people said. He must know what he's doing.

They were right. Raphael's Son did know what he was doing.

Raphael's Son's explanation for how he was able to offer such high interest rates on any size of deposit was that he invested the funds in a way that few others were able. In the era of billion-dollar profits on Wall Street and rags-to-riches stories from Silicon Valley and elsewhere, this was not such an unlikely possibility. Nor was he the only person engaged in that line of work. His investors were no more or less guilty of recklessness than anyone else who ever bought into a racket.

What was different with Raphael's Son was that he sought not only his own prosperity, but also the ruin of his victims. He didn't discriminate against friends or foes, family or strangers. In the end, he didn't even discriminate against his own father-in-law.

For years, he had told Neda that her parents' poverty, however genteel, was an embarrassment not only to him but to Nicole and Kayla.

"It's not right, when people see you're living like a queen while your father's hauling boxes of cucumbers and bags of rice like a work mule. It reflects badly on us."

In 2005 he offered to help the Raiises "become somebody."

If they agreed to pay the mortgage, he said, he would cover the down payment so they could buy a business.

In another day and age, before he lost his pride and buried his ambitions along with his medals and memories, Dr. Raiis would have walked with his head high in front of a firing squad rather than take a dime from Raphael's Son. Even now, with his back permanently damaged from lifting heavy loads and his hands cracked like a farmworker's, his first reaction to the offer was pure indignation.

"Tell your husband we thank him," he said when Neda carried Raphael's Son's message to him and Zeeba, "but that we're not beggars and wouldn't be in his debt to save our lives."

They were living in a rented walk-up on the corner of Van Nuys and Moorpark, and Zeeba had been out of work for five months. What income they had was the seven dollars an hour from Benny Produce. Nilou, who was working for NASA on the Mars Rover project, sent them money all the time, and so did Zeeba's brothers from Iran. Neda would have liked to help, but she never had enough to spare: Raphael's Son gave her access to credit cards, but he made sure she was always short of cash.

He had done this from the beginning of their marriage. At one point, Neda tried to get around it by asking for cash back when she charged groceries or items at the drugstore, but Raphael's Son found out when he checked the credit card statements at the end of the month. He canceled her cards and didn't give her new ones for twelve weeks. He paid the maid directly, so that no cash went through Neda's hands, and he was more than generous with the girls' allowances. But he wanted Neda to remember who was feeding her and how badly she needed him.

Maybe because she felt guilty for not being able to help them, or maybe out of fear that Raphael's Son would take offense at the rejection, Neda insisted that her parents take the offer. She saw them once a week on Dr. Raiis's day off, when she drove to the Valley and spent the afternoon in their apartment that was in perpetual semidarkness because it didn't get direct sunlight. She pressed the point at every visit and on the phone with Zeeba because they both knew that once she—Zeeba—was on board, Dr. Raiis would have to fall in line. He had learned this quickly in America—that the person who calls the shots in a family is not necessarily the father but the one who makes the most money; that he, who had ignored his wife's urgings in Iran and by so doing endangered all their lives and reduced them to this, could no longer decide anything on his own.

You don't get to dictate too many decisions when you're dependent on tips from the adult children of people who once held you in the highest regard. And, ultimately, you don't get to refuse an opportunity such as the one Raphael's Son was handing out when you're past retirement age and still waiting for your big break.

Benny Produce was the smallest and least profitable of all the Iranian grocery shops in Pico-Robertson. The owner was all too happy to sell the place and leave it to Dr. and Mrs. Raiis to revive.

He was nine years late, but Raphael's Son had finally made his wife happy to be married to him: his gesture toward her parents, the ease and speed with which he delivered the money and signed the papers, even the seemingly sincere way in which he shook Dr. Raiis's hand and kissed Zeeba's—"Congratulations, madame, I wish you success; please do not hesitate to contact my assistant Eddy should you have questions"—all made Neda believe that he was, in fact, a better person than she had judged him to be.

The girls were nine and seven, so it was safe to say Neda had not been intimate with her husband for eight years; they had slept in separate bedrooms since they brought Kayla home from the hospital and Raphael's Son moved across the hall to get a good night's sleep while Neda breast-fed. After that, his main function as a father was to write checks and complain about the cost of private schooling and extracurricular activities for kids. He paid for lavish birthday parties and even more lavish bat mitzvahs, but he didn't spend a minute involved in the planning, and couldn't leave the events fast enough.

Is it true that we harbor the greatest resentment for those we need most? Is that why Raphael's Son so hated the community he had so longed to be accepted by? Why—now that he had finally made it, forced the doors open, and inserted himself into every business gathering and nonprofit board and social event—he could barely stand the company?

Perhaps predictably, the one person who was not pleased to see Dr. Raiis rise from store clerk to owner at Benny Produce was Angela. She heard the news from Nilou and immediately warned of dire consequences such as, but not limited to, bankruptcy, prison, divorce, or a murder-suicide for the lucky new owners. At thirty-three and working at a big, fancy law firm, Angela was just a bolder, more assertive version of her younger self. She didn't care how rich everyone in the country had become or how wide open the gates of success lay for every man, woman, and child in the age of easy mortgages. She knew what Raphael's Son was made of and could guess what he planned for his in-laws.

She went to Benny and personally warned Dr. Raiis, who continued to wear a suit and tie every day to stand behind the cash register and scan pound after pound of Japanese eggplant, Indian tea, and Israeli pickles, that he had made the biggest mistake of his life: "This is worse than when you wouldn't listen to Auntie Zeeba and got yourself stuck in Iran"; that he had not only made a pact with the devil but borrowed money from him: "I mean, who told you this was a good idea? I don't know how, but I promise he's got some dark agenda that he'll break out just when you've made this place good and profitable."

Dr. Raiis had a feeling he and Zeeba would be long dead before Benny became profitable. They had owned the place for under a month and already it had sucked whatever strength he and Zeeba had left. She had a permanent set of aches and pains, kept picking fights with the Honduran boy they had hired to replace Dr. Raiis in the back. She didn't talk to anyone unless she had to, and then usually about how a vendor had cheated them or a customer had slighted her. Dr. Raiis had known that he and Zeeba were too old and inexperienced to run a business of this kind, his years of service at Benny notwithstanding, and he had said as much before they accepted Raphael's Son's offer, but now here they were and—what the hell?—they would fight to keep from failing.

"Don't worry so much about me and my wife," Dr. Raiis told Angela, "we've had our turn. You just try to make sure that you and Nilou each have a husband and a couple of kids before I leave you all."

More than anything else when it came to marriage, Angela was among the lost generation of Iranian women who fled the country in their childhood or early teens and became stranded in the netherworld between East and West. Too young to have been shaped entirely by traditional values, too old to understand and adapt completely to modern ways, these women vacillated between seeking the safety of a "wise" marriage and the appeal of "true love," between the good sense of capitalizing on their youth and beauty to ensure financial security and the creation of a young, healthy family, and the temptation to make the most of their brainpower and individual strength. Most Iranian men found them too modern, and most Westerners thought them too traditional.

Because Los Angeles, as Raphael's Son would famously express to the Aramaic brothers, was indeed a third world country. The image was that of a city filled with tall, blond California girls and boys, all rosy cheeks and short shorts and bicycle rides by the beach. In fact, nearly everyone who lived here had come from outside California, blondness was chemically induced, and more than 224 languages were spoken in LA County.

The arrangement made it easier for a foreigner to feel at home, but it did have a few flaws: once they arrived here, members of each ethnic group joined their own little tribes and stayed there, more or less harmoniously, for good. Each tribe was possessive and territorial and forever threatened by the success or expansion of their neighbors. In some parts of town, they acted out their fears with AK-47s and other constitutionally sanctioned weapons of mass destruction—hence the city's distinction as the "Gang Capital of the World." In others, as on the West Side, they took the war into the sandboxes and playgrounds of private preschools, the boardrooms of city councils, and the sanctuaries of synagogues.

Within each tribe, a war of attrition was waged in which Western values first threatened, then encroached upon, then ate the dying carcasses of old beliefs and traditions. Angela knew about that war.

As far as she could tell, her entire adult life had been shaped by this conflict. It was the reason she received a first-class education, had a career, and controlled her own fate. It was also the reason she was alone and childless.

In the late '80s and early-to-mid '90s, when Angela was of dating age, young people in the community were expected to marry other Iranian Jews. Anything else (like marrying an Ashkenazi Jew) was cause for the parents to sit shivah. This always struck Angela as preposterous, given that they had chosen to live in America instead of Iran, but it was largely irrelevant in her case because no "normal" white male had expressed real interest in her anyway. Normal white males, it turned out, thought they could do better than Iranian women.

All those LA natives who complained that Iranians were loathe to mix with and integrate into the larger community—who blamed the parents for insisting that their children marry other Iranians and who blamed the children for bonding primarily with other Iranian kids—all the former immigrants who accorded these newer ones the same lack of regard as they themselves had once been held in, now overlooked their own part in keeping the tribes separate.

Nor were normal Iranian males of suitable ages lining up with applications to marry Angela. She wasn't pretty enough to satisfy the prospective mothers-in-law's physical requirements, and not rich enough to influence their fathers to waive those requirements. Past age twenty-five, she was not pretty enough, not rich enough, and getting too old. Before she knew it, she was twenty-seven and older women were saying things like, "She never did get married," as if she were dead or on the verge of it, had missed the three-minute window of opportunity during which girls were considered worthy of marriage. Then she was thirty, with an Ivy League education and a high-paying job, but as far as anyone in the community was concerned, she was a walking tragedy because she remained unmarried. This way of thinking was not particular to Iranians: postfeminism, most American women also thought of marriage as the best of all options.

When she turned thirty, Angela bought a small house on Mulholland overlooking the valley, and told herself she must learn to accept what she wasn't able to change. Three years later, in 2005, she had accepted that, at thirty-three, she may be heading toward permanent "husband-lessness." She was mostly fine with this. But every once in a while she saw a child, usually a stranger's, who made her heart sink and filled her with a sadness she would not be able to shake for days.

She hadn't seen John Vain since he turned himself in at Lompoc, but she had been keeping count and knew it was almost time for him to be released. He had served eleven years of a thirteen-year sentence. In federal prison, convicts get fifty-four days reduced from their sentence every year for good behavior. Assuming he had received the maximum amount of time off, he would be released at some point within the coming months. Until now, Angela had respected his wish to be left alone, but "enough is enough," she told Elizabeth when announcing her intention to visit John Vain, "he's coming out any day now and he's going to need help getting his life back."

Angela was right about that—John Vain needing help—but she got the release date wrong: she went to Lompoc only to find he had been let go sixty-three days earlier "because the fifty-four-day rule, you see, madame-attorney-from-the-East-Coast, isn't set in stone, we all liked John Vain and the warden did too."

Stricken, she tried to track him down every which way she could think of. She was working as a government attorney then, at less than half the salary she had drawn in the private sector, and she couldn't afford to hire the kind of investigator she thought was needed to track down an ex-con who was determined to remain lost. She felt Elizabeth owed her this, that she owed it, in fact, to John Vain, regardless of his one-time plea for emancipation from their friendship.

Not that Angela harbored any conscious anger toward her mother. Past thirty, she was sure she could understand, even excuse Elizabeth for not giving of herself that which she had never received from her own mother. Angela could see how the losses of the early years, the disruption of exile and the ensuing strife, would stifle in a person, even one as steadfast as Elizabeth, the kind of tenderness a daughter longs for. She could imagine how, having buried one child, Elizabeth might hesitate to attach too deeply to another.

Still, there were facts Angela could not forget even after she had forgiven. One of them was the habit instilled in her from her childhood to be independent to the extreme. The other was to be alone and unattached. This was easy enough in Manhattan where she had no family and didn't like any of her coworkers. But once she moved back to LA, she was always running into people she knew from high school, or people who knew her even though she had no idea who they were, who came up and stopped her in the middle of the street, in a restaurant, anywhere, really, to ask about "your dear mother" until it became clear that they had more personal information about Elizabeth than Angela ever would; and as if that weren't enough of an affront, they invariably went on to inquire about her private life, or what should have been private anyway, like whether she was married yet and if not, "Don't worry, girls marry later these days, some even date Americans, you shouldn't have any trouble meeting a great guy, you're smart and accomplished and have many other assets."

"Translation," Angela would fume on the phone to Nilou, "you may be smart, but you're no looker. Or, someone's bound to marry you for your mother's money."

That last one—about Elizabeth's money likely attracting a husband for Angela—was a fair prediction, given the way things happened in every community in every part of the world, and especially given the amount of money at stake.

Elizabeth's house on Oakmont Drive in Brentwood had the kind of Zen simplicity that costs a lot of money to look inexpensive. All the lines and frames were straight and fine, every surface smooth and quiet, every color neutral and easy on the eyes. The maid wore sleeveless gray Calvin Klein dresses reminiscent of the heyday of Communist China. The male servant wore white dress shirts, gray ties with white stripes, and tailored gray suits. They both spoke with spa voices—the practiced just-above-a-whisper tone that signals over-priced tranquility, tap water flavored with cucumber slices, eighteen types of herbal tea, and chenille bathroom slippers.

Against this backdrop Stephanie Dalal, Elizabeth's self-appointed chief of staff and jealous gatekeeper, stood out like a well-dressed rash. Tall, thread-thin, and salon-tanned like a beach volleyball player in Rio de Janeiro, Stephanie Dalal was one of those painfully conflicted creatures that are found in such unfortunate abundance all along the California coast: women in their forties and fifties who once believed they could and should and would have it all. They had started out smart and educated, attractive and confident—and yes, thin, tanned, and toned—and they had assumed that life—and men—would reward them fairly for all they had to offer. A divorce or two and a string of bad relationships later, they were still smart and educated, and still a size 4, but they now subsisted on undressed salads and nonfat lattes, got spray tans instead of lying in the sun, couldn't run up and down the Santa Monica steps without injuring a knee, and had to resort to paying overly grown young men with underdeveloped brains $180 an hour to help them with "spot reduction" at the gym. Men ten or more years older wouldn't consider dating these women because they were too old, too demanding, and had "too much baggage." Married women their age avoided them, and unmarried ones competed with them for the attention of the very few recently divorced or widowed men who hadn't been snatched while they were married or the minute their wives got sick.

Stephanie wore pencil skirts and lizard-skin pumps, listened to self-help courses in her car, and addressed everyone as "Dear." She served Elizabeth faultlessly but hated her for being ungrateful and stingy—not with money or perks, or vacation and sick time, but with her handsome, wealthy, and single male friends and associates, of which Stephanie knew there were many. In seven years of seeing her every day, Elizabeth had never once inquired about Stephanie's personal life. One might either credit her for respecting an employee's privacy, or assume she didn't ask because she didn't care. Stephanie believed the latter. She was on her way out of the house on Tuesday afternoon when the gate guard called to announce Angela.

"Tell her no," Stephanie barked at the guard. "Mrs. Soleyman is busy and is not expecting visitors."

Two minutes later, Angela's Prius was storming up the driveway like a toy tank driven by a kamikaze pilot.

A male servant showed Angela into the library and closed the door. He returned a few minutes later with a small silver tray bearing a bottle of sparkling water, one crystal glass, and a Daum candy dish with Fauchon chocolates. He put the tray down on one of those minimalist tables that are put on display in museums of modern art, threw an ever-so-subtle glance at Angela who had splayed herself on the love seat like an unruly ten-year-old, and asked if he should pour.

"No," Angela said, combatively. "But please tell my mom I don't have all day."

She was thinking the man seemed like someone who would be named Gerald. He could have been a manager at a men's luxury department store, making minimum wage plus the occasional commission but acting like he owned the business and holding the customers who spent enough in contempt until he was replaced by a better-looking, more athletic version of himself and had to find employment elsewhere.

"You've been with her long?" she asked, trying to soften her voice. She realized it wasn't his fault that she felt like a stranger at her own mother's house—that, for all practical purposes, she *was* in fact a stranger at her mother's house.

"Five years this August," he said, carefully signaling his disapproval of her manners by averting his eyes.

"Hmm," Angela pondered aloud, "I wonder why—"

"We have, indeed, met before, madame," Gerald interrupted. "A few times." He bowed his head perfunctorily and left the room.

Were they really that different—Angela and Elizabeth—when dealing with other humans?

She heard the quick tempo of heels against the gray wood floor, like a metronome set to presto, and felt her heart tighten with emotion.

"I'm so glad you came," Elizabeth said as she emerged through the door. In an instant, she was upon Angela, kissing her on both cheeks, and then she said the phrase that was the trademark of every Iranian Jewish mother: "*Ghorboonet beram*"—May I be sacrificed for you.

"I've been hoping to see you."

It always distressed Angela to hear Elizabeth say, "*Ghorboonet beram*," or use any other maternal term of endearment. To Angela, these phrases felt like an unfair attempt to undermine the cold war she had waged against her mother for decades.

Elizabeth wore a plain (no doubt expensive) beige dress, two-inch heels, soft makeup, and no jewelry except for a watch.

"You've been working hard?" she asked in Persian.

"No. But I want something from you. That is, I want you to fulfill an obligation you've neglected."

At this, the light in Elizabeth's eyes dimmed. She nodded once, then smiled sadly and asked, "You mean about John Vain?"

It always surprised Angela to think how young—fifty-one—her mother was, how wise she seemed at times, how quick to understand and learn. Angela couldn't help but be in awe of her, admire the strength that had helped her survive the many past lives.

"I can't find a trace of him," Angela said, suddenly bereft. "I think you should hire an expert. I would do it, but they're expensive." She glanced around the room as if to verify that Elizabeth could afford it.

"Do you think he wants you to find him?" Elizabeth asked softly.

That she said "you" instead of "us" felt like the coldest of the cold postures to Angela.

"What the hell, Mom!" She only realized she was yelling when she heard her voice echo in the room. "*You* should be looking for him too. You should never have stopped seeing him."

It wasn't the first time Angela had reproached Elizabeth for abandoning John Vain to his wishes.

"I know you want to help him," Elizabeth said calmly.

"Someone needs to."

She had stood up to greet Elizabeth when she came in, and had remained standing. Now she dropped back into the chair.

"He was there for *us*." She realized she was going to cry, and put her face into her hand to hide the tears.

So much longing. So many losses.

"Angela," Elizabeth said with tenderness, "I've been where you are—young, and certain of what you want. I know that need, how vital it seems, how imperative. But I wish you'd believe me when I say that some truths are better left untold, because the more you learn, the more you'll be haunted by what you don't know."

D r. Raiis became the canary in the mine.
In 2008 he received a notice of foreclosure from a bank he had never had dealings with. He assumed there was a mistake, called the bank, and told them so. He thought this was the end of it.

Throughout the easy-mortgage years of the early 2000s, Raphael's Son had taken second and third loans on just about every property he owned. What he did with the money was for him and some bank officers in the Cayman Islands to know, but as he approached the date of the bankruptcy, he began to let the banks take what they wished from among his overly leveraged holdings. Dr. Raiis, of course, had not been informed that the loan on his shop now belonged to a new bank. As far as he knew, Raphael's Son had parted with the down payment in 2005 but registered the title to the shop in Dr. Raiis's name. He sent the mortgage checks to Eddy Arax who forwarded them to the bank.

Eddy was unusually twitchy the day Dr. Raiis rushed over with the foreclosure notice getting soaked with perspiration in his hand. He cursed under his breath the minute he saw Dr. Raiis enter, then said with that Armenian accent that grew heavier the more exasperated he became, "Wait in the hallway with everyone else."

That's when Dr. Raiis glanced behind him and noticed what he had been too overwhelmed to see when he came in: a line of restless, anxious-looking men and women that stretched down the corridor, into the office lobby, and outside by the elevators. Every one of them, he soon learned, had come bearing a letter or a notice they thought was sent to them by mistake.

News of Raphael's Son's so-called bankruptcy arrived in Los Angeles the way most other headlines broke on the West Coast: through the well-oiled gossip network of Iranian Jews in Long Island. Perhaps because they were only the *second* largest community of Iranian Jews in the United States, the East Coasters had a curious and long-lasting fascination with the *Los-Aan-jealous-syiah* that stretched back to before the great migration. At the time, only a few dozen Iranian Jews had left Tehran to seek their fortunes in the United States. Most had settled in New York and gone into the real estate business; many had been enormously successful. But these were the salad days of Iran's economic expansion—of money growing on trees and entitlement being a birthright; of weekend shopping trips from Tehran to London and three-month summer junkets to the French Riviera; of parties that started near midnight and lasted till daybreak on weekdays, and privately owned villages and thoroughbred stables and jewels that made a laughingstock of the entirety of the crown jewels of the United Kingdom. Triumphant as the renegade Iranians had been in New York, they could not begin to impress the families in Tehran or justify having abandoned their ancient homeland—"because we're Iranian, you know, flesh and blood, and always will be"—for the soot-covered buildings and confined living spaces and yellow traffic hazards of Manhattan.

The revolution brought some of those flesh-and-blood Iranians to their senses and sent them packing to Long Island to suffer through snowstorms and hurricane weather, but the majority skipped the excitement and headed for the West Coast. From deep beneath sable coats and mink earmuffs, on the train to Manhattan where they hoped to consult the best plastic surgeons, the New Yorkers consoled themselves that LA's climate had made the *Los-Aan-jealous-syiah* spiritually shallow and physically vain. Held captive by the Ashkenazi bridezillas their sons had brought home, and the robber baron party planners the future daughters-in-law had hired on their dime (because among Iranians, the groom's family pays for the wedding), they consoled each other that the celluloid culture had made the *Los-Aan-jealous-syiah* too flashy and permissive. Over the years, those who saw the futility of denial packed up and moved quietly to LA. The rest remained on the lookout for reason number ten thousand why living in Long Island was a better idea. As it happened, a single reason would have sufficed and that, ladies and gentlemen of the East Coast, was provided courtesy of R.S. Soleyman.

Before they immigrated to the West, Iranians had revered America as the one country on the planet where the law was mightier than the people who wrote it.

"In America," they had told each other with awe, "even the president gets impeached if he breaks the law."

The president, maybe, but not Wall Street players and not, alas, Raphael's Son or the Riffraff. What the great recession of 2008 would prove to many immigrants who hitherto held the American justice system in adulation was that, much like the dictatorship from which they had escaped, it applied mostly to the poor.

After he got no answers from Eddy Arax, Dr. Raiis called Raphael's Son at the office and at home and on his cell phone several times a day. He left messages and tried to convince himself that he had not done a foolish thing. Better businessmen than he, after all, had trusted Raphael's Son with much larger investments; they couldn't all be fools. Rabbis ranging from the ultra-Orthodox to Reform and Reconstructionist praised his financial savvy and his generous devotion to every Jewish cause; they couldn't all be wrong.

He appealed for help to Neda and even to his granddaughters, Nicole and Kayla: "Ask your father to call me back, please—this is urgent, extremely urgent." He went back to the office in Century City and was horrified to find an even larger rush of panicked, outraged clients threatening to break down Eddy's door if he didn't open.

Shaking like a scarecrow in the wind and appearing like he was on the verge of a stroke, Eddy screamed from inside, "I can't give you any money today! I don't have it to give."

Over the next few days, as Raphael's Son proved elusive and word spread that he was preparing to go into bankruptcy while his hillbilly relatives in their ninety-nine-cent-store getup were buying blocks of real estate downtown and elsewhere in cash, Eddy was increasingly besieged by clients demanding return of their deposits. He went from being unusually bitter and short-tempered to a veritable emotional wreck. People screamed at him and he screamed back, they pled with him and he broke into tears.

"There's nothing I can do," he repeated a hundred times a day, then finally turned off the ringer to his office and cell phones. "It's not my money to give."

He lost his appetite entirely and smoked more. He squeezed two or three hours of sleep out of a full dose of Ambien, felt physically ill, and wondered who might care for his mother if he took off for Belize. He called Raphael's Son on his private cell phone—so private, only three people, Joshua Simcha, Hadassah Simcha, and Eddy, knew the number—and yelled at him till Raphael's Son hung up.

"Come here and answer these people yourself," he said.

"If you won't see them, at least return their calls so they leave *me* alone," he said.

"If you're going to disappear, tell me what to do with the books and the office," he said.

Eddy couldn't prevail upon his boss to come out of hiding, and couldn't avoid the creditors even at home in Glendale. He slammed the door on the elderly and the widows because he couldn't bear to look them in the eye; with the wealthier creditors who had lost millions, he poured salt on the wound by saying, "Don't blame me if you're stupid and that bastard is a thief."

Then he got a visit from Cagney and Lacey—the Rat in the Hat and That Fucking Snake—and he began to seriously fear for his life.

A ngela was driving with Nilou to Temple Street downtown, hoping to convince the bankruptcy court to stall or stop Raphael's Son and the Riffraff's heist, when she spotted John Vain. They had stopped at the light on Main and 7th, and she happened to glance up at the orange and white city bus in the next lane. The man by the window looked nothing like the John Vain of her childhood, and yet she recognized him immediately. She put the car in park and left it at the intersection with the engine still running and Nilou in the passenger seat, sprinted up to the bus, and banged on the door till the driver noticed her. He didn't open, but he pointed toward the stop a block away. Angela yelled at Nilou to get behind the wheel and follow the bus, then ran, met the bus, and climbed on before passengers had a chance to disembark. She collided with John Vain on the steps.

At the time he was released from prison he had a few hundred dollars in an old account and a host of old friends with means, Hal and Elizabeth among them, who would have jumped at the chance to help him start over. What he didn't have was the emotional wherewithal to go back and show his face to them, be reminded of who he once was and what he had become, depend—he who had been the king of giving—on handouts.

From Lompoc, he took a bus for the 175 miles into Los Angeles, spent two nights as a guest in the rented one-bedroom house his old kitchen hand Manuel shared with four other undocumented immigrants in the West Adams district downtown. He had lost thirty pounds in prison, his skin was sallow and pale, his clothes fraying and outdated. The rows and rows of cowboy boots he had gone to such lengths to purchase, his expensive suits, the silk ties and tiepins and cuff links he had taken such joy in wearing, were all piled in a heap inside a large packing box in a storage locker off Vine Street in Hollywood. They smelled of dust and mothballs and stale air. Even after they had been cleaned, they hung off him like something stolen out of the back of a truck.

At Lompoc, he had been assigned to the kitchen, so he tried to find work as a short-order cook. His great fear was to run into anyone he had known in his former life, which was unlikely, given the caliber of places where he applied, but it also meant he couldn't get a recommendation or turn to any of his old contacts for a job. In the end, he bought a fake Social Security card from some Russian teenagers and went to work alongside half a dozen undocumented workers at a Tex-Mex restaurant next to a muscle gym on Olvera Street. That's where he was when Angela first started to look for him. He was working fourteen-hour days and saving up so he could move out of LA and go as far as it took, the middle of Death Valley if he had to, to find a place cheap enough that he could afford, put up some plumbing and an old stove, hang up a sign that said, *Warning: Prison Food Served Here.*

They stood on the sidewalk at Main and 8th, Angela in her lawyer suit from Ann Taylor Loft and John Vain in a pair of worn black pants and a faded black T-shirt, and waited for Nilou to park the car and join them. From far away, they resembled old acquaintances who run into each other too often and never quite know where to pick up. Then Nilou arrived and threw herself at John Vain, crying, "Uncle John, I've missed you!" without a trace of anger in her voice, and he opened his arms and hugged her.

He had just started to work as an expo at Artisan House on 6th and Main. The owners were a pair of Iranian kids, and they had hired him despite the fact that he was too old because he was Iranian. He lived on 6th and San Pedro, which could be considered skid row, but he had an apartment with a nice bathroom and kitchen, and he didn't mind stepping over bodies and between tents to get to it.

He gave the report in a single installment, as if it had been prepared and rehearsed and memorized for an occasion such as this. His hair had thinned and his body hinted of a permanent ache or two, but it was the emptiness—the emotional void between him and the girls—that was most telling. It was like going back to a city you grew up in, but that has burned down and been rebuilt since you last saw it.

Too politely, he asked about Elizabeth and the Raiises.

"They're fine," Angela answered for herself and Nilou, "but you don't wanna know about Neda."

If this was an invitation for him to ask, he didn't take it.

They quickly ran out of things to say to each other.

"Shall we go sit somewhere and catch up?" Nilou offered hesitantly.

John Vain was late for work. He didn't have a cell phone but he took Angela's number and promised he'd call.

In the months after Raphael's Son declared bankruptcy, Dr. Raiis tried, Sisyphus-like, to save his shop from the ghost bankers who had somehow come to own it. When Eddy didn't answer his calls and Raphael's Son planted a pair of nightclub bouncers outside his own house to scare away creditors, Dr. Raiis went to the police, the district attorney, Legal Aid; to every one of the members of the Riff-raff Brigade, their spouses and friends. Again and again, he appealed to Neda for help, as if she had any say in her husband's affairs. He wrote an eloquent, heartrending letter in which he asked for her help in return for "everything your mother and I did for you when you still needed us."

Next, he sought out other creditors and suggested they all meet and join forces. The ones who didn't have much to begin with and had now lost it all thought it best to keep quiet and out of the way, rely on Raphael's Son's humanity to give them their money back when the dust had settled. They didn't want to risk alienating him by closing ranks. The wealthier creditors laughed when they heard how "little" the Raiises had at stake.

"I wish that's all I had lost," they said.

Still, Dr. Raiis would not accept that an injustice such as the one Raphael's Son had committed would be allowed in the twenty-first century, in the United States of America, in the we're-so-liberal-we-raise-the-bar-for-everyone-else state of California.

His latest idea was to write an appeal to the president of the bank, reminding him of his responsibilities as a human being, and asking for a face-to-face meeting in which to "arrive at an amicable and mutually agreeable solution."

According to the victims as well as the contingent of bloodsucking, cadaver-eating, let's-steal-the-penny-off-the-dead-man's-eyes lawyers and forensic accountants the trustee had called into action as a result of the "bankruptcy," the genius of what Raphael's Son had done was the intentional failure to keep documents. Ten years into the twenty-first century, all the books at Soleyman Enterprises were kept in old-fashioned accounting ledgers, written in pencil, with no copies made. There was no computer in the office, only an electric calculator, and even that was hardly ever used because both Raphael's Son and Eddy were products of the Iranian educational system and therefore able to retain an enormous amount of information in their memory and perform complex mathematical calculations in their heads.

This absence of documentation had of course been noted by most of Raphael's Son's clients, and while it did scare away a few potential investors, it was overlooked by others as the price of doing business with an establishment that provided such steady, high interest on their money. And besides, they told each other over a few shots of tequila every Friday night at Shabbat dinner or Saturday night at a gathering of seven hundred of their closest friends, "that Eddy is a walking Excel sheet."

As long as the going was good, the investors were happy to rely on Eddy's instant recall, down to the last cent, of every dollar he received or paid on Raphael's Son's behalf. Most of them believed Raphael's Son when he said that he didn't keep a paper trail so he could avoid paying taxes, the IRS be damned, he'd pay taxes on his earnings when Hank Paulson paid his. In case they hadn't heard him tell this story before, Raphael's Son always followed this statement with an account of how Paulson made $700 million at Goldman Sachs while digging the hole into which the rest of the world would sink; in 2006, when he left the firm to become George W. Bush's treasury secretary, Congress passed a law that "happened" to spare Paulson $50 million he owed in taxes.

"For that, and because he was too stupid to see the meltdown coming, Paulson got to keep the top job at Treasury even under Obama."

Once the money disappeared, however, Eddy was left holding the bag. To the creditors, Raphael's Son said he had no way of knowing just how much he owed each investor; to the lawyers, he said they should talk to Eddy, who had, after all, kept the books. To the district attorney, in the single suit brought against him, he suggested the DA would have a better case if they charged Eddy for his shoddy accounting. To Eddy, he explained that there was nothing for him to fear: "You don't have any assets to lose, and if it turns out that one of us has to do time, I can see to it that your mother is well taken care of."

It was true that doing a year or two of quiet time in Pleasant Valley State Prison, better known as the Country Club for its green lawns and lax regulation, might have been an improvement over Eddy's life on the outside. It was also true that, though he had never directly benefited from the fraud, Eddy knew what his boss was up to all those years. And that story about him keeping every number in his head—that was of course pure drivel. Eddy did keep ledgers, only they were handwritten, in pencil, and easily erased or adjusted according to Raphael's Son's instructions.

John Vain's boss at Artisan House had been trying to get ahold of him for over a week when he gave up on reaching him by phone and showed up at his door late one Friday evening. There was no answer when he knocked, and no manager on site, but the door was so flimsy and the hinges so old, they gave way with one good push.

Barely eight hundred square feet and shaped like a T, the apartment consisted of a narrow living room where an ancient yellow and white sofa, backed against one wall, faced an even-more-ancient television set. A small bedroom and smaller kitchen sat to the right and the left of the sitting area. Between them in the back wall, a square window with a cheap aluminum frame overlooked the busy intersection below. The window had to be closed at all times to keep out the dust and noise of traffic, but even then the sound of cars and the smell of gasoline permeated the apartment.

The boss walked in at twilight. In the back, a single bulb screwed into the ceiling cast a white glow onto the plastic folding table. Beside the door, two table lamps on either side of the narrow entrance eked out a yellowish beam. In the kitchen, the fridge was emptied out and clean. Dishes had been washed and left in the drying rack. In the bedroom, the curtains were drawn. The bed was made, the drawers closed. A framed picture of a very young John Vain, his arm loosely around a woman, sat on the nightstand. A second picture—with the same woman and a younger one in a graduation cap and gown—was on the windowsill.

The bathroom was spotless. On the right was a sink and a pair of neatly folded, forest-green towels. Next to it, John Vain hung from a pull-up bar nailed to the ceiling.

John Vain's funeral services, at Eden Memorial Park in Mission Hills, were scheduled for one p.m. on Sunday afternoon. The date and time, along with a brief biography of the deceased, were announced at two-hour intervals on closed-circuit Persian-language radio, on Menashe Amir's program on Israel Radio, and on Radio Iran, 670 AM. An Iranian rabbi recently relocated from New York was hired to recite the customary prayers, with a specific injunction that he was not to exceed his allotted twenty minutes at the grave site.

All this had been arranged by Angela and paid for by Elizabeth. At the funeral house or on the phone with Raab Chaim, she had introduced herself as a close friend of the deceased, which was fine with the rabbi, he didn't need to know any more, given Angela's mother's good credit and the fact that she did not balk at the fee he suggested. With the recession, people still died at the same rate, but "funeral specialists" were often called upon to issue discounts or interest-free payment plans.

Angela had done her best to make the process both dignified and meaningful, but she didn't know the first thing about Jewish law regarding burial of the deceased, and that became a problem on Sunday when having arrived at Eden ready to pray over a handsome casket and a sea of white flowers—a staple at every Iranian Jewish funeral—Raab Chaim was handed a small urn and shown to a 12' x 12' square in a wall. Pale-faced and scandalized, he explained to Angela that "real Jews are not to be cremated or buried in a wall, not if they're observant in the least, not like that Reform and Reconstructionist bunch who're really gentiles at heart—you can go hire one of those rabbis to stick an urn in a wall if you want but you're not getting me to ruin my reputation in this world and the next by violating two of the most basic laws of Judaism."

You had to feel sorry for Raab Chaim: he was a legitimate scholar (as in, he had actually gone to rabbincal school and graduated from it), and relatively moderate in his ideas. You would think this would count in his favor in this day and age, but on Long Island where he started his career, he had found himself increasingly marginalized by a host of younger, much more Orthodox (black hat and *peyos* and all the trappings) rabbis whose message had begun to resonate with the community. It was a fad of sorts—this tendency toward orthodoxy of the kind that had not existed in Iran. Jews who only a few years earlier had prided themselves on being "modern" (to the point of eating shellfish in public and admitting they went to shul twice a year at most) were becoming more and more observant and, as a result, abandoning the likes of Raab Moussa for more unforgiving rabbis with more draconian views.

Having been rendered superfluous on the East Coast in the 1990s, Raab Chaim set his sights on the Jews of LA. He arrived here in the early '90s, barely a step ahead of the winds of orthodoxy that blew westward and that brought with them small and large replicas of the same beard-growing, finger-wagging, fire-and-brimstone-promising individuals he had so wanted to escape—and this time, there was nowhere for him to go. For a while, he dug his heels in and tried to cultivate a conservative-minded but otherwise tolerant base upon which to build a congregation. But the more moderate Iranian Jews he wanted to reach out to had already met and married David Wolpe, the American rabbi, at Sinai Temple. Everyone else—the Iranian Jews in the Valley and the ones on the West Side who didn't revere Wolpe because they found him too "permissive"—had their doubts about Raab Chaim's devotion to the principles he had begun to preach.

Struggling to keep a foothold in LA and having to supplement his income by giving private Torah and Hebrew lessons, Raab Chaim was not in a position to turn down an invitation to conduct any service, but nor could he go down in popular memory as the rabbi who had condoned the burning of a body and buried it in an urn inside a wall.

It was bad enough that the man had committed suicide and that the next of kin consisted only of Elizabeth and Angela, and Dr. Raiis and his family. For Iranian Jews, having so few relations at one's funeral was about the biggest insult imaginable to the dead. In Iran, Muslims and Jews would even hire professional mourners to mix things up at a burial. Theirs was, after all, a culture that measured a man's popularity by the amount of tears shed at his grave site.

They grieved—these Iranians—with the same spectacular intensity with which they entertained. They noted that Americans dressed better and were more social at funerals than they were at parties: to parties, they showed up in shorts and flip-flops, served potato chips and one dish, and called it a day at nine p.m. At funerals, they put the dead through professional hair and makeup. As for the family, if they were going to shed any tears, they would do it in private, then face the world with such pronouncements as, "I must move on to the next chapter of my life."

In the end, John Vain's funeral looked totally American—simple, rushed, poorly attended.

Raab Chaim stayed for the services, but the job of saying kaddish fell to Dr. Raiis. Afterward, he drove out of Eden alone and didn't tell anyone where he was headed. He put thirty-seven dollars' worth of gas in his dented silver Hyundai with the bad alignment and the rattling exhaust pipe, and drove to Century City where he parked along the red zone a hundred feet away from Watt Plaza. He sat there with the engine running and his hands wet and clammy from anxiety, and waited for Raphael's Son to emerge.

Dr. Raiis was not a violent person. He had never wished harm on anyone except Khomeini, Ahmadinejad, and all the thugs and mullahs who had raped and robbed Iran and forced him to flee the country of his and his ancestors' birth. Whatever hardship and indignity had been exacted on him in the thirty years since the revolution, he blamed on the fact that he was a man without a country. He didn't expect America to make up for the injustice done to him by the government of Iran, or for his own failure to become financially secure. But he did expect some justice from the American legal system.

In Iran, a person who could not pay his debts would stay in debtors' prison until he died or made his creditors whole. His cohorts and accomplices would either follow him to jail or be so bereft of *aabehroo* they either escaped the country or came clean. In Los Angeles and New York and Tel Aviv and Taiwan, Raphael's Son and the Riffraff Brigade's only punishment so far had been the ability to go on a buying frenzy—all cash—to take advantage of sliding prices.

Dr. Raiis waited in the car for three hours. His phone rang two dozen times, his wife and children looking for him, but he didn't take his hands off the steering wheel or turn the engine off because he wanted to be ready.

To access the parking lot of the towers, tenants and visitors had to cross a walkway. At 7:15 that evening, as soon as Raphael's Son emerged from the building, Dr. Raiis put the car in drive and floored the gas pedal. He aimed directly at Raphael's Son with the express intention of crushing him like the venomous arachnid that he was.

Instead, the front wheel of his car hit the curb and exploded.

His wife and daughters bailed him out, and hired an attorney. Raphael's Son insisted that the DA press charges, but Angela had a few good talks with her colleagues and in the end they settled for a warning and eighteen months of community service. The judge who signed off on the deal also suggested yoga and meditation classes which were offered at a nominal cost, she took pains to point out, by the Beverly Hills Parks and Recreation Department, even to nonresidents of the city.

John Vain had left no note, confided in no one, made no attempt to put his life or death into a narrative that could be saved or remembered. In the end, all that remained of him, for Angela and Elizabeth and everyone else whose lives he had touched, was the memory of his kindness and the sweet, enduring faith in his own good luck. Maybe, Angela told herself, it was the constant shame, the pernicious guilt, that had consumed John Vain since Lucky 99 burned down. Maybe it was his new surroundings, the memory of that other house in Trousdale, all those wide-open spaces and sun-drenched rooms, a view of the garden from every part of the house, that got the best of him.

What do you call that moment when we let go of the conviction, albeit illusory, that life will only grow larger? That the horizon will always expand?

The shivah was held at Elizabeth's Oakmont Drive house, and was therefore among the most well-attended events of the decade. Every afternoon for six days (the seventh being Shabbat), the house filled with callers who arrived for the reading of the *minhah*. They stayed anywhere from five minutes to five hours, drank hot tea brewed with cardamom, and ate dates and peeled cucumbers served to them by harried, grumpy Armenian women who had been somebody back in Iran but who were now reduced to working as waiters because they didn't speak English and didn't have papers. In the evening, a lavish dinner was served courtesy of Roberto, a young Seventh-day Adventist from Guatemala who used to work at the Russian kosher butcher shop on Doheny and Pico, and who managed to parlay that job into a full-service Iranian-kosher catering business.

Some of the visitors had known John Vain from the glory days of Lucky 99, and came to pay respects. Most were there to satisfy a long-standing curiosity about Elizabeth's personal life, or what little of it they could glean by seeing the inside of her house. Still another handful were old friends of the Soleymans from Iran who had lost touch with Elizabeth after Aaron's death, and used the shivah as a final reunion of sorts. There was Omid Arbab, Aaron's childhood friend who had abandoned a wife and child in Tehran and followed a lover to America before the revolution. There was Miriam (as beautiful as) the Moon, who bore no trace of the good looks for which she had been known, but who still carried herself like a marine sergeant on a mission. There was Lili, the adopted daughter of that Russian homewrecker, Mercedez, who wanted to be a movie star in Hollywood; she failed miserably at the silver screen, but bought entire blocks of the city when they were dirt cheap and left them all to Lili. And then, on day four, there was the man who had come thirty years too late.

He walked in ahead of a row of younger men, all of them in long black coats and black hats, their eyes deflected toward the ground for fear of seeing any women, their faces pale from a lifetime of sitting indoors studying the Torah, following the old man like a flock of black birds as he trudged through the foyer and into the reception hall where he stopped dead, apparently stunned by the realization that in this room men and women sat together without any kind of partition, then lowered his head and turned his chin toward the one behind him, whispered an order of retreat, so that all the younger men stepped back against the wall lest their eyes stray onto a female shape. He waited until Stephanie Dalal, ensconced much too snugly in a black pencil skirt and a silk black top that set off her angry, salon-tanned neck, came up and invited him in. He told her he couldn't—was there a room where men could sit and pray in a holy manner? That only drew a more truculent than usual "You must be kidding me" from the chief of staff. The man remained, neither challenging her nor retreating, drawing attention to himself and Stephanie until she gave in with a huff, led him and his flock to the more intimate sitting room. There they sat for the next three hours, humming prayers in one cadence and speed, the lot of them sounding like an entitled bee colony waiting to be recognized. At dinnertime they filed into the dining room without an invitation but did not touch even the bread or the wine lest it not be kosher enough.

They came again the next morning at seven, and waited at the gates on Oakmont until the attendant called the house and Gerald answered. They had come for the wrapping of the *tefillin*, they said, and again gained entry into the sitting room. They did this for two days in a row, while the rules of hospitality and good taste dictated that the *sahib azza*—person(s) in mourning—welcome them wholeheartedly. The other visitors speculated endlessly about the men's identity, having started with the assumption that they were part of the league of black hatters who went asking for donations at the homes and offices of wealthy Jews all around the city, but that theory was put to rest by some who had seen the men arrive in a chauffeur-driven stretch Mercedes limousine.

On the final day of the shivah, Elizabeth stopped in the sitting room.

"What can we do for you?" she asked, and the old man responded, ever so courteously, "We've come to pray for the soul of my dearly departed son."

Monsieur Moussa Varasteh, OC, Officer of the Order of Canada, an honor second only to the Canadian Order of Merit and bestowed by none other than Her Majesty Queen Elizabeth II, had learned about the passing of John Vain from Angela's column (okay, so there is one person out of seven billion who willingly reads the damn thing) and immediately ordered his assistant to tell his pilot to gas up his Learjet. Then he had packed his brood of black coats and crocheted *kippahs* and, in less than twenty-four hours, checked into the presidential suite at the Beverly Hilton.

He had picked the hotel because it was owned by a Jew, and he chose to stay in it even after he learned, from an overly eager bellman, that Monsieur Varasteh should feel very special because he had been accorded the very great honor of sleeping in the suite where, only four months earlier, Whitney Houston had died. No doubt the bellman had expected the news to titillate Monsieur, inspire him to give a big tip and rush to take pictures in different parts of the suite so he could e-mail them to his friends. As it happened, in addition to being the only person in the universe who read Angela's column, Monsieur was also the only person who did not relish the idea of bathing in the same tub as a dead celebrity. He was so put off by the prospect, in fact, that he briefly contemplated moving to the five-star Bel Air or Beverly Hills hotels, or even the Beverly Wilshire. But he quickly relinquished the idea because the first two were owned by an Arab, and the last one featured a restaurant by that famous chef who—hasn't anyone else in this town noticed?—happened to hail from the same country that gave the world Adolf Hitler.

Monsieur Varasteh was nothing if not a good Jew, but he would be the first to tell you that his religiosity had less to do with faith than with fear.

Twice in his eighty-four years, Moussa Varasteh had clinched the title of God's Worst Subject on Earth, and no amount of prayer and good deeds was going to strip him of those colors.

The first time was when he abandoned his wife and eight-year-old son in Ramsar and went off alone to seek his fortune. He was thirty years old and had worked every day since the age of six. His parents were poor and had five children, so they had sent him, the eldest, to work in a bottle factory ten hours a day. He handed his pay over to his mother every week and had barely enough to eat for himself, but he recognized his responsibilities as a son and didn't complain or slack off. At fourteen, he quit the factory job and went to work as a runner for a fabric seller in the central bazaar in Shiraz. Then he was twenty years old and his mother thought he should get married and have children, which he did, again living up to his duties as a son and husband and father. Two years later, his wife complained that he would never make enough in the fabric shop to feed so many mouths, so he went to work for a tobacco exporter. His job was to sell Iranian-grown tobacco to American and Canadian cigarette makers who would mix in the right amount of carcinogens and sell it, attractively packaged and at many times the price, back to Iranians. The more dealings he had with the Americas, the more Moussa Varasteh wished to leave home and country.

He planned the departure carefully over many months. He picked Edmonton, Canada, as a future home because it was cold enough, far away from Tehran and unpopulated enough, his wife and son would likely not attempt to find him there.

In Edmonton, Moussa looked for a synagogue or a Jewish center, and found a Chabad where he was served his first hot meal in weeks and told where he could find a cheap room to rent. The next day he went into a fabric store downtown, bought a bolt of the cheapest wool he could find, threw it on his left shoulder, and began walking the residential neighborhoods around the city center. He was nearly illiterate, and the only English he spoke was the conversational basics he had learned by dealing with Americans in Iran. He knocked on doors and stopped pedestrians on the sidewalk, sold the fabric by the yard for barely more than what he had paid, and didn't stop till he had cleared out every last scrap. That was in 1960; by the year 2000, Moussa Varasteh was one of the richest men in Canada, recognized by the queen for his contributions to the country's manufacturing trade.

He had money now, but he couldn't fathom going back to Iran to see his family, looking them in the eyes and explaining his absence. It wasn't just shame; distance, if it's great enough, will make the heart forget.

He built Edmonton's largest retail center, owned oil wells and petrochemical plants around the country, gave easily to philanthropic causes, followed Jewish law to the letter, and still not a day went by when he wasn't reminded that he had betrayed and abandoned his wife and son.

His Canadian passport bore no mention of a wife or child, so he married in 1970, and again in 1977. They were young Ashkenazi women with pure souls and untouched bodies who should have given him many children but didn't manage even one. The doctors couldn't find what was wrong with the women and Moussa knew, though he kept it to himself, that he was not sterile—and yet, who is man to think he can bend the will of God? In 1985 he handed his second Canadian wife her Jewish *get* and resolved to accept his childlessness as punishment for having left Jahanshah. Two years later, on a business trip to Toronto, he met an Iranian Jewish widow at the Chabad house, and married her.

The new wife was past the age of fertility, but she had a fifteen-year-old daughter from her first husband. The girl's name was Shabnam, but Feri called her Shab for short. This struck Moussa as unsavory, since *shab* means night in Persian; he believed a person's name affected her fate, which is why, he explained to Feri, Iranian Jews do not give their children the names of people who had had unhappy lives. In Shab's case, the name had already left a gloomy handprint because the girl was given to dark, melancholy moods that lasted for weeks or months. She was forever withdrawn and pensive, distrustful, it seemed, even of her mother. The one thing she had going for her was her talent for art, but she used that to sketch the same few images over and over, as if to tell a story she thought must be heard but that she couldn't tell any other way.

It snowed a great deal in Edmonton, but it didn't rain much, and that was a good thing for Shab because she tended to take the rain personally, slip into a deep depression at the first few drops and remain there, nearly catatonic in her darkened room, and burning God only knows what kind of incense or scented candle that emitted a smell of the sea so strong, it clung to the plaster and wouldn't be washed off.

Moussa and Feri tried to get the girl help. They had her seen by a dozen psychiatrists and twice that many therapists. They sent her to art camp and yoga and meditation classes and put her on a series of mind-body diets. Feri, who took every one of the girl's depressive episodes as a personal affront, was convinced that Shab was "God's punishment for every bad thing I've done." Moussa, who in an attempt to absolve himself of the original sin of having abandoned his first family, had started to adopt orphan and abandoned boys, feared she was sent to remind him of the suffering he had caused to his own child. As for Shab, all she would say about the source of her anguish was, "I have a feeling I don't belong in this world." On her eighteenth birthday in 1990, she got into bed, closed the blinds, locked the door, and cut her wrists with a razor blade.

You couldn't blame the man for not knowing: he had left Iran in 1960, sixteen years before Jay Gatsby blew a hole into Aaron Soleyman's head, then threw himself out the window to defend his honor. Until then, Moussa had not been to Tehran and never even heard of the Soleyman family. Afterward, he went to hide in the farthest corner of a faraway continent, sought refuge from the occasional Iranian tourist under his black hat and bushy beard, avoided all reference to his family of origin. That had been easy with the two Ashkenazi wives who couldn't find Iran on a map and didn't believe it was their place to ask questions anyway, and it had been equally easy with the Iranian one—Feri (for Fereshteh)—who revealed little and inquired even less. She had told Moussa she was from a prominent family in the city of Kashan, which explained, he thought, her private nature—Kashi Jews having been historically secretive—and that they still lived in Iran. Her husband had died when he climbed on the flat roof of their house to shovel off snow, slipped on the ice, and broke his neck. After that, she said, his family turned Feri and her daughter out. Her passport, which she had to obtain with the help of her own father, bore only her maiden name.

Moussa had no reason to doubt Feri's story when they met in Toronto. He was more concerned with revealing his own past transgression to her. Before he proposed, he told her about his Iranian wife and child, "so that you understand that I'll be held accountable in this world or the next."

Feri had no interest in Moussa's divine reckoning; she cared only that he was a decent man with a lot of money, which mattered a great deal if you were getting old and living in a very cold place with an emotionally delicate child. She wasn't stupid enough to reciprocate his honesty by revealing to him her own past: men like Moussa, no matter how guilty themselves, did not forgive women like her. So she listened and nodded and told him yes, she was sure he was already in good standing with Adonai. It was only after Shab had killed herself and Feri was overcome with pathos, when she knew that her marriage would not survive the suicide and that she couldn't stay in Edmonton anyway, that she told Moussa the truth—about the affair she had had with the teenage nephew of her first husband; about Jay Gatsby shooting Aaron Soleyman; about the old widow who had revealed the affair and subsequently promised she was not done with the Soleymans yet, not by a long shot.

In 1977 Fereshteh Gatsby was a divorcée and a widow with no prospects, money, or children, and a scar on her reputation that made the one on Cain's forehead look like a beauty mark. Of all the survivors of the melodrama that was the fight between Aaron and Raphael's Wife, she—Fereshteh—had sustained the biggest losses. Yes, Aaron's children were fatherless and his wife a widow, but Elizabeth had inserted herself into the business and was doing just fine as a single mother. No doubt, she would marry again, have more children.

So when Raphael's Wife came calling, Fereshteh let her into the house, even took some pleasure in hearing her curse Elizabeth. She listened as the Black Bitch proposed an alliance against "that daughter of a mad math teacher," but Fereshteh drew the line at harming the children.

"And what would we do with it?" she laughed at the idea's madness. "Where would we hide it and what good would it do, anyway, except get our necks into a noose?"

Child abduction, like many other crimes, was punishable by death in Iran.

She showed Raphael's Wife the door that time and asked her not to come back. But Fereshteh was still living at the house on Molavi Avenue, within walking distance of the hospital where Raphael's Wife worked nights, and so she stopped by every few days, rang the bell, and pounded on the door till she was let in.

They would keep the kid for only a few days, just long enough to scare Elizabeth and make her understand how vulnerable she was. They would have her drugged and quiet in Fereshteh's house because it was the last place anyone would think to look. Raphael's Wife had a friend working in the Big House who could be trusted to unlock a door and keep her mouth shut. She—Raphael's Wife—could sneak out of work for an hour without being missed, but she would need a car to drive her to Bagh-e Yaas, wait for her, and drive her and the child back.

Just a few days—that's all. They would keep the kid for just a few days.

They would take the younger girl because she'd be easier to carry. It would give Elizabeth a taste of what it was like to be truly helpless and at the mercy of others. Then they would release the child—frightened, still drugged, too young to be able to give a useful description—on a street somewhere.

Fereshteh knew this was a bad idea every time she heard it on Molavi Avenue, and she knew it was a bad idea as she sat in her "getaway car" that freezing February night on the Avenue of Tranquility. When she saw Raphael's Wife emerge from the yard gates of Bagh-e Yaas with a gunnysack tossed over her shoulder, Fereshteh had the urge to drive away as fast as possible and not look back.

But she didn't. She waited for Raphael's Wife to get in with Noor, drove the Black Bitch back to Razi, and took the girl home.

She didn't wake up one day and decide she was going to keep Noor. That's not how the biggest blunders usually happen. You slip one centimeter at a time until you're too far down to pull yourself up and out, so you keep descending. Or you stand still, do nothing while the truth crawls away and out of reach. This is what happened with Feri: she didn't take Noor so much as she was left *with* her.

The response to Noor's disappearance was much bigger than either Feri or Raphael's Wife had envisioned. They expected the police, even the secret service, to get involved, Elizabeth to go searching alone or with people who offered to help, a news alert or two. Then they would turn the kid loose and have a good laugh. Feri would go back to solitary confinement on Molavi Avenue and Raphael's Wife would chalk up one more win for the widow's sigh. It was bold and reckless, and, yes, stupid, but it wasn't meant to be a national affair.

What did she expect, Feri would later ask herself, when a child from a prominent family is abducted from her bed with her mother next door and a crew of servants in the house? When the punishment for kidnapping is as severe as it is for murder. When the missing child's mother is as single-minded as Elizabeth.

For weeks, Feri could not leave her house. She kept Noor half-drugged by blowing opium smoke in her face, tied by the foot to a bed, force-fed. The house was big enough and surrounded by a good two acres, plus the usual ten-foot brick yard wall. Feri hadn't been able to afford a servant since Gatsby died and she didn't have any friends who might miss her. She certainly didn't want Raphael's Wife to come around—she was the main suspect, no doubt being followed.

When Feri did start to go out, on brief errands to buy food or other necessities, she locked Noor in the bedroom and rushed back as soon as she was able. She waited till Raphael's Wife called, then unleashed her anger and demanded that "you wait for me in the alley behind the hospital tonight, I'll bring the kid and leave her there, and after that, she's your problem."

"You do that," Raphael's Wife warned, "and she'll freeze to death or wander into the street and be hit by a car—and believe me, they'll trace her back to you in no time."

They had to wait for the commotion to ebb.

The girl was still like a terrified, trembling cub cornered in a dark cave, but she had stopped wailing every time the opium wore off and was easier to feed. She wasn't throwing up or wetting herself anymore, which was a great relief because Feri couldn't stand to touch the stuff but couldn't suffer the smell either. Then the cold abated and the ice thawed and one morning Feri woke up to a voice on the radio announcing that "the late Mr. Aaron Soleyman's missing daughter has been found."

"If you let her go now," Raphael's Wife called from a pay phone near her house, "now that no one's looking for her anymore, you can bet she'll be picked up by the Gypsies or stolen by a madam and sold."

"Buy her a fake birth certificate and take her to *farangestan*—the West. Lose her there and no one will be the wiser."

The Canadian embassy issued visas faster than the Americans, and they asked fewer questions.

Any minute now, Angela thought as she watched her mother's face through Monsieur Varasteh's account, Elizabeth would raise a hand, stop the hoax, and say, "Please, sir, I've heard enough, you must take your fairy tale and sell it to one more desperate than I." She was so blank-faced, so very still and silent, she could not possibly have believed a word the man had said.

Any minute now, one of the sons would stand up and proclaim that the old man had played a game—"This is it, ladies and gentleman, a bad joke at an especially inappropriate time, we apologize for the inconvenience, we don't do much by way of entertainment, you see—it's read Torah all day long and copulate with the same woman every night, it can get dull from time to time, so we put on our coats and hats and fly 1,800 miles to strangers' homes and hold fake confessionals for fun."

Because, really, if Varasteh had brought the truth, what would it prove but the utter futility of knowing?

All her life Angela had banked on the difference between truth and fiction, and the importance of identifying one versus the other. When her father died and no one would tell her what happened or why, when Noor was taken and no one knew who took her, when they left Bagh-e Yaas and Tehran and the only country they had ever called their own, all that time Angela sustained her senses by telling herself there would be time—if only she stayed strong and able to defend herself—there would be time to learn the truth.

What else is there—once you've counted the losses you could not prevent, withstood the harm you never thought possible—but that bit of solace that comes from knowing the how and the why?

Any minute now, Angela prayed, Elizabeth would call it a night and walk out of this room and this second truth, this other version of what became of Noor. She would go back to the story she had heard from Raphael's Son and believed, the one that had felt like a cataclysmic wave that emerges out of nowhere and hits you every day and slays you all over again. She would go back to the child she had mourned and buried in Iran, mourned again and buried in LA.

That night, as Angela drove home, it started to rain on Mulholland. The street was dark and windy, the lights of the valley a thousand feet away, the road visible only as far as the reach of the car's headlights. But every time a drop of rain hit the windshield, Angela saw a flicker out in the blackness. It went on and off in half a second, but then another one appeared, and the heavier the rain became the faster it fell, the more the flickers lit the horizon, every one of them the phosphorescent blue-white of the trees of Angela's childhood, and after a while there were so many that they hung like a moon fallen from the sky and onto the road before her, light radiating from its cold, bare surface, and it was on this moon that she saw for the first time the shape of the man people called Raphael in the stories they told of Iran, all lit up from inside and surrounded by moths and trailed by the creatures whose existence Angela's Princeton-educated, truth-seeking mind had never contemplated seriously, and he was so real and vibrant, so sure-footed in his journey on this other land, Angela had to pull to the side and stop the car, watch him through the rain that came down now like a sheet, and tell herself, it's true what those old Iranian women used to say when she still listened: it's not where you are that determines what you see, it's where you look and what you choose to believe.

And yes, it's also true what Iranians say about the past trailing you like a spell.

Elizabeth was falling backward into the sea, like an anchor finally released from its mooring, and the closer she came to breaking the surface, the more her body longed for the water. It was midday, the sun a blinding white glare, the waves smooth and lazy in the heat. She floated for a second or two before starting to sink. Then the glare fell away and the world turned black and white.

What had she done, Elizabeth the Great, with the life she was given? What had she made of the years that the others—her siblings, husband, daughters—did not have?

To push through the wall of wordlessness that surrounded her from birth, converge with the soul of another, contain and soothe their injured heart. That's what she had wanted.

It's what she had chased from the first night, that Shabbat at the Big House where she saw Aaron. She knew where the pearl lay within the oyster—that this urgent need was quenched only through the connection between one living thing and another. She had tried; she had wanted to build that bond of tenderness. But it wasn't enough to feel; one must find the words through which to speak, discover the path through which to reach, before the door is closed and all is lost.

Elizabeth had lost her parents and siblings to the curses of a widow who had the door slammed in her face. She lost Aaron to the vengeance of a man who was not allowed to cross the threshold of a forbidden kind of love. She lost Angela to the anger that replaced her yearning for a mother's warmth; lost John Vain to the shame that replaced his unrequited love. She lost Noor once, then lost her again.

What had she done, Elizabeth (the Great; the Ice Queen) Soleyman, but stand on the other side of the door?

She was still sinking, but she could hear the rain coming down in sheets, sense the agitation of the servants who rushed from room to room, shoving towels against the baseboard to catch the water that came through the hinges on the windows. She could hear them yell

at each other to close one door and another, banging on her bedroom
door to wake up—"Wake up, Miss, the rain is falling too fast, it has
filled the soil and turned into a flash flood, there aren't enough drains
in this town to absorb it all, wake up and let's go on the roof, we may
get thrown off by the winds but at least we won't drown, wake up,
Miss, you've seen this rain before and you knew to walk away, you
came from the water, a drop of rain that should have fallen like all the
others into the Caspian but instead landed in a woman's womb, you're
part flesh, part sea, you can't scream your fear or pain or even your
love, when you let go it turns into a flood and takes too much, wake
up, your daughter, the one you lost, must have been the part of you
that's water, you couldn't hold onto her any more than you can to this
flood of rain and mud and broken branches and dead leaves that have
crashed through the roof just at the end of the hallway and are cours-
ing toward us now, you still have another child, this one's all flesh and
resolve and certainty, wake up, Miss, we have to leave now or we'll
be trapped in the mudslide, this house is built like a fortress, it could
withstand machine-gun fire and maybe even a tank's, it's earthquake-
proof up to 7.3, burglarproof as the US Mint, but it can't forestall the
might of a single drop of rain multiplied by millions, wake up, Miss,
the water has pulled the door out of the wall, whatever's calling you
from the other side, whatever shadow or promise beckons, it can wait.
There's still time."

There was still time for Elizabeth, but she would have no more of it.
She drowned in the stormy waters of her own grief, on the night of
December 12, 2008, alone at age fifty-four.

LOS ANGELES

Friday, July 19, 2013

" 'm going to be frank with you—*je vais te dire franchement*," Angela told Leon. "You're out of your depth with this one and don't know it. Any one of these people, from the Riffraff to Luci to Raphael's Son himself, is a world-class villain. They could kill circles around you and you wouldn't be able to do a thing about it."

They were sitting outside her favorite hangout in Beverly Hills, a chocolate and espresso shop on the corner of Camden and Brighton where she had stopped at least once a day for the past ten years. Angela liked the coffee here, and she also liked watching the other customers. The William Morris Endeavor talent agency directly across the street employed dozens of young, great-looking, well-dressed interns who spent most of their time walking the agents' dogs or picking up their dry cleaning. Above William Morris Endeavor was a gym where middle-aged men and women spent four hours a day taking classes with names like "Pump N Grind" and "Core N More," then walked over to the coffee bar for a decaf, nonfat cup of foam with a drop of espresso in it. Among the regulars was an Iranian man, well into his fifties, who wore shiny silver leggings and neon orange shoes he thought would make him look younger to the girls, an Austrian psychiatrist who pretended he was Jewish so as not to frighten away potential West Side clients, an Israeli woman who pretended she was English in hopes of impressing a rich old American into marrying her, and an Englishman who pretended he was a duke of one thing or another and went around in a rented Bentley in hopes of finding a rich woman to pay his bills; for a while, he was engaged to an Afghan woman who—he found out just before the wedding—pretended she was descended from royalty and went around in a rented Carrera GT in hopes of finding a rich man to pay her bills.

Leon had Facebook messaged Angela that morning to ask for a meeting. Now, he was staring at her from the other side of a tiny aluminum table surrounded by people and dogs and baby carriages. Although she tried to contain her volume, she could be heard thirty feet away.

From behind the espresso bar a tall woman with major tattoos and a streak of bright blue hair muttered, "You sound like you need a double."

Angela got up and picked the drink off the counter. "Anyway," she said as she lowered herself into the chair again, "I appreciate the chance to visit, but I don't know that I can be of any help to you."

On the sidewalk next to them Kareem Islam, the elder statesman of Beverly Hills panhandlers, was yelling at a man who had refused to give him money. Kareem and his wife had just celebrated their thirtieth anniversary of "working" (the term they used when speaking to the police) in the city. From the beginning, they each had their designated turf: she, on Wilshire Boulevard across from the Beverly Wilshire Hotel, and he on Beverly Drive outside Nate 'n Al's deli. Together, they made a decent living—enough to maintain a small apartment in the Pico-Robertson area among all the Orthodox Jews. They also maintained a checking and a savings account, and, Angela had learned from the public defender who had of late been representing Mr. Islam, a number of credit cards. Forever polite, upbeat, and eager to engage in endless intellectual conversation (hence the name given to him by an old Nate 'n Al's regular), Kareem had become rude and aggressive over the past year—a result, he confessed, of "business pressures" having to do with a shrunken revenue stream during the recession. To remedy the slump in earnings, he had abandoned his piece of real estate on the east side of Beverly Drive, and relocated outside the parking lot next to the Williams-Sonoma store. When that didn't help, he had started walking his wheelchair (he took it around so he'd always have a place to sit) onto neighboring streets. Now he was off his own turf and not getting the kind of respect he was accustomed to, so he started "to lose it" several times a day.

The object of his outrage that day was tall and heavy, and about to walk into the sandwich shop next door to the coffee bar when he declined to, as Kareem liked to put it, "help me have a better day." Retaliating, Kareem had parked his wheelchair at the entrance to the sandwich shop and was screaming that the man was "too fat and stupid to be eating them mozzarelli-and-tamater-whole-wheat-spinach-my-balls wraps, you can pay eight bucks for a sandwich you don't need but you can't give me a buck to buy a coffee, you fat fuck!"

Angela shook her head. Any minute now, she knew, two cruisers would be pulling up outside the café to take Mr. Islam to the station and book him for creating a public nuisance. His wife too had been picked up a few times in the past year for being overly aggressive with her "supporters." When ordered by a judge to move her place of business to another part of the city, the wife had explained that her current location was most convenient because "my husband and I bank there."

Leon waited till Angela had had enough of the sidewalk spectacle. "Did you know Raphael's Son has a child?"

The rabbi brought the boy—all 4'5" of him in that big yellow T-shirt he wore every day and that he refused to part with at night, clung to as if it were a layer of skin or an extra limb, which, given his story, should not have shocked anyone—and even Angela, who had never been at a loss for words, didn't know what to say to him. He was a beautiful child—those golden-red loops of hair, the long, curved eyelashes that cast a shadow over his cheekbones, the white skin and red lips—but there was also an eeriness about him, a sense that he was not quite real, that he was a boy in a painting somewhere with a cold climate and an artist who longed for sunlight. His name was Jonah, and he might as well have been thrown overboard into a storm and washed ashore on Mulholland Drive in LA.

It was Friday afternoon, right before sundown, and the first thing the rabbi said to Angela was that they were going to have to spend the night, because it had taken him five hours in traffic to get to her from Riverside and now it was almost Shabbat, he couldn't drive till after dark Saturday night, and it was very nice where she lived and all, up on top of this mountain, except he hadn't seen a motel or even a gas station within an hour's walking distance so would she mind very much if they camped—he had brought their sleeping bags—on her floor? There was also a change of clothes, and a blue pillow the boy liked to sleep on.

She let them stay, even though she realized the rabbi had planned it this way. It was his idea that they should meet at her house, and that it should be on a Friday; all she had wanted was to see the boy for herself. She would have driven out to them, would have preferred it that way, but the rabbi was insistent, which made her think there was more to this story than Leon knew or was able to relate.

The rabbi offered to go pick up some food in the Valley, he wasn't kosher, he said, and neither was the boy, so any old place would do, but he was especially fond of Persian food, you know, the white rice with sour cherries and lamb, for example, and was there a restaurant nearby that delivered?

While they waited for the food, the boy sat hunched on the sofa in his yellow T-shirt, leafing through a *National Geographic* with pictures of elephants because Angela didn't have a TV or any children's books. The rabbi used the occasion to tell Angela "more about myself, my name is Cornelius Cohen, I was born and raised near Watts Towers right here in LA, no, I'm not of Ethiopian descent, my birth parents weren't Jewish, they were plain old black folk from Africa, and no, I wasn't adopted by a Jewish family, I grew up in foster care, got into trouble, and ended up at this place called Beit T'shuvah, down on Venice near Robertson, it's a Jewish rehab, not Orthodox, no, not at all, the head rabbi is an ex-con, in fact, but they saved my life, I have a rabbinic degree but no congregation, I play in a hip-hop group and work for the state taking care of kids who've been abandoned like I was, Cohen is what I chose for myself."

At ten o'clock, they were still waiting for the food, the driver having been hopelessly lost somewhere on Mulholland Drive—a twenty-one-mile-long, two-lane highway with hardly any streetlights and dozens of narrow side streets with no signs. One of them was even called No Name Alley, and more than a handful were not paved because that's how the owners wanted it—secluded and difficult to find—why the movie stars and music moguls and porn kings made their homes here. Faye Dunaway had grown old along these cliffs; Warren Beatty had finally married, and Bruce Willis had licked his wounds when his own marriage broke up. This was where Roman Polanski raped a thirteen-year-old girl, and he did it in Jack Nicholson's house, so who could blame the poor Iranian driver from the Persian restaurant for getting lost here in his rattling old Camaro, trying to read a map in the dark with his scratched-up driving glasses?

In the end, Angela defrosted some Trader Joe's dumplings in the microwave and put them on a plate on the kitchen counter. The boy had fallen asleep on the couch with a half-eaten sandwich on the end table, his head resting on the blue pillow that he clutched with both arms, and the rest of him barely visible under the down comforter Angela had taken from her own bed.

As soon as the meal was over, Cornelius Cohen asked if Angela might prepare some coffee, "unless you have that good Persian tea they brew with cardamom seeds and, I understand lately, rose petals."

It amazed Angela that she was so unresisting to the rabbi taking such liberties. It was as if she thought she could avert the impact of some ghastly blow by letting someone else take charge.

They sat at the long wooden table that Angela's handyman, Señor Manuel, had built as what turned out to be—his marriage be damned—an expression of his yearning for her. He was a Mexican guy with too many missing teeth and an affinity for fabric starch and cologne. You could smell him driving down Angela's street from the top of Mulholland, and you could hear the crinkling of his overly starched white painter's pants and white cotton T-shirt from the driveway. He walked with a cowboy's gait and spoke in lyrical sentences that were wasted on Angela because she had no time for or appreciation of his "feminine side," she spoke only functional Spanish and he didn't know a word of English, all she wanted was to have a room painted or a dripping faucet replaced, and here was Señor Manuel admiring the sunrise from the terrace or gazing at the lights on Ventura Boulevard late at night, lamenting the intolerance of the wife who kept throwing him out of the house every time she caught him with another woman, bringing Angela roses and refusing to accept payment for his work if only she would let him take her to a nice dinner.

The rabbi was an employee of Jewish Family Services in Riverside, the county adjacent to San Bernardino where Jonah's mother had lived and died. He had been Jonah's caseworker since 2008, but he had only approached Raphael's Son twice—the time he mistook Eddy for his boss and the second time, last April, when he thought he'd try again and see if the father was more willing to care for his own. The rabbi didn't believe in forcing children onto parents who wanted no part of them, and this one—Raphael's Son—certainly wanted none of this boy, said he didn't even think Jonah was his, refused to come down and see him, let alone look at a picture. He went crazy when he found out that Eddy Arax had gone to visit the boy in 2008, and then he really blew up when he learned the mother had been dead for five years already, what was that half-faced Armenian doing with the $2,000 of so-called child support every month? Donating it? Was it his to donate? It's not like he paid taxes and could use the deduction!

The rabbi thought it best not to mention that they had only ever seen $1,000 at a time from Eddy.

"Whatever he did with the rest I figure is not our business, but now look!" He motioned toward the sliding glass doors of the living room. "Look at him now and tell me he's not something special."

Jonah stood in the middle of the room with his eyes still closed and the blue pillow tucked under his right arm, a silver pin of light glowing, fluorescent, in the center of his stomach beneath the big yellow T-shirt.

"He's always been like this," the rabbi said softly. "I believe it's the divine in him—God's light shining through His best creatures."

Slowly, as Angela gaped at him, the space around Jonah fell away, the world getting darker and more empty until it was just him—a small, incandescent miracle—and the setting realization, for Angela, of what this meant.

They walked Jonah to the couch and helped him lie down, then stood around and watched the light glint with his every breath. The deeper they sailed into the night, the brighter the light became and the greater the possibility appeared to Angela that it was indeed true—what no one had contemplated for a hundred years—Raphael's Son being just that. The inconceivable may be real, the pretense fact.

Slowly, she saw fireflies and moths and other night creatures appear in the garden—small, solitary glints at first, and then, suddenly, flurries of them like flashing bulbs the size of a pinhead—flapping their wings against the glass of the closed door, and soon so many of them had gathered that the garden was lit up.

A few minutes before dawn Jonah woke up and came to the window, put his little face with those large caramel eyes to the glass as if to soak in the warmth generated by the incandescence outside, and when he saw Angela, awed and immobile, trying to get the measure of him and what he meant, he smiled at her as if in prayer—believe in me—and turned halfway to open the door, letting thousands of insects swarm the room just as they were about to turn pale in the first light.

That was at five in the morning. An hour later, the room was awash in color, all the walls and the ceiling, the tops of the cabinets and every empty space now dyed in startling hues, a technicolor chimera that felt strangely, quietly alive. In the yard, the July sky was clear as glass, the air warm even for Los Angeles in summer. Angela got up from her chair and walked toward the sliding glass door. The sound of her steps on the Spanish tile floor struck against the silence in the room, shaking a crack open somewhere in the world, because the next thing they all saw was the rush of color that peeled off the walls and the furnishings and gathered into a cloud above Jonah, hovering like a prayer, then glided in a wave like the giant wings of a manta ray, in a choreographed flight that darkened the doorway, then the terrace. Against the bleached floor of the deck, the early-morning light swept across like watercolor off a page, staining it forever in their memories.

For the next hour or so the cloud drifted west, toward the ocean. On the ground, people stopped and stared at it, took pictures with their cell phones and called television stations to report the sighting, and reporters and entomologists speculated about its nature and origin, while in Angela's living room on Mulholland Drive, little Jonah with the electric heart dreamed of flickering ghosts.

They sat on the terrace, Angela and the rabbi, till the sun cast shadows and Jonah woke up and came to the window, barefoot and holding his pillow, and waved at them with those little hands. Then the rabbi announced they were going out for breakfast. "It shouldn't be so difficult to find my way down to Ventura in daylight, we'll find a McDonald's and bring you something," he told Angela. She barely glanced up when they left.

So Jonah had a translucent heart, she thought. So what? There are nearly seven thousand rare diseases in the world, some affecting as few as two people, and there are thousands of other "syndromes" that have not been named. Within small, historically isolated communities, many a strange and inexplicable condition has passed through generations without drawing special notice. The fact that every case of luminescence known to Iranian Jews had so far appeared in the Soleyman clan was not proof that it did not occur in other families, either in Iran or in other parts of the world.

It's like that other illness, HIBM, that for so long was thought to strike only Iranian Jews. Then an Indian girl was diagnosed, and a Japanese woman, and a Korean, Chinese, Palestinian . . .

And who was to say that Jenna Rose's claim of Raphael's Son's paternity had been true?

Then again, what were the chances?

"I'd say infinitesimally small," Leon said when Angela asked him on the phone. It was barely nine in the morning, and already his voice was grainy and drained.

"Just looking at the kid . . ." he paused. "I thought all that stuff about your father's family was bullshit until I saw the boy."

It always shocked Angela that Iranians she had met only casually or not at all, even ones born in the United States, knew so much about her family history.

"Whatever," she snapped, mostly because she resented Leon's allusion to her past. "What's it to me anyway?"

He must have thought that was an especially asinine question because he said nothing in response. That irritated Angela even more.

If Jonah was proof of Raphael's Son's legitimacy, what of Izikiel and Aaron, and their rejection of him? What of Raphael's Wife who had told the truth and been denied and derided for decades? What of Elizabeth who had perpetuated the wrong?

What of Angela who had taken to the worldwide web with her own perceived truth?

Here was a truth: for fifty years, Raphael's Son had tried to shed the indignity of being a bastard among a people who defined themselves and each other almost entirely by name and lineage, and for fifty years the Soleyman family had denied him this singular rite of passage. In return, he had caused unspeakable pain for Angela's parents, and later wreaked havoc on many an innocent life. But the more injury he brought, and the more millions he stole, the farther he found himself from catching that brass ring. Even after he established himself in the United States, after he moved to Holmby Hills and threw his money around, the Iranians who knew about his past looked down on him; and his white neighbors, who disliked him merely for being Iranian, whispered to each other that he should not have been allowed to move into the area.

The old lady with the lake may be sitting on a fortune made by killing smokers, but she clearly believed that being a foreigner was a bigger crime, and so pretended she didn't see Raphael's Son every time she drove by him in her Jaguar. The woman who owned Little Versailles may have stolen her husband from his first wife and consequently lost him to someone younger and more white than herself, but she ordered her chauffeur to avoid driving the Bentley past Raphael's Son's house because she couldn't abide "the sight of those Persians." Even the crazy Hungarian couple with the invented surname bristled in distaste whenever they saw him on the street. Never mind they were servants in a fourteen-thousand-square-foot house where a teenage Russian boy lived alone; even their fictional pedigree linking them to some Eastern European king or the other was more noble than Raphael's Son's actual heritage.

You might almost feel sorry for him if you didn't know just how base and ruthless he had proven himself to be over the years, or how preposterous his claim of paternity by Raphael Soleyman had seemed until now. To give the claim any level of credence, you would have had to start by believing that a dead man could have engaged in the kind of task that is, for mortal people anyway, required for conception; that he had committed this act with a woman so old, she would have needed divine interference to become pregnant; that this old woman had carried the child not for nine months but for a total of thirteen.

Or you could have gone the humdrum way of regular folk and arrived at the conclusion that Raphael's Wife had bought or stolen or just found a kid somewhere, brought him home, and claimed he was Raphael's just so she could get her hands on one of the biggest fortunes in 1960s and '70s Iran.

"He could have asked for a DNA test," Angela mumbled. "All these years . . ."

"I don't think he believed it himself," Leon suggested.

Better to let the claim stand untested, Raphael's Son must have calculated, than have its falsehood set in stone.

At eleven o'clock, the rabbi and Jonah came back from their Egg McMuffin breakfast. As if invited to stay the day, the rabbi cleared the coffee table and took out a deck of cards from his pocket.

"He counts like the devil," he said of Jonah. "Wanna play blackjack with us?"

It was a good thing this rabbi was so handsome, Angela thought, or his presumptuousness would have been intolerable.

"I never learned anything more complicated than Go Fish," she said sincerely, and this made Jonah laugh for the first time since she had seen him.

She didn't ask them to leave because she wasn't sure she wanted that. And she didn't ask the rabbi what he wanted from her because she thought she knew the answer.

Clearly, the rabbi hoped that the child-support payments, diverted by Eddy Arax and diminished too, would continue even after Raphael's Son's death. That's why he had brought Jonah for her to meet—so she could serve as a liaison with Neda, convince her to do the right thing by giving up the $1,000 each month. They were always asking for money, these religious types, no matter how poor or wealthy the charity.

"I don't have any influence with the father's widow," she said when Jonah went into the bathroom to wash his hands before dealing the cards. She meant Neda.

"I can ask the woman who runs my mother's foundation," she offered. "But I'll tell you right now you'll have better luck asking her yourself because the stupid bitch hates me."

She got up to find a piece of paper on which to write Stephanie Dalal's contact information. The rabbi raised a hand.

"No need for that," he said, and smiled at Jonah who had appeared back in the room. "We haven't come to ask for money."

Angela glared at him for making that last remark in front of the boy. It meant she couldn't challenge or dispute the claim without hurting Jonah. "I just wanted you two to meet."

She announced she was going to take a nap and went into her bedroom, closed the door, and lay on the bed fully dressed. After a minute she got up again and locked the door because she realized the rabbi was just *por-roo*—one who isn't ashamed to keep asking for more—enough to walk in even as she slept.

She was turning the lock and telling herself this was crazy—she had to shut herself inside her own house just to get five minutes' worth of privacy, and even then she had the feeling that Jonah and the rabbi were everywhere, on this side of the door as much as the other.

My father is waiting for me on this side of midnight.

Where had she heard those words?

It's what Izikiel had written the day he predicted his own death. Later, he had come back for Raphael.

"I got to bury Aaron because they weren't waiting for him on the other side," Elizabeth had explained to Angela years later. Jay Gatsby had preempted Aaron's ancestors, killed him too soon, and, because there was no one to claim him, sent his body to rot in the rainstorm of Elizabeth's grief.

That's when it hit Angela: What if whoever had killed Raphael's Son knew that his body would disappear as soon as he died? What if he had driven up to the gate, seen a familiar face—someone with whom he felt safe enough to roll down his window even if they came out of the dark in the middle of the night? He didn't put the car in park, just set his foot on the brake and turned his face to the person in the driveway.

He saw the knife and panicked, pressed on the gas pedal to get away, only the car was still in drive so it crashed into the gate and stopped. Then Raphael's Son sat there, bleeding out until his father reached for him.

"Ohhh myyy God," Angela sighed as she slunk to the floor.

Only two people—Eddy Arax and Neda—knew that Jonah had the incandescence disease.

People said Neda had married Raphael's Son because she was too stupid and servile to say no to him. Angela didn't believe that. She thought Neda didn't think she had a right to anyone better than Raphael's Son. That's why she married him and why she stayed with him—that, and the well-being of her daughters, the knowledge that if she divorced him, Raphael's Son would punish her by rendering her and the children poor and without recourse.

She must have realized, as the years passed, that her inaction, her inability to believe she was worth more than what Raphael's Son made of her, would seep into her daughters' souls, that this was the reason Nicole was so solitary and Kayla so very lost. She tried to make them have a better sense of themselves. All those therapists and music teachers, summer camps in Maine and private school education, the birthday parties that were more lavish than any bat mitzvah and the bat mitzvahs that cost as much as a large wedding—and still, she must have known it wasn't enough.

She should have left and taken her daughters with her. But she didn't have the strength.

Then one day Eddy Arax called with news of Jonah.

"I can't see you," he told Neda, "and you mustn't tell him it was I who told you this."

So Raphael's Son had been unfaithful to her. That couldn't have come as news to Neda.

And he had fathered a child, whom he renounced.

That meant he and Neda could continue as before, live separately under one roof for another hundred years or until one of them died. As long as Raphael's Son kept the boy secret, Neda could hold on to the last, acrid crumbs of her *aabehroo*.

But there was more, Eddy had said. The boy had a luminous heart—proof positive that Raphael's Son was legitimate. For years, Eddy had kept this from his employer. It was his revenge—to deny Raphael's Son that which he and his mother had wanted most. And the $1,000 a month didn't hurt either. Only now, this black rabbi had gotten ahold of Raphael's Son, and insisted that he see Jonah, just once. The rabbi had been shown the door by Raphael's Son, threatened to be sued for taking money he knew was not intended for him or his charity, but the rabbi had promised to come back.

One of these days, Eddy warned Neda, your husband will discover just how useful this child could be, and once that happens there will be no stopping him—he'll claim the kid and bring him home and show him off everywhere he can.

"And then, Mrs. Soleyman, what are you going to do? You won't have the courage or the means to leave him, but you won't be able to hide the kid either. People will know you remained in the marriage even after he showed off the child he had with another woman, and I'll tell you, though I mean no offense, she must have been one hell of a looker, judging by how the boy has turned out."

Twenty years ago, a woman staying in a marriage despite any and all mistreatment was not just understandable, it was expected; she was believed to be better off dead than divorced. But that all had changed in the past two decades. Now there was a limit to how much a wife would endure publicly before she was considered a complete sap for not leaving.

Beyond the years of abuse, the betrayals, the cruelties, Neda realized she was about to face one last indignity.

A long-exploited, desperately dependent employee. A wronged and unhappy wife. It was like those buildings that withstand one massive quake after another, then collapse in a three-second aftershock.

That was one thing Tehran and Los Angeles had in common: they were both cities built on major fault lines.

In the evening, the rabbi claimed some other engagement—to which, needless to say, it wouldn't be appropriate to take Jonah—and asked if he might "impose on the family to look after the young man" for a few hours.

"What am I supposed to do with him?" Angela asked in sincere bewilderment. She knew that the rabbi wasn't going anywhere but home, that he had no other engagement and no purpose but to give Jonah more time with her. "I don't even have the kind of food he eats."

This—how unconnected and unwanted he was, more so than even Raphael's Son in his own day because he, at least, had Raphael's Wife to love him—confounded Angela.

All her life, Angela had heard of and met people who had not one other person in the world they knew cared for them. At work, she had come across hundreds of stories of children who died of abuse or neglect because no one stepped in to help, of old men and women who suffocated from heat or froze on the sidewalk because no one looked in on them.

Still, she was struck by the utter unconnectedness, the absolute aloneness of this child. You could say Rappin' Rabbi cared about Jonah, that he cared more than he was paid to, and that was true. He had been a part of Jonah's life longer than anyone else, served far beyond the call of duty, but even he knew that the affection he could give the boy was not enough. He—the rabbi with no congregation—understood the difference between having one person to see to your needs, and having a family, a community, to recognize you as their own.

Angela understood it too. No matter how often the *Pearl Cannon* had targeted the home team or how many gripes Angela had registered about the complexities of maintaining a "tribal mentality" in twenty-first-century Los Angeles, there was always this: where she came from, the people had each other. That was worth something. Maybe it was worth all the difficulties it caused. Maybe that's why Angela had stuck with the tribe instead of severing all ties.

* * *

They were still sitting at the table, though Jonah had long since given up on the organic, sprouted grain wheat bread and organic, unsalted almond butter sandwich Angela had made for him. She kept the stuff in her fridge because it was a healthy LA alternative to white toast and sweetened, packed-with-hydrogenated-oil peanut butter that normal people lived on everywhere else in America, but she couldn't be caught dead eating any of it herself. The almond butter tasted like sludge and the sprouted grain bread couldn't be forced down a normal throat no matter how much coffee she tried to chase it with. She also kept unsweetened almond and coconut milk instead of the regular stuff because in LA, dairy products were known carcinogens, right after cigarettes and sugar. So she bought the "make-believe milk" once a month at Trader Joe's, tossed it out, unopened, after a month, and went to her espresso hangout where she insisted on regular milk in her latte and chocolate chip muffins for breakfast, lunch, and afternoon tea.

"Do you like In-N-Out?" she asked Jonah.

He shook his head. He was back to hugging the blue pillow, and he seemed even smaller, thinner, than he had the day before.

It occurred to her that he must be terrified of being there, alone with a strange woman, his only friend—the rabbi—having taken off with promises of "checking in" later that night. But it was one thing to feel sorry for a lonely, abandoned child, something entirely different to suddenly be the one designated to save him.

Because that's what she had become, she realized all too well, the minute she agreed to see Jonah. That's why Leon had asked her to "see him for yourself." With Elizabeth gone, Angela was the only surviving member of the Soleyman family—or so she had believed, until Jonah came along. Now, it was the two of them.

She could either release Jonah back into the ocean to be swallowed by whales, or she could bring him home.

LOS ANGELES

Monday, June 23, 2014

The Pearl Cannon
a blog by Angela S.
Monday, June 23, 2014
Today's Topic: Unintended Consequences

Raphael's Son died alone in his car, having done more damage in one lifetime than any person has a right to, and if there's one good thing that resulted from his unfortunate existence, it's that he saved the Soleyman family from imminent extinction.

That's unintended consequence #1.

Before Jonah, there was just me—surly, pugnacious, well past child-bearing age—and besides, who would dare have children with that one?—Angela. I do know what you all say about me. I can't argue with the first three adjectives, but I will say, apropos the question, however rhetorical, about my becoming a parent, that it's been some time since men were de rigueur in the matter of making mothers out of women. But I digress.

Before Jonah, there was only me—one of the few Iranian Jews in this town, I'm certain, who can't boast of having five hundred cousins and just as many aunts and uncles. Believe it or not, this dearth of relatives, my disconnectedness, hadn't bothered me for years, not since after high school when I went away to university and lived among other young people who didn't have five hundred cousins either. It was only once I met Jonah that I realized how truly alone I was, how similar to my mother in that regard.

I don't know why I hadn't seen this before—I who am so very quick to point out the obvious in other people, to blame them, even, for not having enough self-reflection. I always thought I was nothing like Elizabeth. Not nearly as smart or capable or giving—yes, my mother was giving, and I don't just mean philanthropically. This is something else I realized once I met Jonah.

It's not true, what I used to say about Elizabeth—she was no Ice Queen. She was strong and driven, yes, the Hillary Clinton of Iranian

Jewish women, and she never did learn how to convey her affection through words or a simple embrace. "If you'll have me, I would like to be your wife" isn't exactly a love poem, but that's how she proposed to my father, and she didn't even wait to get him alone—she asked him in front of a bunch of people she didn't know. A more eloquent young woman might have waited for the evening to end, the guests to go home; she might have stalked the man in a dark hallway, thrown herself, tousled hair and diaphanous gown and ruby lips and all, into his arms and cried tears as big as ostrich eggs. She might have told him about all the sleepless nights, the breathless waiting, the hoping against hope—and if you won't have me I'll lose my will to live, catch a fever, and take to bed and die of sorrow.

Hillary wouldn't do this, and nor would my mother. It doesn't mean they're unfeeling or coldhearted. I realize this now, but I couldn't see it—that the inability to convey the depth of one's affection is not the same as an absence of caring—until I met Jonah. Before that, I never knew what an awesome—as in, extremely daunting—and terrifying task it is to be the sole guardian of a child, the only person in this world responsible for his life and well-being.

Elizabeth was alone in a way few other women of her generation or background could claim. Most of the others had someone—a spouse, a parent, a distant cousin or two—who might throw them a life vest if things got really bad. After my father died, my mother was entirely on her own. Just like Raphael's Wife.

It's true that Elizabeth had Manzel and John Vain and Auntie Zeeba to stand by her at different times in her life; you could even say, if you wanted to go out on a limb, that she had Hal, the Mechanical Brain. But her impulse toward self-sufficiency, the habit she had developed from early childhood of being alone and able to care for herself, always got the better of us. The same glass barrier that kept her one step removed in her youth followed her—and, by extension, me—throughout her life.

That wouldn't have been such a sin in Iran or many other parts of the world. In most places, people are too busy trying to survive to add "express your love effectively" to their daily to-do list. It's enough to perform, every day, the great miracle of protecting one another against hunger and war and the elements. That's how Elizabeth expressed her love for me—with bread instead of poetry. Only I wasn't able to see this—how difficult it is for one generation to reinvent the wheel, learn from the previous ones' mistakes, speak in rhymes, so to speak, when all it has known is good old-fashioned prose.

Before Jonah I assumed I was the last of the Soleymans of Tehran. Whatever started three thousand years ago in Iran was going to end with me, here in LA. Every right and wrong, longing and war, buried in a cave with me, the immovable boulder that blocks the opening. That's why I was eager to set the record straight, get to the facts. That would be my role, the epilogue I would write to the fairy tale of translucent men and disappearing corpses and little girls who carry the sea in their breath and the rain in their tears.

Now I realize I won't be the end of it. After me, there's Nicole and Kayla and after them there's Jonah and so it goes, each of us casting a line through time that the next one will grab on to, tie into a noose with which to hang himself or others, or use as a lifeline, or both. Which means, you see, that what I do matters much beyond my own lifetime. Because it's not going to end with me, this story that started when the first flicker glistened, so long ago, inside the first Soleyman child and brought out every lost and lonely ghost, sent fathers to step across the line and take their fallen sons.

We know this in the East, that children inherit their parents' sins and sorrows as much as their *aabehroo*, that there's no such thing, really, as starting anew, you may not be aware of the past but *it* knows where to find you. Some of us Iranians might have wanted to forget that once we discovered Los Angeles; I certainly did.

Note that I say "we," as in "we Iranians," which is strange, I know, jarring even to me. Here I am, with barely a memory of the place, having lived in the West the great majority of my life, and still I can't help thinking of myself as Iranian. My allegiance, it goes without saying, is to the United States, to its flag and its government (but not the bankers and hedge-fund operators and politicians who enable the thieves). So is my gratitude and so, though I hate to use a platitude, is my love.

And yet.

I've thought a great deal about this since I found Jonah—how he and I are products of two very divergent worlds, how I could live in the United States for a hundred more years and still be something other than American. How, despite this difference, he and I are children of the same enchanted castle, cousins by blood, though I traveled by land and he by water. Maybe it was a curse, maybe a blessing, our fathers' sins or mothers' innocence; something plucked me from behind the tall brick walls on the Avenue of Tranquility, and Jonah from the sun-beaten desert of Southern California, and brought us together on a no-name street on top of a foggy mountain at the hands of a black rabbi named Cornelius Cohen.

The Ashkenazim complain a lot that Iranians are loathe to "integrate." They're wrong about that. I'm as integrated a citizen as you could possibly find, and so are most others. I know the laws of this country, the language, the history, better than a good number of natives, and I vote more often too. It's true I don't have many American friends but then I only have one real friend. My funeral, I am certain, will be as American as a Fourth of July barbecue: a handful of mourners who dress well but don't mourn, and a buffet of cold cuts.

Maybe I'll ask to be buried at sea.

What we're not very good at—yet—is assimilation. We act American, but we think and feel and maybe even dream in Persian. I'm not sorry about this. We may be codependent, but we also appreciate the value of family; we may spoil our kids, but they'll never doubt our love for them. We may carry the past around like a tether, but because of that we can see farther, and deeper, into ourselves and others.

What I see, when I look behind me, is Bagh-e Yaas, the garden that looked as if it had been snowed on in summer because of the poet's jasmine that bloomed on the vines, the house with the high ceilings and bay windows, the color of sunlight in Iran—because it is, truly, different—Manzel's kindness, her husband's tears. I remember too the phone ringing in the night, the rainstorm that wouldn't relent long enough for Elizabeth to bury my father. The morning I woke up to find Noor wasn't in her bed. The footprints in the snow.

I remember leaving the house in the dark, the screeching of metal as Elizabeth closed the gates of Bagh-e Yaas behind us, the pictures in her suitcase curling at the edges before they were consumed by fire.

They say, in LA, that Iranians feel unjustifiably entitled, that their kids are spoiled at home, their men quick to find a loophole, and their women resistant to rules. It's true for some, just as it is for any crowd. There may be a Paris Hilton or two among the tens of thousands of Iranians in this town and they do stand out, but the rest of us, I want to say for the record, all carry within us a repository of hardship and struggle, of fear and regret and sorrow, that is either inherited or gained firsthand, but that defines us and informs our actions in more ways than is readily discernible.

It took strength and courage for us to survive in Iran, and later in America, and it's going to take strength and courage to resolve now the course of our story, to preserve the good and let go of the bad rather than cling to or chuck the whole.

Because, you see, we *can't* chuck the past. That's another thing I learned when I met Jonah.

I let him stay with me those first few weeks because I was spellbound by the beauty of it—he with the luminous heart, the ghosts and shadows and night creatures that lit up as if in reflection of him, those thousands of butterflies carpeting the walls with impossible colors. Just to look at him sitting on the couch in that T-shirt that's a second skin to him, a perfect little sun holding a piece of blue sky for shelter, was worth going without sleep for days. But I also let him stay because I understood (yes, I do grasp a subtlety or two every once in a while) that his being here, being at all, is a chance.

I had to let the rabbi stay too, because he couldn't just leave Jonah with me and take off, though he often failed to show up for two or three nights in a row. The rest of the time he slept on the couch in my living room and helped himself to my Persian rose-water tea. I don't drink tea anyway; I only bought it because everywhere I go in this town, someone is talking about how we should all drink tea now instead of coffee. So I leave the tea in the kitchen and let the girl at my espresso bar look after my health.

Because of Jonah, I let the rabbi drink my tea and sleep on my couch, and when he suggested that I take foster-parenting classes—three months' worth of Saturday mornings—so he'd be able to leave Jonah with me for longer stretches of time, I even did that. I went back to work for the public defender's office because I realized I'm no authority on truth or lies. I gave up writing the book—*Two Continents*,

One Thief (I still think that's one hell of a title)—because I can't imagine doing that to Jonah; I'll let Leon win my Pulitzer if he ever delivers on the police procedural he's been threatening to write.

Jonah doesn't ask about his father and nor do the girls. They don't ask how Neda has managed to hold on to the house while the creditors have yet to receive a dime of their money, or why she seems to be thriving a little more every day since last June. She gave it a couple of months, then went out and got a haircut and a new pair of cheekbones. Another month or two, and she bought the fish lips and the boobs, the tummy tuck, the new Cartier white-gold-with-diamond-bezel Ballon Bleu. She signed up for Italian classes at UCLA Extension, art classes by Shaheen in Malibu, and It's Just Lunch! online. She turned the house over to the bankruptcy trustee, then sent the Riffraff to buy it back in the fire sale the trustee held to "liquidate" Raphael's Son's assets. The Riffraff paid cash because, as we all know, they have plenty of it to go around. All the money they were holding on to for Raphael's Son, that they would have had to return to him out of fear if not loyalty—it's all theirs now to invest and spend and use to lasso spouses for their not-so-attractive children. I mean, I'm no Marilyn Monroe myself, but among the Riffraff, Hadassah Simcha is considered a beauty and she, no offense to the bird, looks like a woodpecker with freckles.

I hate people who're awful and don't know it.

So the Riffraff bought the house back for Neda and they must have given her a good amount of money, maybe out of gratitude, more likely to keep her from going to the DA.

She might not have known anything about Raphael's Son's affairs before, but now she has Eddy, the human abacus, with those ledgers only he can make sense of, which means the Riffraff had better part with some portion of other people's hard-earned dollars.

For the record, I don't begrudge Eddy one penny of what he's earned, in salary or self-served bonus, throughout the term of his enslavement. True, he could have given all $2,000 every month to Jewish Family Services; but he could also have given nothing. The bottom line is, the man played by the rules longer than most of the rest of us would have. He fought in the most useless, meaningless war of all time, and has that face to show for it. He took care of his sick mother for twenty years, and she's still sick and wheezing and calling for him every five seconds in that cinder box of an apartment they share. He worked for Raphael's Son for two decades, and was about to hear his own ribs crushed under the wheels of the bus, courtesy of His Sleaziness.

He did exact the mother of all revenges on his torturer, keeping from him proof that he wasn't a lie his mother made up, but really, was it the bookkeeper's responsibility to report to Raphael's Son what his own child looked like? Suppose Eddy had told him—does anyone believe Jonah would have been better off? That leaves only the matter of what Eddy should do with whatever overseas bank accounts he might know of.

His choice, however, is not between stealing the money for himself or giving it back to its rightful owners. Not at all. Not if he is to abide by the law of the land. His choice, rather, is between stealing the money for himself or handing it over to the bankruptcy trustee to steal.

The way it works, by law and with the full backing of the American justice system, is that the court appoints a trustee, and the creditors hope to get back some small part of the debt they're owed. That hope is a fool's dream. In the case of Raphael's Son's Ponzi scheme, the trustee ended up pocketing, in payment for his "services," every last dime of Raphael's Son's remaining assets. Eighty million dollars is not a lot compared to the half billion lost by creditors, but it's not exactly pocket change for a hack lawyer with a couple of accountants on his payroll, which is what the trustee is. Then again, why stop at that when you've been handed, by a judge who's probably a crook himself, the gift that keeps on giving? Once he had emptied the "trust," Mr. Hack Attorney filed three hundred—yes, with two zeros—separate lawsuits against anyone with any perceived or real assets, then quickly settled for whatever sum he could blackmail out of them. Then he went on to pay himself the total amount of the settlements in return for his "services" in filing and settling the lawsuits.

If Eddy, or Neda, or anyone—even the Riffraff—point to any money anywhere, all that will happen is that the trustee will get richer still.

That would be unintended consequence #2.

#3 would be Leon finding what he (and I) firmly believe is the answer to Raphael's Son's mystery. For three weeks after the conversation with the Altoid Man, Leon pursued the mythical green Impala down every dimly lit alley and abandoned backstreet of Holmby Hills and its surrounding cities. He sent uniformed cops door-to-door throughout the neighborhood. He studied footage from real, functioning security cameras (as opposed to the cheap dummies Raphael's Son had opted for) outside private homes. He scoured DMV records for every one of Raphael's Son's victims and the LLCs and corporations registered in their names, as well as the Riffraff's, Eddy Arax's, and even Neda's. Then he extended his search to the video archives of the Century City building where Raphael's Son had his office, the rental car company's records, and the closed-circuit surveillance cameras installed on all the borders of the 5.71 square miles of real estate that was the City of Beverly Hills.

O'Donnell was fed up. Kevorkian threatened to quit. But Leon couldn't stop digging.

He had never had a case in which the victim was more worthy of the fate Raphael's Son had met, or where the chances of getting the DA to press charges were more slim. Before Jonah showed up, Leon was all but ready to call it a day, let dog eat dog, or at least wait until someone, somewhere, uncovered a body. Before Jonah showed up, Leon could tell fact from fiction, reason from absurdity. But if the most fundamental assumption about Raphael's Son—that he was not who his mother said—was false, and the most implausible likelihood about Jonah—that he had inherited the luminescence disease from the Soleyman bloodline—was true, how was one to distinguish truth from fabrication? If the most outrageous part of Neda's story was true—that the body had vanished without a trace within minutes of her discovering it—what was to keep Leon from believing the Altoid Man's testimony? The woman he had described to Leon sounded like a dead ringer for one of the Simchas. They had motive (Eddy Arax had made sure of that), method (*shechita* was in their blood), and just the right amount of greed to be willing to kill for money. Yes, many other people besides the Riffraff had motive. Yes, if anyone thought they could kill with impunity, it was Luci and his trail of rotting rodents.

But there was a certain poetry to both the image and the role of the green Impala that Leon could not help but respond to. He explained to me later that it reminded him of the story his mother used to tell about a boy she had known in her own childhood; he had died in an accident while riding his bike, she said, but he came back as a ghost, night after night to his mother's house and to the street where he had grown up, pedaling madly in the moonlight as if to tell a story, assert a truth, that had gone unsaid.

"How can you believe such nonsense?" Leon had asked his mother when she first told him the story. He was eight years old, and already he knew ghosts were not real.

"Because I've closed my eyes and listened," she had said. "I heard the ring of truth and when I looked again, this time with my heart, I too saw the ghost boy."

So Leon took to the phone and checked every car rental agency within a fifty-mile radius of both Los Angeles and Palm Springs. When that proved futile, he made a new round of calls, asking for any vehicle with a body similar enough to the Impala's. He was hoarse from talking and his neck and shoulder muscles were tight as coils, and still he couldn't let go of the car. On the afternoon of Labor Day, he had a revelation: The Simchas were tacky and cheap, but they weren't stupid enough to leave a track as easy to follow as a rental car. If any of them did drive up in a green Impala, it was probably bought, in cash, from one of those secondhand lots that recycle old rentals.

That night, Leon drove to Palm Springs with a folderful of pictures of various members of the Riffraff Brigade, their spouses and adult children, and a list of used-car dealerships in the entire forty-five-mile stretch of Coachella Valley. Five days later, he landed on a dealer who recognized Hadassah Simcha's picture.

Needless to say, Hadassah Simcha and her contingent of underdeveloped, unsophisticated, and utterly unlikable relatives did not waste one could-be-spent-pilfering-some-unsuspecting-orphan's-lunch-money moment fretting over Leon's discovery of Baby Simcha's purchase. So what if some used-car shark claimed he had sold a green car to Hadassah? The family had no obligation to disclose their purchases to the police, and anyway, "Go find the thing if you're so smart, bring it back and put a one-eyed witness on the stand, explain to the jury that the cops have spent two decades claiming the guy is either a liar or a lunatic, probably both but an unreliable character at best, and it only gets worse after that, what with no body and . . ."

Never mind that. Leon knows who the killer is the same way I do: because only Neda and Eddy could have counted on the body disappearing once it was cut up. Because only they knew that Raphael's Son was legit. And precisely because of that—because he knows who killed Raphael's Son and what became of the body—Leon also knows that she is going to walk.

Do you see Leon convincing O'Donnell that the ghost of Raphael Soleyman descended upon Holmby Hills early one Monday morning to whisk away his son's lifeless and bleeding body? Do you see O'Donnell committing professional suicide by taking the story to the DA and asking him to prosecute, say, Neda?

And even if he did—if Leon did manage to put Raphael's Son's murderer behind bars—given how much he abused her and what a foul person he was, would any of us feel that justice had been done?

The real justice, I propose to you, is what I'll call unintended consequence #4. You see, even the most unforgiving of Raphael's Son's victims, once they had become convinced of the probability that he was dead and gone (as opposed to alive and gone to Mexico), put down their arms, buried their rancor, and managed to see him as the infinitely small and eventually insignificant element he really was within the three-thousand-year history of the Jewish people of Iran. From the time they had walked in chains, slaves to Nebuchadnezzar after the destruction of the First Temple, into Babylon, to the years when they rose, in achievement and success, to seats of power in every continent on earth, long before Raphael's Son, there had been others who tried to inflict permanent harm upon this small, strangely resilient tribe. They had all failed—some more miserably than others. In barely a tenth of that time, the United States had produced the Oklahoma City bomber, Bernie Madoff, and legions of Wall Street CEOs. They, at least, had done enough harm to become notorious on an international scale; the most Raphael's Son achieved by way of immortality is to be written up in this blog.

This—being ultimately inconsequential, irrelevant, and unreckoned with—was the one state of being he had wanted most to escape.

They say, among Iranians, that a girl comes into this world carrying her own luck. That can be a good thing, as in the case of the good-luck women who bring great wealth and many sons to their husbands. Or it can be a problem, if you happen to arrive empty-handed. No one says anything about the luck of a boy because it would be redundant—a boy *is* luck. This always bothered me and still does, though I have to admit that in Jonah's case, it's true: he *is* a piece of luck.

Sixty-two years ago in the Square of the Pearl Cannon in Tehran, a lone exiled woman planted her hope at the gates of the Palace of Roses. She fed it with her words and tears, tended it with love or hatred, blasphemy or faith, till it grew into a shy and imperfect boy who became a wicked man who nevertheless yearned for love and acceptance. That I joined the others in denying him acceptance is what I cannot forgive myself.

Because of Jonah, it seems to me, I've been given a chance, in this very new city in this very new country, to collect the first blossom of that old and damaged shrub that was the sum of all of Raphael's Wife's dreams. The earth in Bagh-e Yaas might have been poisoned by the widow's sigh, the house my grandparents and aunt and uncle lived in might have been haunted by the ghosts that were orphaned when Raphael died. John Vain's ninety-nine years of good luck might have been stolen by a puff of the witch's breath, and Dr. Raiis, the healer, might have been trapped in a curse that made him an assassin.

But now here's Jonah, wronged by his father—yes—and proof that Raphael's Son too had been wronged, proof also that the wrongs of the past need not yield new sorrows, that for every hundred wrongs this world will do to you, there will be, one day, a right—a tiny, flickering light in the heart of a small, abandoned child—and that all you have to do (all I have to do) is cup your hands into a bulb around the flame and put your faith in the existence of a dawn, the possibility that every colorless creature will someday become a kaleidoscope and every bloodless ghost will at last find a beating heart, and that I—who have sought for so long a Truth big enough, clear and true enough, to explain for me the inexplicable—that even I will be satisfied with the wonder, and the mystery, and the quiet promise of a pinhead of light in a dark and distant sea.